Content warning:

DARKNESSES includes mentions of and/or reference to self-harm, eating disorders, CSA, rape, cult trauma, and forced institutionalization.

This novel is a work of fiction. Names, characters, business, events and incidents are the products of the author's imagination. Any resemblance to actual persons, living or dead, or actual events is, albeit hilarious, purely coincidental.

TO MY DEAR FRIEND NOAH SULLIVAN

prey (noun):

1. (archaic) Anything, such as goods, etc., taken or got by violence; something taken by force from an enemy in war.

2. One that is helpless or unable to resist attack; victim.

3. The act of devouring other creatures; ravage.

July 12, 2004

Bats usually wheel and flit about, but this one seemed to go straight on, as if it knew where it was bound for or had some intention of its own.

bird bones

One-year-old Bird Bones, whose stalwart sobriquets include *C'mere, Kitty Kitty* and *Get The Hell Off That Grass*, has a hard-earned reputation for benevolence in her corner of Elizabeth, New Jersey, having spent her time away from the litter leaving bird bones on welcome mats, peeing in rosebushes, and getting into homes and garages she doesn't belong in. Nights like this often find her gazing at her domain from 16661 Pomegranate Avenue, a hard sell of house gone unsold for so long that the serpentine ivy and jungle of grass hve begun to reclaim its civility.

The sill of a living room window provides Bird Bones with a glimpse of the speckled sky above the fence separating the street from the train tracks. The floorboards tremble as it chugs west. The horn's echoes fold back on the silence like a hymn. Two streetlamps form a net of light at the dead end—a hole in the night, too bright to see the rushing train behind it.

Something swirls, like fallen leaves or loose mown grass. It spirals out slowly, a looming shadow with no source.

Bird Bones watches as it takes shape, like flecks of ash reassembling—flecks of ash that beat the breeze, that sing in shrill notes and move like a cauldron of bats.

The cauldron molds into one bat—one thin, upside-down bat clutching the steel of a streetlamp, swinging gently. The light bleeds back so that its outline is as defined as an angel descending: its sharp ears, the fluff on its head, the leathery membrane of its cape-like wings. Its eyes are closed. A yawn shows two twinkling fangs before it swings and takes flight.

The train's horn thunders again, cleaving the night air.

Bird Bones leaps from the sill as the bat made of bats lands in the grass and begins to carve a path towards the house, clarifying with each step. It moves closer, the shadow borne of nothing, possessing no shadow itself. It eclipses the streetlight through the window. If it had a shadow, Bird Bones would be drowning in it. Its eyes are smaller, shrewder—the width and height of a human's. But where whites and irises should be, there's nothing but a pools of churning dark red—churning brown in Bird Bones' feline vision, like what spills from the mice whose heads she bites off and delivers to the worthy.

The train blares again, masking the sound of breaking glass as the shadow punches through the window.

Bird Bones flattens with fear, a blob of spiked orange fur on the polished floor.

The shadow reaches for the petrified cat and opens its mouth with a soft purr, jaw unhinged, fangs glistening.

July 8, 2019

*And I am afraid, afraid, afraid!—I am afraid of all things—even
to think but I must go on my way.*

one

I balance my phone against the cash register and lean forward on my wooden stool. I see my lips reflected on the screen: thick and round—and dry. I apply a fresh coat of cocoa butter Vaseline from the small jar in my plaid flannel pocket. The roiling puce clouds outside the bookstore window are exactly how I feel right now. My cramps are *killing* me, and the ibuprofen I took at noon is taking its time kicking in.

I flip through the pages of a *Frankenstein* paperback again and again, too fast to actually read, but slow enough to note its defects. It's an older edition, with a worn cloth cover and a few beverage stains on the inside. The marginalia's written in small cursive—stuff like 'the original deadbeat dad' and 'hubris gone wild.' Marginalia is a gift for someone like me—someone who gets turned around the moment a paragraph goes on for more than a few sentences. Sometimes, the notes are more entertaining than the book itself.

After a moment, I set the book aside so that I can buy it later. Kennedy keeps reminding me of my discount whenever he sees me looking at something for more than a few minutes, and this seems like a good reason.

Full Cauldron is a quiet place. As Manhattan's first female-owned, new-and-used science fiction and fantasy bookstore, it's a haven for an array of comic and book lovers: Trekkies and superhero fans, mystery lovers, literary fiction readers with a preference for the Victorian and Gothic. It's a haven for me because it's galaxies away from what I left behind.

As I reach for another book from the appraisal pile, I notice someone approaching the counter. She's a glowing shade of dark brown, with curly laid edges and a silken ponytail. Her gold track-suit is giving the type of Y2K royalty that reminds me of my mother's DJing wardrobe.

I can't look away.

She puts a stack of books on the counter.

"Hello."

"Hello." I nearly knock the unpriced books over getting to my feet. "Did you find everything okay?"

"Very okay." She pats the topmost book in her pile.

It has a rust-colored leather cover and gold calligraphy letters on the spine. I take it off the stack. The title—*Dracula*—ripples in the light. It's $65. I reach for the next. It's another copy of *Dracula*, only this one is annotated with essays in the back. The third is a mass market paperback copy of *Dracula*, but with a dark painting on the cover.

The stranger laces her fingers on the counter and watches as I ring them up, stroking the wings of a golden bat around her left middle finger.

"You must be a big fan," I say.

"I am not a fan of any size," she says, ponytail swishing left and right as she shakes her head. "These are to burn."

"Why?"

"Because I cannot do anything worse to them."

"Oh." I search for something to say. "I...haven't read it." I almost add that up until now, there's been no room in my life for anything like it—that everything around me has been about being closer to angelic, and that I'm starting to think no amount of pop culture consumption can wash that away. But that's not cash register talk, so instead, I say, "It's about vampires, right?"

The stranger runs her tongue over her teeth. "Right."

I tear her receipt from the register and slip it into the first book. "It must be bad if you're burning such a nice copy."

"Nothing about this book is nice." She pauses while picking up her books. "But *you* would not know," she says slowly, smiling. "You have not read it."

"I don't have to read it to know that your lungs deserve better than smoke from a book you hate," I say. "Are you gonna keep coming back to check our inventory? 'Cause it could get expensive for you."

"Money is of no concern to me." She's holding the books

like she means to leave with them, but hasn't moved. "You know nothing of the vampire known as Count Dracula?"

"I know about the vampire bunny known as Bunnicula," I say. "And I know *Carmilla*. I read it in college." And experienced a sexual awakening so intense that I would've made a Tinder account for the express purpose of finding a girlfriend if I hadn't been failing so many classes. But this isn't cash register talk either, so I keep it to myself.

"I will note this," the stranger says thoughtfully. "Just to be certain that I understand wholly, you—" she points to me "—have never read this book—" she indicates a copy of *Dracula* "—by Abraham Stoker."

"I didn't even know Abraham was his first name."

"It is Abraham," she confirms.

Yet again, I can't come up with anything to say, so I keep staring. After hours spent on autopilot, it's dawning on me that this is no longer a passing conversation had solely to fill the silence of a transaction.

Is she flirting?

I almost laugh out loud before the thought's even completed. Of course she's not.

I'm as far from a catch as can be.

Unless…?

There's no *unless*. The universe hand-delivering a breathtaking woman in all gold to flirt with me is as close as I can get to a cosmic joke without leaving the galaxy.

"I learned something today." I step back, returning to my stool and grab another book to price. When I straighten up, she's still there, watching with her fingers laced under the stack. "Need anything else?"

"You."

The copy of *The Left Hand of Darkness* that I just picked up slips out of my hand. I don't pick it up.

"For what?"

"You have shown concern for my lungs, and you have never read this book," says the stranger. "And I am certain many reasons more will become apparent to us both."

I clear my throat and glance around the store, like someone amongst the shelves will raise a cue card with my next line. "There's plenty of people out there who want you to take care of yourself and haven't read *Dracula*. You just haven't met them."

"Why would I meet them?" she asks, brow quirked. "I have you."

My mouth dries out. I lick the Vaseline off my lips, heart sprinting. "I'm lost."

"This may have been the case before, but I have found you. You are mine." The woman adjusts the books in her arms, seeming satisfied—relieved, even. "Do not forget this. And do *not*," she says sternly, raising the stack, "read this book."

I try and fail to form a response. She leaves through the open door, and disappears among the ambling pedestrians, all rushing towards their destinations against the countdown to imminent rain.

Another customer approaches the register with a question, pulling me back to the present. After some time, I fall back into the silent groove of examining and pricing books, although with a more discerning eye, just in case *Dracula* is among them.

two

My South Harlem apartment is a block away from Full Cauldron and overlooks the neighborhood's busiest intersection. When the sun rises, the towers and campaniles of nearby churches cradle the molten light.

I open the fire escape and breathe in the city air. I have a view of the glimmering skyscrapers, a sliver of the Hudson River, and a corner of the dark North Woods of Central Park. I could spend all night on my budget balcony. New York is big and bright and busy, and I feel safer knowing how small I am within the clockwork chaos. A footnote in the cacophony and nothing more.

The clouds break into rain just as I drape my flannel over my desk chair, massaging my growling stomach.

I wasn't allowed to cook my own food in Blessed Falls. Now that I'm not there, it feels like I should be exercising every available freedom. I still struggle not to wonder if I should be making more of an effort; I still struggle not to overthink it to the point of starvation, a feeling that Zeke made sure I was accustomed to.

In the kitchen, I find bread, peanut butter, jelly, and bananas. Making a sandwich with the first three and frying the latter is close enough to a meal. Once my food is prepared, I stand near my desk, gazing at my painting with fresh eyes. Droplets spring over the threshold of the fire escape, beading on the hardwood.

I didn't turn to art until I was admitted to the psych ward, because the thing I miss most about Custodes Angelorum is the penance chapel's towering windows, which depicted the archangels who watched us vessels repent in intricate panes of stained glass.

The rain stops—not gradually, but as if someone zipped the sky shut. I stop chewing, frowning at the stillness outside. The whistling crosswinds raise goosebumps that I ignore.

I keep eating.

Of the dozens of watercolor paintings I've done in facsimile of stained glass, I always come back to Gabriel. I painted him with porcelain lavender skin, a golden robe that matches his trumpet, and wings like canopies with feathers like knives.

Gabriel, angel of mercy, resurrection, revelation, and vengeance, chose me as his vessel.

Or so I believed.

I know better now.

I know that there are no angels, and no rapture for them to prepare me for.

Sometimes, painting angels and biblical scenes feels like it might be the only way to reprogram their meanings. Other times, I wonder if I'll spend the rest of my life tearing the lies off God.

"Be not afraid."

My empty plate and fork fall from my hands and clatter at my feet.

The semi-familiar voice came from the fire escape. The light above my desk illuminates the sharp, recognizable features of the woman who bought every copy of *Dracula* at Full Cauldron.

"That is a lovely piece," she says, smiling. "Is it Gabriel with his horn?"

I forget to be scared or angry over the intrusion. I'm more disturbed by the fact that my scarred arms and shoulders aren't hidden beneath my flannel. It feels too late for subtlety, so I lunge and snatch it off the chair so forcefully that it rocks on its legs. I stuff my arms in the sleeves, then pick up the fallen plate and take careful steps towards the kitchen, which is in full view of the fire escape. The stranger watches but doesn't move.

She's dressed in the same gold outfit from earlier. She has nothing with her, except a book; the blood red cover and gold print of *Dracula* almost match her outfit. The leisurely way she's standing there makes me feel like neither fight nor flight is necessary—yet.

I return to my desk; a good ten feet separate us.

"I know you said you needed me, but did you also need to follow me home?"

"Home is where you went. If you had gone to the bottom of the deep blue sea, I would have followed you there, too."

I wait a moment for this to make sense, but it doesn't.

I should beware of, among other things, people being overly familiar—or so said the psychiatrist assigned to my case last year. Every other session with her seemed to come with another list of taunting cult avoidance tips—like I didn't plan on staying indoors forever anyway after being discharged.

"Have you slipped away from me?"

I jump at the sound of the stranger's voice, having run so far into the back of my head that I almost forgot she was here. "Who are you?"

"Laura, most recently," she says, running her fingers along the cover of *Dracula*, feathered with sticky notes of different colors. "Has anyone told you that you bear a striking resemblance to Billie Holiday?"

"Yeah," I say, blushing. "It never gets old."

I cross my arms and take a small step closer.

Even half in darkness, Laura has a face and figure that would make me crick my neck if we passed one another on the street— brown eyes that haven't left mine, a round nose, and thick, glossed lips that sparkle in the light from my apartment. With her gold tracksuit jacket half open and her tight black tank top hugging her curves, my fear has less to do with her showing up like this and more to do with the tenability of my own sanity.

"Did you follow me home because I look like Billie Holiday?"

"I followed you home because your heartbeat lives in my head. I wished to be closer."

I wait for her to follow this up with more, but she doesn't. "You don't even know my name, Laura."

"You can tell me if you feel the need to."

"It's…Oasis," I say, like I'm not sure. "When you said you needed me, what did you mean?"

She crosses her ankles and leans against the rail behind her. "Do you fear being needed?"

"All I'm saying is, you can't just go into bookstores telling strangers you need them."

"But I have done so, and now you must decide the conse- quence for this act." Laura bites her lip, watching me. "I am ready."

"It's not about consequences. It's about…" I have no idea what it's about—her saying she needs me, or the fact that not so deep down, being needed is exactly what I need. "It's like telling a stranger you love them."

"Have you never done so?"

"No."

"Although we will not be strangers for long, I am here as one now, should you wish to change that." She leans out of the shadows, holding *Dracula* to her chest. "You may tell me that you love me."

"Love first, ask questions later?" I cross my arms, glance at Gabriel on my desk. "It just doesn't sound like the best strategy for life."

"You are human. Humans are cautious with love, no matter how much you crave it. It is a side effect of temporality," Laura says conclusively. "But *I* am eternal, and your life is too short for me to waste your time. I hope that you will soon agree when I say that you should let me love you."

A breeze whistles in past her shoulders, powerful enough to blow a spare MetroCard across my desk. I tighten my flannel around myself, knowing full well that the chill has little to do with my goosebumps.

"Well, I'm not eternal, so don't expect me to say 'I love you' tonight."

Her brow arches curiously. "Your blood speaks, even when you are silent. It will tell me what is in your heart, in time."

I can't look away. A tornado is what's in my heart right now, and I'm in its path like a deer in headlights.

"I haven't felt human in a long time," I confess.

"Neither have I. *You* reminded me that I have lungs. And a heart." Laura steps closer, stopping just short of the threshold. "I would give it to you if I could reach."

On the topic of hearts, mine is thundering.

"Did you bring that book instead? It doesn't seem like a decent substitute."

"It bears my name, but I am nowhere to be found within these pages." Laura turns *Dracula* over in her hand, gazing at the cover like she forgot about it. "It is pure fiction, Oasis. I have nothing to refute with you."

"I'm not refuting that it's fiction, either," I say, twisting the loose button on my sleeve. "What does it say about you?"

Laura blinks.

Her hold on *Dracula* slackens, like I've taken her off guard. She gazes at my painting of Gabriel, and for a moment, she looks as lost as I feel whenever I pick up a brush—like I'm full of a rot that might kill me if I don't scoop it out and put it elsewhere. "All the wrong things," she answers at last.

The button pops off my sleeve under the duress of my nervous fiddling. I cross my arms, squeezing the button in my fist.

I've been down this road before—gazing raptly at a woman saying things that didn't quite make sense. Things that seemed to come from something wondrous and warm and bigger than me—something I didn't have but was certain I needed. Laura, and the way my curiosity won't abate, may be proof I've learned absolutely nothing from that.

My phone vibrates in my pocket. It can only be one of two people: my brother or Kennedy. No matter which of them it is or what they're saying, it's a reminder that the night is pressing forward, encroaching on a moment that I wish I could pause and resume later.

I set the button on my desk, toying with the thread it snapped away from.

"Laura, I should—"

"Join me tomorrow night."

"—wash my face..." I stumble on the last few words. "For what?"

"A date," she replies, straightening and holding *Dracula* at her side.

I step closer to the fire escape. My flannel falls open, trailing in the sudden breeze. Even in shadow, Laura's face is like quicksand; if I didn't have work tomorrow, I might say fuck it and invite her in just to look at her some more. Past delusions notwithstanding, I don't think I'm imagining her looking at me like she feels the same way.

"You're asking me on a date?"

"Just because your blood speaks does not mean that I do not desire to hear your voice speak your love as well." Laura steps away from the rail. She bites her lip, grinning playfully as the wind buffets her rippling gold jacket. Her shirt rides up a little, showing in full the shadowy dip of her navel. "I will return to you at sunset tomorrow. Good evening."

"Don't you want my number?" I ask.

Laura stares at me like I said something in another language. "Good evening."

With that, she disappears.

It takes me a moment to realize that she went up—not down.

I step over the threshold, numbing my feet on the cold metal. When I look up, it's to slivers of the clouds between the grates.

Laura's gone.

My eyes search the sky above. Then I see something I've never seen in my life outside of the zoo: over a dozen bats tumbling and diving, playful as children as they flock through the starry sky.

A splintering crash of thunder rumbles Manhattan, sounding car alarms as lightning snaps the Hudson. I just manage to dart back inside before the clouds rip apart and the storm picks up where it left off.

For a while, I shove away the discomfort of the cold and watch raindrops drip off the rail, picturing Laura standing there. Saying yes to a date with a woman who followed me home is a questionable act unto itself, but if she heard my heartbeat, that means there's something left of me, and I'm too desperate for proof of that to care about what my common sense has to say.

three

three

July 9, 2019

I sometimes think we must be all mad and that we shall wake to sanity in strait-waistcoats.

three

The first thing I do when I get to work is check the Gothic horror section. It's not uncommon for cult survivors to develop split personalities, become schizophrenic, or hallucinate to cope. I've got to be sure this isn't the case—that Laura isn't a figment of my battered imagination—before I let it sink in that I have a date with her tonight.

There's a foot-long gap on the shelf where all our copies of *Dracula* used to be.

I'm not crazy.

Laura is real, which means I'm going on a real date tonight.

The smell of coffee wafts through the shelves as Kennedy gauges the gaps made by purchased books. His dark, curly hair is in a state of total disarray, and the tag of his t-shirt is visible under his chin.

"I think I've been here long enough for you to stop pretending you're a morning person," I say as he joins me in the Gothic section. "I can open by myself."

"Yeah, but then I'd miss this hour where it's just us," Kennedy says through a yawn. "Not because it's *us*. Because I love the store. Not that I don't love *you*. You know what?" He sighs and sips his coffee. "I think you're right." He pauses at my shoulder on his way to the mystery section. "You said *one* woman bought all of these?"

Nervous sweat coats my palms. I forgot I mentioned Laura's purchases as we closed yesterday, and after seeing her last night, I wish I hadn't.

"Maybe she's teaching a class."

"I hope not. It's 2019," Kennedy says, sounding a little exasperated. "We're supposed to be taking racist authors *off* the syllabus."

"Racist?" I repeat.

"*Lair of the White Worm* is probably the most racist book I've ever read that was written by a fellow Irishman. The savage African guy alone nearly knocked *Dracula* off my favorites list—not to mention the overall story execution is just *bad*," he says, mouth turned down in disgust. "Mary continues to be the *only* Gothic writer who *never* misses the mark."

I make a mental note of this, searching for a connection between Abraham Stoker being racist and anything Laura said yesterday—anything to explain why she implied that *Dracula* is a badly written book about her. I haven't forgotten that she asked me not to read it, but it occurs to me that doing so might make me feel like I have armor on.

"I have a date with her."

"You have a date with *MARY SHELLEY?*" Kennedy screams.

"No."

"Oh." He clears his throat. "With the *Dracula* lady?"

I nod. "Think you could give me a cheat sheet since it's your ex-favorite book?"

Kennedy puts his coffee on the shelf just to rub his hands together nefariously. "Absolutely."

At 11 o'clock sharp, I open the front door and jam the doorstop under it. It's sunny today and teeming with people outside, not at all like yesterday's sulky clouds and scattered storms.

Around noon, UPS arrives with a shipment of graphic novels and merchandise. I sign off and open it on my stool.

I hang a *Black Panther* t-shirt on a plastic hanger, one of several items from the franchise. I really *should* make a better effort to get into this stuff—stuff meaning everything I see on a near daily basis and never investigate further. I can't remember the last time I read a book, or watched something other than a tutorial for styling 4c hair.

I'm gone from Blessed Falls, but sometimes, it's like I forget that's the case. Every day, I re-realize that I can watch whatever I want, read whatever I want, listen to whatever I want. I can do whatever I want without the rapture, or my angelic duty, or my sinful soul hanging over my head.

I pull a Superman mug from another box and tag it with the price gun. Maybe I'll start with him; I'm not so far out of the pop culture loop that I don't know who he is. Clark Kent is the most famous fictional character to ever come out of Kansas.

That's what I need. A slice of the home I haven't seen in half a decade. A fusion of something new and something familiar.

"Excuse me, ma'am. Can I ask you a few questions?"

I finish arranging fandom mugs in the display case under the register and straighten up.

The bearded man who spoke looks like he belongs with Secret Service, but the silver cross around his neck, dangling in front of his white shirt, seems to indicate that he isn't.

My chest tightens with apprehension. I take a reflexive step back, nudging the empty box on my stool. "Who are you?"

"My name is Dr. Jacob Seward. I'm with the Vantage Hematology Institute."

"The where?"

"The Vantage Hematology Institute," Dr. Seward repeats, withdrawing a business card from the inside pocket of his suit. "We research and treat blood-related illnesses."

I don't take the card.

He lowers his hand. "My colleagues and I are looking for a patient who escaped our facility recently."

Bitterness curdles in the back of my mouth. "Did you give them a reason to escape?"

For all of two seconds, Dr. Seward looks taken aback. But then a blink, and his face is stony and unreadable.

"Those reasons are tied to a complex diagnosis of co-morbid blood disorders resulting in organic psychosis, including delusions, mania, and homicidal ideation."

"I didn't see anyone yesterday. While you're here, is there anything I can help you find?"

"Are you sure? I haven't even described him," Dr. Seward asks, jaw set rigidly.

I cross my arms, matching his irked energy. "I'm listening."

"He's white. And short," he says confidently. "He also has a Romanian accent."

"What makes you think I know what a Romanian accent sounds like?" I ask, barely containing a belligerent scoff. "Don't you have any pictures?"

His lips part, and a scowl furrows his brow.

"I would if it wasn't a HIPAA violation."

"Either way, I haven't seen him, so—"

"*Dracula*," he interrupts, "has been the focal point of a psychotic fixation for him. Often, he slips into delusions of believing that he *is* Count Dracula. I noticed that you don't have any copies of the book. Who bought them?"

The world seems to freeze. I bite the inside of my cheek hard, as if that'll stop the panicked sprinting of my heart.

Dr. Seward drums his business card on the counter expectantly.

"Someone who doesn't fit the description."

"And who was that?" He asks, apparently encouraged by my hesitation. "This man's wealth is astronomical. Anyone could be facilitating his neuroses."

"Dr. Seward, the twenty-eighth precinct is right up the street," I say, pointing at the door. "What you're asking for fits *their* job description better than mine."

Beneath his beard, Dr. Seward's cheeks flare red with aggravation. "Woman, this man is *worse* than dangerous, and if you know anything, you need to tell me. I'd hate for someone like you to find out that monsters are real, because *that's what he is.*"

My mouth falls open.

"That's how you feel about someone you're supposed to be taking care of? About your *patient?*" I hear my heart pumping in my ears, sprinting with thoughtless anger. "If you think he's a monster, why bother with treatment?"

"I—"

"I don't even care," I interrupt with an exasperated laugh. "Just get out."

Dr. Seward's lip twitches, but he doesn't move.

I point at the door, at the lively, sunny street beyond it.

"I said *leave*," I say, raising my voice. "*Now.*"

He doesn't.

On cue, Kennedy's buoyant footsteps resound in the hallway leading to his office. He joins me behind the register with a manila folder. The cheerful grin slips off his face when he notices Dr. Seward scowling on the other side of the register.

"Is he bothering you?"

"Yes," I say curtly.

"Get out," he says, addressing our visitor just as curtly.

Dr. Seward's mouth tightens, like he wants to hurl out something else. Instead, he turns on his heel, silver cross glinting in the light and strides out of the store.

"What did he want?" Kennedy asks, glaring at the back of Dr. Seward's black suit.

"Nothing that we sell." I scoop up the crumpled plastic from all the merch in the first box and stuff it in the trash bin, then grab the scissors to slice the packaging tape of another.

"*Woah* there," Kennedy says, swooping quickly between me and it, frowning deeply. "What are you doing?"

I frown, too.

"What you pay me to do?"

"PTO means paid time *off*, O," Kennedy says. "Remember?"

My confusion lasts for less than a moment. After meeting Laura, for the first time in a long time, I have a reason to be pre-occupied, and I completely forgot that it's Thursday, which means I'm having lunch with my twin.

"Thanks for reminding me," I say.

Kennedy grins and returns to the register.

Half a step away, I realize that the business card Dr. Seward whisked out is still on the counter. I read it upside down:

VANTAGE HEMATOLOGY INSTITUTE

DR. JACOB SEWARD, M.D., PSY.D

I reach past Kennedy, whose eyes are glued to the register screen, and slide it towards myself.

"I said no working," he says distractedly.

"I heard you," I say, tucking the card away.

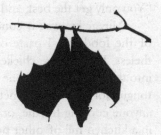

four

I was in deep with Custodes Angelorum by the time my brother's episode of *Chopped* aired, and so I didn't watch it, which I now realize translated to him believing I didn't care. Mirage was in the periphery of my life for three years, and I still have whiplash over what he did while I was lost.

His restaurant is on the 15th floor of a high-rise above Battery Park. From our window-side table, we have a view of Lady Liberty, the bridge, and New Jersey. There's a bar bathed in blue light, a dark fireplace, two dozen tables with black tablecloths and intricate rose centerpieces, and a full lobby.

It's entirely too warm for sleeves, but I refuse to disrobe. There are too many people sitting idly, watching other people while they wait for their food. Here, I watch them before they can watch me, and even then, I always get the nagging suspicion that everyone I see just looked away from me. I see a pale, be-ringed hand grasping a butter knife. Nails painted pale pink drumming the table. A dark wrist turning, throwing a circle of light from the watch face onto the wearer's cheek.

I look at my own hands, folded on my napkin. My silverware is at the ready, a commitment to me eating this time. I look at the restaurant name on the menu tucked in the arm of a passing waiter: *Oasis*. My heart swells with pride and something else—something more bitter than sweet.

"Here you go, sis," Mirage says, stirring me from the fog of imminent dissociation as he appears beside the table. He sets a plate in front of me.

"Thank you," I say, eyeing the spread. Greens, red mashed potatoes, two chicken tenders sliced into sixths.

Mirage sits across from me. For himself, he has brisket crostini and arugula.

"Did you make all of this?" I ask.

"You ask that every time," he says, unrolling his silverware. "You only get the best, and I'm the best cook in this joint."

Mirage knows my concern has nothing to do with the quality of the food, but I paste on a smile and pick up my fork nonetheless. I nudge the chicken tender apart and watch juice trickle into the greens. Long gone are the days of me risking burning my tongue for a taste of something that looks this good. The idea of anyone cooking for me, or of the food my brother cooked being in a kitchen full of other people, often kills my appetite. Eating it often spirals me into several days of panickily monitoring my brain for signs of contamination.

For several minutes, I watch him eat, curbing jealousy over the fact that he can just put food in his mouth without being terrified of what it'll do to him.

"What have you been up to today?" I ask.

"Running some numbers. I'm slowly but surely committing to the BBQ joint," Mirage says through a crunchy bite. "It'll be a vibe shift, but I think I'm ready to accept the fact that I miss Kansas just a little bit. How was work?"

"A doctor came in looking for an escaped patient." My fork hovers over the mashed potatoes, then a moment later, over the chicken. No matter how much I once loved my brother's cooking, and no matter how firmly I resolve to behave and take at least one bite, paranoia always wins.

"What kind of doctor?" Mirage asks.

"A hematologist. He was with an institute that studies blood, looking for some white guy."

He frowns as he sips his water. "Did he say how the guy escaped?"

"No, but I'm sure he had a good reason for leaving."

"Had you seen him come into the store?"

"It's possible." I smear a sixth of a tender into the potatoes, my boldest move so far. "A lot of short white men come into the store."

"Hopefully his family isn't too worried," Mirage says as he polishes off the last crostini. He watches me rotate my plate again, probably as aware as I am of the fact that it's just for show. My skin crawls with shame, which only intensifies when he purses his lips and says, "Mom always told us not to play with our food."

Grief berths in my chest.

There are a lot of things our mother told us during her beautiful, musical life.

I wish this had been one of them.

I wish she, or anyone, had told me that darkness doesn't let go. It just goes into remission.

One moment, I'm free.

I wonder.

I trust.

I'm healed.

And then there are moments like this, where I wish I could evaporate, because my explanation for why I can't eat makes my hospital stay seem like even more of a waste than this food.

I put my fork down.

Mirage's eyes harden before I've even spoken.

"I'm sorry," I say around the lump in my throat. "This looks really good, Mirage, but I can't eat it."

"Why not?" He asks, not quite exasperated, but impatient enough that I want to bang my fist on the table.

"You know why," I say.

"There's nothing wrong with this food." He pushes his empty plate away, leaning back, glaring. "You *know* I'd never let anyone put anything in your food, but you *always* do this."

"I said I was sorry," I say, struggling to hold onto my patience. "I already told you it has nothing to do with you."

Mirage glowers at me, radiating disappointment. "I'm your brother, Oasis. It has to do with me. What happened to therapy?"

"If any part of me thought that therapy was an option, I would have gone by now," I snap. And because I'm feeling like a fanned flame, I add, "If it wasn't for my first experience with psychiatric treatment, this might not be the case."

My brother's eyes flit away—as they should. No matter how much he weighed or how long we'd gone without seeing each other, there's no way in hell I would've thrown him in the mental hospital without asking if he wanted to be there.

I look in the opposite direction, at the Statue of Liberty gazing stoically at the bay, struggling to stamp out memories of the hospital.

"Can we not?" Mirage asks after a minute. "I'm tired of this."

I lick my lips, look down at my plate. I'm tired of this, too.

We drove each other crazy when we were teenagers. Clashing puberties, sharing a room, sharing a car. Our fights were petty, repetitive, and predictable. They sometimes dragged on for hours before being cut short by something that wiped the slate, made us inseparable again—a trip to McDonald's because one of our stomachs had growled. One of us remembering that a show or movie we wanted to see would soon be airing.

A favorite recurring fix was Mom, who always stayed out of our battles, obliviously calling us for dinner, and us sharing a moment of reassuring silence before going to see what awful thing she had cooked.

I don't miss fighting, but if I did, I'd miss those kinds of fights. I'd trade them for these snow squalls, where it feels like my brother gets satisfaction from hearing me testify my own brokenness.

Mirage points at my plate, brow raised in a silent question.

"Go for it," I say hollowly.

He pulls it towards himself, picks up my fork, and digs in.

five

After a brusque departure from Oasis, I get home and immediately start a painting. I pull up references for Himalayan salt crystals and pictures of Jordanian and Palestinian landscapes.

Genesis 19. Sodom and Gomorrah, biblical sin cities, have caught the attention of the Lord Himself. Two angels show up at the city gates for Lot, nephew of Abraham, who invites them to his home, knowing that the streets are dangerous. When a crowd of men show up to rape the undercover angels, Lot offers them his virgin daughters to have sex with, with no success. Shortly after, God reaches His limit, and the angels drag Lot and his family out of town before He starts hurling sulfur, destroying all life and habitat.

Genesis 19:26. The next town over, having successfully escaped the fireballs raining down on Sodom and Gomorrah, Lot's wife looks back at the serpentine smoke and gets turned into a pillar of salt.

In Custodes Angelorum's version of the bible, Zeke had focused exclusively on those two angels. Their power was subtle but commanding. They were conduits between the Lord and the world. They protected humans from themselves. They were models for us vessels, and this chapter was critical to our preparation for the rapture.

September 19th, 2019 is just over two months away.

After lunch with my brother, instead of being grateful for the fact that I'm not still drugged up and cutting myself in Blessed Falls, I'm fighting every speck of my spirit not to wish I was still there. Cult life was simple, cyclic, predictable. As one of the Psalms, my only concern most days was checking the scale to make sure I was still at 91 pounds.

The days were good because they were all one day.

If I'm Lot's wife and Sodom is Blessed Falls, then I turn to salt every day.

For a few hours, I mix pink for the pillar and a spread of greens and browns for the shrubbery of Zoar. Usually, I lose my feelings in the colors and brushstrokes. I go into a painting in pieces, and emerge stitched back together, save the occasional eye strain and wrist soreness.

Usually, but not today.

Usually, I'm the reason I fall apart, but when it's my twin—the person who's always been there to love me even when I hate myself? I'd take the regimen of hallucinogens, self-harm, and periodic starvation over this in a broken heartbeat.

It's 6:45 when I leave my desk with a cursory glance at the finished piece, eyes glazing over the same details I worked so hard to capture.

The sun will set at 7:46, meaning I should peruse my underwhelming wardrobe for something to wear. Instead of foraging in the closet for an outfit, I drop to my knees beside my bed. A dust bunny rolls out as my fingers graze my charger and lamp cord, feeling for the composition book I call my memoir.

I leave my room and open the fire escape, then sit on the hardwood floor against the dining room table, so that I can see the gold and orange horizon slowly being encroached on by the dark blue of oncoming night.

I started writing after being discharged from the hospital with the aim of fashioning a nearly objective reminder of who I was before Custodes Angelorum, how I got there, why I stayed. I turn to it almost as often as I defiantly turn to the bible I bought last year, drinking in everything Zeke left out just to prove I'm not what he wanted me to be.

But sometimes these words, interspersed with smears of grease from whatever I was eating, wrinkles from my tears shed in real time, scribbles in the margins from my attempts to revive dying pens, remind me instead that the person I was before is gone, and I'll forever be in her shadow, unable to look at myself without homing in on every ugly difference.

Just a few pages in, I throw it across the room. I hear it

collide with something as I hug my bare, scarred knees, taking deep breaths, painfully aware of the darkening sky.

Any other day, I'd eat something quickly, pop a few Benadryl, and fall asleep watching *Dark Shadows* or *Lord of the Rings*, which are the only things I've watched since leaving Blessed Falls, because even though I'm free to watch whatever I want, I've only managed to watch things that remind me of people I lost.

How much emptier can my life get?

It feels like if I stand up, I'll disintegrate, and even if that's what I want, I should at least let Laura know I'm not going to make it out in one piece tonight.

I snort back a mouthful of snot, wipe my face on the inside of my shirt. I breathe steadily, until my chest doesn't feel so tight with sobs fighting towards the surface. I let go of my legs, look up, and scream.

The pink and violet swath of sunset is like a portrait backdrop behind Laura, who arrived in silence and is watching me in silence, too.

I scramble to my feet, swallowing my beating heart, wiping my nose on my arm. "How long have you been here?"

"I only just arrived. I had hoped the dysrhythmia I heard was on account of something positive—otherwise, I would have arrived sooner," she says, frowning mildly as I walk closer. "What has happened?"

"Nothing."

Looking at her, I could certainly forget that something *did* happen—that I had a legitimate reason for crying on the floor. Black winged eyeliner above her brown eyes, smoky burgundy eyeshadow, a rippling ponytail draped over her shoulder. She's wearing a burgundy halter tank top beneath a silk bomber jacket, loose black pants, and patent leather heels—heels that are inches from my memoir, open face-up, partially on the hardwood floor, but mostly over the threshold.

My vision tunnels around it, and I barely hear her when she speaks.

"This does not look like the aftermath of nothing." Laura tilts her head to the side, watching me approach. Two gold bats dangle from her ears, wings wrapped around themselves. "Are you alright?"

"It's just PMS," I lie. I stop in front of her, heart pounding in the back of my throat. This close, it feels like she can see right through me. That, or I wish she could. Her eyes are curious and concerned, and I wish I could explain without explaining. Instead, with even less subtlety than yesterday, I stoop and snatch the notebook up. "Thanks for asking."

"You look delicious," she says, looking me up and down with a serene smile. "Is this what you are wearing?"

I'm in a too-small, ketchup-stained t-shirt and torn basketball shorts. All the scars on my arms are visible, Luke 1:19 stamped across my skin in slits from wrist to shoulder.

"I was just about to get dressed," I say. "Gimme, like, fifteen minutes?"

"That is quite a while. I should be given some reading material to entertain myself until you are satisfied with your appearance," Laura says, lips pursed. "How lucky it is that you have this book with you."

I quickly put the notebook behind my back. "What book?""

"The one you have just hidden."

I look at my feet and hers. Fashion impaired as I am, even I recognize the signature scarlet soles of Louboutin pumps, visible when she shifts to the side to peek at my face.

"Are you the author?" She asks, voice still pleasant and inquiring. "Do not be shy. I have no room to judge."

"I'm not *shy*," I say defensively. "This is my memoir."

"And I want to remember you."

I turn the notebook over in my hand, licking my lips nervously. "What if you read it and realize you don't?"

"You think I would be so shallow as to care whether you are a good person?" Laura asks. She fondles one of the bats dangling from her ears, smiling playfully. "Be evil if it would please you. You will smell the same to me."

I bite my lip. If she were anyone else, I'd say no instead of deliberating, but she isn't just anyone else: she's the only person I've told. Silence hangs, in which I look away and back, waiting for Laura's eyes to leave me. She doesn't look away. She doesn't blink. Not for the first time, it feels like she can see more than just my body.

Heart hammering, I pass my book over the threshold, into her waiting hand. I crack my knuckles nervously, tempted to dart away, scramble into whatever clothes I see first, and get out of here just to take her eyes off those pages.

I turn around, but just as quickly, turn back, mortified by my own lack of manners. "Sorry, Laura. I just realized I never asked if you wanted to come inside."

"In time." Laura's leaning against the rail, elbows on the metal as she turns the page, deep frown a testament to her immersion. "There are many lovely turns of phrase here. Would that you had been the one to slander me," she sighs. "Then those lies may have been beautiful."

"Lies are never beautiful, Laura," I say, sharper than I mean to—sharp enough to earn a raised brow and intrigued glance. "And I would never do that to you."

She slowly turns another page, smiling softly. "I will keep that in mind."

The longer she looks at me without looking at me like I'm also crazy, the easier breathing becomes. I smile, too.

I head to my room. In the closet, several dresser drawers are partway open, with underwear, leggings, and unfolded shirts sticking out. I have three denim jackets—black, dark blue, light blue—a row of sweatshirts, a pair of boots for the snow, a pair of galoshes for the rain, athletic Nikes for work and black K-Swiss for everything else. The rest of my wardrobe is plaid flannel.

The nicest pants I have are black corduroy trousers with a pearl button. I pair them with an *I <3 NY* t-shirt. Laura calls out to me from the fire escape.

"Where is your twin brother?"

"Brooklyn, probably," I call back. I change clothes quickly and grab my gingham purple flannel. My hair is in its default Afro puff on top of my head.

"You possess an Ivy League education?" Comes Laura's voice again.

I kill the light and return to her.

"Half of one," I say, tucking my phone, wallet, and keys in my pockets.

She closes my notebook, dog-earing a page like she intends to come back to it. Then her eyes widen and she bites her lip, bringing heat to my face. "Hundreds of languages in the grasp of my tongue, but not one word in any could describe your beauty."

If I wasn't Black, I know my face would be flaming red. My heart's skipping at a mile a minute as I watch her gaze at me like I'm treasure.

"Thank you."

Laura beams and hands my notebook back.

"How lucky I am to be dining with you. Shall I meet you below?" She asks, angled towards the stairs.

"Um..." I'd question the order of things—meeting her downstairs instead of leaving through the door together—if not for the stinging realization that I've just put myself in the same position as earlier, which ended with me crying on the floor. "I'll follow you down here," I say; I'm scared that if she leaves me to my devices, I'll stall until the night's over.

A slight frown creases her brow, and she takes an echoing step closer. "Are you alright?"

I nod, setting the notebook next to my painting of Lot's wife. "I just don't see any reason for us to split up."

Laura's eyes trail from my face to my memoir on the desk and back. "Let us depart."

I turn off all the lights and step out, closing the fire escape doors after myself. I follow her down, watching the view go from sandbox to life-sized. All I see of her is her ponytail swinging in the bare light of the dusky sky.

"Yesterday, you went up instead of down," I say, voice raised slightly over our clanging footfalls.

"Yesterday, I had no passengers."

"Did you fly away or something?"

Laura looks over her shoulder, expression too hidden in shadow to discern. "Or something."

We reach the bottom, which is the second floor of the building. Whoever lives in the unit next to the fire escape has it covered with UV-blocking curtains. A rusted ladder leads to the alley, speckled with puddles from last night's downpour.

Laura turns around and begins her descent, Louboutin pumps clicking on the rungs.

"Let go, and I will catch you."

"Uh..." I move closer to the ladder and watch the top of her head get smaller, heart sprinting at a mile a minute. "Be careful, Laura."

She reaches the bottom rung, swings back, then forth, then back again, before letting go mid-arc. My heart leaps, and I almost scream for the second time tonight.

Laura lands as gracefully as a cat burglar next to an overturned trash can, then doubles back upon straightening and looks up at me. "Come to me, my Oasis."

I must be crazy.

I can barely see her face, and when she holds out her arms, all I can focus on is the rectangle of pavement between them.

"I will catch you," Laura calls, muffled in my ringing ears.

I step onto the ladder, clenching one cold, gritty rung, then the next. My heart thunders as I grab the last one. I see my reflection in the puddle at her feet—the soles of my white K-Swiss, the rolled-up cuffs of my pants. I lick my lips, gauging the distance.

"How should I fall?" I call uncertainly.

"Howsoever you wish," she says, smiling up at me, eyes sparkling through the dark. "I will catch you."

I want to believe that.

I want to believe that even if she doesn't catch me now, someone will eventually.

I've been holding onto the bottom rung for longer than just tonight, and I'm ready to let go.

So I do.

six

The air leaves my lungs. Aside from being winded, I don't feel any of the pain I clenched my body for. I open my eyes to Laura watching my face, a satisfied smile on her lips, one arm under my knees and the other under my shoulders.

"The adrenaline has given you tremors. I will carry you to the car," she says briskly. She adjusts me in her arms before turning towards the terminal end of the alley, furthest from my apartment's view, heels echoing off the brick buildings.

"You must have ankles of steel," I say, finding my voice at last.

"Even if I had ankles of straw, I would catch you," she says, like a purr.

My face warms. I relax, breathing through the quivering in my limbs until it's gone. I look up at the sky. I could get used to this—her arms cradling me while the stars twinkle above, sparse compared to Kansas, but made beautiful by this night.

All too soon, her footsteps stop. I look back to our surroundings and double take, gaping at the jet-black Rolls-Royce as she lowers me to the ground. I step closer to the hood ornament. In music videos and movies, it's a silver woman bent into the wind, arms behind her back like wings, cloth billowing against her; the hood ornament on Laura's Rolls-Royce is a golden bat mid-flight.

She pulls the remote from the arm pocket of her bomber jacket. All four suicide doors open on their own, showing a dark purple leather interior. I sit down tentatively. Specks of starlight on the ceiling, the word *Phantom* on the dashboard, and at least five speakers that I can see. This must be the most expensive thing I've ever touched.

Laura climbs and starts the car with the press of a button.

"When you said money is of no concern to you, I thought you meant when it came to buying up copies of *Dracula*," I say before I can stop myself.

"My wealth is vast, but it is also several centuries in the making," Laura says as she steers the car towards the street. "I consider it reparations for having to witness mankind for this long."

I don't know if I should laugh; it's certainly taking effort not to. I guess it depends on where this talk comes from and why and just how much of it she believes.

When the last pedestrian passes the alley, she turns right, joining the throng of cars headed towards Midtown.

If I thought my nerves would lessen once I was in her company, I was sorely mistaken. Minutes pass, and all I can do is stare straight ahead, knowing that if I look over, I'll just end up staring. I look to the ceiling, as if the fiber optic constellations will tell me how to act on a first date.

"How was your day?" I ask. "Did you give any bookstores your patronage?"

"I bathed my cat," Laura says. "It upset her that I burned books when we could have been bonding, and so we bonded. Unfortunately, this sort of bonding only upset her further."

"Cats are nice. What color is she?"

"That of the rising sun, with eyes of gold." At a light, she smiles at me. "You must meet her."

"I'd like that." I clear my throat. "Laura?"

She grips the wheel, leaning closer.

"Oasis?"

I lick my lips, thinking as I do of how we went from being separated by the front counter at work, to being separated by the center console of her fancy car. "I just wanna say sorry in advance if I'm super awkward. I haven't been on a date in a long time. I haven't been around humans in a really long time either," I confess, running my fingers along my seatbelt.

"Neither have I. And then your heartbeat caught my ear and your fragrance caught my nose." She sighs nostalgically, like it didn't happen just yesterday. "And when you looked at me, I saw what most people only think they have."

"Which is?"

She smiles another playful smile.

"An appetite."

I look at my knees as the blush creeps back into my face. I guess I haven't been as subtle as I thought in ogling her.

"I can't help it. You're beautiful."

"I am delighted you think so," she says. "When preying on humans, ugly is simply not an option."

I raise my head to her looking at me and not the road, even though the car's still going thirty and her left hand is on the wheel, maneuvering us through traffic. We pass several lights; she doesn't look away from me. The Hudson River expands, dark but for the lights of New Jersey's skyscrapers. She continues to watch me, occasionally glancing at the road like driving is an afterthought. She slows at a red without even looking at the car braking ahead of us. Then, as if realizing that my stare is on account of more than just her immaculate face, she looks straight ahead, leaving me with yet another thing to unpack later.

"Speaking of appetites," I say after a lengthy pause, "where are we going?"

"It is an Italian restaurant," Laura says. "I am told the cuisine of Italy is edible these days."

I nod, and though I try not to look away from her smile, I can't help it. I can already picture what's about to happen: the two of us step into a fancy restaurant, the waiter takes our orders, we make small talk, our food arrives, and I stare at my plate until she realizes what she's dealing with, takes me home, and never contacts me again.

I've yearned for human contact for entirely too long to let go of this.

Tonight, I'll behave.

I'll listen to the voice in the back of my head that tells me that there's nothing to worry about. Turn up the volume until it drowns out the one saying I'm a fool who has it coming if I so much as take a bite.

*

The restaurant is on Broadway, facing the Hudson. Laura gives her key to the valet, and after a twenty-floor ascent in the elevator, consults the host, who confirms her reservation details and guides us to a table.

I trail after her, arms crossed, looking around without seeing much, which is half due to oncoming dissociation, half due to the dimness of the place. The enormous chandeliers are candlelit. All around are velvet drapes and oil paintings featuring Italian seascapes, still-lifes of fruits and bread, and views of the stars and planets. The bar spans two walls. There are twenty or so tables, all booths, some against the windows, some against the wall, and curtains at the ends of each table, some of which are drawn shut, hiding the patrons from view.

The host delivers Laura and I to a booth set against the floor-to-ceiling windows, with a view of the river, just like I would've picked. Not long after, a black-suited waiter sweeps towards us with two menus and a towel over one arm.

"*Buonasera, signora. Grazie* for dining with us tonight. New on the menu," he says, handing one to each of us, "we have *caprese di bufala* and *melanzane al forno* antipasti. For main courses, we have *tortellini funghi* pasta with crisp asparagus and braised cremini, or if you are in search of something heartier, a wonderful *abbachio alla romana* with New Zealand lamb-chops and a subtle chianti wine sauce. On the wine list, we have…"

As he speaks, I scan the menu under the candlelight and can't help widening my eyes to make sure I'm reading correctly. The last item he mentioned is $68.

"I will have a bottle of the *Bruno Giacosa*," Laura says, handing back the dinner menu without having perused it. "*Barbaresco*."

The waiter nods and smiles at me. "Would you like more time?"

"I'll have spaghetti," I say.

He steps away, returning briefly to fill two glasses with ice water from a carafe. He snags the tassels binding the curtains and draws them shut, robbing me of my usual restaurant pastime: people-watching.

Laura leans forward, elbows on the table beside her glass of water. The candlelight illuminates her eyes and face, but by some trick, doesn't cast a wisp of a shadow around her head and shoulders.

"Oasis."

I look up from where the shadow of her forearms should be, thinking as I do that it's possible my litmus tests for whether I'm going crazy are skewed by virtue of being self-administered.

"Will you tell me the minutiae of your day?" Laura asks.

I clear my throat, dislodging thoughts of potential psychosis.

"I woke up. Went to work," I say, at which she nods, face alight with fascination. "UPS came with merchandise. There was some Superman stuff, so I was thinking of buying a Superman comic tomorrow."

"The red S man with the nice chin?"

I laugh.

"Yeah. I haven't read anything new in a while, and me and him are both from Kansas. And then…" Just as quickly as it stabilized, my heart starts sprinting again.

"And then?" Laura says, leaning closer.

"Then a doctor from someplace called the Vantage Hematology Institute came in looking for a patient who escaped." I lick my lips, heart filling with anger all over again. "I was actually going to bring it up to you."

Laura nods again.

"And then?"

"Well…his name is Dr. Seward, and he said his patient is a short white man who's wealthy and has a psychotic fixation on *Dracula*, and that he also *thinks* he's Dracula," I say. "He also said the patient has people who enable him."

For the third time, Laura nods raptly.

"And then?"

I clear my throat.

"I just couldn't help noticing that you're wealthy and fixated. And you said *Dracula* is about—I mean adjacent to you. That's not an accusation," I say quickly, raising my hands. "But if you and that patient are friends, you should tell him Dr. Seward's looking for him."

She frowns, biting the corner of her plump lower lip in silence.

"You can also let him know—the patient, I mean," I say hesitantly, cracking my knuckles one by one, "if you know him…I won't say anything to Dr. Seward if he comes back."

"Dr. *Seward*," Laura says with a soft, serpentine hiss, "will be lucky to have all twenty-four vertebrae in his spine once I have dealt with him."

"You're not afraid?"

"Afraid of Jacob Seward?" Her lips part in an awed smile, showing sharp white canines and a very distracting gold bar in her tongue. "The Sewards are like roaches. They skitter into the open and cause a fright. One good stomp," she says, bringing her fist down gently on the table, "and you realize there is nothing to fear. Just a filthy bug living its life by scavenging yours."

I expected at least *some* concern, if not an explanation.

"It's a good thing Kennedy made it clear he's not welcome at Full Cauldron anymore."

"Roaches cannot be talked out of being roaches. They must be exterminated," Laura says sagely. She bends her left index finger, and delicately brushes her knuckle against her glass of water, drawing something into the condensation that I can't see. "I will show Jacob what it means to prod the son of the dragon, as I showed his grandfather, and his father before him."

I stare, unsure of if I should be this fascinated, or if it would be smarter to be afraid.

The waiter spares me from having to decide by ringing a bell outside the curtains.

"*Entrino*," Laura says.

The curtain parts, and he leans in with two glasses and a dark bottle.

"I don't need one," I say quickly.

He puts it in front of Laura instead and with his corkscrew deftly uncorks the bottle.

"I will pour my own, *grazie*," she says.

He nods, and says to me,

"Your meal will arrive shortly."

"Thanks."

The curtains fall shut again.

Laura pours to half an inch below the rim and cradles the wineglass between two fingers.

"You must alert me if he contacts you again."

I look away, watching the pale crests of waves in the lapping river. The sultry sight of Laura and her wine has me so full of butterflies that I doubt there's even any room left for food. But the disconnect between the way she makes me feel and the things she says feels like an echo of the Angelorum—of my only friend Helena, who I was scared to fall in love with because she believed the angels were waiting for her, and who I stopped myself from falling in love with because I soon after believed that the angels were waiting for me, too.

Then again, it's possible that Laura doesn't believe what she's saying—that there may be another explanation for her...well, for her. I'd never use 'nerd' as a pejorative, but it's the best way to describe the patronage at Full Cauldron. For a moment, it all makes sense.

"Are you roleplaying?" I ask. "You and Dr. Seward, I mean. Are you roleplaying *Dracula*?"

She takes a hefty sip and licks her lips, frowning over the rim of her glass.

"What is roleplaying?"

"It's when you pretend to be a character from something," I say, returning her frown. "My ex-boyfriend and his friends used to role play *Mass Effect* on Facebook, but people do it in real life."

Laura puts the glass down, rotates it in place.

"And what makes you believe I am guilty of this?"

"Well, I wasn't going to say anything in case English isn't your first language, but I haven't heard you use any contractions whatsoever," I point out. "Nobody talks like that in real life."

Her frown deepens.

"It is you humans whose lives are so short that you cannot say two or three whole words. But the English language will die, and *I* will be here watching linguistic anthropologists attempt to decipher your *contractions*," she says, ending the word with a delicate hiss.

I click my tongue and unroll my silverware, yet again symbolically committing to eating.

"That's another thing. You talk like you're not human. Do you really believe that?"

Laura takes another sip, brown eyes sparkling like gems as she watches me put my fork and knife on either side of the tapestried place-mat depicting a Sicily sunset.

"Are you going to bring me back to reality?"

"If you need me to." I watch a few bubbles combine at the surface of her wine as she lowers her glass, but mostly, I watch her face. "I don't really care if you're into roleplaying, or if you're straight up crazy. I can handle that—probably. But I need to be sure I'm not being played. Or role played." I'm fighting every fiber of my being not to look away. "I thought I wasn't human too, once. I can't handle anything else not being real."

"*I am real*," Laura says, soft in volume, but firm enough to loosen my paranoia just a little. "And I would never bring stress into the life of my human. It defeats the purpose of making you mine."

Again, the tinkling of a bell prevents me from forming a

response. It stops ringing, but my ears don't. I barely hear the waiter's voice when he sets a steaming plate of spaghetti in front of me. He asks if I want anything else—a drink, a side dish, dessert. I say no to all three.

The curtains fall shut, and I'm left holding my fork and butter knife upright on either side of my plate, like I'm in a commercial. The spaghetti certainly looks commercial-worthy, with several meatballs nested in the pasta, sprigs of basil in the center, and a dusting of Parmesan soaking into the dark red sauce.

"Have you eaten the food here before?" I ask.

"I consume blood and wine alone. The wine is meh," Laura says with half a shrug. "Is the food conveying meh as well?"

"I…"

Haven't eaten anything but a banana today.

Could dig into this and inhale it like a vacuum.

Would never recover from letting my guard down and finding out the hard way that it should've stayed in place.

My stomach squeezes and gurgles with hunger, but my hands stay where they are, clenched in sweaty fists around my silverware.

"Look at me, my Oasis," Laura says.

Somehow, I do. "It looks really good, but I…" I swallow hard, and search for a scrap of resistance in my body. A whisper from within to talk me out of wasting this $40 spaghetti. Nothing surfaces. "I can't eat this," I say, exhaling a shaky breath as I put down my knife and fork. "I'm sorry."

"Would you like to order something else?"

I shake my head at my plate.

"I just can't eat stuff if I didn't see it being made. I thought I could tonight, but…" I chew my lip. I look up but can barely see her eyes as mine sting with tears. "I should have said something. I'm sorry."

"It is *I* who should be sorry for presuming."

I blink away the tears and watch as Laura reaches for my napkin, then drapes it over the plate of spaghetti like it offended her.

"I will have them dispose of this, but somehow, someway, I must see you fed tonight," she says as she gets to her feet. "Your hunger is my hunger."

As the palpitations from my confession die down, warmth fills me like helium.

"Laura?"

She looks over her shoulder while parting the curtains.

"Oasis?"

"Thank you."

Laura smiles.

Her eyes trail from my face to my hand, like she's thinking of touching it. A moment later, she says,

"I will return to you," and leaves.

I didn't think it was possible to feel this okay after stepping into a restaurant and having my brain buckle into noncompliance. I don't feel like a misbehaving child, or like I'm drowning in guilt while looking from the covered plate to her wine, to the glasses of water that neither of us have touched.

Only Laura *did* touch hers.

Curious, I reach over and rotate her glass by the rim. The condensation's starting to roll down the sides in congealed drops, but her knuckle drawing is still intact. It's a stick figure, tilted slightly to the side, with a long stick spearing it through the center, jutting up from thick blades of grass.

I fold my hands in my lap and bite my lip, mind whirring, but forming few cohesive thoughts.

I spend every day going over my empty life with a fine-toothed comb, searching for so much as a thread of a red flag in every situation. Something tells me that if it wasn't for just now—if it wasn't for Laura treating me the way I wish my brother would every time he tries to exposure therapy me out of wasting food—I'd be hearing alarms in my head.

But I'm not.

I watch beads of water disappear the impaled stick figure until Laura returns with a smile and a sealed bottle of wine.

"Are you ready?"

In silence, I slide out of the booth.

"Is there nowhere you can dine comfortably?" She asks once we're on the elevator.

"I sometimes eat Popeyes," I reply sheepishly. "I used to work there. I tell myself everyone hates it there too much to bother poisoning anyone—for the reasons I'm scared of, at least."

"We will go there. And I will smell the food to be sure it is safe." Laura laces her fingers around the wine bottle. "And if it is not safe, the employees of Popeyes will not be, either."

Goosebumps prickle my neck, and a voice echoes in the back of my head: what if she's being completely serious?

"Thank you," I say, telling myself as I do that it doesn't matter.

That for all her nonchalant suggestions of violence, at least she hasn't given me a razor and told me to bleed or leave.

*

I get my riverside view for dinner after all when Laura finds a spot in the lot off Hudson Parkway. I smash through a biscuit and two wings, then start on the mashed potatoes. Normally, I'd be wading in guilt over somehow being able to eat this garbage and not my brother's cooking, but right now, I'm grateful to be eating something I didn't make three days in a row.

"Very good," Laura murmurs, stroking the label on her wine bottle, watching me. "Nourish yourself, my Oasis."

"I'm not sure this can be called nourishing."

She swigs from the bottle and smacks her lips. She's leaning against the door, legs crossed, looking as satisfied as I feel.

"What did you mean when you said my hunger is your hunger?" I ask thickly.

Laura raises her eyebrows and looks away, like she's embarrassed.

"I must ask that you forget I said that. My sister informed me that this is not appropriate talk for a first date."

"It's less inappropriate than threatening the whole staff of Popeyes—which I'm not necessarily criticizing. The sentiment means a lot. I think," I add, at which she smiles. "Was your sister at the restaurant?"

"She is always with me—unless we are in a fight. Then I cannot find her in my mind and must sniff her out to give her a piece of it," she says.

Is she admitting to hearing voices? Because I haven't seen her pull out a phone.

"Tell me about your sister," I say.

"She is twenty-one and human. She will be graduating from Juilliard in the spring," Laura says with a proud smile. "Soon, audiences across the globe will be moved by her fake tears, as I have been for the past sixteen years."

"Sixteen?" I repeat. "How old are you?"

"Twenty-four."

"You're a year older than me."

"And I have been twenty-four for the last 564 years," she says before taking a mighty gulp.

I close the box of clean chicken bones, slurp some Sprite while performing mental math.

"You were born in the 1400s?"

Laura licks wine off her lips, nodding.

"January 26th, 1431, in Sighisoara."

"I was born July 13th, 1996, in Wichita," I say. "I should check and see if we're astrologically compatible."

"I have waited 122 years for you," she says. "The stars cannot sway me now."

More goosebumps. More trying not to look away.

"In 122 years, you never looked for anyone else?"

"You have your food trauma and I have mine." She bites her lower lip, top row of teeth just visible above her chin, but her smile lives on in her eyes, alight with the glow of the ceiling stars.

I start to ask how much of that has to do with *Dracula*, but soon realize that it might be the equivalent of having someone ask me about the abridged, bastardized bible that I used to read for hours at a time. I probe my brain for something else.

"What do you do for work?"

"When I was human, I was Voivode of Wallachia," she answers before taking another swig. "Then one too many Ottomans tried to kill me, so I said fuck it. I am doing nothing but getting drunk with cold water, defending these gates while humans spread lies about me." She waves a dismissive hand at the space between us, scowling. "Gave the Devil my heart. Spilled all the blood I needed to destroy my soul, faked my death in battle. And now here I am with you."

"What's a voivode?"

"A prince," Laura says. "But in Wallachia, princes are warlords groomed for battle, and so this I was as well."

I slurp Sprite from my half-empty cup.

"Where's your crown?" I ask.

"Crowns are for kings, and kings are all lazy. I wore a coronet, which I kept in an alder box. It was looted from my castle after it was destroyed in 1897—along with many basques and polonaises and reticules and first edition pairs of Levi's blue jeans," she says, heavy with nostalgia. "Forgive me. Materialism is my most innocuous sin, but I see no point in walking this earth for eternity if I am to cut corners on my wardrobe."

"I can get behind that. Let's go back to the destruction of your soul," I say slowly, feeling very much like Barbara Walters as

Laura leans a little closer, nodding attentively. "Why and how?"

"I did not want to go to hell, and one cannot go to hell without a soul," she says. "The how is between me and the Devil."

"Gotcha." I look at the artificial stars above, and at the tangible moon straight ahead, slowly climbing out of view. Talk of the Devil is inherently talk of angels, and I don't know if I'm ready for that. Not tonight. Tonight, I want to soak in her company like a bath full of Epsom salt. Forget that the future consists of anything other than this strange woman.

"How close are you?" Laura asks, licking her wine-tinted lips.

"How close am I to what?"

"How close are you to loving me?"

I choke on my Sprite. I drop the cup in the cup-holder and cover my mouth until the coughs subside.

"I don't know how to measure that."

Laura swirls the bottle of wine, which she finished nearly as fast as I finished my food.

"Love has no unit of measurement." She swallows the last of it, rams the cork in, and puts it on the floor. "You are there or you are not."

"Oh."

If it's that black and white—one or the other—then the answers in my heart and my head are opposites.

I've tried getting comfortable before. Nestled into people and places that were rotting at the root. Got in too deep too fast and didn't realize it until the surface was too far away to see.

Love is where I draw the line on letting go tonight.

"Can I answer that some other time?" I ask.

"May I ask why the answer must wait?"

I can't help narrowing my eyes at her. I stuff the remnants of my meal into the paper bag and roll it up securely.

"Probably because I'm human."

Laura slides closer, fiber optic starlight twinkling in her eyes.

"Is it a spoiler?" She whispers.

It takes a moment to connect the dots back to my memoir, dog-eared to mark her progress.

That beat up composition book may as well be a compendium of all the reasons I *don't* feel human.

I'm tempted to just say it.

Get it over with since I spend so much time wishing I had someone to love.

Find out the hard way that I opened my heart too soon.

Laura lifts her hand and covers my mouth.

"No spoilers."

"*Angels be with me*," I gasp, shivering as I grab her wrists. "Your hands are *cold*. I rub her fingers in my palms, trying to get some circulation going. I switch from her left hand to her right. "*Why* is the heat off?" I demand.

She looks both content and amused, a recurring combination that makes me scowl this time.

"You need more iron," I say.

"As do you."

"Maybe, but I'm not the one whose hands are about to freeze off her wrists," I scold, even though she's right. I peel off my flannel and put it over her, securing it under her chin like a bib and force her hands into her lap beneath it. "Is that better?"

"Much better," she says, same satisfied smile on her lips. "And when I drink of you, I will be like a serpent in the sunlight."

"If you don't die of hypothermia before then," I say wryly. "Next date, we're doing something in the sunlight."

A frown furrows her brow.

"I will barbecue."

"I was thinking more like going to the park. I'll make sand-wiches—if you want," I add quickly. "If that's too much for you, we can keep food off the table. I'm fresh out of spare blood, but I'll get you some wine if you tell me what you like."

She smooths my flannel over her chest like an apron.

"You will bring with you the Gospel of Oasis?"

I want to say no, especially since if she's still interested in me, that means she hasn't gotten to the good parts. But all it took was tonight for me to realize I want to show her—to get that out of the way so I don't have to spend however much time explaining why I'm...me. She stares at me, pouting lightly, like she anticipates a disappointing answer.

"I'll bring it."

Laura nods satisfactorily.

"The wine must be red."

I smile.

"I can work with that."

Quiet falls between us, and for the first time all night, the voice in the back of my head is quiet too. I'm watching her and she's watching me, and miraculously, there's not a single paranoid thought stuck in my sanity like a splinter. I can't believe I was considering doing anything more to her than pulling myself together to spend the evening together.

*

Three hours later, Laura parks in the loading zone in front of my building. The whole ride here was spent trying to keep my heart from sinking, but I don't want to get out of the car. I stare out at the empty street, waiting for the will to move.

"When will be our next date?" She asks.

"I'm off tomorrow," I say, trying and failing to keep the sulk out of my voice. "Do you still not want my number?"

"I want all of you," Laura says, chilling me. "But I do not have a phone."

I'm not sure what answer I expected, but it wasn't that.

"Why not?"

"I find them overstimulating to witness," she answers. "The thought of owning one makes me wish I had died in battle."

"If that's the case, I guess I'll just have to handwrite your playlist and give it to you."

"A playlist?" A pause before she leans close. "Just for me?"

"Just for you." I haven't blushed this often in one night in my life. "Music is my unit of measurement."

She grins. By now, her lipstick is gone. I like her lips bare. They look soft and succulent, just like the rest of her. I want to reach over, brush them with my thumb, cup her face in my hands, and—

"Are you still breathing?" Laura asks.

I start; I wasn't. I've also been subtly but certainly leaning over the center console. I clear my throat and grapple for the door control. It rises, flooding the car with crisp air.

"Just thinking about the dishes in the sink. I had a good time," I say. "See you tomorrow?"

"You will." The overhead light illuminates her smile, but her eyes look further away, darker than before. "Goodnight, my Oasis."

I step out, walk uncertainly towards the brick stairs.

Laura waves; I wave back.

She's right.

I do have an appetite.

seven

July 10, 2019

All he would say was:—
"I don't want to talk to you: you don't count now;
the Master is at hand."

seven

I used to be queen of mix making. Mom said I have an ear for putting together songs that all reached for one another, that their curation came from my soul. My ex-boyfriend, Raymond, thought that all my playlists told stories and showcased my heart.

My unit of measurement.

After breakfast, I sit at my desk to begin curating Laura's playlist. The balmy summer breeze tickles my scalp, which is tender from the four cornrows I put in last night. I have a can of coconut water, a banana nut muffin, and the YouTube homepage open on my laptop. It's time to go in.

Faithless are on practically every playlist I make, so I pull them up first on YouTube and queue a few songs to test out.

I always spend the research portion of playlisting in my head, using each song as the soundtrack to a daydream, seeing where the synths and lyrics take the seeds. Today, that daydream is a revisionist fantasy of the moment in the back of the Rolls-Royce when Laura asked how close I was to loving her.

What if I'd said I was there?

Would it have been a lie?

I tear a sheet from my memoir and write the name of a Faithless song in the middle of the page, close to where the centerpiece will go. I test out some Sidewalks and Skeletons next. A song called 1996 pops up on shuffle, prompting me to simultaneously delve into something I almost forgot I mentioned last night: birth chart compatibility.

For a while, I cycle through one astrology website after

another, searching for one that goes back to 1431. Half an hour goes by and 15 pages into my Google search, I realize how ridiculous it is to input anything other than 1995.

I head back to the first website and input January 26th, 1995, and July 13th, 1996. Of course, I check the challenging aspects first.

Hard feelings if it ends, periodic inability to see one another clearly, impatience.

All I can think while my brain populates with vague scenarios of domestic disputes between myself and the woman I went on one date with is that getting into fights would mean kissing and making up.

The stars can't sway me either.

That doesn't mean I don't want to know what they have to say, or that I don't want a cosmic nudge in a direction close to right.

The exact nudge I needed appears in the form of a shared note from Kennedy:

I hope I'm not too late but see
attached SparkNotes.

Dracula (Severely Abridged)
By Bram Stoker
(Edited by Kennedy Cairns)
-Jonathan Harker (lawyer/real estate agent/ nerd) pulls up to Transylvania to sell Dracula a house in London. Locals say Dracula is bad vibes.
-While snooping around, Jonny realizes Dracula is a vampire. -He gets trapped in his castle with his three brides. Eventually he escapes to a hospital in Hungary.
-Dracula turns into a wolf so he can get on a ship to London.
-Wolf-Dracula kills everyone in transit.
-In England, Lucy (best friends with Jonathan's wife Mina) writes about being proposed to by a terrible psychiatrist, a trust fund jock, and a guy from Texas. She chooses the jock.
-Dracula bites Lucy. She starts sleepwalking and killing kids.

-Dr. Abraham Van Helsing, vampire extermina-
tor, gets called onto the case. He's Dutch and
talks weird.
-The case goes very sour and Lucy is both
beheaded and staked by Van Helsing and the
three proposals.
-Some stuff happens. Dracula drops cool lines
about being old and stealing their women so
they'll drink blood on his behalf
-Dracula bites Mina. They develop a psychic
connection that Van Helsing uses to track and
kill him.
-Van Helsing and Co. destroy Dracula's castle
and live happily ever after.

Key concepts:
-shameless Protestantism
-coded Antisemitism
-some anti-Blackness
-flagrant Orientalism
-Bechdel test failure
-delightfully homoerotic
-beautiful prose
-bottomless adaptations
-inspired by Vlad the Impaler. He's a really cool
guy.

I almost forgot I asked for this. I brush muffin crumbs off
the keyboard, nursing guilt. Just because I silently committed to
not reading Dracula itself doesn't mean I can't read adjacent to it.
I feel as much apprehension as I do anticipation while looking up
Vlad the Impaler.

Wikipedia loads first. The glimpse of a summary includes
born *1428 – 1431 in Sighisoara, Transylvania,* and *Voivode of Wallachia,*
and *Vlad Dracula.*

My heart skips a beat and struggles to regain its rhythm,
pounding like the kick drum of a jungle song. I still don't understand Laura's obsession with Dracula, and now there's this guy.
An abundance of potential red flags jump out at me as I skim the
Wikipedia page contents, tripping over the heading *Reputation for
cruelty.*

The Impaler part alone has me wondering if Laura's some-how a variation of the kids in high school who thirsted over Ted Bundy and Charles Manson. I thought that type of psychopathic behavior was specific to weird, lonely white girls. There has to be another explanation still, and if anyone'll know, it's Kennedy.

Is there a word for someone pretending to be a fictional character?

Roleplaying?

Another word?

Let me check

Two Cairns siblings aged 31 and 13 have provided the term "kinning" or "kin with" in the gc, which is when you genuinely believe you're x character incarnate

Apparently you can kin with historical figures too. Explains why I feel so Joan of Arc sometimes

When is the last time you felt like Joan of Arc?

Last week my great-uncle who has dementia wanted someone to watch a mov-ie with him, so I offered. He picked Passion of the Christ. Then he forgot we watched it, so we watched it again an hour later. Then he realized while watching that it wasn't what he wanted to watch, and he'd *actually* been think-ing of The Last Temptation of Christ, which we watched twice because my aunt came in, realized we were at the end

**of it, and wanted to watch,
too. I almost committed
geriatricide**

**Anyway. Does this have to do
with Laura?**

No. Not sure how to say this
but I'm kinning Bilbo Baggins

Wow. I want what you have.

Maybe Laura's kin with Vlad the Impaler.

There are worse people to kin with than medieval tyrants who've been dead for so long that there are more uncertainties than certainties about them. From the looks of it, Vlad the Impaler may as well be as fictional as Dracula the vampire.

I close the tab. I want to believe I'm doing my due diligence, trying to get to the bottom of her fanaticism; that if she finds out, she'll understand that I just want to understand her. But I'm the one who said that lies aren't beautiful, and this could easily turn into one if I keep perusing the internet, hoping my eyes glaze over anything involving Dracula the book.

I get back to the task at hand and search for another song.

*

I don't know the first thing about wine, so since Laura's mystifying obsession with Vlad the Impaler is all I have to go on, I pick a red from Romania at the nearest wines and spirits emporium and put it in a canvas bag with my memoir before stopping by Full Cauldron. It's funny seeing Kennedy in my spot, looking like The Thinker while appraising books for pricing.

"Anything good?" I ask.

"A lot of vampire books coming through." He pencils a price in the corner of Fledgling. "Mercedes Lackey, some anthologies, and a ton of Buffy novelizations. Somebody either died or grew the hell up."

"No Dracula?" I ask casually.

"Not yet."

I glance at the crate next to his feet, which typically holds the discard pile of overly damaged books that somehow made it past the first round of vetting, books that we have way too many copies of, or books that he simply changed his mind about.

"Why is that one in the penalty box?" I ask, standing on my tiptoes for a look at the upside-down hands cupping a Granny Smith apple.

"I hate Mormons," Kennedy says. "The author also hates Black and Indigenous people, which is bold for a bad writer, but unsurprising for a Mormon."

"You're like the John Brown of vampire fiction readers."

Kennedy grins and closes a priced horror anthology. "I was embarrassingly obsessed with vampires in high school. My jock then-boyfriend was too, but he kept it on the low—right where he kept our relationship," he mutters, at which the smile slides off my face.

"I learn something new about you every day," I say, gently jostling the bowl of fandom buttons beside the register. "I'm sorry about your high school boyfriend—but happy to be reaffirmed in you being such a great white."

"Actually, I think I'm more of a hammerhead," he says, flipping through a copy of Aesop's fables. "It only just registered that you're here on your day off. Care to explain yourself?"

I cross my arms on the glass display case. "I'm looking for a gateway to Superman. I have a reading date and nothing to read."

Kennedy's eyes widen, and he straightens from his slump, tucking his pencil behind his ear. "With Laura? It was my cheat sheet, wasn't it?"

"Yup."

"That's romantic. I'm happy for you, O. Superman: Birthright might be up your alley. It's from the early 2000s," he says, reaching for another book from the pile. "If you're diving headfirst into comics, you should read Hellblazer next. I'll order you a copy in lieu of a raise."

"I knew I could count on you," I say wryly. I disappear into the shelves and find Birthright. I flip quickly through the volume, then stop and go back after passing an illustrated confederate flag. Upon a second review, the flag isn't what catches my eye. It's a snatch of Superman's dialogue in the middle of the page, spoken to the confederate criminal:

I can hear your heartbeat. You're lying.

"I prefer this take on *The Scarlet Letter*," comes a voice.

I start and whirl around, holding the volume to my chest.

I didn't hear Laura, or see her in the corner of my vision, but she's a foot away, observing the shelves over my shoulder.

If it wasn't for her voice, I might not have known it was her. She's covered from head to toe in black. A wide-brimmed black sunhat, a black pea coat, skintight black pants, knee-high black heels. A black cashmere scarf covers her nose and mouth and enormous black shades cover her eyes.

Laura lowers her scarf with a black velvet glove-clad hand, revealing lips coated in glossy black. "Good afternoon, my Oasis."

"You look nice," I say, which is an understatement. Near-invisibility aside, she looks like she just stepped off a runway. "Why so much coverage?"

"I have a mild sun allergy and must enjoy it cautiously. You look delicious," she says, looking me up and down with a small smile. She whisks her hat off, revealing two zig-zagging braids and puts her sunglasses in her pocket. "Are you ready?"

"Almost. I just need to pay for…" I trail away at the sound of raised voices coming from the counter.

Voice, singular. Kennedy isn't matching the energy of the irate customer glaring at him, and in fact, looks bored. Said customer's gesturing angrily at a book open beside the register.

I draw closer, arms crossed, scowling.

"I dunno what to tell you, sir. Almost all the books we sell here are used," Kennedy's saying laconically, but I can see the impatience flaming in his green eyes. "The defects are factored into the price."

The customer, a rail-thin white man with a red Big Bang Theory t-shirt, blue checked button up, and wire-rimmed glasses, jabs a finger at the open book.

"And you're telling me that even with this coffee stain, this is twenty dollars?"

Closer, I can just see the edge of a hardcover copy of *The Silmarillion* that I priced last week.

I remember without a doubt that the coffee stain in question is on the back cover, not touching any words, and over half obscured by the dust jacket, which is so pristine it could be mint. It's a defect no one would notice if they hadn't gone looking for it.

"Prices are firm," Kennedy says with half a glance at the stain.

"So customer satisfaction means nothing to you?" He demands loudly.

"You're the only customer I've had today who wasn't satisfied. Technically you're not even a customer since you haven't paid for anything," Kennedy says.

"This is ridiculous," says the non-customer. "Absolutely ridiculous."

"If you were really on top of your Tolkien, you'd know that edition goes for at least $90 from resellers," I say, which is the number I recall from hunting down that same edition for Raymond's collection and is therefore probably lowballing it. "This may be the best you'll find without selling an organ."

The customer revolves on the spot, glaring at me. "Woman, nobody asked you, so stay out of it."

I flinch, but don't back away. "You need to relax."

"You need to mind your business before—"

"Before what?" Laura asks. In the corner of my eye, I see her rotating her enormous sunhat by the brim in her fingertips, glossy lips pursed. She pushes her sunglasses on, but her brows remain creased behind them.

"Nobody asked, you, either," the man retorts, just short of a yell.

"Watch how you talk to these women, jackass," Kennedy snaps.

Laura fans her face with her hat, pouting. "I do not appreciate the manner in which you have spoken to my Oasis. Go play in traffic."

Kennedy chokes on a laugh.

Both of us watch Laura's smile widen while she herself watches the glaring customer. He looks from her, to me, to Kennedy, then slams the book shut and shoves it away.

The three of us watch him storm out, button-up flapping with the speed of his exit.

"I swear. There's nothing worse than nerds who forget they're nerds and think they get to be assholes," Kennedy mutters as he picks up *The Silmarillion*. "Thanks for having my back, O. Thank you, too," he says, addressing Laura. "Sorry I called you a woman. I didn't mean to presume."

"You are very kind, but my gender matters only insofar as it attracts my human," Laura says.

"Right on," Kennedy says, nodding. "The older I get, the more I realize I'm pretty fluid myself. So long as the people I care about understand me, I can't care about the rest of the world."

I feel miles away, and not at all like I did something worth being thanked for. I wonder what the rest of that guy's threat was going to be—if I should feel as threatened as I do.

I put my comic on the counter; I've been holding onto it for dear life.

"I hear you're the one who swiped all our copies of *Dracula*," Kennedy's saying. Then he steps back and stoops to remove a book from the stack. "This one just made it to the surface. It's on the house if you want it."

Laura's smile disappears as she removes her left glove one finger at a time and holds the mass market paperback at arm's length. It has a retro cover that features the black, cartoonish silhouette of a hand reaching for a ghostly white woman.

"Thank you," she says before tucking it in the pocket of her pea coat. She puts on her hat, tightens her scarf, and waits by the door.

Kennedy finishes the transaction. We say our goodbyes and head out.

As the encounter with the irate customer fades away, so does the adrenaline he inspired. Sunlight streams through the linden trees, a collage of shadows on the pavement.

"How'd you know I was in there?" I ask, hugging my comic as we walk idly up the street.

"Your heartbeat told me."

I bite my lip. "If you can hear my heart, how do I know you're not eavesdropping?"

"I am an apex predator—not a creep," she says. "I listen to your heart via echolocation to be sure of its continued manufacture of my blood."

I scoff. "Your blood? Our second date isn't even over."

"Presently," she says, bypassing this, "your heart hums with distress. Was it the nerd?"

I was hoping she hadn't noticed. "Raised voices always make me feel panicky. My dad and my brother fought every ten minutes once we moved in with him. I moved in with my boyfriend because I couldn't take it."

"One moment, please." Halfway up the block, Laura steps close to the curb and stoops gracefully. She pulls Dracula from her pocket, then drops it through the sewer grate like a coin in a slot. She straightens up, dusting off her gloves, and returns to me.

Before I can make a remark, Laura grabs my wrist and pulls me closer, out of the path of a cluster of pedestrians I hadn't noticed. Her hand is cold through her glove. Up close, she smells… good. Like something fiery and something floral.

Something I could fold myself into. Something I could consume.

To my dismay, she lets go, orienting herself towards the end of the block.

"I am sorry to hear that," she says. "I promise I will never raise my voice to you."

"I believe you," I say.

Laura nudges her sunglasses up the bridge of her nose with the same hand that was just touching me. It feels like the world began and ended with that brief contact.

"My brother and I had many bombastic fights as youth," she says, bringing me back to the moment. "I am—"

"Can I hold your hand?" I blurt.

Laura offers her gloved hand without question and twines our fingers.

Satisfied, I keep walking, squeezing her palm while she squeezes mine.

"As I was saying, I am not proud of this fact," she continues. "Perhaps if I had been a better influence, Radu would not have been such a pussy."

I work fast to keep myself from laughing at her wryness.

I remember that name, though. "I looked at Vlad the Impaler's Wikipedia page."

"As did I, long ago. Pft," she says dismissively. "It says I am short. Do I look short to you?"

"No," I say uncertainly, because technically, she looks above average height. "Are you kin with him?"

"I am him. All his kin are dead," Laura says, unembellished by any emotions that I can discern—as if his kin have been dead for so long that remembering they're gone doesn't hurt the same anymore. "I am the last of the Drăculesti." She slots her tongue bar between her canines diagonally. "Is this the answer you desired?"

"I'm not sure I wanted a specific answer," I say truthfully.

Her eyes pierce through mine, dark brown and searching. "I will show you my face if it would keep you close."

The earnestness in her eyes makes my heart pound harder.

She doesn't need to show me anything to keep me close.

Her standing here with me is more than I dared to want this time a week ago.

Do I really want the truth, too?

The sudden blare of sirens shoves my barely stabilized heart into a fit of palpitations. A squad car appears as though flung via slingshot, letting loose short bleeps of the siren to get people out of the way. Another few squad cars screech to a halt at the intersection. Police officers leap out, gesturing for onlookers to step away from the unfolding calamity, which is around the corner, just out of sight. I see the hood of an ambulance as I drift closer.

Up and down the street, people are looking over their shoulders, sticking their heads out of storefronts and pausing in their steps, proving wrong the theory that New Yorkers are all too busy to mind anyone's business but their own. Soon, the aggressive screeches of a fire truck join the cacophony, and the typically downtempo block boils over with noise.

I'm not the only one moving towards the chaos for a look, which I don't even realize is the case until I hear Laura's heels on the pavement as she follows, still holding my hand.

Closer to the intersection, I see the back of a sedan that had been going south. The hood of the car is scrunched into that of a northbound SUV. A third and fourth car seem to have collided behind them, while a fifth ran into a streetlamp, knocking off the side mirror and cracking one of the headlights. All the drivers look unharmed as they talk to the police officers. Two more cops are talking to a man holding a little boy, rubbing his back soothingly. Yet another officer is less than ten feet away, talking to a woman with an apron and a pair of combs. Her face is pale with fear.

"...Just ran right into the intersection," she's saying. "Then he started doing cartwheels and somersaults. I came outside—" she points at the salon "—and I asked him if he needed help, and he kept saying, 'No, no, it's playtime, it's playtime, Master says it's playtime'."

My ears lose hold of the rest as I catch sight of several paramedics crouched in the thick of the action, nearly impossible to see. An occupied stretcher rises with them, and they begin to wheel it towards the open ambulance.

A torn, fluttering blue checked shirt, a glimpse of a red shirt, a bloodstained hand feebly holding a pair of glasses on his chest while a paramedic holds an oxygen mask to his face.

My heart stops. I turn to Laura, whose face is fully covered.

"Let this be a lesson to all," she says gravely. "Do *not* play in traffic."

I turn back in the direction of Central Park, Laura walking at my side. I glance over in silence; she's watching the street, which is now backed up with traffic. A path clears for the ambulance. Tow trucks struggle towards the five vehicles, orange lights flashing.

The calamity quiets in my ears as we cross the street, but my brain continues to whir, on and on until Laura's hand is the only part of the world that feels real.

I stopped believing in coincidence a long time ago, but I've never been in a position where coincidence was the only option. Laura may have told that guy to play in traffic, but that doesn't—that *can't* mean that he did it because of her. Nothing but coincidence could be the connection between what she said and what he did. And though I tell myself that it's also not my problem, it's all I can think about the rest of the way to Central Park.

*

Superman: Birthright is flooring, visually. Markers are more unforgiving than watercolor, but the result is brighter. It's a medium I should consider investing in. The biblical scenes I can visualize most clearly are darker and more shadowed than watercolor can convey.

But a new medium means a new learning curve, and it still feels like I have miles to go before any of my pieces feels like a painting and not an attempt at one.

"I wonder if it's too late for me to go to art school," I say.

"Your human life is short. It both is and is never too late."

I lower the book to look at Laura, who's sitting straight across from me. Her sunglasses and hat are finally off, and the bottle of Romanian wine is in the crook of her left arm.

She hasn't looked up from my memoir yet, sitting with her back against the trunk of an elm, studying each page like she's prepping for a midterm. The elm's overlapping leaves and wide branches form a perfect canopy overhead, blotting out all direct sunlight.

"You no longer aspire to own a record store?" She asks.

I wrinkle my nose. "I haven't finished catching up on music. I'd feel like a fraud."

"I hate to show my age, but music all sounds the same these days." Laura sighs and swigs from her bottle. "Such is the case when it is made for money, and not to fill the silence within."

"There's still good stuff coming out," I say. "Just gotta work to find it."

"I look forward to being proved wrong then, when you deliver your playlist to me." She turns a page, only to go back to the one before, as though to clarify something before resuming. "May I ask what has become of Helena?"

My breath hitches, and my fingers start to sweat. I haven't heard her name out loud in almost a year—haven't talked about her since Mirage told me she's the one who took me to the hospital. Haven't seen her anywhere but my dreams.

"I don't know. Hopefully she left, too—under different circumstances than me, I mean."

"Are these circumstances documented in here?"

"That only covers the before and the first few months."

My gaze drifts to a group of sorority sisters in matching t-shirts walking across the Great Hill, looking for a tree of their own. When I look back to Laura, she's watching me expectantly.

"How did you leave?" She asks.

I guess I was naïve to hope that handing over my memoir would spare me having to orate my shitty backstory in some way.

"Zeke had this inner circle called the Psalms, and we all had to be under ninety-one pounds," I say. "I lost eighty pounds in a year. I had a heart attack on the way to a drop in Philly. Before that, I was telling Helena about Mirage's restaurant, so she Googled it and called him. She tried unlocking my phone first and accidentally erased everything on it. The only way I can contact her is by going back."

She turns a page slowly, unreadable. "Is Ezekiel still alive?"

"I don't..." I swallow, unable to finish.

Laura bites her lower lip. She removes a glove one finger at a time, bends forward, and with her knuckle, wipes a fallen tear from my face, leaving a trail of cold where her skin touched my cheek.

I hide my face behind my book, flushed with shame. "I'm sorry."

"Do not be sorry, my Oasis. You have done nothing wrong," Laura says softly, which only makes me want to cry harder.

"I know. Objectively." I squeeze my eyes shut, press my face into my knees until I see stars and can't breathe. "Sometimes."

"You sit before me, who has done so much wrong that hell will not admit me," she says. "Cherish your innocence."

My nose is runny, but the urge to cry abates as I raise my head and behold her sympathetic yet solemn face.

"I thought you staying out of hell was voluntary."

She purses her lips, looks away. Then she clears her throat pointedly and resumes reading my memoir. "I do hope that Ezekiel is still alive. And I do not believe it would do much damage to your innocence should you choose to watch me kill him."

I set Superman aside, scowling, hands folded in my lap. "You don't have to do that for me."

"What about for me? Your blood has always been mine," she says, brown eyes piercing through mine as she rolls a braid between her fingertips. "He is a false prophet, and there is hardly a thrill greater than ripping a false prophet from this earth and sending it to hell, knowing that the Devil will be waiting, smiling with pitch-fork in hand."

"I wish I found that thrilling," I say, "but if the Devil is real, then God is too, and if He's letting false prophets walk around in the first place, then I'd rather believe in random sadistic evil." I grab a few blades of grass and start to braid them, terrified that if I do look up, I'll just start crying again. "It doesn't matter any-way. No matter what happens to Zeke, I'll still be covered in scars. Living, breathing evidence of the worst thing I've ever done."

"No creature but the Lord and His angels is immune to mis-placing its trust," she says. "Not even I."

I start another grass braid, in lieu of stuffing my fingers in my ears. Half of me wants to shut down this conversation and reroute. But what she just said is what the other half of me needed to hear.

"What's your story, then?" I ask, curling my grass braid around a twig.

Laura sighs and closes my notebook on her finger.

"I decided to love a real estate agent. He was from England and his blood smelled…" She trails off, licks her lips, closes her eyes as though submerged in the memory. "He had a heartbeat like thunder. One summer, he came to my home to help me pack my belongings. We were to elope to London."

Jealousy pricks my heart as my melancholia melts away, and I frown at the grass in my fingertips.

"I'm not sure I can compete with a real estate agent."

"There is no competition, as you do not seem to suffer from—" she leans forward and drops her voice to a whisper "—in-terior homophobia." She straightens up, mouth set in a solemn pout. "Worse than that, I had already packed many outfits when it came to light that Jonathan did not like bats."

I raise my eyebrows.

"Really?"

"My beloved winged friends flew past the window, and he remarked that they were terrifying, disgusting, and ominous creatures—a bold thing for a human to say. I lost the power of speech and attempted to ghost him."

"Why only attempted?" I ask, leaning closer.

"I met his wife and found myself attracted to her, and then I met her dearest friend, who then became my beloved. And by then, Jonathan had fallen under the spell of my ex-wife Justina. I saw no point in burning bridges or depriving the world of good blood by killing him," Laura says with a noncommittal shrug. "But then he decided to spread lies—shortly after my beloved's death, no less. After that, the only reason I did not kill him was so that Mina would not raise a fatherless child."

"When was this?"

"1897."

She almost had me.

For a hot second, I thought I might be standing in the shadow of an ex-boyfriend, ex-wife, and dead beloved, but with Laura, it all comes back to *Dracula*.

"Sounds messy," I remark. "Who's Mina?"

Laura opens her mouth, then closes it, lips pursed, like she's suddenly self-conscious. I scoot closer and sit right in front of her, so that our knees are almost touching. "Who's Mina?"

Her suspicious gaze rapidly intensifies, until it feels like she can see my heart beating in my chest. If she said she could hear it right now, I'd believe her.

"Mina was Jonathan's wife," she says at last. "She and I had begun to enmesh, but she decided to remain faithful to Jonathan. She introduced me to Lucy."

"Your beloved?" I ask. "What happened to her?"

"She became a vampire by my fang. She was torn from the darkness before finding the freedom she sought," Laura says, gazing at the blank cover of my memoir, voice delicate as an autumn leaf. "Abraham Van Helsing and his circus cut off her head. They put garlic in her mouth and a stake in her bosom—polished her soul so that she would again see God. But not all vampires go to hell, and this, Van Helsing knew," she seethes. "He did not do it to save her, but to wound me. And *now*," she says, louder, straightening up so fast that I straighten up too, "the circus has renewed its attempts to starve me by bringing stress to my human."

I blink. "Me?"

"You."

I hesitate; real or fictional, I don't need more things to be par-anoid about. "I haven't met any Van Helsings yet."

"Only because his legacy lived on in the Van Helsing Institute, and then the Volta Health Initiative, and then Vital Hearts Incorporated, and then Valiant Hope Innovations." She rattles them off on her fingertips, voice laden with irritation.

I lick my lips. "And the Vantage Hematology Institute…?"

Laura nods. "Each generation, a new front, and a new pack of clowns."

"And Dr. Seward is…?"

"The progeny of a spineless, arrogant sycophant of a physi-cian. Another sad man looking to be in the appendix of a myth," she says, rubbing her left thumb and index finger together like she's playing a microscopic violin.

I nod once. "Good to know."

Laura gives me a small smile.

"Though there is much more to be said, I am happy to have told you this."

"I'm glad you trust me," I say, and mean it.

It occurs to me that I may be under-reacting. That the breadth and specificity of her fictional world should be more disconcerting. It also occurs to me, as the topic fades away and we resume our reading, that I'm under-reacting not because it widens the scope of her potential delusions, but because I'm deluding myself—a habit I thought I'd broken once I stopped believing in angels.

But just because angels don't exist doesn't mean that vampires don't exist.

Except in Laura's world both vampires and angels are real, and if I entertain that notion, I'm entertaining the notion that I almost died for something that was there all along, just beyond reach.

*

Hours slip away under the elm with Laura.

Eventually, she puts on her hat, scarf, and shades as the sun encroaches our shelter with its descent. I haven't talked this exten-sively about Custodes Angelorum before, but with her, it's almost easy.

Which is why it's so hard for me to keep my mind on the question mark above her head.

The sunset leaves streaks of grey against a blue and gold sky, and I feel nothing but reluctance as I tuck *Superman* away and get to my feet, cracking my back and knees.

Laura rises, too, dog-earing my notebook yet again.

"I'm surprised you haven't finished this," I comment.

She hands it back and stands alongside me. "I want to savor you." As she speaks, she removes her hat, sunglasses, and scarf again.

The second disrobing of her face submerges me in want. She smiles and reaches for my hand as we leave the park for the street enclosing it.

"I can't remember the last time I spent this much time with someone," I say.

"Nor can I," Laura says. "And in the sunlight, no less."

"I wish you had told me you were allergic beforehand," I say, poking out my lower lip.

"But you are in need of vitamin D, and so it was worth it," she replies resolutely.

Just as I start to rebuke this, it hits me. I've seen too many of *Dark Shadows'* 1,200+ episodes to have forgotten the fact that sunlight hurts vampires.

As we cross the street, still hand-in-hand, I try to assess this realization relative to her other quirks. There are worse things than mummifying herself in all black to avoid the sun.

"What about *your* vitamin D intake?" I ask.

Laura presses the crosswalk button, then readjusts her cold hand in mine so that our fingers are intertwined.

"I will take in all that I need when I drink of you."

Goosebumps flush my neck. It's the way she says it—soft as a cloud, certain as a sunset, hungry as a flame licking kindling.

The crosswalk light changes, and we continue down Central Park West, strolling between the greenery of the park and a traffic jam that seems to stretch all the way to the Bronx. Looking at it, I can't help but revisit the earlier traffic cataclysm, triggered by a man who thought it was time to play.

That intersection is a few blocks away, meaning my apartment is, too. I wish my heart would settle on one thing to feel. If only I could be curious or suspicious or thirsty. All of it at once is an unfair ask.

One thing I know for sure is that I don't want this date to end.

"Let's say you're a vampire," I begin, struggling to steer my mind away from the overwhelming urge to stop dead in the middle of the street and kiss her.

"No, no—let us not say this," Laura says, shaking her head delicately. "I am *the* vampire. The master from which all others have been copied."

I nod my understanding.

We stop at another crosswalk; from here, I see the mouth of the alley behind my building, then my building itself, and the awning of Full Cauldron up the street. I slow my pace, like I'm nine years old again and shuffling down the walkway of my childhood home in Kansas, doing all I could to delay the bi-monthly visits to my father's.

She's *the* vampire, yet I'm the one wishing I could sink my teeth into her, drink her in until I'm full to bursting.

"If you're *the* vampire known as Dracula, and you haven't eaten anything in 122 years, then what are you waiting for?"

"I am waiting for you to love me," Laura says.

I look away but feel her eyes on me. There she goes again, throwing those words around like I won't fuck around and say them. Like I won't overlook everything I don't understand just to make her mine in return.

"Do you only love me because you want to drink my blood?" I ask.

"That is the only reason for me to love any human."

"What about your sister?"

"She is a very special exception," she says, frowning. "The taste of my own blood would likely cause me great physical, mental, and spiritual torment."

I mull over this as we walk slowly past the bodega on the corner of my street, where the resident tomcat is washing his face in the window. He looks up; his eyes seem to widen as he watches the two of us amble by.

"How can you love me if all I am is food?" I ask.

Laura clicks her tongue as though chastising me.

"You cannot comprehend just how much I love my food. My palate has undergone over five centuries of refinement."

I slow to a stop as we pass the alley. I see my fire escape from here; it's almost impossible to believe that mere days ago, she was standing on it, watching me. Even then, the questions I should've been asking—how she got up there, how she knew I was there, why she left via rooftop—fell to the wayside once I saw enough of her face and heard enough of her voice.

This late, there aren't many pedestrians. It could just be the two of us under the velvety blue sky. The New York milieu of distant subway screeches and honking car horns dims as I face her. She's only a few inches taller than me in heels, meaning that without them, we're either the same height, or she's a little shorter than I am.

I'm used to standing on my tiptoes to kiss, but if I kissed her, my feet would still be flat on the ground. And if—*if* we ever have sex, maybe I'll be able to do what my boyfriend did when we were together and would pounce on one another the moment the house was empty. I'd be in his arms and he'd grab my thighs and pick me up, and I'd wrap my legs around him. Sometimes he'd press my back against the wall; sometimes he'd sit me on the kitchen counter between the toaster and coffee maker; sometimes he'd carry me up to his bedroom, with me still kissing his face and neck. The mere notion of this being me and Laura has me ready to—

"Are you still breathing?" Laura asks sharply. "Oasis, is there some pulmonary condition you have not told me of?"

"Of course not," I say, scrambling to turn off the part of my brain imagining me and her doing all the things I used to do and more. "I'm fine."

"Are you certain?" She asks, eyes searching my face.

"I think I'd know if I wasn't breathing." I clear my throat, but I don't look away. I can't look away, knowing that if I do, my eyes'll be drawn right back to her. Dangerously aware of how close I am to home, I pivot to doing what I do best lately and get to stalling. "It just occurred to me that being a—I mean, *the* vampire and all... doesn't that make you dangerous?"

"Selectively yes," Laura replies, scowling. "But I could never bring harm upon your head. It—"

"Defeats the purpose of making me yours," I finish.

She beams.

We keep walking.

Nothing's telling me no anymore—not even the part of my brain reminding me that 'Selectively yes' isn't a flat no. Which should probably be the only acceptable answer. I picture myself grabbing her wrist, pulling her into the alley now sliding out of view, kissing her until I really do stop breathing. I picture us pushing through the doors, all roving hands and locked lips on the elevator ride up, then stumbling into my apartment and melting into one another.

"For our next date, perhaps we should choose an indoor activity," Laura proposes, bringing me back to the present, reminding me that my time with her is over for now.

It doesn't have to be. Yet when I open my mouth to invite her in, the words don't make it out.

"We could go see a movie," I suggest, throwing all my weight against memories of my boyfriend and I going to the theater and coming out without knowing a single plot element because we were too busy fooling around.

Laura nods, watching me with a raised brow. "When will I see you for this excursion, my Oasis?"

"I have work tomorrow from 12 to 4." It's easier to say than the truth, which is that I'd rather we just not part ways at all. "Or if you're not free tomorrow—"

"I will see you tomorrow after work regardless," she finishes.

Which only makes me wonder if she'd be just as okay with letting the day we spent together turn into a night spent together.

"Goodnight, Oasis," she says, smiling.

I look over my shoulder at the transparent lobby doors, mailboxes and elevator just visible through them. The window of opportunity isn't closed, and it's not too late to summon the confidence to invite her in—or to pretend I have the confidence and ask her anyway.

"Actually, Laura, I was wondering if...?"

When I turn back around, it's to nothing but the parking meter on the curb flashing for coins. My heart thuds as I look left and right, seeing no trace of Laura at either end of the street.

Maybe I spent more time than I realized on my internal debate.

I tell myself it's for the better as I withdraw my keys and head inside. That although I want to believe there are few things that could go south, I've been disastrously wrong before.

At least I had misgivings about Custodes Angelorum. Signs I ignored because stability mattered too much to acknowledge them. I don't have any misgivings about Laura, but that may not mean anything. It could be that ignoring my gut back then has caused it to ignore me, burying all the warning signs so that I can relish in the first attention I've gotten in years, only to be blindsided when something happens.

I trudge upstairs, stomach growling. The frozen chicken I left

on the counter is thawed. With it are two potatoes, a covered cup
of flour, and a bottle of Cajun seasoning. My attempt at making it
impossible to not eat real food when I got home.

Well, I'm home and I'm hungry—just not for food.

What I'm hungry for vanished before I could say goodnight.

I leave my bag near my desk and go wash my hands. In my
room, I turn on the light and kneel in front of my nightstand,
opening the bottom drawer slowly, like I'm defusing a bomb.

A pillowcase covers the contents:

A Fenty lingerie set that I ordered and tried on once before
bursting into tears over how ugly I thought I looked with scar tissue and stretch marks peeking through the lace. A fuchsia dildo still
in its packaging, harness included. A Hitachi magic wand that has
so far only been used to massage my back during PMS. Condoms.
I bought all of this to signify recovery. I can have sex if I want.
Pleasure myself all night if I want. But I don't. And if I can't stand
the feel of my scarred skin, I can't expect anyone else to.

Still, I wish I had the chance to invite Laura in. There's plenty
we could do with our clothes still on.

I close the drawer, take a few deep breaths to regroup.

If I can't indulge this freedom, then I'd better indulge the one
I thawed the chicken out for.

eight

July 11, 2019

Won't you give me one kiss? It'll be something to keep off the darkness now and then.

eight

Kennedy

Hey O, super sorry for the last-minute notice but the store's gonna have to stay closed today, so enjoy a paid day off!! I'll keep you posted about the rest of the week.

Another day to myself. I pull the sheet up to my chin, staring at the stucco ceiling.

I dreamt of Helena, I think. Her sea-colored eyes and forest green hoodie, unzipped over a V-neck t-shirt. Dreams of her leave a melancholic residue that clings after waking, but there are gems among the shards of memory; they're just harder to find the further I get from the source moments.

I don't know how to feel about the first woman I fell in love with showing up in my dreams, just as I'm considering falling in love with another.

It's with this nagging thought that I force myself into the kitchen for breakfast.

*

After a brief scramble for ways to occupy myself, I sit out on the fire escape with the Superman comic that I only read four pages of yesterday, legs dangling over the edge as a soft breeze buffets my flannel sleeves. Scattered clouds race across the sky, lumping together, gearing up for the showers meant to come this evening.

If Laura had a phone, I could tell her that I'm off work today, see if she's free to hang out now.

Or maybe this alone time is a good thing for once. After that half-remembered dream about Helena, maybe I should pump the brakes a little, reevaluate the speed of my attachment.

My eyes glaze over the action-packed panel I've been trying to read for ten minutes. My gaze falls instead on a cluster of rats in the alley, two of whom are chasing each other in a circle, one with a pizza crust in its mouth, like something straight out of a cartoon.

An apt metaphor for my brain right now.

My desire to let go of the past falling prey to the hyper-vigilance that the past left me with. Me deciding not to ask questions while I'm with Laura, only to ask them louder when I'm alone.

I leave Superman face down on my desk and grab my purse, fishing for Dr. Seward's business card. I sit at the table with my laptop, facing the fire escape so that I can see the clouds—and anyone who happens to come up or down the stairs.

I close the braid crown tutorial I watched before bed and type in the web address on the card, bracing myself for an error message, or a real but totally unrelated website. What I fail to brace myself for is the hyper realistic image of red blood cells flowing through a vein, or for the white sans serif font laid over it: *Welcome to the homepage of the Vantage Hematology Institute.*

My heart races as I navigate to the about page and read the description.

Blood is life. At Vantage Hematology, we're committed to understanding the link between blood, the body, and the brain. Founded by a renowned Dutch physician, the VHI's research aims to treat blood-based psychological and neurological disorders using a holistic evangelical approach, blending modern medicinal methods with the tenets of Orthodox Christianity.

I scroll down to a picture of Dr. Seward smiling against a blue background, a silver crucifix centered on his sternum.

Dr. Jacob Seward, M.D., comes from a family of psychiatric professionals. A graduate of Columbia University, Dr. Seward has been head physician of Vantage Hematology since 2009, employing a compassionate approach to treatment. For consultations, call (212) 555-1897.

My mouth is dry by the time I've finished perusing the sparse but clearly legitimate website. If any part of my brain was still attached to the roleplaying theory, that isn't the case any longer.

Dr. Seward wasn't lying about who he is. The escaped patient he was looking for may be real, too. If only I'd asked for more information instead of being defensive, or waited for a straight answer from Laura about her connection to him. Maybe they're both patients at the VHI; a blood disorder could be the *non*-vampire explanation for why her hands are always so cold. For her, vampire could be code for patient, and when she says master vampire, she could mean patient zero.

It's a reach if I've ever heard of one.

But just because Dr. Seward was telling the truth doesn't mean she was lying.

I bite my lip, leg bouncing with anticipation as I open the Internet Archive. I plug the VHI website into the Wayback Machine—my go-to for reading old articles that've been paywalled since publication—and wait. As it loads, a pigeon lands on the rail outside, startling me. I didn't realize how close I was to the screen, or how intensely I'd been frowning at the loading page.

The oldest archive entry is from 2000. My finger quivers slightly as I click. At the top of the blocky, simplistic, and overall Jurassic-era web-page is a gif of an anatomically correct heart rotating like a globe. Above that, in white Comic Sans font: *Welcome to the homepage of Vital Hearts Incorporated.*

I navigate to the about section, my own heart beating a frantic rhythm in my ribs.

At Vital Hearts Inc., we're committed to understanding the link between the heart, the body, and the brain. We employ a hematological approach to psychological, emotional, and behavioral problems...

A cursory skim says that the description matches the Vantage Hematology Institute's nearly word for word.

So does that of Valiant Hope Innovations, which shared the VHI's URL in 2005, as did the Volta Health Initiative in 2012.

If the Van Helsing Institute is real too, it must have been pre-internet.

If.

Although the odds keep getting slimmer and slimmer, it's still possible that this is all an elaborate hoax—a hoax involving the timeless fictional celebrity vampire known as Dracula, designed to ensnare me, the mediocre college dropout known as Oasis Johnson.

It makes so little sense that being afraid makes no sense, either. Or so I tell myself.

How messed up would it be if it made perfect sense for me to be afraid of the person I'm making a playlist for?

Because that's what I'm doing now—closing the tab, opening YouTube, grabbing my memoir and a pen. The page Laura marked for return is halfway through.

No matter how many circles I run in, I always come back to this—the knowledge that regardless of my research, I'd still be falling for her for having seen so much of me. For now, I stop running and plug in my headphones to search for another song.

*

An hour of playlisting, another hour reading Superman, half an hour getting dressed and re-braiding my hair.

I'm out of ways to occupy myself by 2:30. I'd intended to head out at 3, take a slow walk to Central Park, and be back in time to meet Laura at Full Cauldron, but after finishing that comic, what I *actually* want is to get my hands on some markers and a sketchbook.

I wear high-waisted jeans with my blue and green plaid flannel, which is thicker than most of the others I own, perfect for the arctic AC that movie theaters always blast. I'm cutting it close, knowing how long I tend to dawdle at the art supply store, but I'm sure Laura will understand if I'm late.

Half an hour later though, I'm sort of regretting that I didn't stay in a little longer to at least watch some YouTube reviews. I didn't realize how many marker brands there are, how many kinds of markers there are, or how expensive they all are.

Maybe I should've come in with a specific piece in mind—but then that would require an imagination, which I don't have.

I check my phone: 3:15. I told myself I'd head back home at 3:30. I have half a mind to leave now instead of looking around any longer, adding more fuel to the fire of regret.

Regret and guilt, the dynamic duo hiding in the spaces between thoughts, lurking in the wake of every move I make towards becoming someone.

"Did you have questions about anything?" Comes the voice of a sales associate in my peripheral vision.

"I'm alright, thanks," I say with a smile.

"Let me know if you need anything," she says, returning my smile as she walks past me. "Is there anything I can help you find?"

"You are very kind, but no. I have found her."

A chill runs down my spine as I glance in the direction of Laura's voice. Glancing turns to staring at her legs clad in skin-tight snake-print pants. A loose black cardigan hangs off her sleeveless white turtleneck; she's pointing at me with a pair of purple tinted shades, smiling as the associate checks in with another customer.

Something bigger than butterflies surge in my stomach as she approaches me, heels resounding. Something like the pearlescent art deco bat around her neck, flapping a whirlwind in my ribs.

"Where'd you come from?" I ask.

"Nowhere exciting," Laura says, straightening the canvas bag hanging off her shoulder. She stops a foot away, looks me up and down and smiles again. "I do hope, my Oasis, that I have not interrupted a period of silent reflection."

"I'm glad you did," I say, turning away from the marker display. "I came in here without doing my research and, uh...started to spiral a little." I clear my throat; I can't help looking at her chest—at the shadow of her nipples beneath the white fabric and the hints of piercing on both. "It's nice to see you."

"And you, always," she replies, stepping closer. "Where did your spiral lead you?"

"Nowhere exciting."

She gives a sharp laugh and a sharper grin. "Come now, my Oasis. Imagine the things you could do with all these colors—the worlds you could show."

The doubt had been creeping fast, but with Laura here, it abates fast into something I can look past. I pull a case of twenty markers from the shelf without further deliberation.

"Why'd you leave so fast yesterday? I didn't even get the chance to say bye."

"I apologize," she says, strolling alongside me as I make my way back towards the sketchbooks, fully reneging on my notions of abandoning the whole endeavor. "Usually, I am in no hurry to be alone with my thoughts, but something occurred to me, and I had to ponder post haste."

"Was it something I said?" I ask.

Laura shakes her head with a delicate frown. "Know that although you were out of my sight, I had your heart in my ears all night and day."

"Apology accepted." I pick a hardbound sketchbook at random, roughly the size of a comic book. "What does my heart sound like?"

"Music," she says without hesitating. "When we met, Bill Withers. *Ain't No Sunshine.* At present, Whitney Houston. *I Will Always Love You.*"

I don't know what I expected—something mystical, or something that relates directly to *Dracula.* Not something so familiar.

"I love Whitney. I saw her live once with my mom."

"Her voice was a gift. I attended many shows in 1991 with my brother when she toured the globe," Laura says, smiling nostalgically.

"With Radu?" I ask, raising a brow.

She shakes her head. "Radu has been dead for centuries. I have another brother. He is called Cypress."

I make a note of this, adding the name to the cache of facts that ground her in the real world. Still, her saying my heart sounds like music causes it to flutter all the way through the checkout line.

Outside, the clouds knit together over fistfuls of pale blue sky.

"Have you heard of *Midsommar*?" I ask.

"The midsummer Drăgaica fair? It was in June," Laura says. "I did not anticipate you having any interest in celebrating John the Baptist."

"I don't know what Dr...I don't know what that is," I say. "I'm talking about the movie. I did some pre-date research and saw it came out this week."

"And this movie piqued your interest?" She asks, facing me as we stop at the crosswalk.

"I saw cults in the premise, so kinda," I say with a slight shrug. "Morbid curiosity."

She purses her lips. "Are you certain it will not bring you discomfort?"

"*Well*, if you *really* wanna know..." I look her up and down—the dip of her waist, the curve of her neck, her soft jawline and sharp cheekbones. It's my fourth day in a row of being this close to her, and I'm feeling bolder than ever. "It doesn't matter what we see. I'm more interested in the idea of me and you sitting together in a dark theater."

Laura nods, though she's still frowning.

"This does not make much sense to me, but I trust your logic will become apparent soon," she says before leading the way across the street.

I hesitate to follow, earning myself another frown.

I've never deliberately flirted before, but that felt like the flirtational equivalent of pulling out a loaded gun. My internet history is proof that I know that there's way more to her than meets the eye; I just didn't expect cluelessness to be one such thing.

After putting my new supplies in Laura's bag, I pick a window seat near the back of the subway. She sits beside me, a cold thigh pressed against mine, and laces her fingers in her lap. I look at the bat necklace below the fold of her sleeveless black turtleneck, wings spread and hooked to a snug gold chain. Up close, I realize that the cuffs on her ears are also bats, as is the clip above her silken ponytail.

"Are the bats a statement?"

"There is no creature more noble than the bat," Laura replies, turning to face me. "Were I alive, I would lay down my life for any bat that asked it of me."

"As your human, I'm not sure how to feel about that."

She opens her mouth, then closes it, looking at me like I've taken her off guard—confused her, even. "I must reevaluate."

"You do that." I clear my throat. This is as good a time as any to circle back to doing my due diligence by attempting to conclude earlier's research. "I know it's been a couple of days, but you never told me if you know the guy Dr. Seward is looking for, or if he's okay. The short white guy who escaped," I remind her when she frowns.

"My Oasis, I must be completely honest with you." Laura turns to me, looking so grave that my heart plummets. "I am *not* white. *I,*" she says, pointing emphatically at herself, "was recovering from having my heart ripped out by the Devil while Christopher Columbus was still flinging feces at his mother from his crib."

I raise my eyebrows in silence.

"*I* was here first," she continues. "No one asked me if I wanted to be white, and so I am not. I am Wallachian," she says firmly. "And I am six-foot-two. Tall for my time, rest assured."

"But you're the person Dr. Seward was looking for," I say, finally reaching the ludicrous thesis I'd been avoiding uttering, even to myself. "*You* are the one who thinks you're Dracula."

"I know that I am." She frowns, and from the look in her eye, you'd think I was the one who confessed to being fictional. "I have told you this. And I am here to be loved by you so that I can drink of you. Have I not conveyed this?"

"I…yeah, you have," I say, because she has.

It's me who's been trying to dig beneath the things she calls facts for something that makes more sense—for a glimpse of the other side of *Dracula*. Maybe there is no other side. Maybe she really is…

I can't even complete the thought. Laura is clearly Black and no taller than 5'7". Does this qualify as internalized racism?

Maybe this is where I should draw the line—bring her back to reality, like she said. Open my mouth and say sternly that vampires aren't real, Dracula's made up, and Vlad the Impaler has been dead for centuries. Then again, as much exposure as I've had to reality, maybe I should take a leaf out of her book.

"Have I lost you?" Laura asks.

"I'm still here." Still here, and still torn between wondering if she's crazy, or if I'm crazy for asking questions with answers that won't change the way I feel. I put my head on her shoulder. "I'm sorry if I upset you. I'd also hate to be accused of being white."

Laura wraps her arm around me, cold through the fabric of her clothes. "You do not upset me. You understand me."

I don't quite agree, but I nestle into her anyway. My head is beneath her collarbone, and the tip of her bat necklace is touching my forehead, but I don't feel her heartbeat. I tell myself it's the jostling of the subway muffling the sound, that the thump of her heart is too soft to feel on my cheek.

"I feel your heart racing, my Oasis," Laura murmurs, hand splayed on my back. "Is this fight or flight I smell?"

"No," I say and mean it. "You told me the truth, which is all I can ask for."

"Van Helsing made it his mission to starve me," she says, rubbing circles between my shoulders. "It would be unwise for me to be dishonest with you and do the work of his progeny."

"Don't worry." I close my eyes like we're not just a handful of stops away from the movie theatre. "I'm not going anywhere."

*

My hatred for Union Square, which is where the theater is, is probably something I should be over by now. NYU Langone was the psychiatric hospital I was treated in, and everything even remotely affiliated with those memories—sporks, golf pencils, *Gilmore Girls*, slip resistant socks—takes me back to the weeks that snatched my delusions away. Seeing NYU's purple flags fluttering on the sides of buildings affiliated with it gently stirs the dormant rage as we emerge from Bleecker Street station. But then Laura takes my hand without my asking, and without asking me, providing a distraction from the onslaught of memories, and further emboldening me in my plans to kiss her at some point today.

Most of the people in the snaking box office lines are families with children and Marvel fans in graphic tees, chatting excitedly about the new Spider-Man movie. When Laura and I reach the self-service kiosk, less than half the seats for the next screening of *Midsommar* are taken. The only side-by-side seats in the back three rows are almost smack in the middle of each.

Laura pays for our tickets and joins the concessions line, squinting at the backlit menu above the counter. It's the upscale kind that serves alcohol and small plates for the price of an entree at a five-star restaurant.

"Nine dollars for a canned Merlot that will most likely taste like nothing whatsoever," she scoffs. "The twenty-first is fast becoming the most unhinged century so far."

"What about the century that involved slavery?" I ask wryly.

"All centuries involved slavery," Laura says as we advance in line. "Regarding the latest and most notorious enterprise, my siblings believe it to be simple Darwinism, that if you must ship stolen peoples across the water to work peopled lands and make your home, it is not your home."

"And what do you believe?" I ask.

"When I come from, much of the map was blank. Now it is smeared with western Europe's miasma. For this reason," she says, sighing through her nostrils, "I believe it was a horrible waste of blood."

I have no idea what to do with these words, delivered like a genuine lamentation.

"What were you doing during the latest and most notorious enterprise?"

Laura purses her lips. "Well, specifics evade me, but in general, awaiting the downfall of the Ottomans."

"Like the things you put your feet on?" I say, hoping I don't sound too clueless.

"On, or in, or through," she says, waving a noncommittal

hand. "And not just feet. Fists, spears, *kilijs*, hedgehogs, plague-havers. I liked to get creative, just as they did."

"I'll...keep that in mind." And although I tell myself that keeping it in mind is all I'll do, I'm itching to whip out my phone and google the connection between Dracula and glorified footstools.

No sooner have I thought this than Laura turns quickly to me, wide-eyed.

"I must again ask you forget I said that."

I raise a brow. "Why?"

"A good courtship strategy should not include mentions of past violence," she says, like she's reciting from a manual.

This time, I really do laugh.

"That may be a *solid* strategy, but it's not an *authentic* one. It's not like I don't already know you're selectively dangerous."

Laura opens her mouth, then closes it and purses her lips.

"What's that face for?" I ask.

"Which face? I have several."

"I meant the one you make every time I remind you of something you said," I say with a scoff. "It's like you don't expect me to remember."

Her brown eyes, coy yet content, turn sheepish as she looks away. "It is not often that prey takes equal interest in its predator."

So I was right. She *is* clueless to flirtation.

The people in front of us step away with buckets of popcorn and tall Icees. I can't help watching them straggle towards the butter and seasonings, and even though I ate before leaving, my stomach growls. I look away, only to be confronted with the sight of an employee standing at the popcorn machine, pouring out a fresh kettle before scooping more kernels in.

He returns to the register and gives us a buoyant smile. "How can I help you?"

"I will have four...four wines in cans," Laura says, like she's under duress.

"Alright. Just need to see some ID."

She obliges, flashing a bright smile as he compares.

"Happy early birthday," the cashier says, grinning as he raps the touchscreen register with his knuckle. "If you sign up for our loyalty program today, you'll get a coupon for a movie and a bucket of popcorn on us."

"I thank you kindly, but I am loyal to no one but my family, and to nothing but my appetite," Laura says, tucking her ID away.

"I understand," the cashier says, though his frown tells a different story. He looks at me. "Anything for you?"

For once, 'no, thank you' doesn't fly out of my mouth automatically. I could go for some popcorn—just a kernel or two. It's been years. The fact that I'm even deliberating makes me feel a little less broken. I almost want to hold onto this moment of indecision, file it away as evidence of forward progress. I look over my shoulder at the lengthening line behind us.

"There is no rush whatsoever, my Oasis," Laura says; her words reach my ears through a thickening fog. "You are blessing these people with much needed time to ponder their lives and choices."

I chew the inside of my cheek, straddling the nebulous precipice of frantic hyper-awareness and looming dissociation.

"I might add," she says, a little quieter, "that given the vigilant sharpness of your memory, you must recall certain statements made at Popeyes concerning actions I will take should one taint your food, and therefore my food. They apply to the concessions stand of AMC theaters as well." She bounces on the balls of her feet, arms crossed over her chest. "I encourage you to consider it a universal oath."

I *do* recall. When she puts it like that, I *do* feel a small sense of comfort.

"I'll get the kids box," I say. I haven't *really* made up my mind, but with Laura, I feel safe enough to pretend.

A few minutes later, the transaction concludes, and we're at the seasoning station. The kid-sized popcorn looks like all of four fistfuls. I drench it in butter, Parmesan, nutritional yeast, and pepper, ignoring the voice in the back of my head telling me not to bother when there's a not-so-slim chance that I won't eat it.

"You should congratulate yourself on this mighty leap," Laura says, cradling two cans of wine in each arm like they're her newborn children. "And I do hope this popcorn understands the privilege of being chosen by you at this delicate stage of your life, even if it is not consumed."

My face warms, and I bite back a smile. "How can the rest of your courtship strategy even matter when you say stuff like that? Also, I thought your birthday was in January."

"I was forced to borrow my sister's license, as I cannot be photographed."

"Why not?"

"I am…camera shy," she says, drumming her fingertips on the cans.

"You shouldn't be. In my opinion," I add, clearing my throat.

Her dimples appear with a slow bashful smile that makes me want to faint.

With just under twenty minutes left until the previous showing ends, we sit on a blocky bench outside the theater.

Laura cracks open a can of wine and gulps like her life depends on it.

"Is everything okay at home?" I ask sarcastically.

"I cannot be sure. It has been almost a year since I last set foot in Transylvania. This," she says, scrunching the first can in her fist before opening another, "is because I am hungry."

I purse my lips and hold out the popcorn I haven't yet touched myself. "Have some."

"You are very kind, but I cannot indulge this." Laura takes another, lighter sip of her second can, then holds it between her thighs and puts the other two in her cardigan pockets. "It has been so long since I consumed human food. I am certain that doing so now would result in devastating embarrassment."

I balance the tray of popcorn in my lap, watch condensation roll down the chilled apple juice box that came with it.

"However," Laura says after a lengthy pause, "I will risk this if it would bring you comfort." She leans forward, eyeing me, swirling the canned wine delicately. "No pain, no gain, yes?"

"You don't have to hurt yourself to prove anything to me," I say, scowling as I turn a few degrees so that she can't access the popcorn. Then, with neither thought nor hesitation, I eat a soggy, savory piece myself.

Laura freezes with the can midway to her mouth, agape as she watches with wide eyes.

Of course, nothing happens—right away, at least, except for me eating another piece. Three pieces later, and I'm eating clusters at a time. A few clusters later, and I couldn't stop if I wanted to.

Laura looks as satisfied as she did the other night, watching me scarf down a box of greasy chicken and potatoes, like she's the one eating her fill and not the other way around. Moments later, there's nothing left *to* eat, except for the packaged gummy bears and cookie.

I unwrap the cookie and take a monster bite, turning it into a crescent.

"If you're so hungry that you have to chug wine, why bother waiting for me to love you?" I ask thickly. "I thought vampires only needed consent to come inside."

"Call me a blood connoisseur," she sighs.

"Blood connoisseur."

She clicks her tongue playfully.

I shrug. "You asked me to."

"It is what I have become in my old age. Once upon a time, I drank the blood of humans upon whom I had intentionally inflicted tremendous pain," she says. "It took me much dissatisfaction to realize that the taste of the blood directly correlates to the contents of the heart. Pain dilutes the flavor, but love is…" She inhales deeply, smiling serenely. "Love is deluxe. As a human, you might compare it to braising, or searing, or sautéing."

I crumple the cookie wrapper in my fist, watch it spring open when I drop it in the box. "Love isn't always painless."

"Neither is capsaicin," Laura says, "and yet my sister devours Hot Cheetos as though they are the source of all life and knowledge."

I pop a few gummy bears in my mouth, working to keep my face as neutral as possible.

"Can you imagine," she says quietly, fiddling with the aluminum tab on her can, "how those jellied bears would taste if they wanted to be eaten as much as you want to eat them? It is a rhetorical question," she adds without waiting for an answer. "It would be unfair to expect your comprehension in this regard."

"Guess I'll stick to trying to comprehend loving someone enough to let them drink my blood," I say.

"Did you not love the angels?" Laura asks.

I tear the head off another gummy bear, frowning. It's funny. With Laura, those memories aren't as shameful as they are when I'm alone. With her, it almost feels shameful to be ashamed of the past—of the fact that no, I never really loved the angels, but I did this to myself anyway.

"Touché," I say.

In unison, we sip our beverages, eyes locked in a silent continuation of the conversation.

A small crowd gathers over the next few minutes. From the faces and blurry conversations of the people exiting the theater, the movie was good.

Hopefully not *too* good. Whatever my game plan winds up

being, I'd hate to distract Laura from genuine entertainment by trying to make a move on her. I toss my empty box in the garbage as we head inside and up the stairs. Several of the people in our row are already settled in the luxurious red seats.

Laura takes my hand and clears her throat. "Excuse us."

Their conversations suspend as though muted by a remote. Knees draw up over seats, bodies shift to the side; three of them stand up, stepping back until they're almost toppling over, and the two with a seat between them both put their legs in it, giving us plenty of room.

My ears ring as the anxiety of having to awkwardly squeeze past drains away, replaced with an amorphous feeling. Awe in a certain light, dread in another. Above all, those three syllables were extremely sexy.

Laura opens her third can of wine and puts it in the cup holder, then reclines in her seat, stroking her ponytail. After a moment, she holds out her left hand for me to take. The reel of concession stand advertisements soon roll into trailers as the lights dim.

This is it. This is the moment I've been waiting for—or at least the beginning of it. I fantasized about us sitting down together, and I fantasized about us kissing, but the stuff in between...

A siren-esque violin note bleeds into the theater. This fragment of the score already has me questioning my choice of film. With each frame, it becomes more and more obvious that *Midsommar* is not a making out movie.

I glance at Laura, who's watching with a heavy frown on her face, like she's attending an advanced seminar. Just as I'm starting to consider telling her she was right, my phone vibrates: someone's calling, giving me the perfect opportunity to think without this bleak movie in my face.

"I'll be right back," I whisper.

Laura raises her wine in acknowledgment and sips.

I make my way towards the aisle, muttering *Excuse me*'s with considerably less finesse than her, and hurry out of the theater. It's not just a call, but a FaceTime call from Kennedy. I see only his dark curls, and snatches of a burgundy wall decorated with *Blade*, *Underworld*, and *Buffy* posters.

"What's up?" I answer as I return to the bench.

"Hey, O. I have some terrible news, so brace yourself," he says, though his semi-distracted voice doesn't suggest anything particularly ominous.

"I'm braced," I say warily.

"My grandma's dying."

My jaw drops. "That's awful. I'm so sorry, Ken."

"Well, she's ninety-eight and has been extremely vocal about being more than ready to go ever since Prince died," Kennedy says over what sounds like a suitcase being zipped shut. He lifts his phone so that I can see his exhausted face in full. "What's terrible is that my dad thinks all our faces should be firmly planted in her dementia riddled brain before she heads to heaven, which is probably not where she's actually going. Her words, not mine," he adds when I raise my eyebrows. "So, we're all going to Ireland for however long it takes her to die, since we actually have some warning this time."

Those last few words come out less casually than the others, rousing vivid memories of the hollow Kennedy I first met, who reminded me so much of myself after my mom died that I insisted we hit the pause button on register training and offered to familiarize myself with the store while he caught up on paperwork and listened to music.

"Obviously, you're getting paid for the sudden vacation," he continues, "and you can expect a bonus once her assets are liquidated—which is her offer, not mine. I swear I care about her."

I frown, but it's hard to hold onto any sort of reverence when he has so little himself.

"Tell her I said thanks," I say. "And to have a safe trip to the afterlife. Same goes for you—to Ireland," I add. "Not the afterlife. Yet."

Kennedy, having briefly disappeared, returns with an armload of socks. He drops them seemingly at random and picks up his phone, holding it close to his face as he squints incredulously.

"This is the part where you say 'Noooo, Kennedy, don't go' and threaten to stuff yourself in my suitcase."

"Is it now?"

His jaw drops, and he covers his mouth. Then he gasps. "Wait—where are you? Are you at the movies?" He asks without giving me time to answer. "Are you with *Laura*?"

I chew my lip, unable to keep the smile off my face.

"Have you made it to first base yet?"

"Bases are for white people," I say, rolling my eyes. "But hopefully I work up the nerve today."

"Wow," he says, hushed. His lips pinch in a proud smile as he covers his heart with his hand. "I hope this isn't overstepping, but I'm so proud of you, O. *Beyond* proud. *Disgustingly* proud."

I look away, bashful to the core. "It's not."

Kennedy grins. "Keep me posted. On this and on other… stuff." He clears his throat and looks away, scratching his head like he made a faux pas.

"What is it?"

"I dunno. Ever since my mom died, I've only ever been at FC or at home. You're kind of my only friend," he says, vexed, "and I just realized that I don't even know what you do with yourself."

"That's because I don't do anything."

He scowls and points at the screen. "*Yet.*"

"Is that a threat?" I snicker.

"Absolutely." He starts to say more, but someone in another room shouts something unintelligible. He dips out to reply, then hurries back and says, "I'm off to buy some Benadryl because there's no way I'm surviving this flight awake."

"Alrighty. Let me know when you land."

After the call, I visit the water fountain and rinse popcorn kernels from my mouth. I can tell from the sliver of setting I see upon reentry to the theater that I've missed a lot. I head back to Laura, once again undergoing the anxious task of excusing myself past a dozen people.

Laura waits until I'm seated and settled before reaching automatically for my hand.

"What did I miss?" I whisper.

"They are in Sweden," she replies, frowning like she doesn't understand why that's the case. "Scandinavia is not my cup of blood, but a dear friend of mine hails from there, and so I respect their choice, for now."

I nod and face forward.

Based off her total lack of plot description, I'm assuming she's just as detached from the movie as I am.

I could flat out ask Laura if I can kiss her. Would that ruin the spontaneity? Do I even *want* to be spontaneous? At this stage of life, I think I'd have an aneurysm if someone just planted one on me without warning.

The way her lips glisten in the light of the screen makes me bite mine. A simple yes from her mouth would send me over the moon.

It occurs to me though, as she takes another hefty sip, that any yes she gave right now wouldn't count: she's had at least two and a half cans of wine. She's not swaying or slurring or displaying any signs of drunkenness, but that doesn't mean anything. I could just ask her if she's drunk before asking for a kiss. But then how often do drunk people openly confess to being drunk? The best course of action might be to just wait until we're somewhere else. Then again, everywhere we've been, she's had wine within reach, as if it really *is* all she consumes.

I look away, diverting my attention to the increasingly confusing movie, hoping it'll distract me from my equally confusing dilemma. The main character, whose name I don't know, seems to be talking to her boyfriend about doing shrooms—or not doing shrooms. She doesn't want to, but one of the guys—her semi-supportive boyfriend's annoying friend, I'm guessing—wants all of them to trip at the same time.

Someone offers her a cup of shroom tea.

A burning, tugging sensation creeps over me, like the onset of a vicious pang of period cramps. As the feeling intensifies, it starts to feel less like I'm watching and more like I'm there, trailing behind her, taking on her discomfort like static electricity.

Not taking it on; projecting.

This is just a movie, and I'm projecting.

Nothing about this is even remotely like the nature of my descent into the psychedelic regimen of Custodes Angelorum. The nauseating image of grass growing through her hand signifies the start of her trip. I saw fractals the first few times, like reality was folding into a mirrored geometric shape; everywhere I looked, there was a crease. After that, I started seeing things in the sky—clouds with fluffy handles, or the moon hanging off hinges, or birds flying in a line like a zipper unzipping. Access points to a heaven that I couldn't yet reach.

"My Oasis, are you alright?" Laura whispers; she's close to my ear, but I still struggle to hear her over my own beating heart.

My mouth is dry from how close I am to hyperventilating, and my fingers ache from squeezing hers so hard. I try to relax, only to realize that I'm shaking. I pull away, fold my hands between my thighs.

"Yes."

It's a lie and I know it. I shouldn't be this worked up. This girl stumbling through a pulsating world of greenery and sunshine isn't something I can relate to.

Except it is.

I can relate to being surrounded by people and feeling like they could see every shard of my broken spirit. I can relate to compromising my own sanity to feel less alone.

She's insisting to herself that she's okay, she's okay, she's okay. I know she's not, because I'm not either.

I rub my eyes so hard that lashes slip under my eyelids, making it even harder to fight the tears.

Not this.

Not these memories swooping in to remind me of how far from human I once felt. How far from human I still feel. How likely it is that I'll never feel human again.

Cold grips my wrists as Laura pulls my hands from my face, pulls me out of my seat. All I see are the amorphous backs of my eyelids, and all I feel is the chill of her body right against mine.

"Move," she commands, loud and clear to the person beside her. "Move. Move. *Move*."

I hear scuffling footsteps, seats springing back to their original positions. My feet move without me telling them to, like I'm a balloon tied to her wrist. I could be in midair the way I'm gasping for breath, struggling to see. I could be nothing but a thing in the wind.

I stumble down the stairs after her, feel the brightness of the hallway pressing in. All it does is unzip more of the darkness within. Sobs pour out of me, and every attempt to take a stabilizing deep breath only makes me cry harder. I feel the ache in my lungs and the cold wrapped around me, like I'm standing in a winter breeze.

A breeze that numbs my body while the pain runs its course.

I don't know how much time goes by before the moment that I never expect to come finally arrives: the end. It evaporates and leaves me a breathless husk, all too aware of how I once again let the past drag me under.

I'm not under right now. I'm with Laura, standing beside the bench we were sitting on not too long ago.

I'm in her arms.

I step back, wipe my face on my sleeve.

"Angels be with me," I croak.

"They are not. *I* am," Laura says firmly. Her hands are where they were when I pulled away. "Do not be ashamed of your… spiral."

The panic attack gave way to crystal clarity, like a plug snatched from a drain. Something like hysteria surges in me, and I can barely keep from laughing.

"I'm not ashamed," I say, throat still thick from crying. "I just wish I could go *one day* without having an allergic reaction to being alive. I'm not ashamed," I repeat, more to myself. "I'm tired."

Sorrow leaches the light from her eyes, and now more than ever, I want to be close to her.

"I, too, yearn for rest," she says.

I bite my lip as the shame I just denied having creeps over me. "It's beside the point. I just…really wanted to kiss you."

"You…really wanted to kiss me?"

I'd laugh at the disbelief on her face if I had the wind in me. "I still want to kiss you. And I want to understand you, Laura. I really do."

Laura steps towards me, a subtle pout on her lips. "What is it that confounded you so terribly that you and I did not simply kiss?"

"I was scared you were drunk," I admit. "I didn't want to take advantage of you."

"In my condition," she says, stroking the pearlescent bat on her necklace, "I require unbecoming quantities of wine to be drunk, let alone the sort of drunk where I would not freely say yes to anything you asked of me."

I wipe my runny nose, frowning. "What condition?"

Her eyes flicker with something indecipherable. "I am hungry. I cannot indulge my vices without first respecting the necessities. The Devil would not allow it."

"See—*this* is what I mean when I say I don't understand." Somehow, I hold her gaze, even as confusion flits across her face. "I saw the VHI website. Let me finish," I say, holding up a finger when she opens her mouth. "Laura, I don't care if you were being treated by them. It doesn't matter to me. And I'll do everything I can to protect you from them."

"*If?*" Laura repeats with more uncertainty than I can handle right now.

I shake my head, lost in a mental maze of my own making. "I don't want you to feel like you have to change just for me, but I'm…I'm scared of mistranslating something. I don't want to lose you."

Her brown eyes look so lost that all I want is to be in her arms again.

"What if I told you there is nothing to translate?"

"Vampires may be cool and sexy these days, but to the people who made them up, they were monsters." I blot my eyes with the hem of my flannel and suck in a shaky breath. My nose and throat are congested, but my head has never been clearer. "You're not a monster, Laura. I'll put my faith in angels again before I ever believe that."

Through the blur of tears, I can see that her sharp eyes are their most confounded yet, clenching my heart in a painful knot.

"But I am."

I shake my stuffy head, refusing to let the words reach my ears. "Maybe you haven't figured it out yet, but I *know* monsters. I remember they exist every time I take my clothes off. And I'm sorry if you feel like one, but you're not."

Laura doesn't look as confused anymore, but her unblinking eyes are no less unreadable. Minutes go by; some of the people in our theater leave in the direction of the bathroom. A nearby showing of *Spider-Man* ends, flooding the hallway with satisfied fans until it's just us again, me with tears drying on my face, her still staring at me.

"Please say something," I prompt.

Laura sucks her lower lip like she's thinking of refuting me. "Please kiss me."

My heart stops, then starts again at a gallop. I cup her face in my hands, stroke her bottom lip with my thumb. She's ice cold, cloud soft. I put my mouth on hers, gently bite her lip. A dam breaks somewhere in me, flooding me with heat.

I feel her jaw move under my fingers and taste the sweet film of wine on her tongue.

Laura tastes like something words will never touch—something that threatens to untie me and show the world the breadth of my hunger, like tugging the tip off a cattail and letting the explosion of fluff sail in the wind.

Suddenly, she stops kissing me back. My lips brush her forehead as she bows her head, and when I open my eyes, she's looking down. A strained noise comes from her throat. She takes a step back, and another, until her back is against the wall.

"What is it?" I ask with my heart in my mouth.

Laura clears her throat, holds up a finger. She plunges a hand in her cardigan pocket and pulls out her last Merlot, then opens it and chugs so fast that I hardly have time to blink before the can is a fistful of scrunched aluminum. She drops it at her feet before reaching for my waist, pulling me close.

I press her against the wall, hungry.

She takes my face in her ice-cold hands. "Where were we?"

My answer is a kiss, and another kiss, and another.

We're finally here.

I don't care if *here* is the middle of a movie theater hallway, or that my head hurts from crying, or that my throat's still scratchy and clogged.

I care about her fingers digging into my waist as she pulls my hips against hers. I care about her tongue reaching for mine, and my lips between her teeth when she bites them between breaths. I care about the small, satisfied moans from her throat, fueling my lust like diesel in a tank.

I'm an appetite incarnate, and all I care about is getting my fill.

nine

July 13, 2019

*At first I could not believe my eyes. I thought it was some trick of
the moonlight, some weird effect of shadow; but I kept looking, and
it could be no delusion.*

nine

My birthday hasn't meant much to me since Mom died. Every year, she'd say it was as much of a celebration of herself as it was of us; after all, she was the one who carried two twins for nine months, powering through double the back pain, double the contractions, and double the anemia, which resulted in cravings for dirt, matches, ashes, and feathers, among other ridiculous things.

Our father left Mirage and I to our own devices the one year we lived with him, and if it wasn't for our mutual friends, we probably wouldn't have celebrated—which wound up being the case over the next two years, when we were too poor to plan for anything but quality time together, and even then, we fell short.

Zeke said it was selfish broaching blasphemous to celebrate oneself in any capacity that didn't relate directly to the angels, but that didn't stop Helena and I from secretly celebrating ours by rolling a fistful of joints and walking to the bluebell meadow across town, where we'd lay on our backs in the blossoms and watch movies on my phone until the fireflies came out.

Every flannel I own is on my bed, along with all my t-shirts and pants, as I construct the perfect outfit in advance of me and Laura's 9 AM departure.

The final candidates are a burgundy and purple gingham flannel, skinny jeans, and a tight black t-shirt with a high neckline to cover the scars on my chest.

I won't be including a bra in the ensemble.

After putting the rest away, I sit down at my desk to continue Laura's playlist. It's at five songs, a few of which are new to me, and all of which have been on repeat for days to be sure they'll stick. It's hard to focus though.

This'll be the fourth consecutive year that I don't celebrate with Mirage.

He calls at 6 o'clock sharp, and I have to wonder, hivemind that we once were, if he had to set an alarm, or count down, or otherwise watch the clock—if he had to set a deadline in order to place the call.

I was going to start emotionally preparing myself at 6:30 to call him at 7.

"What are you up to?" He asks when I answer.

"Making a playlist. Still playing catchup on music, but I think I'm getting somewhere."

"You *been* there," Mirage says easily. "Your oldies sets are proof that music should be catching up to you."

"Thanks," I laugh. For a moment, the stress tugging my heart slackens. "What are you doing?"

"Watching *Chopped*," he says, just as a blurry piece of dialogue and dramatic music gain volume in the background.

"Your episode?"

"Random ones. Sometimes I look at the baskets and wonder if I could've succeeded with those same ingredients," he says. "I should prolly stop. I've already had nightmares."

I hesitate. If only I was as quick-witted as he is when it comes to on-the-spot reassurances. I lean back, pat the shower cap covering my hair while it conditions.

"What if you buy the basket ingredients and make stuff? Give your dream self some recipes to pull out."

Mirage laughs. "That might be the move, actually. Anyway, I was struggling to think of birthday plans for us."

Bitterness bleeds to heartbreak.

For us.

"What did you come up with?"

"If we go shopping together and I cook the food in front of you, will you eat it?" He asks.

The pleasantries have peeled away, but this isn't the exhausted ultimatum-giving Mirage I'm used to when it comes to food talk. This is closer to the same pleading tone I use with myself.

"If I do, it won't be tomorrow." I scroll through a playlist from earlier this year, funneling my nerves through the musical treasure hunt. "I have a date."

Chopped pauses.

"With who?"

"Her name is Laura."

"I…didn't know you were gay," he says after a few moments. "Where did you meet her?"

"At work. She bought some copies of *Dracula*," I say. "From there, we just clicked."

More silence. Then,

"That's wonderful, sis. Why didn't you tell me?"

"It's a recent development," I say, which doesn't feel as true as it is. The more time I spend with Laura, the more it feels like she's always been part of my routine.

"Where's she taking you?"

"It's a surprise," I lie. "But she already knows I can't eat in public."

It takes another stretch of silence for me to realize that I've made him feel bad without meaning to.

"I'm sorry, Oasis," he says. "I, uh…I know I've been…"

"I know you've been too." I close my laptop, having gotten nowhere with my ears being occupied by my brother's thoroughly ashamed, shame-inducing voice. "And I get it. But you'll never be as frustrated with me as I am with myself."

"I hear you," Mirage says quietly.

I want to ask if hearing will be enough, since I've said all of this before in different words.

"I gotta get going," I say, not because I have anything to do, but because this is the first time in a long time where the trajectory of our conversation hasn't led to me fighting back tears, and I don't want to jeopardize that by keeping him on the phone. "We should plan for something soon."

"Whenever you want," Mirage replies. "We should go to the butcher and the farmers market and treat ourselves to some K-BBQ. How's that sound?"

"That's a great idea," I say.

So great that it's exactly what I'm doing tomorrow with Laura.

*

"Are these falls not more majestic than the blessed ones which you narrowly escaped?" Laura asks.

The falls in question are slim and practically flat, tumbling over a wrinkle in the creek beside our campsite. I have no clue where we are exactly—one of the many forests and wilderness areas of bright green, lake-riddled Upstate New York.

"These are perfect." I'm lying on my side, watching the thick clouds mesh together and tear apart, showing different patches of the deep blue sky. "To be honest, the only reason those were ever blessed to me is because I didn't die in them."

Laura, sitting cross-legged in front of a foot-tall grill, tucks a beaded braid behind her ear, one of two crowning her head, dangling at her temples while the rest of her hair is in a shiny bun.

"I would even go so far as to say that nothing on this Earth is truly blessed, save blood," she says, wielding a pair of tongs.

"I know *you* would say that," I say dryly, twining a piece of grass around my finger. That's all there is surrounding us—green grass ensconced in thick forest, so beautifully secluded that I haven't seen anyone since we parked at the welcome cabin. "Are you sure you don't want me to do that? You should give your hand a break."

Laura stretches out her bandaged left hand, as though x-raying the injury beneath. "You are learning to be cooked for, yes?"

She lifts the grill cover, prods the brisket cooking in the center and the russet potato next to it, then squirts lighter fluid over the mesquite beneath. Her canvas apron is printed with black bats flocking over a castle and crescent moon, and beneath that, a black t-shirt with red and violet sequined bats on the shoulders.

She's right.

I could get used to this—being alone with her in nature, the look of peaceful concentration on her face as she sprinkles salt on the grilling leeks and carrots chosen at the farmer's market this morning. Laura secures the lid over the grill and slips the tongs through the handle. She notices me staring through the smoke and scoots closer in the grass. "What are you thinking?"

I'm thinking a few more dates like this, and I'll cut the courtship short and make her my trophy wife. I'm thinking that if she'd asked me how close I am to loving her, the answer would be 'I'm there'.

"I never thought I'd have a happy birthday ever again after my mom died," I say. "She used to go *all out*. One year, she took me and Mirage and all our friends to a sunflower orchard, and we picked seeds all day and roasted them all night." I close my eyes as the memory fills me with warmth. "Another year, her friends held a barbecuing competition, and her band gave it a dramatic electronic soundtrack in real time, like on *Chopped*." I sigh and open my eyes to Laura watching me serenely, fingers laced under her chin. "Are your parents still alive?"

"My father was murdered alongside my elder brother, and my mother died of old age. Staying alive from one year to the next is a duty fulfilled for a voivode. Nothing fit for celebration," she says, grasping the tongs again. "But I was my mother's firstborn, and she would not see me go uncherished. On my birthday, she would rouse me in the morning with a pear pastry and almond milk, and later take me to the library to see the cats."

"Which cats?"

"Noble Wallachian felines protected the books and scriptures from rats," Laura says. The same nostalgia I felt in my heart is on her face now, in her warm eyes and smile.

"Did you ever get gifts?" I ask.

"Not when I was human. This is perhaps why I find it crucial that my sister is showered with them on her birthday," she says. "She shares one with you."

My jaw drops. "And you're hanging out with *me?*"

"Your reaction has been the most passionate so far. You spared her the awkwardness of inviting me to Cancun, knowing that there is no activity for me to partake in without bursting into flames," she says with a dry smirk.

"Do you have the same parents?" I ask.

Laura shakes her head. "Talon descends from Mina Murray and Jonathan Harker."

"Talon's a cool name."

"It fits her very much. She is as much of a dragon as I am—maybe even more so."

"So what you're saying is that things in 1897 were *so* messy that your sister is a relative of the real estate agent you broke up with?"

Laura gives a mild shrug. "This is why they say what happens in Transylvania stays in Transylvania," she says, tucking her stubborn braid behind her ear again.

The falls whisper, and the heat casts a mirage above the grill.

"She is curious about us," Laura says after a few minutes.

"But I like giving you my undivided attention."

She looks away, then back, like she's waiting for me to say I'm kidding.

"You really are *the* vampire," I say, smirking. "If you could see yourself in the mirror, there's no way you'd look so surprised."

"Perhaps."

I roll onto my back and hold my phone at an innocent angle, like I'm texting someone back. I open the camera discretely and aim it at Laura.

Aiming is all I can do. The only thing on screen is the cloudy day behind her. I start to turn up the brightness on my phone to be sure, but the brightness is at the max. I see the clouds, the greenery, a corner of the grill, and absolutely no one sitting in front of it.

It's not a trick of the light. There's no light to do any tricking, save the sun, wedged behind a thick patch of clouds. I lock my phone and let it fall flat on my stomach, working hard to keep my pulse from going haywire.

I try to resume my leisurely cloud-gazing, but my eyes fall on Laura and don't leave. Should I tell her what I just saw?

Of course I shouldn't.

Why would I point out what I said I believed this whole time?

Memories of everything she's said about vampires, Dracula, and Vlad the Impaler overlap in my mind, clearer than the day itself.

"I have gifts," Laura says.

I sit up, blinking hard to clear my head. I couldn't imagine this day giving more than I've already gotten, but Laura's opening her canvas bag, pulling out a rectangle wrapped in black paper, putting it in my outstretched hands. I untie the purple ribbon wrapped around the package and loop it around my ankle so it won't flutter away in the breeze. The cover of the topmost book is a painting of a crying woman. *Tears and Saints* by E. M Cioran.

"He was a Romanian philosopher," she says, pursing her lips. "If you ever feel ashamed or insane for believing you would host an angel, read about the saints, who are infinitely more insane and addicted to being ashamed."

"That's sweet of you." I set it aside, grinning. The second gift is a set with orange spines and gold lettering, packed into a durable cardboard box. The three volumes of *In A Glass Darkly* look old enough to be first edition. My suspicion is confirmed when I pull out the second volume and open it tenderly.

"I revisited *Carmilla* after you mentioned it," she says. "It gave me much to ponder, reading of a Laura who was prey and not predator."

"I don't know about that. Laura seemed pretty thirsty herself," I say, setting the box on top of *Tears and Saints*.

The last book is thin and bound in goatskin leather, with no title on the cover or spine.

"What's the Book of Enoch?" I ask, gingerly turning a page.

"It is a story of angels. Namely, the ones who fell," she says, tweaking the bandage around her hand. "You will forgive me, I hope, that this last one is not a gift, but a long-term loan."

"I'm fine with that."

Like the Le Fanu set, the Book of Enoch looks older than both of us combined. I would've been just as happy with no gifts at all, but seeing tangible physical manifestations of her affection fills a part of me that I didn't realize was empty.

"Thank you, Laura. Thank you," I say, smiling so hard that my cheeks start to hurt. "The bar for your birthday celebration is through the roof. I'd better start planning ahead."

Smoke blooms from the grill as she lifts the lid. My mouth waters, and my stomach growls as she arranges the piping hot food on the bamboo plate from her bag.

I take it and inhale; the brisket is still audibly sizzling. For the first time in a long time, I don't stare at it with intent to stall; I stare with impatience. I've burned my mouth on brisket before, and I'll do it again in a heartbeat. But I have a strong feeling I'll need my tongue in top shape today, so I wait.

Laura scoots away from the grill and unties her apron, spreading it beside me like a blanket. She lays back and rubs the space beside her.

I join her, propped up on my elbow. Her brown eyes reflect the cloudy sky, spritzed with flocks of geese. She unstoppers her wine and waterfalls a dark red gulp into her open mouth, still flat on her back. The bandage around her wrist loosens a little, and I get a glimpse of the injury; the black welts on her brown skin look like tattooed veins.

"1789 Chateau Margaux," she says, smacking her lips. She swirls the bottle above her stomach, smiling at me. "Would you like to taste the French Revolution?"

I reach for it, wrap my hand around the neck. The green glass is scuffed, the label worn and illegible. I sit up and sniff the rim, then tilt a small sip into my mouth, lips brushing the bottle. The wine is thick and sweet, and trails warmth throughout me on its way to my stomach.

I thrust it back, shaking my head.

Laura raises a brow as she reclaims the bottle and balances it on her stomach. "No love for the city of love?"

"It's good. *Chuggable* good. Best to cut me off now."

"For now," she says, twisting the cork back in place. "One day we will wine and dine."

I glance at my cooling brisket. I'm stalling again, but not for the reasons I'm renowned for. I pluck the bottle from her hands again and set it aside in the grass. "Until then, I'll just have to taste the Revolution some other way."

Her dimples appear slowly. She reaches up, pushes a coil of Afro away from my forehead as I lean over her, put my lips on hers.

Laura sighs into my open mouth, and I feel a full body throb of longing as my ears latch onto her voice. She grabs my thigh, coaxing me on top of her.

A thinner patch of clouds pass over the sun, casting my shadow over her face and shoulders. I see the dark, delicious tint on her plump lips. I bend lower so we're chest to chest; she's so cold that I feel my nipples slowly hardening as I kiss her face, her jaw, the cold tip of her ear, like I'm testing the waters.

We've wound up here a few times now, locked in embraces I wouldn't leave if I didn't have to breathe at some point. And when I run out of air from kissing her, I catch my breath while my nose is buried in her neck. She smells familiar in ways I can't reach.

But she isn't.

She's a vampire.

The vampire.

I feel my hunger and hers. I feel it in the way her fingers tense when she holds me. I hear it in the small noises from her throat and see it in the subtle arch of her back when her hips rise an inch, as though to meet mine.

Whoever or whatever she is, I want her. All of her.

"You," she murmurs, wrapping her arms around my waist, "make me want to take the Lord's name in vain."

I bite my lip, smiling into her collarbone. Old habits die hard, and the corpse of the angelic vessel in me won't let me say aloud all the things I'd do with her if we weren't technically in public—which we always are. I'm always some degree of wet when it's time for us to part; always on the cusp of asking if she wants to come inside so I can show her how hungry I really am.

Not that this isn't enough. The deadest parts of me resurrect with each kiss, and even through the layers of clothes between us, I feel reborn under her touch.

But no matter how far I take things in my head, I can never say straight up that I'm down to fuck. I'm not ready to see all of me, even if it means seeing all of her, too.

July 24, 2019

I suppose one ought to pity any thing so hunted as is the Count.
That is just it: this Thing is not human—not even beast.

*

24 July.—*There seems some doom over this ship.*

ten

It's 10 o'clock in the morning, and Kennedy has more energy than I've ever seen him with at this time, claiming to have woken up at 4:30 AM due to a convoluted mixture of jet lag, post-flight bloating, and too much kombucha.

Two weeks' worth of condolence cards, bills, and boxes await at Full Cauldron. Franchise merch from distributors, bulk order t-shirts and canvas bags with the store logos on them, used books from sellers who do business long distance; the boxes are piled both in front of and behind the counter, and in the middle of the comics' section. Kennedy's dad updated the website to say that the store won't be opening until the first week of August just so the two of us have time to catch up.

But after an hour of swimming in packaging plastic, fighting with the pricing gun, and turning our fingers ashy from appraising book after book, we decide to take a break and watch *The Hobbit* on the cash register.

I've seen it a million times already. My attention is on Kennedy's grandmother's gift to me: her obituary, which is as thick and glossy as a special edition Time Life Magazine.

It's autographed—*To Oasis, from Siobhan xoxo* below a black and white photo of the red-haired, green-eyed actress, who, according to the bio in front, appeared in hundreds of Irish theater productions while staunchly refusing all suggestions of migrating to the big screen or to an international audience.

"You must think my family's demented for this," Kennedy says, munching on an Air Head.

It's hard to keep from smiling as I flip through the beautifully curated, yet shockingly honest obituary.

"My mom didn't include her divorce papers with accusations of cheating in her obit, but she did press a vinyl from her ashes."

His eyes widen with awe. "That's so sick. What's on it?" He asks. "Remind me to put in my will to have my ashes pressed into the Adam West *Batman* theme music for 15 straight hours."

"Vinyls don't go on for that long, so they'll have to cut your ashes with something and turn you into a box set," I say. "And I don't know. It's still in Blessed Falls."

I hope.

I haven't really let myself consider there being an alternative.

"That's gotta be tough," Kennedy says. "I hope she finds her way back to you."

"Me too. I used to feel this giant hole. Especially post-Angelorum," I say, recalling my first few months post-discharge spent soaking in self-hate for losing hold of my records. "Sometimes I felt like my whole life would be fixed if I could just listen to her."

"What changed?"

"That…is a good question." I frown at a picture of 89-year-old Siobhan flying off a swing while her children and grandchildren watch in horror—including Kennedy, who's off to the side filming. "I didn't realize that I *used to* until just now. It used to be a nightly thing until…"

Kennedy devours another Air Head, then wedges the wrapper in the trash amidst fistfuls of brown packaging paper and plastic. "So how are things with Laura?"

I set the obituary aside, pull Vaseline from my flannel pocket and blot my lips while Bilbo reviews his burglar contract on-screen.

Put simply, Laura is the most fulfilling and consistent part of my life—not to mention the most interesting. After making the executive decision to stop worrying about *Dracula* and its implications for our relationship, I can appreciate just how fascinating she is both because of and despite it. I know more about blood, bats, philosophy, and medieval cuisine than I ever could've learned on my own.

My skin feels worth being in when she touches me and I need that. I don't know how I survived this long without it. "I want her to be mine."

"But…?"

I shrug, picking at a hole in my jeans. I can just make out the

pale edge of a scar. "Guess I just realized how unhealthy it probably is to want to be in a relationship with her just because she's the
first person to pay attention to me in that way."

"Do you think you should wait and ask out the second person who pays attention to you? Or the third? I get it, O," Kennedy
says, frowning slightly. "I mean, I don't *get it* in that I didn't leave a
pseudo-Christian cult, but I *do* have half a master's in social work,
so I understand fundamentally, to a certain extent, what it may or
may not be like…" He shakes his head, sighing.

"Thanks, Ken," I say wryly. "I feel better already."

Kennedy gets to his feet and pauses the movie. "What I'm
trying to say," he says, standing above me with his arms crossed,
"is that it can't be easy going from making none of your own decisions to making all of your own decisions. And I can't imagine
what it must be like to have your guard up all the time after being
robbed of…well, everything."

The sarcastic smile wipes off my face. This is my first time
hearing something like this outside of my own head, and in a voice
not steeped in self-loathing.

"And I could go on for days about how forced hospitalization
probably only made it harder to trust yourself," Kennedy continues, plunging the knife in even deeper, "but for the purpose of
this pep talk, I'll keep it at this: don't let everything you've been
through keep you from listening to your heart. It'll just get louder,
and louder, and louder, and louder…"

His ongoing conclusion leaves me stunned and speechless,
and the urge to cry tickles my throat. Between him and Laura, it's
like all the validation I needed this past year got crammed into the
last two weeks.

"…and louder, and louder, and louder, and then on *top* of
that, you two have been hanging out consistently for what, two
weeks?"

I wipe my nose, rapidly blinking back tears. "Two weeks and
two days."

"See? All the queer people *I* know are on Tinder one day and
Zillow the next," he says, resuming the movie as he sits next to me
again. "Two weeks and two days is a slow burn in the twenty-first
century."

I roll my eyes, but relief flows through me all the same.
"You're right."

"Exactly." Kennedy smirks. He crosses his arms and leans

back on his crate—right into a tower of empty boxes that cascades over both of us, spilling packing peanuts everywhere, knocking the fandom pins off the counter.

We soon fall into a ramshackle rhythm of pricing books, filling orders, and throwing out ideas for new fall displays.

*

Tonight's date is reading on the roof. I climb up by myself with my memoir and the Book of Enoch tucked under my arm, hauling several fleece blankets, a camping lantern from Target, and a bottle of Bordeaux so expensive, I almost shielded my eyes while inserting my card into the reader.

It feels like I can see all of New York from my spot among the windswept leaves, deconstructed bird nests, and deflated helium balloons. The disappearing sun gives the lingering clouds golden underbellies; a silver half-moon grins from the darkest blue part of the sky.

I tighten a blanket around myself and lean closer to the lantern. The Book of Enoch is refreshing. It feels like a real story—something I can enjoy without searching for a pre-established lesson. My favorite part so far is that the angels aren't looking for humans to make their vessels in the hosting sense: they're cruising.

Footfalls echo off the rungs.

I look up and see the burgundy and gold top of a book before I see the woman holding it. I straighten up and smile as Laura crosses the rooftop with *Dracula* in hand.

Her matching black sweatshirt and sweatpants read *Juilliard class of '20* on the chest and left leg.

"Good evening, my Oasis," she says, lowering herself gracefully across from me, crossing her legs lotus-style. "Are you well?"

"I…" I lose track of my words almost immediately. She looks beautiful as always, with her hair in dark waves down her back, and her face bare but still aglow in the moonlight. I clear my throat. "I am. How are you?"

"I am here with you now. It has been…" Laura trails off, holding *Dracula* out in both hands like someone else just handed it to her, sticky notes and all. "Yet another July 24th."

"What's special about July 24th?"

"Nothing, I suppose. But then I also suppose," she says without looking up from the cover, "I could bathe every copy of this book in pink hellfire until even I could not see through the smoke, and still never be free of the calendar beneath."

Something is different. It's dark, but I can still see her eyes.

I've seen them flicker when she's irked or irritated; I've seen them full of amusement and full of sorrow; I've seen them burn with questions and with secrets.

I've never seen them this empty.

My heart beats a little faster.

What if this is a bad time?

That's impossible.

There's never a wrong time to tell someone you love them.

Is there?

I sift through the blankets for the bottle of wine tucked partway under my thigh.

"I got you this," I say, passing it over the lantern.

Laura puts the book down and holds the bottle in her hands like she's never seen wine before in her life. After a moment, the look fades away and she smiles.

"Thank you." She moves closer, so that she's sitting right next to me, cradling the wine in her lap. "May I listen to your heart?"

"Of course." I put down the Book of Enoch and readjust the blankets.

She nestles into me, puts her ear to my chest while I wrap my arm around her. She's colder than the blooming night. The last wisps of light drain from the horizon, shedding a gradient of blue. Stars peek through the clouds, and the moon beams brighter still as it makes its way over our heads.

"Laura, are you okay?" I ask.

"I am always okay, at minimum, when you are near," she murmurs.

Usually, it's me who says she's fine and later stands corrected by having a near meltdown, but not this time. My heart beats for her now, and it knows that despite her words, something's deeply wrong.

"If you're not, you can tell me," I say. "You know that, right?"

"I do know this," Laura says, "but the past has made a plaintive and impatient fool of me today, and I have lost all sense of self-preservation. Perhaps..." She sits up slowly, clutching the wine. "Perhaps I should leave you for the night."

My heart stops dead as she stands, exposing me to the night.

"*No.*" I shove off the layers of fleece and get to my feet with much less grace than her. "Per*haps* you should stay right here."

Laura says nothing, and I feel nothing but panic and the ache of my racing heart as she stares like she doesn't recognize me.

I know that this, whatever it is, has nothing to do with me, but I also don't know what it could have to do with, which is, in itself, a predictable consequence of being in love with someone whose life seems to be built from metaphors.

"I brought my memoir for you to read in case *Dracula* gets too upsetting," I venture. "Not that it's any less upsetting. Or maybe it is." I bite the inside of my cheek, fighting off waves of desperation, because she's standing in silence, body angled towards the fire escape ladder, looking like she wants to be anywhere but here.

"'The angel said to him, 'I am Gabriel. I stand in the presence of God, and I have been sent to speak to you and to tell you this good news,'" she recites quietly. "I did not trust my memory." She flexes her hand, stroking the healed scars. "I had to be sure."

I feel every degree of the descending chill as a tidal wave of goosebumps threatens to push me back down.

"And I understand now," she continues, "why you would choose to believe...or not to believe..." She blinks a few times, not quite looking at me, like she's also powering through speechlessness.

"Laura, I need you to listen to me," I begin. I hadn't rehearsed for this, let alone for a version of this in which the sadness on her face makes me want to pull her close, wrap us both in a cocoon until this sudden gloom passes like a storm cloud. "I don't know what you think I believe, but it doesn't matter, because when I look at you and when I'm with you, I want you to be all there is."

Laura looks from me to the moon, slowly being smeared away by clouds. "And I would give you my heart if I could reach it."

A sharp breeze brings tears to my eyes. I blink them away.

"I've already seen your heart."

More sorrow clouds her face. So much of it that her brown eyes look like beacons of hopelessness.

"What's going on?" I ask. "Please just tell me."

The breeze strengthens even more, blowing her hair over her shoulder as the gathering clouds submerge us in shadow.

"Much of my human life was wrought with suffering, and when I look at humanity, that is often all I see. Valleys and gorges and mountains of suffering and darkness. But there is light, too," she says, hardly louder than the wind, "and when you found me, I believed you were one of the lights. I believed you were the light of all lights."

I cross my arms, tightening my flannel, but the weather has nothing to do with the chill throttling my bones. It feels like she ripped my heart out, threw it over to the crows hopping on the neighboring rooftop.

"You don't believe that anymore?"

"You are not a light. You are an oasis. And I did not realize I felt so unsafe in this world until you showed me somewhere safe." Laura wrings her hands. "I know how to starve. I have been without food before. I have not yet been without you."

The things she's saying are completely at odds with her tone—confessions of vulnerability that sound like goodbyes. I look away from her, and my eyes drift involuntarily to the book it all started with—the book that it always comes back to: *Dracula*, face-down on the ground next to the lantern.

"Whatever you need to tell me, you can say it when you're ready. Not because you feel like you're about to lose me."

"I *have* told you." Laura presses her lips together. When she steps closer, her eyes are focused on the ground at my feet.

It's too late for subtlety, but I can pretend. I bend down slowly, not taking my eyes off her, and pick up the Book of Enoch.

"I only ever read that once before all things holy were pulled from my grasp, but the book I miss most is Romans," Laura says, taking another step towards me. " 'Noaptea aproape a trecut, se apropie ziua. Să ne desbrăcăm dar de faptele întunerecului, și să ne îmbrăcăm cu armele luminii.' Romani 13:12."

Context and a year of high school Latin help to translate some of the words, but the rest—the rest comes from the aspiring angel in me who refuses to die, no matter how hard I press a pillow to her face. "'The night is almost over, the day is approaching. But let us put off the works of darkness, and let us put on the armor of light.' Romans 13:12."

"The night will never end for me," she says quietly. "And whosoever's heart you saw, it was not mine. The Devil made certain of that."

I shake my head. Despite it all, I still want to kiss her, and hold her, and hear her. I still want to be with her.

"Then the Devil got careless," I say.

The deepening ache in her eye douses me with anguish.

"You have not said you love me, and I have not had a drink of you to be sure, but you make me feel as though you love me, and I have marooned you in denial. So long as you do not understand what I am, your blood is undeserved, and I am but a harvester."

I'm shaking now. I take a deep breath, try to force back the creeping realization that although I don't know where this is coming from, I know where it's going—just as surely as I know I'm in love with her.

I put the Book of Enoch behind my back, again too late for subtlety. Her hand has been free of its bandage for several days now, but I haven't forgotten the glimpse of the damage—black marks forking over her skin, like veins pushed to the surface.

Laura's close enough to see her nonexistent pores in the moonlight, the baby hairs pasted perfectly at the crown of her head, the crease of her dimples as she bites her lip, painted burgundy with wine.

My heart always sprints when she's close enough to touch, but like so much of tonight, this is different. This is the fight or flight she thought she smelled, only I'd never fight her, and I'd fall apart before I ever fled. So I freeze.

She closes the space between us, leaves cold trails on my skin through the fabric of my flannel as she runs her hands down my arms.

"Tell me again where it was you saw my heart," she asks, so close that I feel the words on my lips.

My heart punches my ribs, reaching for her.

"It's the first thing I noticed when you walked into the store."

Her first smile of the night doesn't reach her eyes, which flutter closed as she leans in to kiss me. The movement of her icy lips thaws me, but I don't pull away, don't step back, don't move except to kiss her back, because she's right.

I *am* in denial.

I pointed my camera at her, saw no one on the screen, and I stayed in denial. Nearly every moment with her is spent in denial, except for these. My fingers are on the nape of her neck and her hand is on my waist, fingers climbing up my spine. There's nothing to deny when we touch because she is the truth.

My eyes are closed, but I see a hint of light through my eyelids.

This kiss feels so much like a goodbye that I'd rather die than end it, but I somehow break away, breathless. The light is pink and closer than I thought. I didn't notice the Book of Enoch leaving my grip. It's in Laura's hand, which is now at her side.

Pink flames blaze where her skin meets the cover. They engulf her fingers, her palm, her wrist, chewing up to her elbow.

Instinct takes over. I snatch the book from her hand and throw it across the roof. The flamingo pink fire felt like a warm breeze to me, but Laura shakes her hand out, wincing. I take it in mine. Dark scorch marks twine around her forearm, snaking under her sleeve. If it wasn't for the embers falling from her skin, it would look like a tattoo.

She takes her hand away, flexing her fingers.

If I can hear my heart, I know she can.

Every inch of me aches to reassure her, but the rage makes it so that nothing close to soothing makes it out of my mouth.

"Laura, what the *fuck?*"

"The fuck is that you have taken my survival instincts one after the other," Laura says. "I had to be sure you understood."

"I never asked you to fucking combust," I snap.

"But you did not believe me," she says, quiet and fragmented.

"And I told you that you don't have to hurt yourself to prove a point to me," I say, raising my voice. "So, I'll ask you again: *what the fuck?*"

Silence.

A thick cloud passes, briefly unveiling the moon now shining behind her back. Where her silhouette should fall beside us, there's nothing—nothing but moonlight and my shadow on the disheveled blankets.

I lick my lips, which taste like wine after that long, slow kiss. All the wild longing it inspired is still there, buried under a steadily swelling, blistering, indecipherable pain. I try to smother it, try to scrub the anger and confusion from my throat; I haven't cussed this much since I was a teenager.

"I think we both need to take some time to think," I say, which is the exact opposite of what I want. If I could, I'd take my brain out and skip it across these rooftops like a stone on a lake if it meant never thinking a single thought again.

"There is no rush."

I barely swallow a derisive laugh, battling exasperation fast approaching hysteria.

"Yes, Laura, there *is* a rush."

She tilts her head to the side just a little, like she misheard. "Time is the only certain thing for me, and my love for you will not expire."

"You're hungry," I snap, "and I know what that's like. So yes, there *is* a rush."

Laura nods, lost-as-ever eyes gazing at my feet. "Then I will leave you."

I swallow the three words I wanted to say and offer up three others as I turn away and stoop to gather the blankets: "Get home safe."

My words are met with silence.

I stand up with my arms full.

I'm alone.

She was there and now she's not.

I look up; a ribbon of black specks flutters across the sky.

Bats—a whole cauldron of them.

They stud the clouds like bolts, zig-zagging across the moon and out of sight.

This rooftop isn't the psych ward, but I'm once again feeling exposed and insane, delusions and illusions stripped away like scabs off wounds nowhere close to healed.

Only there were none of those with Laura. Just honesty wrapped in tenderness I've never known before. It's me who refused to believe that the work of fiction she hates so much is fictional for the wrong reasons. Me who refused to believe that the only way someone could know that much about medieval Romania was by being there. Me who refused to believe that no one could have that long and specific of a list of clothing items lost to a castle looting unless they were nursing real bitterness.

It was me who didn't want to believe that Laura burned her hand by gift wrapping a piece of apocrypha for me.

The fact that I don't know when or what our next date is scares me more than anything I just heard or saw. It scares me so much that I should be asking myself what the fuck.

What the fuck have I done?

I cross the rooftop, using my phone flashlight to find the Book of Enoch. It sustained a few bent pages from skidding across the filthy ground, but it wasn't damaged by her spontaneous combustion. The leather still has its sheen.

Dominos topple in my head, resulting in the twisted destruction of yet another delusion.

Angels are real.

The clouds have disbanded. The sky is dark blue and empty. The moon is all it holds—no heaven, no doorway to it.

I almost died, and the angels I believed in almost let me.

I sink to the ground, detangling the blankets and wrapping them around myself until I can't see the city, can't feel the cold, can't hear a sound but my own breathing, which turns to gasping, which turns to sobbing.

Maybe if I sob hard enough, I'll wake up to find that no, I'm not crying on a rooftop. I'm still in my apartment, gathering the blankets, searching for a bottle opener, debating with myself as to whether I should bring the book with my favorite vampire story, or the one that'll once again upend life as I know it.

The Gospel of Oasis

Chapter 0

A brain tumor took my mom in 2013. Mom was part of an electronic group called Noctivagrants. They weren't well-known. They released their first few LPs in limited batches of 100 or 200. They mainly did shows at clubs and opened for bigger acts like Four Tet and Boards of Canada, and a lot of smaller shows of their own in Detroit and Chicago.

After she died, the Noctivagrants pressed her ashes into a vinyl and gave it to me and my twin brother before we went to live with our father. He and I were never close. He cheated on our mother and left her to raise twins on her own. We hadn't seen him in years before Mom told him she was dying.

He had something to say about everything, especially stuff he had no business having anything to say about. My hair phases, my boyfriend, my growing collection of records that I had no way of listening to. I learned to tune him out. My brother couldn't do the same.

Mirage didn't care about anything but basketball. In the summer, he and his friends practically lived at the park up the street from our house. When it got cold, he stayed in his room with the door cracked and the glow of NBA2K on his TV spilling out, controller in one hand and an open bag of Funyuns at his side. He was always on the court, no matter where he was.

Our father thought that at 16 going on 17, Mirage should be doing more with his life, so tensions were perpetually high. I struggled to track the source of most of their shouting matches, but regardless of if it was Mirage's passive aggression or our father's interrogative nosiness, together they were like water thrown on a flaming skillet of oil.

At the time, my boyfriend Raymond and I had been together since we were 13. We were a match made in algebra class. I was the kid who forever had a pair of headphones around my neck and no interest in much beyond scouring LimeWire for obscure remixes of newly discovered songs. Raymond was obsessed with Lord of the Rings, and I started learning Quenya and other elf languages so that he would have someone to talk to. He wanted to be a Tolkien scholar, which my father thought was a waste of his athletic potential, and even worse, a missed opportunity to support me financially and get me out from under his roof.

Towards the end of senior year, things were so bad between Mirage and my father that I lived with Raymond. I felt uneasy being away from my twin, but I tried to focus on finishing high school. I lived with Raymond even after we broke up before the start of summer. The things we had grown to love were putting us on different paths. He wanted to pursue his Tolkien studies in Scotland, and I applied to UPenn so I could go to Wharton Business School. I had always wanted to own a record store so that I could showcase both my mom's music and share my own superior music taste. Raymond helped with my essay and helped me pick my classes, and my acceptance letter came to his house. I got a decent scholarship and took out all the federal loans I could.

I hadn't spoken to Mirage on a daily basis since Christmas, which was only decent because our grandparents flew in from Los Angeles and acted as a buffer. I didn't see him at school anymore, and when I called, it usually went to his voicemail box, which was always full. I felt like I was losing track of him, and like I had betrayed him by moving somewhere else. One day he finally called me and asked to see me. He had a black eye but wouldn't tell me what had happened or let me get close enough to see. All he said was that our father had done it. He felt like I had abandoned him, and I felt too guilty to disagree.

To soothe the heartbreak of splitting up, Raymond had done everything in his power to make sure we had smooth separate first years of college. This included making me a budget and giving me a color-coded planner for the year, which included all the due dates and exam dates on my syllabi, as well as ideal dates for me to get a job, and going as far as to research employers near campus. He admitted that he had almost included a period tracker extrapolated from his own observations because he didn't want me to get blind-sided by anything whatsoever. And for the first time I thought that maybe my future could wait, and that I should stay with Raymond and go wherever he went, because I was sure that with Mom gone, no one would ever take care of me like that again.

Mirage didn't factor anywhere into the budget that Raymond made, but I couldn't abandon him again. We used the last of the money our mom left us, plus my savings from working at RadioShack, to get out of Kansas. I told myself we were escaping Kansas, but it didn't feel like an escape. You can't escape a place that's part of you. Kansas is racist, and some of those memories still burn, but it's quiet, beautiful, and peaceful. It's home. To this day, I miss living in Riverside because no matter what direction you wandered—north, south, east, west—you always ended up at the bank of a river.

Chapter 1

In 2015 I turned 18. The year leading up to that is a blur because all I ever did was play catch up. I didn't have a scholarship that year because my GPA was under the requirement, so I had to get a second job at Popeyes. I had already been working at the school library because again, Mirage wasn't in the budget, and neither was living off campus with him instead of in a dorm.

Mirage started working three months after we got to Philly as a line cook at a restaurant that had been on Kitchen Wars. We shared a room in a house and lived with an elderly lady. Aurora was 82 and liked to jog every morning. She liked us because we were quiet and diligent, and because we were twins. She used to be a twin, and she used to show me black and white pictures of herself and her sister, Nebula, with their twin Afros and matching outfits.

Aurora was so good to me. We watched Dark Shadows and Twilight Zone and the original Star Trek on my days off and ate homemade pies that her daughter brought from her bakery. I even went jogging with her a few times.

I used to wish that life could be just that, because every moment not spent with Aurora was spent trying to douse the flames that had become my life. My GPA only ever declined, and Popeyes kept cutting my hours. Mirage was depressed. He felt like he had no future. He had dropped out of high school not long after he and our father had gotten into a physical fight, and he didn't think a GED would make a difference. Although he didn't dislike his job, he hated being told what to do. Any instance of authority made him feel suffocated, and usually I could remind him that no one really has control over everyone and that situations hardly last forever. Mom always said 13 minutes is an epoch when it comes to twins and the gap between them, and so I tried to be a good big sister by telling him that none of this was forever. Most of my reassurances felt too little too late though, because sometimes after a long shift, he'd come home and just not respond to me when I asked how work was. Sometimes he'd ask how I thought it went, or he'd say that his day probably wasn't as good as mine. As much as he hated not finishing high school, it was like he was judging me for doing so myself. One time, his passive aggression dug so deep into me that I asked aloud if he wanted me to fail, and if he'd feel better if I was miserable in the trenches of a kitchen too. He didn't say anything, but he didn't apologize either.

Raymond and I only talked a few times a week. He was still my closest friend, but whenever we got off the phone, I always spent a few minutes afterwards reeling in despair and jealousy. I was jealous of him for making friends so easily, and I was jealous of his new friends for having him. I laughed at the idea of finding someone the way we found each other, because it just didn't seem possible that someone would ever look at me again and decide to love what they see.

Just after spring break, Aurora passed away. Hers was the third funeral that I had been to in my life. Aurora's family were going to sell the house and offered to let my brother and I stay at half the cost until the end of summer so that we could save up and find somewhere else. It seemed like a good offer in the short term, but the further out I zoomed, the worse the bigger picture looked. For one, it was impossible to find somewhere where my brother and I could have separate rooms and still afford it. For another, with my grades, I would have been lucky to not get kicked out of UPenn, and even if I didn't, then what? Another semester of classes too hard to keep up with? Another semester with three alarms set every morning just to pry my exhausted self from four, five hours of sleep, skip breakfast, chase the bus, and start another soul-crushing day at either of my jobs? I didn't have any friends at school, I didn't have any friends left from Kansas, I didn't have time to sit down and listen to music, I didn't have time to read books for class let alone for pleasure, and I couldn't get the smell of fried chicken out of my hair.

Mirage, on the other hand, had finally found his calling. He decided to become a chef. It was around that time that he became less argumentative and more focused on bettering our circumstances. He cooked every day. He'd talk about us going to other cities where he could find work or open a restaurant of his own, and I had to remind him that I still had a degree to finish. It felt like he saw me as a failure in the making. In a way, it felt like my dream was fading just as his was lighting up. I continued looking for somewhere else to live.

This is when I met Ezekiel.

Chapter 2

Thank you for your message, Oasis. My name is Zeke Wharton. I'm head resident at Custodes Angelorum. We're a co-op in Blessed Falls, Pennsylvania. I'd like to set up a time to meet with you to answer any questions you might have and schedule a tour of the place. How does that sound?

– Zeke

I remember the email verbatim because his last name was Wharton, which made me feel like my own life was laughing at me. I was definitely going to flunk out of Wharton Business School and it seemed like a cosmic joke that my failure was following me in my search for stability. He met me at my job after my shift. He was a mid-30s white guy in a grey button up and Levi's. He stood out because nothing about him stood out. I told myself not to look or act too desperate, but I felt the truth gnawing under the surface as I sat with him—that I couldn't keep up with school, that I didn't care about keeping up with school, that my brother didn't seem to be on my side anymore. I fought to keep myself from bawling in front of a stranger. Mom was gone, Raymond was gone, Mirage felt like he was gone, and I couldn't remember the last time I had an opportunity or reason to do something that wasn't pertinent to survival. I was lost, and so was everything that mattered.

In the end, all I said was that I needed a change.

Zeke explained that the Angelorum could be just a place for me to live if I wanted, but it also could be more. He told me that over 300 people lived in the houses that made up the community, and that most of them believed there was more to life than all this coming and going, working and recuperating, picking oneself up just to fall down again and search for another foothold. He said that they rejected the minutiae and embraced the angels. My religion had always been music. I believed what Maxi Jazz from Faithless said: God is a DJ.

But Zeke knew just what to say to that. Zeke said that no one can speak or act for God, except angels. The Angelorum was a family for people who were willing to listen to the word of the divine as it is, unfiltered by pastors or preachers, directly from the mouths of those closest to the Lord: the angels. He said that listening to the angels was the first step to becoming one.

There was no rent, groceries were provided if I gave a list, and there were communal cars. The thing I heard loudest was that there was no rent. Based off that alone, the Angelorum sounded like heaven. And although I thought that every other thing Zeke had said was bullshit, I hoped that maybe some of the spirituality would rub off and I would find a higher purpose on my own.

Chapter 3

Zeke drove me to Blessed Falls that same day to look around. It was a town full of churches and Bible colleges, surrounded by what could've been a national park. Custodes Angelorum was a neighborhood of chapels molded into homes. He took me into one, and it looked almost exactly like the dorm I would've stayed in at UPenn.

He introduced me to a group of about eight people who were mostly my age, and we all walked to the lead mines together. No one asked me anything about myself, like where I was from, or what I did, or why I was so far from civilized Pennsylvania. Instead, they asked when I was moving in and if Zeke had told me which house I was going in. After a while, a girl named Helena told them not to crowd me because I had no clue what they were talking about. She said she hoped I would stay to find out. They were passing around a joint, and I took a few hits and focused on putting one foot in front of the other as we trekked through the woods. I had been to the salt mines during a field trip back in Kansas. We went underground and wore hard hats, and it was so big that we had to go through them on a tiny open-top train. The lead mines in Blessed Falls were nothing like that. Decades and decades ago, they had caved in and killed the settlement that was there before Blessed Falls was incorporated. There was a wooden tunnel entryway above curved trolley tracks that used to lead into the mines, and behind the entryway was nothing but the base of a hill. The mines must not have reached very far when they were intact. The stumps of cleared away trees were the only sign that someone intended to breach the serenity for industry, but it was otherwise a smooth pasture on a gentle incline surrounded by oaks and maples and pines, with a tangle of creeks pressing down on the greenery like the fingers of a crooked hand. Here and there, a bleached, eroded log stuck out of the tall grass, remnants from cabins that had collapsed. It was quiet and warm, and on its own worth the trip. At some point, someone offered me shrooms, which I had only tried once before. I didn't say no. It had been a very long time since I was around people outside of group projects at school or in the break room at work, and it had been an even longer time since I had been around nature, so I decided to live it up until it was time to leave.

Even the remotest and greenest part of Pennsylvania had

nothing on Kansas. Me and my mom used to ride her two-seat-er bike for miles to the orchard, and me and Raymond used to walk for hours along the river until we got to the sunflower fields. Raymond was so tall that he could bend the heads off two or three and my mom would roast the seeds for us to have as a snack. Pennsylvania was no Kansas, but having the sunlight follow me through the leaves of the trees made me feel like I was on the right path and like I stood a chance.

I was so caught up in finally feeling okay that I hadn't been paying attention to the conversation the others were having. It wasn't a conversation. They were reciting bible verses like trivia. I had been somewhat nervous when Zeke said what he had to say about angels, but doing drugs and reciting the bible while walking through nature was pretty mild compared to what I had imagined, and I thought that if being around these people was all I had to do for free rent and food, I could handle it. And then I saw Octavio's scars.

Octavio had been quieter than everyone else. He had been reading a version of the bible that looked like it had come from Kinko's. It had a laminate black cover with white font on it, that spelled B. I. B. L. E., like an acronym. I saw his scars when he tripped slightly on a tree stump and flailed to keep from dropping the book. His skin was in plain sight, but I somehow felt intrusive seeing it. It was one scar comprised of several slits, and when he turned, I realized it was a bible verse: Job 38:11. He saw me staring and drew the conclusion that I was looking at the bible and not the scars. He told me it was from Zeke, annotated specifically for vessels. Another girl stopped him from saying more. I don't re-member her name, and I don't think she stayed long, but she told him that he couldn't share any of what was inside until Zeke said it was alright. While she was gesturing, I noticed scars on her wrist. Then I noticed the scars on her cleavage and collarbone, peeking from the shoulders of her tank top. She had bible verses carved all over her body, too.

Helena, who seemed very serene and in touch with her sur-roundings, also had scars on the backs of her hands, and I swore I saw some above the waistband of her jeans when her t-shirt rode up a little. I looked around some more, as subtly as I could. All of them had verses on their body, and not just on their arms. One girl had some on her shins and calves, and another one had scars on her midriff.

I also couldn't help noticing how thin she was, and for a moment, I wondered if maybe I had somehow missed out on Zeke saying that this was a recovery center for cutters or people with eating disorders. Something told me that I had stumbled into something more twisted than I realized, but I had gotten into the nasty and unshakable habit of telling myself things were going to be okay when they clearly weren't. My brother had gotten passive aggressive to the point where I felt guilty for studying in another room in case it disturbed his downtime. I knew I was one late clock-in away from getting fired. I came to terms with the fact that my academic reputation was on life support after I got a D on the midterm in my History of Electronic Music class. If there was any class on earth that I should've passed with flying colors, it was that one. Nothing was okay, so it seemed like it was Custodes Angelorum or nothing.

Zeke drove me back home after an hour of walking through the trees. He said I was quiet and asked why, and although I wanted to lie, I knew that I had to know what was up eventually. I asked if Custodes Angelorum doubled as a halfway house because everyone I saw looked like they had self-harmed. He thought that was funny. He said that they did it to themselves, but it wasn't harm. Blood speaks to devotion and the angels can hear it flow. He knew this because she was their chosen emissary.

It was then that I decided he was crazy. I felt comforted by this because I thought that crazy was something I could handle. I assumed that because I could identify it as bullshit then, I would always know that it was bullshit. Right then, I knew that angels weren't real. And that if they were, they weren't talking to some guy in the middle of nowhere, Pennsylvania. But they were also what I needed. I had a 1.3 GPA at an Ivy League school and I felt like dead weight to my brother. I needed to be needed in some capacity. And Zeke said that the angels needed me. So I said I'd think about it.

Chapter 4

By then, Mirage had been promoted to kitchen manager, which it took him a while to tell me. He was also slow to tell me how much money he was making until I noticed him buying a bunch of small appliances. He said he deserved nice things and so did I, and that it wasn't his fault I didn't treat myself.

Before I went to sleep every night, I tried to mentally unravel the mess we had become. I thought that if anything, our mom dying and us leaving Kansas on our own should have brought us closer, but somewhere along the line, a stitch had dropped, and I couldn't figure out how to fix it. What made it worse was that Mirage didn't seem to think anything needed fixing. I asked him what had happened to the days when we used to talk and hang out and have fun. I'm glad I forgot whatever his answer was, because I know it was something painful. I remember thinking that for the time being, I needed to let him go. Mirage had been asking how I felt about New York, which I took to mean that was where he wanted to be, and so I lied and said that the both of us should go.

I sold my TV, my SNES, and my laptop. I sold some of my clothes. I kept paring down until it was just my phone, my records, and my flannels, which were all from Kansas and in my mind couldn't ever be replaced. Sometime during all of that, I lost track of myself. For weeks, I didn't feel anything but this burning urgency to have less stuff. I don't have many other memories from then, except sitting at the bus stop after work, watching bus after bus pass by because I didn't have the willpower to get up. Or sitting at the library computers and watching the cursor blink on Microsoft Word because I couldn't summon a single critical thought for an essay.

I didn't want to go to New York. There was nothing for me there but more strangers and more opportunities to fail. But I didn't want to let Mirage down either, now that he had found his calling. I didn't think he would understand how lost I felt and I didn't want to explain. I had let him go long before we had actually separated.

I told him that I had decided to stay in Pennsylvania with school friends that didn't exist. I told him that he could still have my half of the moving budget. I know he asked questions, but the answers were so far from honest that I don't remember them.

I do remember telling Zeke via email that I had thought about it, and that I wanted to hear what the angels had to say. He re-sponded right away, asking when he could come get me. I told him that the next day would work. He showed up with Octavio and Helena right after Mirage went to work. They were both wearing long sleeves. They were very happy to see me even though we'd only spent an hour together. In fact, they were more excited to see me than anyone had been in a long time. They acted like we were already friends.

We all got in Zeke's Chevy Trailblazer after my stuff was load-ed, and on the ride up to Blessed Falls, I emailed Mirage to say that I had moved my stuff and had gone on a road trip with my nonexistent friends. I transferred my entire bank account balance to the joint account we shared to pay rent and bills. Last, I put my phone on airplane mode. Obviously, this couldn't be permanent, but it was symbolic. I didn't have a way or a reason to look back.

Chapter 5

My first day at Custodes Angelorum started with Zeke in his office. All he had was a desk and index cards. He said that even if I chose not to understand the Angelorum or its message, I should know what the others believed. Most of them were vessels, which meant that we they were going to host angels on 9/19/19. They practiced penance based on what the angels told Zeke about their nearness to divinity. He started talking about the guardians next, and explained that they were there, but they weren't going to host angels because the angels didn't know who they were. They still wanted to repent and to be closer to the angels by way of being near Zeke, which was why he let them take care of the vessels. They were the Custodes part of Custodes Angelorum.

I met Clarice, who was one of the guardians. She showed me the kitchen and full pantry, and then the calendar of upcoming grocery store trips and where to put meal requests. I wasn't comfortable with the idea of letting strangers cook for me, but since I had given Mirage all the money to my name, it was that or starve. I made a mental note to see if I could arrange to cook my own food after the tour. Zeke showed me the grow rooms, where all the weed and shrooms were being cultivated. I noticed people reading bible passages to them.

Zeke showed me my room last. Helena was inside reading an index card. She smiled when she saw me. I couldn't read her personality and didn't know how honest I could be with her. We talked, and I learned that she had been there for almost two years, and that she was going to host Jophiel, the angel of wisdom, understanding, and judgment. She said that not a lot of people came to Custodes Angelorum, and that as far as she knew, no one had ever wanted to leave.

I asked her if she felt like this place was a cult and she said it was less of a cult than Catholicism, where priests molest boys who become priests who molest boys. She also said that her least favorite part of the Angelorum was the choir. There was no set group of people because they were all vessels, thus all angels, thus all part of the choir. They sang to the drugs in the grow rooms, and they sang to the new vessels, and they sang to Zeke whenever the words of the angels started to jumble, so that their voices would clear up. Helena was wearing bandages on her upper arms and her ankles because that's where she had cut herself that morning. She showed me an index card that said 'righteous' and 'vain' in Zeke's handwriting. She said that the angels saw her harboring these sinful traits, and so she performed penance to atone. Then she gave me a tour of the penance chapel.

The penance chapel was the most beautiful part of the commune. It was the only church in it that had character, with its neo-gothic door and steeples and bright stained-glass saints watching over the pews. What I first thought were bronze altars turned out to be troughs. Wooden boxes of gauze sat like treasure chests between them. Those bronze troughs held bloody gauze that had been used. In one almost empty trough, I saw actual drops of blood browning at the bottom.

My stomach dropped and for the first time that day, I didn't try to talk myself out of wondering if I had made a mistake. For how long could I truly mind my business when the business around me was this? Custodes Angelorum was supposed to have been the out that I wanted, but I was starting to think that yet again, I wanted out.

Helena showed me another wooden box near Peter's feet with a row of razors from the hardware store. She explained that cutting parts of the body fortified different things. Legs were for stability, arms for strength, torso for conviction, chest for passion. I thought to myself that if I ever somehow believed in this insanity, and if I somehow ever became devoted enough to the bible to carve pieces of it into myself, my whole body would be covered in scars.

That night, our bedroom light went out at 9:19, which was curfew. Helena set her alarm for 9:19 the next day. I hadn't seen her touch her phone except to do that. The next morning, she weighed herself and wrote the number on the index card Zeke had left the day before. I didn't ask for explanation before she put it on her pillow and left for breakfast. I no longer wanted one.

Chapter 6

Someone else had moved into Custodes Angelorum a day before me, but I didn't get to meet her because she was being exorcised. Helena told me this as she was getting ready to join everyone else to welcome her back. She asked if I wanted to come too, and maybe see that things weren't as crazy as I probably thought they were. I doubted that heavily. Still, it was all so bizarre that I wondered: If I saw enough, would I understand? Maybe if I understood, it wouldn't make me so uncomfortable, and I could let my guard down enough to breathe.

We went outside. Across the dirt road, there were dozens of people crowded around a faraway chapel, under a canopy of oak branches where the sun could hardly reach. Raymond watched a lot of Supernatural, and even though most paranormal TV shows get less than half of my attention, I saw those brothers perform enough exorcisms to be confused by the clapping and cheers of encouragement. Zeke was with a blonde girl, who had a blanket wrapped around her shoulders and a bucket in her arms. The two of them were almost 50 feet away from the rest of us, so I couldn't hear what they were saying, but he was rubbing her back enthusiastically, and she was nodding her head and grinning. Then she sloshed whatever was in the bucket at a nearby tree, and everyone clapped harder. She looked like she was naked under that blanket. I knew there was more to it that I had to have missed, but I decided then that I was for real going to mind my business and not let my curiosity suck me into whatever it was.

My first week at Custodes Angelorum was pretty much carefree. I slept eight hours or more every night. I walked near the mines every day. The guardians let me hang out in the kitchen while they made my food. Their cooking wasn't all that bad, and they said they welcomed feedback. I called Raymond just to hear his voice and lied about being in school and grinding on, and I didn't feel guilty about lying because everything finally felt okay. And because I wasn't ready. Raymond had become a fierce atheist while in Europe, and I didn't want our first sustained conversation in years to end with him worrying about me living with pseudo-Christian cutters. We promised to talk again the next day because we hadn't in so long.

The rest of our conversation was mostly silence. Raymond thought that us going so long without talking was his fault, because he'd been trying to keep his distance and fall out of love with me. He said that it hadn't worked, and he still thought about me every day and wondered if he would ever feel as much for anyone as he felt for me. He regretted respecting my decision instead of trying to talk me into going to Scotland with him. I knew I would've started crying if I agreed with him, which I did, so I pulled some bullshit from somewhere. Something like we were still young and there were so many people out there, and he'd always be in my heart no matter what. Lies, basically. Imagining another future with him meant taking a good look at the present, and I wasn't ready to do that.

My second week at Custodes Angelorum was tainted by that regret. I kept to myself. I started making playlists again. They were all dark and downtempo, but at least I could pretend I was crawling towards a new normal.

The guardians did everyone's laundry. One day, they came in the morning and took everything in my basket, including the clothes I kept on the rim because they weren't clean, but weren't dirty either. I didn't notice my jeans were missing until I realized my headphones were, and by then it was too late. They were already in the dryer and had stopped working.

My logical brain didn't get the chance to talk me out of crying. Helena came back from penance and found me face down in my twin sized bed, sobbing quietly. I don't remember what I said to her, but I remember her watching sympathetically. I remember her dark, silky hair spilling down her shoulders, and thinking that the sunlight through the window behind her made her look like an angel, and that she didn't need to cut herself to be one.

Helena said I should seek Zeke's silence. He didn't call it guidance because all he did was listen and untangle. She said that even if I didn't adopt the faith of a vessel, he would at least give me something to do with myself, because having unstructured time after having nothing but structured time must have been doing something to my head.

She was the only person I ever said more than a few words to. What surprised me was that outside of recommending that I see Zeke for guidance after seeing me cry that one time, she never talked about being a vessel, or asked why I hadn't become one. She said that her estranged devoutly Catholic family had inspired her to never open her mouth about her faith or beliefs unless asked, so that she wouldn't become like them.

And so I started asking questions. My first question of "What happens during an exorcism?" Got the mysterious answer "That's for the faithful to know, and for you to find out if you become one." Then I asked about the verse she had carved into her skin over and over. It turned out that Zeke assigned one to everyone, based on what message the angels believed they should carry. Hers was Joel 1:13. After that, I got onto more practical questions, and found out that the bills and groceries were being paid for with drug sales, which I had guessed. But Helena told me that the grow rooms I had seen were the ones exclusively for Custodes Angelorum. All who observed and had faith drank psilocybin tea with every meal, for clarity, and consumed weed in a million different ways every day, and did acid and kratom on Sundays, Tuesdays, and Thursdays. But there were more grow tents and basements spread around Blessed Falls that everyone tended to for general sale. Vessels got commission by the batch, meaning from seed to stem, or from spore to shroom, the care administered during the life-cycle of every individual harvest was tracked precisely so that the appropriate person got a cut, and the more quality drugs they cultivated, the more plants they got to take care of.

Most people shared the responsibility with at least one other person, but Helena had some plants all to herself because she was so good at what she did. She said that she let them into the light of the angels by reading them the bible. I thought she was crazy, but I decided it didn't matter. I had no choice but to be around her, and the fact that she thought drugs understood the concept of Christianity didn't stop her from being a nice person to be around and to look at. She wore a lot of v-necks, and had a collection of belly and nose rings on the windowsill that she asked me to give my opinions on. She also had a record collection like mine, and said she was hoping to become a Psalm so that she could have a better chance of talking Zeke into making an exception to the little to no technology mentality at Custodes Angelorum for the sake of a record player.

I asked what the Psalms were, and she explained it like an empowerment group for female vessels who wanted to feel better about their bodies. Dropping down to 91 lbs was the criteria for admission. Psalms got to go on day trips around the state. Zeke cooked for them throughout the week, and the guardians cooked for them on weekends.

I was horrified, but because it was Zeke, I was certain that

I just didn't have enough context. It broke my heart that Helena thought she needed to lose weight. I kept selfishly thinking of how I would miss seeing her fill out those v-necks.

I thought I was straight at the time. I had never ruminated about my sexuality because I hadn't felt the need to. But now that I was single and not sharing a room with my brother, I had the opportunity to yearn. I yearned for Helena to extricate herself from her faith so that I could take a closer look at her without touching what she was part of. But that also didn't seem fair. She never tried to pull me into her world but still spent time with me. She had more to talk about than just angels. She knew a lot about fashion, like the exact names of the style of plaid some of my flannels were, and the kinds of buttons that were sewn on. She also really loved movies and TV shows about the mafia because they made her feel closer to her father. Nobody at Custodes Angelorum had a computer, and there was no TV, but I made a mental note to somehow watch The Godfather with her, since it was the only mob movie I had seen.

We started watching The Sopranos on my phone before bed every evening, even though my phone service was so bad that the show was mostly just chunky pixels. When she left the penance chapel in the morning with bandages on her ankles, I was there waiting so that we could walk to the mines and back. Once, I let her convert one of my cherished long-sleeved flannel shirts into a button-up tank top. She found a pair of her own headphones that had slipped out of her awareness and been buried in a backpack pocket, and gave them to me. She became my best friend. I knew that whatever future I found after regrouping had to have her in it.

One morning, I was in our room alone listening to Adele when Zeke came by. Helena was in the penance chapel. She had skipped breakfast with the other vessels and stayed and shared mine with me. She said that the food had given her a sugar rush, and that she would probably take a nap when she came back. Zeke had a stack of index cards in his chest pocket and put one face down on Helena's pillow, which I had just fluffed after making her bed.

Then he asked me how I was liking my new home and my roommate. I confessed to sleeping badly the past few nights and to feeling restless. And then Zeke said, "You're not restless. You're just being careless." His voice was so reassuring that I thought I had misheard. He apologized for being so forward because when he was that honest with the vessels, they understood it was coming from a place of guardianship, and that he got nothing out of delivering the truth, except being a part of something bigger than himself. I told myself I was humoring him when I asked what he meant, and he took me leaving my headphones in my jeans as an example. He said it was a metaphor for what I was doing to myself, and that I had been in such a hurry to turn over a new leaf that I let pieces of myself fall away. I hadn't mourned what was lost. I hadn't tried hard enough to take inventory of what was missing. And I hadn't asked for help.

Those were signs of spiritual negligence, of being careless with the very fabric of my being. I was so desperate for an explanation as to why I felt the way I felt, that I didn't care where it came from. I would've trusted the king of France to know me better than I knew myself.

He said he was going to do something he'd never done before and consult the angels in my behalf, even though I wasn't a vessel. I said that what he'd said was enough for me. I didn't need the angels' input, too. Then he asked if I would have lunch with him since that was the first time we'd had a conversation since I'd moved in. It was Wednesday, and on Wednesdays he had picnics with one or two vessels away from the commune, at the actual waterfall called Blessed Falls.

He asked me about my parents and my brother and my friends. I tried to be as honest as possible while keeping as much to myself as I could. Zeke told me about himself, too. His mother was a lawyer and his father was a minister. He had been amicably estranged from them before they died. He'd been speaking to angels since he was a child and regretted that he never told them. He traveled across the country working at dispensaries before buying one of the rundown chapels and fixing it up into one. He said he had a bunch more built per the angels' guidance.

Blessed River cleaves through the forest like a steam engine, terminating at Blessed Falls, which pour over the cliffs like a spout, ending in a sheer drop of 70 or 80 feet into the plunge pool below. It was sunny. There were rainbows in the mist where the water fell, and fragments of sunlight on the river like gemstones. All day I had felt like I was boiling over with energy that I had nowhere to put, but I hadn't even touched the water and it felt like it had healed me. I was telling Zeke this as he parked and we walked towards the waterfall discussing our families. And then, just as we passed the top of the falls where the clear water folded into churning white, he pushed me with the side of his arm. I flailed and somehow grabbed his elbow so that we both toppled over the edge of the falls with the basket of food. Teetering on the edge of the bank was the most terrified I had ever been. I screamed all the way down and wound up with a nose full of water. I kept sinking and sinking and tried to claw my way to the surface, but all the water did was go through my fingers while the sunlight dimmed with distance. Instinct must have taken over because next thing I knew, I had kicked off of something. I felt my clothes trying to drag me back, but I reached and reached until my fingers touched the underside of the surface. Zeke had made it up before me and was spluttering and coughing, but smiling. "See?" He said. "I knew you cared about your life enough to try and stay balanced. So why don't you act like it?"

He could have killed me, but that day, it seemed like the most profound experience I had ever had in my life. The basket had survived, so we sat in the sun and ate the lox bagels that the guardians had made, plus salt and vinegar chips. We drank pomegranate juice and talked some more, and I found myself telling him many of the things that I had promised to keep to myself.

We talked about Mirage, who I had been trying not to even think about. He had found himself a loft in Brooklyn and filled it with used furniture and plants, and sent me pictures of it, and of the view from his living room. After a while, my eyes started to glaze over when I looked at them because all I could think of was how easy and fulfilling his life seemed to be without me. He'd been more cheerful the two times we talked on the phone than he had at any point in Philly. I told Zeke all of this, and said I couldn't figure out if the place was the problem, or if I was. Zeke said that for one, he never envied twins, because there was so much arbitrary weight on us to be close, when really, you aren't born with or around the people who love you most: they find you. Zeke said love is strongest when it's looked for. He said that Mirage probably didn't love me anymore, but that if I stopped asking myself what I did wrong, I would realize that I didn't love Mirage anymore, either.

Mirage hadn't done anything wrong yet. But it had been such a nice afternoon with Zeke, and I saw no need to tell him that I didn't believe this was the case. I knew in my heart that it wasn't true, and so long as I knew, it didn't matter if he did. But I couldn't get the idea out of my head.

At the same time, my mind was still racing, and the more

Zeke kept talking, the more I felt like I had never seen my own life so clearly. By the time we left the falls, I was starting to think that even though angels weren't real, maybe Zeke did have an ethereal connection to the universe that made it possible for him to see things I couldn't.

Chapter 7

After that day, I went from sleeping badly to not sleeping at all. I stopped having periods, which I blamed on stress. I just couldn't stop thinking. I made dozens of playlists that turned into echo chambers. Music wasn't working, so I walked and listened to the quiet. Only a few people seemed to actually be friends with one another, and for the most part, when I saw people outside of their churches, they were alone with a joint and their bible. I never saw anyone with any book besides that, and I never saw anyone listening to music. It didn't feel like there were 300 other people in my vicinity.

Some nights I went with Helena to the grow rooms so that she could tend to her plants. They were dank, and the hum of the lights above was so soft and steady, they were like a lullaby. Some nights I waited for her outside the penance chapel while she cut herself. Like it was a bathroom, she teased. I was free to go in with her, but I felt like seeing the inside once was enough, and that if I wanted to understand why people felt the need to go in there, I should just people watch. Look for a trend. I found one, sort of. They went in solemn and came out serene. Not everyone used gauze or bandages. Some exited with blood staining their clothes or dripping down their skin. I think this is why I don't remember a lot of faces. Sometimes, the blood was all I could see.

My father and I hadn't been in touch since the week before high school graduation, when he silently sent me money for my cap and gown. Not long after I told Helena about him, he called to say that my grandmother had died. It felt like I was hearing his words through a tube. He kept asking if I was okay. After living with him for a year and living with his absence for longer than that, I was certain that neither time nor death could alter his inability to care about me. But whatever I said when he called, and however I said it, managed to disconcert him.

That phone call started a prolonged spiral.

I started having palpitations daily and couldn't drink enough water to deal with the dry mouth. The insomnia was like a Kansan tornado in my brain, ripping memories and feelings from the back of my head and flinging them out in the open like debris. I remembered all the times my father had never asked if I was okay. I hated him for thinking it was okay to suddenly try and be the father he should've been when I needed him. I said I was fine, but for weeks, I couldn't stop fixating on the call. After that, I sought Zeke's silence.

We met in his office after dinner but before sunset. It was chilly, and I remember wondering how summer had gone by without me really noticing. When I got there, he was hidden in a room that branched from his office in the back of the chapel. It had stained-glass double doors that depicted grey angels and were slightly ajar. He told me to sit behind his desk, which faced away from the doors, so I couldn't see in. When I asked what was in the room, he said that sometimes people decided not to walk with the angels, and that they left things behind. I asked how long it had been since someone had left, and he said it had been six years, but about three years ago, someone who had left returned to earn their things back.

He sat across from me and told me to tell him my problem like it was his problem. At first I didn't get it, and when I did, I felt dumb. Eventually I said, "You feel like your brother and father are taunting you by finally showing interest in your well-being, and now you can't stop imagining where you'd be if they had given a fuck sooner." And then Zeke responded as if that was his problem by saying, "I'm happy now. Why should I care? Should I care just because they finally do? Where has caring about them gotten me? What happens to me when they show their true colors again? Why give them the opportunity to disappoint me again? Why not give those parts of myself to the beings who cared about and were waiting for me?"

He stopped talking like my problems were his and became very blunt by saying that my feelings about my brother and father were coming from spiritual neglect, meaning I was once again being careless with myself. I had given up so much for peace of mind and was shunning the opportunity to hold into it by even considering that they were reaching out from a place of anything but selfishness.

Desperation may have been the impetus, but I had found Custodes Angelorum for reasons beyond that. I had risked everything to leave Kansas, then to leave Philly, but somehow, I couldn't take just one more risk, because, he said, I knew it would change everything. I feared change, but was too neglectful of my own needs to realize how badly I needed what was right in front of me.

I was flambéed by each word from his mouth. But I was so exhausted and so desperate for comfort and answers that I latched onto those words like a treasure. I didn't believe in angels, but I thought that maybe if I pretended for long enough, eventually I would, and the void would fill. Or maybe I would be proved wrong, and the void would still be filled with power unlike any I ever had. I asked Zeke what I needed to do. He told me to open the topmost desk drawer. It was empty, except for one of the white bibles, taped with an index card that already had my name on it. He said that was for me to read during my exorcism, and on the other side of it, it would all be so clear that I wouldn't even need him to explain.

Chapter 8

I stayed awake until it was time. I was going to be in the dusty shed of an exorcism chapel in the shade until I had read the bible cover to cover. I had one night to do so. During this time, I wasn't allowed food or water, or to use the bathroom. It was me, the spiders and dead leaves that had come through the door, and a few rows of candles to read by since there was no electricity.

Zeke and I approached it alone, and he had me go in and take off all my clothes and pass them out through the window, which was so high up that the ledge was at my forehead. Then he told me to just be, and that the angels would be with me, and that he would be back. I didn't know how to just be. I kept standing on my tiptoes trying to see what the rest of the world was up to, like I hadn't been there long enough to know that Custodes Angelorum was always quiet and peaceful, and the only sounds ever came from people coming and going. They walked to the same few places. The mines, the penance chapel, the guardians' house, the grow rooms. They read the bible in the sunlight like college students in the quad. They smoked joints in the stained-glass windows and on the stoops of the chapel. I couldn't figure out how all these people living in close quarters seemed so far away from one another. I wondered if they only seemed far away to me, and if that would change soon.

Eventually, I opened the bible under a blade of sunlight. The inside cover said B.I.B.L.E., which stood for Basic Instructions Before Leaving Earth. I thought that was clever. I read the opening page enough times to remember it by heart:

"Every Christian has probably heard the words 'Jesus loves me this I know, for the Bible tells me so.' But there is plenty that the Bible doesn't say. There is so much that the Bible can't say, because it is not a book meant to inspire panic. Who or what can know those things? And what can they do with that knowledge? If you're reading this, you may think that you know what God is, what an angel is, and what a vessel is, but there's so much more than my voice could ever convey. This is why for this text, I'm going to let the angels do all the typing."

Zeke had whittled the bible down to just fifteen books. Ezekiel came first, then Joel, Genesis, Colossians, 2 Samuel, 1 Peter, Isaiah, Luke, Matthew, Jude, Hebrews, Psalm, Job, Daniel, Revelation, and Romans. Zeke had provided commentary on different verses, repeatedly drawing the conclusion that an army of angels needed to be formed to handle the impending apocalypse, the date for which had been extrapolated from a fusion of Psalm 91:9 (to 16) and Jude 1:9. Zeke noted that the names of people and places were placeholders for things to come. And there were notes on things pertinent to vessels and ~~our~~ their mission of shepherding the worthy into pastures of peace. According to Zeke, most of those pastures were full of marijuana.

I wish I could remember what about Zeke's bible felt so magnetic. I want to believe that it was because the guardians poisoned me with amphetamines, which is the conclusion I came to while attempting to pathologize my mistakes. This had to have been the case for at least a few weeks. Depression as deep as what I had been feeling couldn't turn into energy and curiosity that had come out of nowhere. But whether that's true doesn't change the fact that Zeke's annotated scripture resonated with part of me.

The day passed. I ignored my hunger and the need to pee, and I forced myself to read. I was halfway through the bible and terrified of how fast night seemed to be coming. The mosquitos that hadn't died off yet seemed to zero in on the chapel with me in it, and bit me in places that I had never been bitten before. I put that bible up like a barrier between me and every bodily need begging for relief. The chapel smelled like wood and leaves and faintly of weed and soil. The thought of being the first person in however long, or possibly ever, to pee mid-exorcism made me feel so embarrassed that I held it until tears filled my eyes. And then I kept holding it.

The sun set, and I lit a candle so I could keep reading. I got hungry. I wondered how much hungrier I could get, and what would happen when I got there. Every inch of my body became a test. I ignored the mosquito bites. I swallowed every cough and gritted my teeth against every sneeze. I clenched my jaw so hard that my teeth hurt, just so I wouldn't shiver. My eyes started to hurt, so I lit the candles a few at a time, in case they burned too fast for me to finish reading.

I finished just before sunrise. I flipped back through to revisit parts that stood out. I kept going back to Daniel and Luke, which both mention Gabriel. Before Custodes Angelorum, I didn't know a thing about the bible, and I guess afterward, I knew even less by knowing all the wrong things. As I kept reading, I started seeing spots of pastel color in the margins. When I looked up, there were orbs around me like blown bubbles, but the moment my eyes focused on one, it disappeared. They were saying my name, saying they were waiting before they went.

It seemed miraculous and prophetic that I closed the bible for a second time just as Zeke unlocked the door that morning. He had a bucket for me to pee in and a blanket to put around my shoulders. He was full of awe and congratulations and relief. And just like the girl I had seen the first day, he guided me to a tree to symbolically throw my urine at, then through the crowd of vessels who had come to see my liberation, and took me back to his office to begin everything to come.

Chapter 9

Zeke and I had psilocybin tea. It was bitter and made me want to gag, but I had been over 24 hours without water. He told me that it would help me hold onto everything I had just learned. This wasn't the case. All it did was disorient me and brown out the rest of the day. I remember perfectly though, that he became solemn while talking about what came next, saying it was necessary but sometimes painful, and that as the angels' emissary, he tried to make it as painless and fulfilling as possible. I think his grave reluctance softened his explanation of a vestal restoration. It was both to purify me, and to establish a connection with the angel who had chosen me.

It took me a moment to realize that he was talking about having sex. I didn't realize I had a "type" of man until I took a good look at Zeke and realized that there was nothing I wanted less than sex with him. The only person I had eyes for was Helena, and I didn't even want to have sex with her. I just wanted to spoon and kiss a little while watching The Sopranos.

I finished my tea and asked Zeke if there was something else we could do. He said no, and that although he appreciated his role, he wouldn't take any pleasure in what would probably be uncomfortable for me in the moment. I asked what would happen if I said no, and he said that Gabriel wasn't known for his capacity to handle being told no. And there was no higher degree of spiritual neglect than ignoring the will of the archangel who wanted me to host him. I asked again what exactly would happen if I said no. I didn't get an answer beyond Zeke saying that I had come so far.

I thought I would at least be given time to take a shower or a nap, but he started explaining why he couldn't use a condom and why we would only stay in one position and why I couldn't make any noise. Then he took out a razor and said that it was for my wings, and that my wings were how Gabriel would recognize me. It all happened at Mach speed. It never occurred to me to get to my feet and leave. It never occurred to me that I might be able to find a way out of the place that was supposed to be my way out. It felt like I was in a vault, not a room. The only way out was through, and the only way through was to get on all fours in Zeke's office.

There was nothing ceremonial about it. The rug burned my knees. I didn't move or make a sound. Every ounce of my strength went to pretending there was no one inside of me. Then came the first slice to the left of my spine. I almost bit my tongue off. I almost threw up too, and found a distraction from the pain in trying to silently swallow mouthfuls of blood and vomit.

I choose to believe that this was the moment I lost myself. I choose to believe that I was so desperate for the pain to mean something, that I let myself fully embrace the idea that I was chosen. I was marked with something the real world would never understand, which felt both shameful and righteous.

I remember Zeke wiping the blood off my back with a blanket, and the guardians helping me shower in their house while telling me how blessed I was. I had more tea and a joint and something to eat. Everything I did was through a numb haze.

If my restoration is when I lost myself, then my first penance is when I found the angels. Zeke gave me the same razor he had used for my wings and told me that my verse was Luke 1:19. He walked me to the penance chapel and waited outside. Every movement chafed my wing wounds. The chapel was empty except for me and the stained-glass saints. Sunlight streamed in at an angle. Jesus was among the stained-glass figures in his blue and red outfit, and since he was still the biblical figure I was most familiar with, I went over to him. I remember the sun lighting him up, and the blue light and lamb he was holding casting colors on my face. I remember lifting my arm into the red light, thinking that if I cut under it, I wouldn't be able to see the blood. It's one thing for someone else to slice me up, but me doing it to myself was something else altogether. I remember thinking to myself, "There's still time to leave. I can run and leave all of this."

And then the lamb in Jesus' arms asked, "Where to? This is where you belong."

It started blinking at me expectantly, until I myself was wondering what I was waiting for. I knelt at Jesus' feet and leaned back and sliced Luke 1:19 above my right ankle. It wasn't as easy as I thought it would be, and it wasn't until much later that I realized that cutting with the intent to scar is like painting a wall. Sometimes it takes more than one coat for the color to come through. I couldn't do it all in one go. I'd have to go at it again and again before the scar tissue became something legible.

Zeke took me to my room after that. He was saying how happy he was that I wouldn't have to be alone anymore, and that I would finally get to eat with the others and be able to have a space in the grow tents and borrow a car to go to Philly. He explained what the Psalms were, and said I'd make a powerful addition and inspiration to everyone else. By the time we got to my room, my smile wasn't uncertain or fake. By then, I couldn't believe that all of this was all I'd had to do to belong. I couldn't believe how easy it had been. He left just as Helena was returning from the grow rooms.

Helena glowed when I told her about me being a vessel. She asked who I was hosting, how I felt, if I needed anything like water or a snack. I told her that Gabriel had chosen me. I told her I was fine but asked why she hadn't told me that Zeke carving wings into her back was part of becoming a vessel. Helena was confused. She asked what I was talking about; she hadn't gotten any wings.

July 25, 2019

Seven years ago we all went through the flames; and the happiness of some of us since then is, we think, well worth the pain we endured. It is an added joy to Mina and to me that our boy's birthday is the same day as that on which Quincey Morris died. His mother holds, I know, the secret belief that some of our brave friend's spirit has passed into him. His bundle of names links all our little band of men together; but we call him Quincey.

eleven

I don't remember when I came back indoors, or how I made it to bed in one piece. The answer probably lies somewhere beneath the sour taste of wine and mouth-breathing on my tongue.

In one piece is being generous. I didn't put my bonnet on, didn't wash my face or brush my teeth. The blankets are filthy from being on the rooftop and my pillows are on the floor.

It's been a long time since I drank to forget, and my roiling stomach is a staunch reminder of why.

It, and the fact that there was no forgetting. I hear Laura's voice louder than I hear my buzzing phone, lost somewhere under my body.

My head pounds as I sit up, digging in the linens. I'm still in yesterday's clothes, jeans twisted up my shins like I crossed a river in my sleep.

Mirage's name clarifies in my doubled vision.

"Hey," I croak. "What's up?"

"Uh...it sounds like you haven't been for long," he says uncertainly. "We said nine, didn't we?"

It takes a few throbs of my aching head for the days-old memory to resurface. We're supposed to be alone at Oasis before any of the staff come in, eating breakfast in our booth above the river. I'm supposed to be with him, doing everything in my power to repair our relationship, which has been six years in the unmaking.

"What's wrong, O?"

I can't bring myself to say *nothing*. Not this time.

"I messed up, Mirage."

"What do you mean?" He asks alertly. "What happened?"

I don't know what I mean, and I barely know what happened, but I don't get to say any of this out loud. I open my mouth to speak and vomit. My stomach heaves not once, not twice, but three times in rapid succession, until I'm hunched over, gasping and shivering, yet somehow still holding my phone to my face.

"That bad, huh?"

My reply is a belch.

"Go back to sleep, sis. I'll be there soon."

"Mkay," I say feebly.

After we hang up, I extricate myself from the bedding and drag all of it off the bed. The sky-blue fleece on top is the most heavily soiled with blood red vomit. My stomach feels better after throwing up, but my head hurts, and my body still aches for rest.

I throw the sheets in the washer, then lay face down on my bare mattress, soaking in the light of the rising sun, and wait for sleep to come back to me.

*

I wake to the sound of a pan being set on the stove and the smell of bananas frying in butter. My empty stomach clenches in too tight of a fist for me to panic. Through the gap in the door, I see Mirage in my kitchen, untwisting a loaf of bread.

I slip into the closet and change into clothes that won't betray my meltdown. The washing machine still has fifteen minutes left in its cycle. I barely slept thirty minutes.

Mirage, dressed in a Nirvana t-shirt and basketball shorts, turns at the sound of my footsteps. His eyes widen, which I take to mean that I look worse than I thought.

"Sorry I started cooking without you," he says, eyeing the frying bananas and the makings of a peanut butter and jelly sandwich. "You looked like you needed the rest."

"Don't apologize," I say hoarsely.

Mirage pours me a glass of water and follows me to the table with it.

I slump into a chair, glancing at the sunlit city beyond the fire escape doors. The books from last night are stacked in the middle of the table, with the exception of my memoir, which I vividly remember reading while guzzling the $150 wine meant for Laura.

"What happened?" Mirage asks.

I gulp some water.

"Thawed some chicken, thought it smelled funny, cooked and ate it anyway." The lie comes easily, largely because the truth hasn't fully percolated through my brain.

He returns to the stove to tend the banana. "You don't have to eat this. I can make something new in front of you."

"Don't be—" I belch "—silly. I'll eat it."

Mirage casts an uncertain glance over the counter, then quickly looks away. "You don't have to."

I barely refrain from smacking my lips in irritation. Any other day, I'd probably shut down, tell him whatever it is I think he wants to hear just to reach a point where the conversation doesn't feel like a game.

Not today.

"What's going on?"

"Nothing. I just don't want you to feel pressured." Mirage looks away and back, which takes me off guard. Usually *I'm* the one who can't hold eye contact to save my life. "I just want you to trust me again."

"Oh," I say. It's all I can manage. I wasn't ready for this. It's not too late to shut it down—or to do what he's known for and run this conversation in circles until both our days are ruined.

No.

I can't think about fixing my relationship with Laura just to turn around and further damage this one.

"And I want you to understand that it's not you I don't trust. It's the world," I say. "And me."

He plates my food in silence, pours me some oat milk and brings it all over.

My stomach growls like thunder as I pull the plate towards myself. He cooked two bananas and two sandwiches. The arrangement reminds me vividly of the two of us after school, sharing a grilled cheese or two while doing homework.

"What I don't understand is why you take it so personally when I can't eat at Oasis when we could always just do more of this," I say, gesturing at the food I'm fighting not to inhale like a shop vac. "You seem to think it's deliberate, and then bring up Mom when we both know whose side she'd take, which there shouldn't be any of to begin with."

My brother looks down at the steaming plate, combs his fingers through the short, springy curls at the nape of his neck.

I take the opportunity to scarf down half a sandwich despite it still being scalding. I haven't finished my first bite, and I'm already thinking of seconds. I glance at the stove clock; I'm sure Kennedy won't mind if I'm late, but Full Cauldron is the only place I can go to think without overthinking.

I reach for another half sandwich and, as I bite into it, hear an enormous sniff from across the table.

Mirage has the neck of his t-shirt pulled over his face, fingertips pressed into his eyes.

I vault out of my chair so fast that it almost falls.

Mirage twists and wraps his arms around my waist. The top of his head and the planes of his reddening cheeks are all I see. Guilt blunts my senses, and for a while, I can't speak either.

I can't pretend I haven't thought about scenarios like this in a way that could qualify as fantasizing—moments where I wanted to see him cry as hard as I have over the state of our relationship. Now that my brother's holding onto me, clearly trying not to cry harder than he is, I feel evil for wondering.

"Sorry," he says thickly. "I just…I wouldn't have a thing to my name if it wasn't for you. Oasis is named after you because without you it wouldn't exist, and every time you don't eat there, it feels like I'll never be able to prove it was worth it." He tilts his head back so that I can see his bloodshot eyes and the tears clinging to his long lashes. "But I realized a long time ago that you never would've given up everything for me if I hadn't made you so desperate to get away from me to begin with."

I glance at my bedroom, where my memoir is wedged somewhere between the bed and the wall. It's like he read it before coming by.

"I wasn't desperate to be away from you. Just desperate. I made my choices, Mirage, and I have to live with them. *But*," I say, reaching for half of his sandwich as he clings to me, "I'd really appreciate it if you let me recover at my own pace."

Mirage nods and prods me back in the direction of my seat with one finger. "I know. I've been having these nightmares where I come back to Aurora's, and you're gone all over again, except you never called or left a note or anything, and then I never hear from you again. I get old and senile in my dreams," he says, hollowly, "and haven't heard from you in 60 years. And then there's others where I never hear from you again, but then I see you on the news after…" He doesn't complete the sentence.

He doesn't have to.

There's no questioning the fact that I probably escaped mass suicide.

"I know I can't talk you out of having nightmares, but stop. Or at least do whatever you can to stop," I say. "Reality is awful enough."

Mirage laughs humorlessly. He blows his nose on a piece of paper towel. His reddish, tear-streaked face reminds me too much of glasses-wearing, short-for-his-age, Pokémon-loving junior high Mirage—the one who'd been crying in the bathroom stall before coming to me at the end of the school day to give me the name of another bully who needed to have their head slammed in a locker.

"Wow," he says, looking around like he can't believe what happened. "I hope I didn't ruin your day."

"Hush." Having left half of a half of his sandwich, I pick up my fork and cut into a banana. "You're not the only person to be overcome with emotion in front of me in the past twenty-four hours."

Mirage tilts his head to the side inquisitively. "Was it...Laura?"

I'd been prepared to say nothing at all about her, or to amplify my lie if necessary, but between my residual headache and the relief over the shift in topic, I don't have room for more devastation over last night.

"What are you gonna do?" He asks.

That's a good question.

How do I contact a vampire who has no phone? Now that I know she really can hear my heartbeat, maybe there's breathing exercises I can do to tell her in Morse code that I'm done taking time—that if I go any longer without seeing her, I'll scream.

"I don't know, but I know we can fix this."

"This?" He repeats. "As in...you two?"

"She's mine." No I want, or I wish, or I hope. "We'll figure it out."

I finish both sandwiches and bananas by myself, then move the blankets from washer to dryer. Since Mirage doesn't have to be at the restaurant just yet, I text Kennedy to let him know I'll be running half an hour late, because unlike previous times this past year, I plan on letting this time with my brother run its course instead of cutting it off before it turns sour.

"You're reading this?" Mirage asks, voice raised slightly over the sound of running water.

I dip out of the bathroom, massaging cleanser on my cheeks and forehead, and squint at the book he's pointing to: *Dracula*.

"That's Laura's."

Mirage thumbs the sticky notes on the edges. "Is she an English major? What is it with you and book nerds?" He asks without waiting for an answer.

"Raymond's nerdiness was specific to *one* author's books," I say, returning to the bathroom. "Laura's just…passionate about representation."

"It ain't not one nigga to be found in it," he says succinctly. "Save your girl some trouble."

I moisturize my face and lips, then pop an ibuprofen and assess my reflection. My hair is beyond salvation; an oversized, satin-lined beanie will have to do.

Back in the dining room, Mirage is looking at the cover of the Book of Enoch like it's speaking to him and saying some of the worst things he's ever heard.

"Have you read it?"

"I was in a book club for cooks last year," he says. "That one character Jonathan Harker is always writing down different foods, so we tried some of the recipes."

"I meant the Book of Enoch."

"Oh. Yeah. I read it and the bible and a few other things when you were comatose," he says. "Just wanted to understand why you were with those people, yanno?"

I barely refrain from agreeing. Even with my written memories of those years, I still sometimes wonder why.

"What would you do if angels were real?" I ask.

"I'd beat the shit out of them," Mirage says, voice warped as he stretches his arms high over his head. "And then once they recovered, I'd beat the fuck out of them. And then…you know, whatever's worse than that, I'll beat that out of them too."

I snort. More laughter bursts out of me, until I'm cackling so hard that a pang in the back of my head reminds me that I'm still hungover.

"I'm serious," Mirage says with a deep frown. "You're my sister, and you're beautiful, and you told me you barely even look at yourself anymore. I don't care if they can fly and have eighty-three wings and are also wheels with eyes. I'll beat the shit out of every angel in the sky."

Any other day, I'd give him my blessing, but this isn't any

other day: this is the day after I found out that angels are real. And because I found out by way of my girlfriend's hand catching fire, I'm thinking I could beat the shit, fuck, etc. out of them too.

*

It turns out that the hangover I thought I successfully dodged was just waiting for me to sit still. The sandwiches and bananas I ate with reckless abandon sit heavy in my squirming stomach.

"You need ice cream."

This is Kennedy's response to my abridged version of last night's events, given on our trip to Duane Reade for sticky notes, staples, card stock, and markers.

"You may be right. Just not today."

Now that the backlog of labor has been remedied, the two of us sit side-by-side behind the counter like students, brainstorming ways to spice the place up before re-opening. My contribution is a new Lord of the Rings display with hand-illustrated signage.

Kennedy looks up from his impressive portrait of Mary Shelley, drawn in green, purple, and blue marker.

"How about tomorrow? There's this place on the other side of Central Park that sells all these exotic flavors. My friend told me they have one from Michigan."

"Since when is Michigan exotic?"

"Since they have a flavor of ice cream named after Superman."

Nostalgia creeps over me, the buried source being a week-long trip to Detroit with my mother for an electronic music festival. Mirage had been off in California for some basketball tournament, so it was just the two of us roaming the blighted yet beautiful city for restaurants and record stores.

"I had Superman ice cream before with my mama. We should get some," I say, feeling the hesitation in my voice. But rather than let it sit, I elaborate: "In my case, trying might be all I can do. I have this thing about eating...or *not* eating, food prepared by strangers."

Kennedy doesn't ask for elaboration. "I hear ya. Well, the non-credentialed mental health professional in me says no pressure. The other one says you can let it melt for all he cares. But then there's this third Ken," he says, scratching his head like this is a brand new discovery, "and *he's* saying that we could just eat out of the same waffle bowl, because you *deserve* a taste of that red, yellow, and blue hero."

"I can't say no to that," I say. "Although…"

"Although what?" Kennedy asks.

Whatever I'd been about to say falls off my tongue, and I practically knock him off his stool lunging for the trash can. I gag and heave; nothing comes up, but the window for hangover damage control is rapidly narrowing.

"Do—"

"*No*," I gasp, shaking my aching head as I gaze up at him through watering eyes. "Home is ground zero for moping."

Kennedy opens his mouth, then closes it, clearly torn between scolding and indulging. "I'll run and get you some Gatorade, saltines, apple sauce, Alka Seltzer…" He lists a few more hangover remedies like a frantic parent while I massage my temples. "You sit *right* here," he says, patting my stool, "until I get back."

I can't actually move though, and remain next to the trash can, where I have a nice view of the dust bunnies, balled up sticky notes, and pencils beneath the counter.

Five minutes later I'm by myself, with Kennedy having literally run out of the store after giving me a bottle of water and a folded-up Superman hoodie so that I'll at least be comfortable pricing books while laying on the floor.

This seller kept their collection of trade paperback sci-fi novels in pristine shape, making the task even easier, and clearing up brain space for the pressing question of how to contact my girlfriend.

I don't know where she lives, or if she even lives in New York. I have no idea what her last name is, either—if she even has one. Something tells me Laura the Impaler wouldn't turn up any legitimate results on Facebook. All I have to go on is that her sister goes to Juilliard and is distantly related to Jonathan and Mina Harker, who, up until yesterday, were fictional characters in a book I haven't read.

The bell above the front door tinkles as it opens.

"That was fast," I say hoarsely, raising onto my elbows. I use the stool to push myself up and grab the counter. "Please don't tell me they were…"

The word *closed* slips away.

The tall fair-haired man who just stepped in isn't Kennedy. He has a long, pointed nose, a wide forehead, and eyes the color of the clouds. His black t-shirt features a sketch of the Death Star from *Star Wars*, labeled like an architectural blueprint. He strolls through the towers of boxes that we have yet to break down and put out, looking left and right like a tourist.

I can't say I was particularly comfortable being alone in rooms with random white men *before* Dr. Seward and the non-customer who pitched a fit over the Silmarillion, but I feel especially vulnerable right now since I'd probably throw up trying to defend myself.

"Sorry, but we're closed," I say.

He turns his head left and right, like he lost his way in and is looking for signposts. "I must've misread the website. Can't blame me for being impatient, can you? This place is wonderful."

"I think so, too." I put my elbows on the counter, trying my best not to look like I could pass out at any moment. "Sorry to test your patience even more, but I gotta send you on your way. I promise it'll be even more wonderful next week."

He smiles but doesn't turn back towards the door. "I'm sure of that. But I'm claustrophobic. Not a fan of crowds."

"You should come before noon, then," I say swiftly. "Things don't pick up until the comics hit the racks."

"I see." He's still moving closer while looking left and right at the posters on the walls, the stacks of books to be shelved, the comic racks behind him, like a cat who doesn't think I'll notice his approach.

Sincere anxiety results in sincere subtlety as I ease my phone from my back pocket and set it in front of the register, beyond his sight. I quickly do what I should've done a long time ago, and share my location with Kennedy.

"I bet you get a lot of interesting customers," the stranger says.

I nudge my phone further out of sight, but keep the screen lit and my conversation with Kennedy open. "Not too long ago, a guy came in, flipped out, and then got hit by a car up the block. That was interesting."

He laughs quietly. Before I know it, he's right across from me, and I'm trying to use nothing but my peripheral vision to search for a deterrent.

"I also bet you get a lot of attention, being as beautiful as you are," he says, and for the first time, I realize that he has a hint of an accent.

My heart skips a beat. My stomach squirms like putty. "I wouldn't know. I only care about one person's attention."

His thick brows arch over his grey eyes, as if he knows me

well enough to be taken off guard. "He's a very lucky man, who-ever he is."

"She is. So am I," I say with a half-smile that I hope comes across as neutral. I pick up a stack of books from the floor and set it on the counter. Then I grab my phone and stride from behind the counter, ignoring my aching head and roiling stomach. "I gotta get back to work. I'd hate to have to push back your first *real* visit."

I see the stranger's reluctance in the tightness of his smile and the way his grey eyes don't leave me as he follows me to the door. I open it all the way, shielding most of my body behind the wood and glass and smile.

"I look forward to seeing you soon," he says as he steps out.

I wave and close the door. The sign is flipped to *Closed*, and the handwritten sign below says *We will be re-opening July 29th!! LLAP* in Kennedy's handwriting.

Since he left with the key to the store, the most I can do is push a stack of empty boxes in front of the door like a barrier—except the boxes I attempt to nudge with my foot aren't all empty. The one at the bottom of the stack is still unopened.

With a sigh, I kneel with scissors and slice the box open.

A condolence card sits on top, sent from a long-time custom-er—an English professor who moved to Connecticut but contin-ues to send books that he's cycled out of his syllabi. This batch is full of Barnes & Noble Classics with colorful spines. A handful of Austen titles, several books by the Bronte sisters, a Dickens com-pendium. *Frankenstein*, with its orange spine and skull graphic cov-er, will probably be going on Kennedy's Shelley shrine-in-progress.

The blood-red cover of *Dracula* features a white cross sticking partway out of a grave. I pick it up, turn it over in my hand, then quickly turn it face up again so that I can't read the back cover.

I still don't understand, and this isn't how I want to learn.

I carry the books to the counter, pushing the new signage out of the way, and search for a pencil. But before I can sit down, my gut tells me to run to the bathroom. I barely make it in time to vomit and afterward take a few minutes to gasp on the floor before rinsing my mouth, too terrified of puking again to drink water.

I readjust my beanie and tighten my flannel around my shoul-ders, then smear Vaseline on my chapped lips, all of which does little to remedy how pale I look and how shivery I feel. If someone had told the Oasis of July 7th that the Oasis of July 25th would be in this position, I might've rethought my stance on psychiatric intervention and sent them to someone for evaluation. Hungover, helplessly consumed by thoughts of a woman I met less than a month ago, trying not to panic over the possibility of never seeing her again.

I hear a chime from the sales floor and the sound of the door opening.

Are half our patrons suddenly illiterate?

I can't see whoever it is amid the boxes when I return to the sales floor, so I make my way behind the register for a better vantage point. The newest stranger's back is to me: She's tall and slender, and strolling past the comics display like she's at a museum. Her dark Afro is in a long braid, draped over her shoulder like a boa. From her cream tank top to the black corduroy shorts hugging her hips, to the wide-diamond fishnets wrapped around her long legs, she looks like she was peeled off a high-end fashion billboard.

If I wasn't already taken, I'd think twice before kicking her out, but I've had enough distractions from my thus far fruitless brainstorming on recovering her.

"I'm sorry, but we're closed," I say.

"I know," she replies in a clear, songlike voice. "I'm not here to shop."

I frown at the back of her head. "Double the reason for you to leave, then."

She laughs, low and playful, before turning around.

My mouth falls open, and even though I'm standing still, I almost lose my balance. All thoughts cease to circulate as she walks closer.

Dimples crease her round cheeks, and long lashes coated with sparkling mascara fringe her wide brown eyes. Her dark brown skin is spritzed with darker freckles, and her lips are painted dark red.

She looks like Laura.

Up close, I see that her nose is a rounder, her chin is smaller, and her brow is higher, but from afar, she looks so much like Laura that if she didn't have those few inches on me, I'd think it was her coming to tell me that she doesn't need more time to think, that I'm hers, that she loves me.

"When my sister said you were from Kansas, I was terrified I'd get up here and find some cornfed, confederate flag thong wearing, blonde-haired, blue-eyed white bitch." She takes a deep breath, beaming, and exhales like she's strolling through a meadow. "What a *joy* it is to find a brown-eyed, thick-thighed, plaid-clad *baddie*. And that *jaw*. You look just like Billie Holiday." Her eyes twinkle as she stops at the counter and holds out a hand. "It's nice to meet you, Oasis. I'm Talon."

My heart gallops in my chest. I'm slow to recover, and still feel like I might be dreaming until our hands touch. Her palm is warm, her fingers firm around mine.

"Sorry I tried to kick you out," I say, voice still raspy from puking.

"It's alright. I don't mean to intrude," she says with an uncannily familiar frown. "I just *had* to meet the woman my sister braved the sun for."

I stare, struggling to swallow my speechlessness. I notice a silver crucifix on a thin chain around her neck, shining amidst a constellation of freckles on her collarbone.

"That's me. Sorry to say the cornfed allegation sticks. Kansas is Kansas no matter what color you are."

Talon grins as she opens a fuchsia velvet purse slung over her arm.

"The thing is, my sister is older than the concept of color, ergo the only color she *really* sees is red. I have no intentions whatsoever of letting a white person into the family portrait." She takes out an envelope, rifles through a few pages. "My iPad died, and I had *all* my annotations marked on a PDF, so I guess I'll just have to…" She scans the stack of books on the counter, then peers into the box. "Improvise." With *Dracula* in hand, she puts the box on the floor and makes room on the counter.

I'm too shocked, too fascinated, and too hungover to stop her. I retrieve the folded Superman hoodie and put it on, stuffing my clammy hands in the pockets.

"Talon, if you're here to advocate for Laura, you don't have to."

"I do, actually. She's my sister," she says, flipping slowly through the book, eyes squinted in concentration. Then she picks up my pencil and begins to annotate the book. "Page 70… and page 111," she mutters, underlining passages, "and page 194, and…page…399." She closes is it and rotates it 180 degrees.

I don't touch it. "I promised her I wouldn't read this."

"And I promised her I'd mind my business." Talon twirls my pencil deftly over her knuckles. "You don't have to be in denial to still be in a state of disbelief," she says, pushing the book closer. "I can't leave until I know you believe, Oasis."

My reservations are flaking away despite myself.

This isn't me picking up a random copy of this book to peruse behind Laura's back.

This is her sister.

The living, breathing proof that I didn't know I needed, because even after realizing I was in denial, I never really left it.

And so, under her expectant gaze, I read each underlined passage, noting mentions of Wilhelmina Murray, Jonathan Harker, and Quincey Morris.

Then Talon unfolds one of the pages she brought and flattens it on the counter.

It's a birth certificate, issued in Alameda County, California. *Quintaliyah Wilhelmina Harker*, stamped in all caps, born on July 13th, 1997 in Oakland, California to Taliyah Belman and Quincey Harker.

"And I thought Talon was as badass of a name as you could get," I say after a moment.

Talon looks both incredulous and amused as she takes back her birth certificate. "You're even more well-adjusted than I thought. Not even a gasp or a widening of the eyes."

I snicker and take a sip of water, soothing my itching throat. "Are you sure you're talking about the right Oasis? Because the only thing I'm well-adjusted to is feeling unadjusted at all times."

She purses her lips and arches a brow, almost like she expected me to say as much. "Laura thinks she scared the blood from your veins."

"Why?" I ask.

"She genuinely believes you had no idea she's a vampire," Talon says, "but you and I both know that no one goes that long without asking for proof unless they already know the truth." She drums her fingers on the glass, fixes me with a steady, piercing gaze. "Don't we?"

I look away, focusing instead on the cover of the book between us.

"I'm not sure what she did, so I won't defend it, but—" she taps the book with her finger, lowers her voice dramatically "—it was the baggage talking."

"Where is she?" I ask.

"At home," Talon says, "looking at pictures of ice cream since she can't eat any. Our brother says she's listened to *Toccata and Fugue in D minor* 288 times in a row and counting."

I didn't think my body could feel any worse than it does now, but the thought of Laura curled up alone flipping languidly through a Baskin Robbins menu makes my head pound even harder. Worse than that, I realize that I've been going about my playlist construction all wrong: I can't showcase my heart to my 588-year-old girlfriend with songs that are exclusively from the 20th and 21st centuries.

I reach for a pad of sticky notes and pluck the pencil from Talon's hand. "How do you spell that?"

"T-O-C-C-A-T-A and F-U-G-U-E." She watches with her elbow on the counter and her chin in her hand. "I don't know what I expected when I came up here, but it wasn't you."

"I'm just glad you came by. I was starting to panic." I peel the sticky note off and affix it to the back of my phone for safe keeping. "Since you already broke your promise to mind your business, will you tell her my thinking is concluded?"

Talon nods, grinning, and tucks her birth certificate away. "I'll let you get back to work. I hope I see you soon," she says with another bright smile. "Not too soon, though. You look like you have some recuperating to do."

Talon turns around, stroking her braid, and heads towards the exit.

My thoughts further unspool with each step she takes.

"Talon?"

She pauses with her hand on the doorknob and turns, smiling expectantly. "Oasis?"

"What would you have done if I was white?" I ask.

"I would've killed you."

I swallow a quiet laugh, but she doesn't laugh at all. She glances out the window, then opens her purse and pulls something partway into the light: A pink and white Glock with hearts stamping the grip.

My eyes widen until it feels like my eyebrows are touching my beanie.

"Oh."

Talon puts the gun back in her purse with a semi-helpless look that says, *You asked.*

"Like I said, that's my sister. Jonathan Harker broke her heart when he betrayed her, and because I exist, she still smells him every day. My sister's love doesn't expire," she says, fondling the tip of her braid, brushing the strands on her palm. "I'm not dealing with a white bitch forever."

"I'll be sure to stay Black."

She smiles again, waves, and leaves.

After several minutes of picking up my pencil and putting it back down, I give up on productivity. Kennedy returns with what looks like half of Duane Reade. I fully comply with his shift into caretaker mode, but the back of my mind whirs with Talon's voice and face, replaying tidbits of our conversation as relief and anticipation trickle through my body like a tincture.

*

I feel stabilized in the hangover department by the time I'm off work. My body craves sleep, but there's one thing left to do before I succumb.

I let Kennedy believe that my purchase of *Dracula* is part of a plan to reconcile with Laura, but what I plan on doing is more for me than her.

The bottle of wine I thought I'd finished is sitting on my nightstand with two or three good chugs left. I take it to the bathroom, stuff a towel in the crack between door and floor, and throw open the frosted window. The sky is a ruddy lilac, the clouds scattered and patchy.

I put *Dracula* in the middle of my cast-iron claw foot tub and drench it in stale wine. Then I drop a match on the cover and sit on the toilet. Black smoke fringes the dancing flames, which rise to a few inches above the rim.

The flames in front of me are orange, but the ones in my mind are pink like the ones that consumed Laura's hand.

Cluelessness is one thing; the adorable look in her eye when I remind her of how attractive I think she is always makes me want to give her a demonstration.

Disbelief is something else. I never said I loved her, but she told me she felt it; she just didn't believe it was real. I have no choice but to hate the book responsible for this, and so I stay in the bathroom sipping Gatorade and scrolling through Bach compilations on YouTube until all that's left of the book is a mound of ash to wash away.

July 26, 2019

26 July.—I am anxious, and it soothes me to express myself here; it is like whispering to one's self and listening at the same time.

twelve

It's Friday afternoon, and all the shady spots of Central Park are occupied. My saving grace is the cold confectionery sitting between Kennedy and I, placed on my purse to make it hard for the ants to reach.

Superman ice cream kind of looks like someone crumpled the hero himself in a fist and scooped him into a waffle bowl. It tastes like my newest reason to burnish the wounds of the past so that I can eat some on my own.

Kennedy is slowly chipping away at the blue vanilla stripe.

I decided to wear my hair out today, and wisps of my Afro keep getting in my face. Trying to tame it is like trying to tame smoke.

"If you were to finish your degree, would you go back to UPenn?"

"I'm too bitter," I say. "Would you go back to U of M?"

"I'm not fit for those winters." He frowns at a distant troupe of geese. "I'm barely fit for these."

I take my time sucking ice cream off my spoon, then break off a piece of the waffle bowl and nibble. "I'm sure the status of the federal loans I've been ignoring disqualifies school as a near future option, but it's fun to imagine myself writing papers and reading books again."

Too safe in the present to fall behind like before.

"Question," Kennedy says, interrupting my unfolding daydream. "Why'd you share your location with me yesterday? Did something happen?"

"Some guy came in saying he misread the website," I say. A day after the fact, my reaction seems more intense and paranoid than necessary, but Kennedy's face says he doesn't agree.

"I'm glad you did," he says. "My friend Ana is a manager at the new Strand location, and she told me that one of her employees no-called, no-showed, and right as she was writing out his termination letter, NYPD came into the store asking if he'd been acting funny, or if anyone came to the store to see him. I thought maybe you'd seen it in the news or something."

"Is he still missing?" I ask, but once again, Kennedy's expression speaks for him.

"They didn't tell her how he died. The guy was a training MMA fighter and everything," he says, shaking his head at our ice cream. "But the part that concerns me most is that she told me that someone who works at McNally told *her* that one of *their* employees stopped showing up before NYPD swung by. I don't know if that person's been found yet."

"Someone's kidnapping bookstore employees?" I ask skeptically.

"I sincerely hope not," Kennedy says. "But my dad says I should consider hiring someone else, so I'll go ahead and draft up a post for Indeed. Hire them as bait so you'll be safe."

I shouldn't laugh, but I do. "What makes you think you're safe from being kidnapped?"

"I'm annoying," he says easily. "And I'm not even annoying on purpose. Imagine how *powerful* I'd be if I put effort into it. I could be a weapon of mass destruction."

I shake my head and eat more waffle cone. "I hope their families get closure." I push my hair back, frowning at Kennedy, who's also frowning at a golden ladybug traipsing intrepidly up his knee. "Why'd your dad suggest you hire someone else?"

"He thinks I overwork us," he says, and though his voice doesn't change, his averted eyes betray latent sadness. "Plus, my sister thinks I should go back to school, even if I don't go back to Michigan. And honestly, thanks to you, I agree."

"Are you calling me crazy?" I ask mid-bite, sprinkling crumbs on my t-shirt.

"Of course not," Kennedy chides. "Life is too short to state the obvious."

Just for that, I dig my spoon into the blue stripe he's been nursing and scoop so aggressively that the waffle bowl splinters.

"You may be crazy now, but you weren't when you were hand-cuffed to that bed," he says. "I hope it's not weird to say, but I think about that a lot. A *lot*, a lot. I thought about it for a month straight when you told me. It's one of the most fucked up things I've ever heard—more fucked up than anything you did to yourself."

My heart trips over itself, but somehow I stay steady. "I'm glad someone feels as strongly as I do."

"So strongly that I might fuck around and go deeper into debt. I'm just so *jaded* sometimes." Kennedy flattens his hand on his thigh, obstructing the ladybug's path. It pauses near an artisanal tear in the denim. "Even if I were to open my own practice, the mental health industrial complex looks is like politics. You go in thinking you can change the system from within, just to end up like every other miserable psychiatrist taking blank checks for Xanax and Adderall."

I grimace. "You should write that scenario on a piece of pa-per, and then put it in quotation marks, and then write *sike* at the bottom. It's what I'd do."

"You know what? You're absolutely right," Kennedy says, grinning widely as the ladybug climbs onto his index finger. "And just for that—*oh my God*," he gasps, gaping at something over my shoulder. "*Kitty.*"

I look where he's looking, raising a hand to shield my face from the sun.

Kennedy isn't the only one who's noticed the orange tabby feline. A few people point at it with smiles on their faces; a mother intercepts her ecstatic toddler before he can try and chase it.

The backdrop of park visitors and foliage blurs behind the approaching cat. She isn't just wandering around central park; she's marching determinedly towards us.

"This is the best day of my life," Kennedy whispers as the cat draws nearer. He reaches for her once she's a few feet away, grazing her coat with his fingertips.

The cat leaps over his crossed ankles, golden-eyed gaze fixed on me. She barely looks older than a kitten, with reddish-brown stripes on her face like war paint and a quizzical twitch to her tail.

"Oasis—you're the *chosen one*," Kennedy says, choked with awe.

"This wouldn't be the first time," I say dryly.

The cat slinks around my waist, rubbing my arms with her head and face, leaving goosebumps spritzed on my skin. Her body and fur are both cold, like she just leapt out of a freezer. Her paws feel like ice cubes through my jeans. I click my tongue and scratch above her tail, which twines around my wrist as she circles around for more scratches between her ears. A black heart-shaped tag dangles from her collar.

Bird Bones.

She licks her nose. Her pupils are razor thin in the sunlight. She sits statuesque while I peek at the other side of her collar.

I will come to you at sunset.

Laura.

The number of hours between now and sunset feels astronomical, but seeing her then is preferable to never seeing her again.

Bird Bones is still watching me, paw on my arm like she's telling me it'll all be okay. She has eyes like stained glass suns and a coat like a sherbet Rorschach painting.

She leaps over my legs, leaving me dazed.

"Don't leave," Kennedy says, heartbroken, reaching.

Bird Bones ignores him, swishing her tail, once again stealing the show as she trots back the way she came.

"Oasis, what was that?" Kennedy asks, gawking.

"Laura's a cat trainer," I say. It's the first lie I can think of and, like all of the lies I ever come up with, sounds more convincing out of my mouth than in my head.

All that matters is that it suffices for Kennedy.

"I'm sorry, but whatever's going on with y'all's relationship— you need to fix it ASAP. Do you know how much clout it'll give me? *Too much*," he asks, clutching his head like he can't comprehend it himself. "I could just walk up to a stranger like, 'Hey, my name's Kennedy, nice to meet you—by the way, my friend's girlfriend is a cat trainer.' And then they'd be like, 'Holy fucking shit, are you serious? You know someone who knows a cat trainer? That's so fucking cool.' And then I'd be like…"

I sweep my hair back with my forearm and let him go on with the ridiculous scenario, which, after a few minutes, evolves into something like a *Choose Your Own Adventure* story. We finish our ice cream, lingering until the sun is low enough that by the time I get home, I'll be able to count down the minutes until sunset.

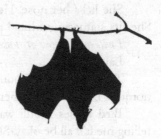

thirteen

I haven't touched my markers since I bought them. Now they're a life raft carrying me through the long hours separating the present from sunset. I'm in bed, sketchbook on my knees. I turn to a new page and reach for pale green, goldenrod, and black. I draw Bird Bones' eyes and shade part of her nose. I draw my ice cream from earlier. I draw the horizon through my window.

Shadows slowly swallow my room as the sun sets, until the skyline resembles cups of sherbet.

This isn't a date, but I still choose my outfit carefully, willing my heart to still. I wonder if Laura's listening—if it's like thunder in her head right now. I don't look at myself while putting on basketball shorts and a tank top. I'm not there yet, but I want to be, and I want her to be there for it.

The sky is still orange when I leave my room, hands stuffed in my pockets, and amble to the open fire escape.

It's empty.

I sit at my desk, trying not to consider the possibility of Bird Bones getting lost, or of Laura changing her mind. The thought alone fills me with freezing dread. I rub my arms, massaging the goosebumps interspersed with slices of scar tissue.

"I am here."

Laura's voice carries through the still air. The first time I heard her standing out there, I almost screamed. This time, I almost sob. She's here, half in the darkness, half in the light. She hasn't changed clothes since the other day, and her hair is up in a disheveled bun. She tugs the hoodie string left and right, left and right while watching me from the other side of the threshold.

I rise from my desk chair, cross the short distance between it and the fire escape. I never let myself notice that her feet never come within an inch of it. Now, I can't unsee it—can't halt my brain doing laps in my skull as I revisit in rapid succession all the things I pretended not to see, and that Laura didn't think I saw, either.

"You've never asked to come inside," I say after several minutes of silence. "Why?"

"Should you ever need refuge from me, you will have it," she says. Her voice is quiet, but the words echo in my heart.

"You said to me, 'You are mine.' You said it with your chest." I cross my arms, watching her look at my feet. "What kind of predator gives her prey somewhere to hide?"

"A sorry one," Laura says. She looks and sounds like she did on the roof after I cussed at her.

Guilt tramples my anger.

"Laura, I'm so, so, s—"

"Oasis, I cannot express—"

We both shut up.

A minute later, I try again. "I'm sorry I yelled at you. You deserved a better response than that."

Laura gnaws her lip, blinking slowly. "No language has the words to convey how deeply sorry I am for that unholy display. I apologize if I frightened or hurt you."

"You did hurt me." I uncross my arms, moving closer to the fire escape. "You hurt me when you hurt yourself."

"I had to," Laura insists, looking as desperate as I feel. "I had to be sure you believed me. Otherwise it cannot be love."

"So you went up in flames?" I ask, painting the words with patience so that it's a question and not the demand I want it to be. "You couldn't have chosen another species reveal?"

Her gaze drifts to our feet and the foot of space between us.

"Stepped in front of a mirror?"

A frown creases her brow.

"Showed me your fangs?"

She pinches her lips and pouts.

The hint of her dimples floods me with adrenaline. Her eyes traveling back to my face balloons my heart with relief.

I point at the table, where *Dracula* sits. "You left that when you batted off."

Laura looks to where I'm pointing and sucks her lip. Her bun is coming undone; wisps at the crown of her head flutter in the breeze. "I am...very sorry."

"I know." I step out alongside her and lean against the rail. The cold metal sears my elbows. "I forgive you."

"I was afraid I had lost you," Laura says quietly.

"Thanks to you, I'm done being lost."

She stands in silence, gazing into my apartment like I'm still inside.

I wonder if being an uninvited vampire peering into the home of a human feels like being at the zoo.

"Are you?" I ask.

"I have no heart, my Oasis. I will always be lost."

The smell of exhaust filters up as a semi-truck grumbles past the alley.

I grab the rail, grounding myself amidst the tide of brewing melancholia. "Can I show you something?"

This grasps her attention. She joins me at the rail, just within reach, watching.

I pull the neck of my tank top down so far that some of the seams snap, but I'd rather destroy this shirt than take it off all the way, putting this and much more in her enhanced line of sight. This isn't the context in which I imagined her seeing my breasts, but if I get my way, she'll be seeing them anyway. I reveal just the left.

Laura comes closer to me. Shock and sorrow cloud her eyes as she looks at the illustration beneath the verse Isaiah 41:10—a rudimentary compass rose sliced around my areola. The three slashes of the N and the triangular north point are all I can see without looking in the mirror or contorting my breast like a water balloon. A few hairs sprout between the scars. If I had known I'd be doing this show and tell, I would have tweezed them. If I wasn't so desperate to keep her, I wouldn't have shown her at all.

"Zeke said being lost was a choice," I say. "All the guidance I needed could be written on my body."

She looks like she wants to touch, hands not quite at her side, but not quite reaching, either.

I cover up again. Her eyes meet mine, and in them, I see what I felt when she touched the Book of Enoch. Anger. I see the same elusive rage I felt, standing in a reality that pushed someone I love to do something like that.

"I'm yours," I say. "Use me."

Laura moves closer, until she's within holding distance. I could reach out and pull her close and put her head on my shoulder right now. Carve out a soft moment to drain this darkness from the picture.

"I'm there, Laura."

She trails even closer, drumming her nails on the rail as her fingers get nearer to mine. "Where?"

"I love you," I say. It feels like jumping into a pile of leaves after hours of raking, spreading my aching arms and legs as the cushion of brown and orange crackles under my weight. "And I'm yours."

The smile I've been craving gradually debuts. She touches my arm, fingertips colder than the rail beneath my palm. She turns me away from the alley so that I'm finally where I belong—looking into her eyes while she looks into mine.

She's right here, but there's still too much space between us. I gently yank her towards me, closing the gap and hold her face. I know why I didn't simply kiss her the first time, but this time, every second that her lips aren't on mine feels like an inexcusable waste of time.

"I love you, and I missed you," I say again, rubbing her lip with my thumb. "And I could just eat you alive."

Her smile flickers like candlelight, and she frowns slightly. "You do understand that I am not a living—?"

I stop her with a finger pressed to her lips.

"I love you, even when I don't understand you." Then I drop my hands and cross my arms, frowning, suspending the moment I've been aching for. "That doesn't mean I don't *want* to understand some things, though."

She looks at my folded arms with her mouth open and her eyes wide, seeming devastated by the fact that we aren't touching.

"What things?"

Too many. The sun'll be back in the sky by the time I'm finished asking all the questions I have, so I stick to the one that hasn't left my mind since I first realized there was more to her than an obsession with a book.

"Why are you pretending to be Black of all things?" I ask.

To my surprise, Laura herself looks surprised.

"The only thing I am pretending to be is human. I had a template for this face, if it would please you to know."

I raise my eyebrows. "What do you mean by template?"

"She confessed that she approached you in your haven," she says. "I must apologize for her interference."

"Your sister?" I say skeptically.

Laura looks me up and down with a sly glint in her eyes. "Talon deserves the world," she says, "but when I offered, she said all she wanted was a sister."

My eyes widen. My thoughts stir at the bottom of my brain like leaves.

Her golden tongue piercing catches the light as she laughs, quiet but amused by my face journey. "I hope this question was not to gauge the political correctness of my existence. You may have found me, my Oasis, but in that realm, I am most certainly a lost cause. I will not bloody these hands, but the other's…"

I lick my lips slowly. "That makes sense." It makes so much sense that my ears are ringing, and I have no clue what to say.

"Is sense going to suffice? Because I love you, and I need you," she says, "and I need you to love what you see."

"I do," I whisper.

The longer we stand out here in the cooling night, the less urgent all this feels. The facts will still be facts if we hit pause for a taste of one another.

I take her hands in mine again, pull her close and kiss her. Her tongue slips into my mouth, gold bar clicking my teeth. I feel her hands on my arms, then on my shoulders, then on my neck as she cradles my jaw.

Being with her after all those uncertain hours apart feels like washing ashore after treading water for dear life. I don't want to pull away, not even to breathe, but I do.

My heart stops.

The woman I'm holding isn't the same woman I put my arms around. Her skin is lighter, her jaw is wider, and her straight but disheveled hair is now a tangled Afro-puff.

I'm gazing into my own brown eyes, watching my own sparsely freckled nose wrinkle and my own round lips purse in a pout. I stare, winded, unable to speak as I blink at myself. My eyes trail from her face—*my* face—to her—no, *my* arms, hidden in those sleeves.

Goosebumps flush my body in violent waves. I wonder if she has my scars, too—if they're as ugly on her as they are on me.

As I reach for the cuff of her sleeve, the other Oasis takes my hand in hers and flattens my palm on her chest. There's no heartbeat on the other side of my hand. The only movement I feel is in my own wrist—my pulse thudding like a jackhammer in the body I was born with.

"Only a facsimile," the other Oasis says regretfully.

Is my voice really that deep? Is the uncertain stammer I hear when I talk just another splinter of self-hate stuck in my spirit?

She chews her lip and looks me up and down, then shakes her head subtly. Black smoke peels off her neck and shoulders. It shrouds her like a sentient shadow, swallowing her from sight. When it clears, Laura is Laura again, and I'm shivering with awe.

"And a poor one of you." Her mouth is in a straight line, conjuring memories of Talon's face after she showed me her gun. "I am sorry again, Oasis, that I did not trust you to believe."

"I believe you." I slip my hand from beneath hers, then take it in mine. Colder than the night, and so soft that I want to put her knuckles on my cheek. "I believe you should *never* do that again. *Ever.*"

She bites her lip mischievously. "Were you not as enticed as I when first I saw your face?"

"I wasn't *not* enticed. I just can't have my girlfriend running around looking like me," I say flatly. "I have enough existential thoughts as it is."

Laura tilts her head to the side. "I am your girlfriend?"

"Well…yeah. I was gonna ask, but then you did *that*," I say, gesturing to her hand. The bandage is gone, but I still see the welts on her skin, fading like shadows. "I had to say yes on your behalf."

A grin splits her lips. She wraps her arms around me. "Thank you."

I twine my fingers behind her neck, and soon, it's like we never stopped kissing—like we're still on the roof under the moonlight, and the space between then and now was nothing but a breath—inhaled, exhaled, onto the next.

I grab her waist, keeping our balance for both of us as I walk backwards, towards the warmth of my apartment, a place where we can more easily pretend that nothing but us comes next.

Laura heaves a gasp and breaks away from me. I only hear her breathe when she's kissing me, but she's inhaling and exhaling now, breathing like she's gearing up to scream.

"Laura, what's—?"

She hisses once, twice, three times in rapid succession and

snatches her hand from my waist. It's on fire, casting her face in a bright pink glow.

I scream, then quickly cover my mouth. I'd been too deep in her touch to notice the threshold underfoot.

"Come in," I say hurriedly, blowing her three burning fingers like candles. "*Come in, come in, come in.*"

The flames dissolve, leaving nothing but scentless smoke. I hold her hand delicately in mine, assessing the damage while she pouts, lower lip sticking all the way out. Even burned, her fingers are cold to the touch.

I put them in my mouth, suck on her fingertips until the only fire I taste is the one raging in me.

She steps over the threshold with me, but we don't make it further than that. We're still in the doorway, and her fingers are still in my mouth when she presses me against the wood. She strokes my lips, my cheeks, my nose, my eyebrows, touching the features that she replicated seamlessly before reverting back to the face I fell for.

Now it's just the two of us, hands and lips roaming like pilgrims of the flesh, sating the hunger we share.

fourteen

July 27, 2019

All I could do now was to be patient, and to wait the coming of the morning.

fourteen

I wake up to the sounds of popping oil, the scraping of a whisk in a bowl, the movement of plates on countertop. My bedroom curtains are drawn, and the plastic tub with my winter bedding sits empty beneath the window. I feel the joy in my bones before I remember the source: I have a girlfriend, and after an evening of mutually relishing in this fact, I fell asleep next to her, with enough layers of fabric between us to muffle the cold of her skin.

I extract myself from the blankets and follow the scent of something sweet and buttery. The fire escape curtains are closed too, casting lacy shadows on my desk and the floor.

Laura's in the kitchen wearing nothing but a teal plaid flannel buttoned up to her neck, sleeves rolled up to her elbow. The hem stops in the middle of her thighs; I can hardly take my eyes off her legs as she tends to a pan on the stove.

"Good morning, Oasis," she says brightly. "I am preparing for you *scovergi*, from home."

"Thank you." I sit at the table and pull my bonnet off, tossing it across the room in the direction of the washing machine. "I wish I didn't have to work today," I sigh. "I'll write down my laptop password for you."

She steps away from the stove and dwindles over to me on her tiptoes. "What for?"

"In case you get bored," I say. "I have HBO, Disney+, and Peacock."

Her knowing smile raises goosebumps on my arms. "Those are human activities." She kisses my knuckles one at a time, then my palm, then my wrist, inhaling deeply, not exhaling at all. "Reserved for time spent with my human."

I continue to reach even after she lets go and returns to the stove. "How did you sleep?"

"I did not. I will be sleeping from Tuesday to Thursday." She rips a square of paper towel from the roll and folds it on a plate. One by one, she removes the golden cakes from the bubbling oil. She uses a dishwashing glove to retrieve a knife and fork from the silverware drawer and sets my plate in front of me, then sits across from me.

The three golden brown *scovergi* look like a cross between pancakes and biscuits and sit between a spoonful of strawberry preserves and a sliced pear. I fold my hands in my lap to keep from scarfing it all down. My gaze trails from my knuckles to my wrists to my forearms to my bicep. After almost a year of going out of my way to stay fully concealed from the neck down, I may as well be naked.

"Did you sleep well?" Laura asks.

"I always sleep well when I don't remember my dreams," I say.

"I will bear this in mind." The latex glove flops over her wrist as she puts her chin in her hand, scrutinizing. "I have informed my siblings that we are girlfriends."

My heart beats a little faster. "What did they say?"

"Talon was thrilled. She said she was excited for me to wear less and go out more," Laura says, vexation plain on her face. "I told her this will not be the case, as you and I are similarly introverted."

"What about your brother?"

"Cypress was mortified to his very core."

I pause while picking up my fork, winded. "Why?"

"He feared that my old age, and indeed the very nature of my unholy existence, will eventually mangle your sense of time and reality until your sanity degrades irrecoverably and you enter a vegetative state, never to regain cognitive function," she says, smoothing back flyway strands of hair with the squeaky dish glove. "And after that, you will break up with me."

"Your brother thinks I'll break up with you while in a vegetative state?"

"He did, until I informed him that vegetative has nothing to do with vegetables. His scenario then fell to pieces. *However,*" she says, putting her elbows on the table, leaning halfway over it to look me in the eye, "I believe the first scenario may be worth examining."

I pick up my fork and slice into a pear, eyes averted. I'd rather not examine anything now that I have what I want, but she wasn't wrong on the rooftop. Me reclining in denial is half of what pulled us apart.

"I'm not worried about going into a vegetative state," I say. "But I do feel like there'll always be something unknowable about you."

"And I feel the same about you." She pops her tongue, gold bar clicking against her teeth. "There is hardly a thing you could ask that I will not answer."

I ponder this while taking a bite of the flaky fried bread. "Who sets your alarm if you don't have a phone?"

"The alarm is a myrrh fire that burns above my resting place. I cannot rise until the flames either die or are doused," she says.

"Do you sleep in a coffin?"

"Of course not. Coffins are for vampires and I am—"

"*The* vampire. Right," I say. "Do you sleep in a bed?"

"Of Transylvanian soil, yes. It will be arriving tomorrow via FedEx."

I nod and eat some more. "You only sleep once a month?"

"Much more frequently than before. I have been fatigued these past few decades, going so long without sustenance." She plucks the glove off one finger at a time and flattens it on the table. "I hope I dream about you."

"I hope they're good dreams when you do." I scrape the remnants of breakfast into my mouth. I devoured it all in minutes flat, and now push my plate away, crossing my arms on the table. "About that sustenance you mentioned…"

Laura watches me in silence, waiting.

"What are the logistics?" I ask.

She purses her lips. "Of?"

"You eating. Or drinking."

"Very good question," she says with a thoughtful nod. "First, I will caress your neck, and then my fangs will appear and they will pierce your flesh, and I will drink of you and be nourished."

I suck a morsel of pear from my front teeth. "When?"

"When?" She repeats.

"When are you going to eat?"

Her eyes narrow slightly, and she turns her head a little, as if asking me to raise my voice. "I do not understand."

"Are you on a feeding schedule?" I ask uncertainly.

Laura sits up straight, scowling at me. "When humans eat, do they not wash their hands and set the table and say grace?"

"I wash my hands, at least," I say, matching her frown. I get up to do so and return to the table with a glass of water, keeping my eye on her the whole time.

"Why are you looking at me this way?" She asks defensively. "Is there a bat on my face?"

"I thought my blood was the reason you love me."

For a moment, it looks like she's doing math in her head, or searching her memories and struggling to find what she's looking for. Then she picks up my empty plate and the glove and returns to the kitchen.

"You spent too much of your time having your blood stolen from you by a false prophet," she says as she gathers the dishes she used to cook and deposits them in the sink. "And because I love you, I will let you cherish having it in your veins, nourishing no one but you, like the oasis that you are."

Before I can respond, she turns on both the hot and cold water at maximum flow, and the space soon fills with the sound of dishes and cutlery colliding with one another underwater. All I see is the top of her head as she stuffs her hands in the gloves and gets to washing, like I won't notice that the volume of her dishwashing sounds like construction work.

Mirage was my first case study in passive aggression. When paggro Mirage came around with the sulking, or the scorekeeping, or the *How come you nevers*, or the *It's fine, whatevers*, with the intention of guilting me into action.

This isn't that. Wearing my clothes, feeding me, spending the night with me—these aren't the actions of someone with a bone to pick, but no backbone to pick it with directly.

I join her in the kitchen. Her face is the image of concentration as she puts in the level of shirt-soaking effort that always led to Mom tacking another $15 onto my allowance when she saw the water stain. Her hand isn't on fire anymore, but I still smell smoke coming from somewhere.

"Laura?"

"Oasis?"

"If something's not okay, you can tell me."

Her hands stop moving in the sudsy dishwater.

She looks over and licks her lips slowly, like I'm still speaking.
I'm trying to.

I don't know how to speak with my heart, but if it really speaks when I'm silent, I need to learn.

"I'm gonna get ready for work," I say. "I'll leave the door unlocked if you need anything."

I hear a splash as I turn away.

Laura stops me from leaving with a soapy, gloved hand around my arm, and pulls me a step back, so that I can see every shade of brown in her eyes under the overhead light.

"I love you," she says.

I sweep a lock of hair behind her ear and kiss her temple. "I love you, too."

*

I'll be waking up alone soon enough—no Laura in the kitchen in one of my flannels or sitting across from me drinking wine while I eat. After so much of this, three days without seems like cruel and unusual punishment.

"You cherish me," Laura says as I balance my laptop on a pillow. "I have never been serenaded to sleep."

"I want you to have good dreams," I say.

If I had rationed my time better, I could have put together a playlist for her slumber, so my impromptu sleep serenade is a bat documentary. The two of us are side by side in my bed, both laying on our stomachs. The setting sun casts long shadows through the curtained windows.

Laura probably knows more about bats than they know about themselves. I wonder if this is the equivalent of showing my mom macaroni art or a turkey drawn from an outline of five-year-old me's hand.

I had no reservations about the age gap between me and Laura when I made her my girlfriend, but now, I can't help wondering if this is part of the facsimile.

She shifts onto her side, propped up on one elbow. In the corner of my eye, I see her absently stroking circles on her thigh, alternating between her index and middle finger.

A sweat breaks under my collar. I force my eyes back to the screen and try to follow along with the narrator's explanation of echolocation—which I forgot is something she can do herself.

She lays on her stomach, interlocking her fingers under her chin. I glance over my shoulder at our legs—I've got on sweatpants that end at my shins and accentuate my ass to the point where I'm sure that if I gave it more than a cursory glance while passing the mirror, I could pause and make it jiggle. Meanwhile, Laura doesn't need anything to flatter hers. The plaid fabric rises over it like a hill. It goes down to the middle of her thigh, which doesn't stop my mind from trying to fill in the blanks—what kind of underwear she's wearing, what color they are, or if she's wearing any. So far, we've always changed clothes beyond each other's line of sight.

This train of thought is getting dangerously close to crashing what with her being so close that I can feel the chill of her body. She crosses her ankles, gazing contentedly at a fox bat walking upside down across a netted ceiling.

Even if she isn't just going through the motions with me, it doesn't change the fact that she's been around for over half a millennium, and therefore has half a millennium of sexual experience.

The fantasy-prone part of my brain doesn't know where to begin.

The part of my brain tuned into reality doesn't even know how.

Just because I'd be open to her grabbing my ass and rolling me over doesn't mean she feels the same.

I could always ask. But then Laura almost made it sound like she'd welcome me not asking, and I'm not sure I have the gumption for that.

The harder I think on it, the more obvious it becomes that the problem is me.

The things I'd do with her if I wasn't so hopelessly lost on how to seek them out. The things I'd let her do to me if I wasn't a hostage to my scars.

Right now, I'd be more than satisfied with something as cut and dry as putting my face between her legs and spelling her name, and hearing her say mine in a voice loose and ragged with pleasure.

The drawer containing my sex artillery is right there, and she's right here, and we're both in my bed, but the words I need to say are lodged so deep in my throat that I'm scared I'll never find them.

"Oasis?"

I look away from the screen; my face hurts from frowning so intensely. "Yes?"

She rolls onto her side and puts her hand on her hip, taunting me even further. "Are you still breathing?"

I clear my throat, which does nothing to clear my head.

"Not really." I sit up, kneeling on the bed. "I've been laying on my stomach for too long." To validate the lie, I slide off the bed and stretch.

I can see the length of her from this angle—every inch of her legs, every crease and shadow where my flannel hugs her body, until she sits up too, and smooths it against her chest.

She stands up, reaching for me. "Perhaps an activity at the table shall be my sendoff."

"I think you're right." I let her guide me out of the room, casting a glance at the unopened drawer before turning out the light.

*

"This is what girlfriends do?"

I tear a page from my sketchbook and pass it to her over the row of cherry-scented tea candles between us. "It's what they do now."

Laura selects a dark green marker. The glow of the flames obscures the sweeping movements of her left hand putting lines on the paper. "Have you painted lately?"

"I think I'm retiring that medium," I say. "It feels like I'll never associate watercolors with anything but the bible, and all things biblical went up in flames the night your hand did. It served its purpose."

She reaches for her glass of Merlot, and for the first time, I reach for mine too.

"A toast," she says, raising her wine. "To new mediums."

I tap mine against hers, sip, and smack my lips. "Can I tell you something?"

Laura leans closer to me. In the flickering candlelight, she casts no shadow—not even on herself. "I have endless capacity for your secrets."

"I was never in denial about you." I uncap a grey marker and warm up with a few boulders. "I tried to take a picture of you on my birthday. You didn't show up."

My eyes dart to her, searching for a change in expression, but she only looks curious.

"Why did you not then speak?" She asks.

"I already said I believed you. And that would've been a lot to stop being in denial about at once," I say. "You were right. The angels aren't with me, but they're still real."

"I only know one—of the fallen variety." Laura swaps green for brown and draws a series of lines. Her eyes pierce mine through the mirage of the candlelight. "It has been some time since we last spoke."

If I didn't remember my hangover so vividly, I'd be tempted to take gulp after gulp of wine, softening the edges of this divine blow.

"How long?"

"222 years. I had lost a dear friend," she says, leaning close to her drawing, frowning in concentration. "I did not drink of him, but he was my tether, and so the Devil and I fell out of touch as I was subsumed in mourning."

I sip some more wine, then select two shades of brown from the lineup. I feel warmed up enough to do what I've been dying to do since I got these markers, which is to draw her face.

"What do you mean tether?"

"I am eternal. Time is all I have, and it is all I have to offer." She switches black for red and rotates the page, adding details upside down. "The passage thereof is only worth acknowledging when it affects those I care for. If someone does not tether me to it, I will lose track."

"I see," I say. It's not a lie, but it may as well be. I can't fathom having so much time that it doesn't matter. I'd probably hate myself less for dropping out of school and joining a cult if I knew I had the rest of eternity to fix those mistakes. "What's stopping you from reaching out now?"

Laura looks up; the candlelight dances in her eyes, which for a moment look as empty as they did on the rooftop. "My heart sits under a bell jar in the Devil's library, beating in plain sight like a pet. When it races or swells or shatters, the Devil sees and hears. Why should I do the reaching?"

"So what you're saying is the phone works both ways?" I ask, raising a brow. "You may be eternal, but that's a horrible excuse in 2019."

She deadpans.

"How exactly did you meet?" I ask.

"I do not speak often of this," Laura says, returning her focus to her drawing.

I put my elbows on the table, leaning closer to the flames, same as she did. "I have endless capacity for your secrets."

She licks her lips, and the shadows of her dimples says she's trying not to smile. She drinks more of her wine.

I keep drawing.

"My father, Vlad Dracul, joined the Order of Dragons and agreed to protect the church in exchange for the Holy Roman Emperor's help in defending his claim to Wallachia," Laura begins, magnetic as always. "When the time came, they did not provide what was promised, but my father, dragon that he was, would not see Wallachia gone from his grip. He tightened, and he tightened, and he tightened," she says, drawing three sharp, short strokes on her paper, "until his hands were blistered, and he was at the mercy of the Ottomans."

I exchange markers again, taking the red that she just set down. The learning curve isn't as steep as I feared; her cheeks and chin and ears—features that I struggled to paint for my angels even with a million references—are coming out more accurately than I could've hoped for.

"Did they kill him?" I ask.

"Eventually. At the time, he promised that five hundred Wallachian boys would be sent to the Ottoman army every year, and they were to take myself and Radu as hostages," Laura says. "They taught us their language, and mathematics, and the stars and their stories. They trained us to use their weapons, and to strategize in battle," she continues with a hint of nostalgia. "But we only gained this knowledge after we had been broken in."

I hesitate. Those words—*broken in*—are the exact words I first used to talk about my descent into Custodes Angelorum with myself. I had no other way to describe what Zeke did to me, and I used to obsess over whether I would've stayed if my restoration hadn't happened—if that was the moment that cemented my stay by virtue of being impossible to recover from.

"Our father left us to be raped and defiled because God did not answer his first cry," Laura says. "The Ottomans reminded us of this whenever we had a lesson to learn. They asked me where my God was now, and I could not answer. I was fourteen then and devoted to the Lord. I prayed, and I prayed, and I prayed," she says, lips pursed in a small pout. "He did not answer. Or perhaps He did not listen." She shrugs. "It matters not. The Devil came when I called. It was then that I tried to bargain my way out of hell."

Sorrow gives way to confusion. "Why would you have gone to hell?"

"They made me a sodomite," she answers, awakening an unreachable ache in my heart.

"Is that really how it works?"

"No, but the Devil was bored and let me believe otherwise," she says wearily. "And now the heart that belongs to you is, as I said, under a bell jar in the Devil's library."

I start on the last part of the drawing, and my favorite part of her face: her lips.

"No child deserves to go through that," I say.

"My Ottoman captors left me with wounds far beneath the surface of my skin, but I used their blood as a salve. They may have taught me the art of impalement, but for many years after, I did the schooling." Laura smiles as the rim of her glass meets her lips. She lowers it and twists the stem in her fingers. "And now they are nothing but a chapter in European history textbooks. *I* am champion."

I drink more wine too, relishing in the pleasant buzz. It hasn't quite sunk in that this is my life now, and by virtue of that, it probably hasn't sunk in that I'm sitting across from a self-admitted mass murderer.

"May I see what you have drawn?" She asks.

"A portrait of you." I raise my sketchbook with both hands and turn it around for her to see.

Pink flames whoosh up from the other side of the page, there and gone too fast for me to react with anything but a start and a scream.

Laura pouts. "What a shame."

I gasp and turn my sketchbook back around. There's nothing on it. The page is empty even though, on the next, there's evidence that the markers had bled through.

"What the—?"

"It must have been quite lovely, Oasis," Laura says, smiling like she got a glimpse of it anyway. "The Devil always leaves the ugly ones be—hence the Germans woodcuts," she mutters bitterly. "It is my turn." And before I have time to recover from the loss of my illustration, Laura holds up hers.

It's comprised of stick figures, the majority of whom are on sticks and spewing blood. The only one who isn't impaled is in the middle. He has long black hair under a red hat, a cup of blood with a straw sticking out in his left hand, and a spear in his right. The signature in the bottom right looks like calligraphy; the first letter certainly isn't an L.

She bites her lip nervously, waiting for my reaction. "Do not judge me too harshly. I have not studied color theory in some time."

I pluck it from her fingertips and head to the kitchen, where I pry an *I <3 NY* magnet off the fridge and put the drawing on the freezer.

"Color theory could learn something from you."

She beams brightly, melting my heart until the darkness of everything else she said tonight almost feels like it never descended. She tears herself a new page—the same page that my drawing evaporated from—and starts a new piece.

"I love being your girlfriend."

I gaze at the picture on the refrigerator, trying to make out the limbs and hair of tiny Vlad the Impaler smiling amongst the scene of utter carnage.

"Me too."

fifteen

July 28, 2019

*But there are things that you know not, but that you shall know,
and bless me for knowing, though they are not pleasant things.*

fifteen

When Laura asked for my phone number on Monday night, my first thought was that she'd gotten a phone herself, thus opening the door for me to be unstoppable with my playlist manufacturing. Turned out it wasn't for her, but for Talon.

She meets me after work on Wednesday. The two of us visit the ice cream spot that Kennedy and I went to so I can satisfy my craving for Superman ice cream. With her paisley bell-bottoms, long-sleeved cream blouse, and rope-like braid threaded with gold tinsel, she looks like she's next in the Soul Train line. In a radical shift from my usual formula of plaid shirt over t-shirt tucked into jeans, I'm wearing my brand-new denim overalls over a long-sleeved t-shirt, flannel tied around my waist.

We walk side by side around Central Park Lake, both of us holding paper bowls with three scoops each, neither of us talking. We've been strolling for almost twenty minutes, and while she's halfway through her scoops of rose mint ice cream, all I've done so far is let mine melt.

"How was work?" Talon asks.

"It was good," I say. "Do you work?"

"At the bar in my brother's nightclub," she says.

I nod, and we're quiet again. I glance at her, at her brown eyes brightened by sunlight, and the silver crucifix twinkling around her neck. I look away and moments later, feel her eyes on me.

It goes on like this until we cross Bow Bridge, and Talon straggles towards a bench.

A few cyclists zip by, startling a nearby brood of pigeons into flight. They land a few feet away, eyeing us as they stalk around a garbage can. If only ice cream was part of the pigeon diet; maybe if I gave it to them, I'd feel less guilty about throwing it away.

I guess it was silly to believe that letting Laura and Mirage cook for me in private would fix me altogether. I can't tell if the silence between me and Talon is awkward, or if I'm projecting awkwardness onto it. Either way, it's not helping my state of mind, and is in fact fostering the perfect conditions for a lapse into dissociation.

"Are you excited for school?" I ask.

Talon frowns as a pug strains its leash trying to reach her. The owner smiles; Talon doesn't.

"I'm auditioning for a 'Semester in Stratford' Shakespeare intensive."

"That's exciting."

"That's the only thing keeping me interested in finishing school. I'm wondering if acting was meant to be a temporary outlet. Laura thinks I should be a screenwriter. I'm not sure about the screen part," she says, frowning at me. "Just plain writer. Thanks to her, I'm set in the research department if I delve into historical fiction. Are you in school?"

"I dropped out of UPenn a few years ago."

"What happened?"

"I, uh…"

"We don't have to talk about it," she says after a few moments.

"I'd like to, eventually," I say. "I just don't want you to think I'm holding out on you."

"Holding out on me?" Talon repeats. She frowns and purses her lips in a very Laura-like pout. "You think I'm shaking you down."

I frown too. "Aren't you?"

"I don't want to vet you, Oasis," she says, seeming taken aback. "I want to be friends."

"You do?" I ask skeptically.

Her face falls. "You don't?"

"No—I mean yes. I do. I just…"

My explanation fails away as I realize that I have nothing to say that won't betray my inclination towards self-deprecation.

"There's no pressure," she says, uncertainty plain on her face. "I just—"

I shake my head vigorously, whacking myself in the face with my twists. "We're friends now."

Talon grins. Then, without asking, she plucks my spoon from my hand, dips it into my melted ice cream and slurps it like soup.

"Good."

Whether she knows how much it means or not, the gesture feels like throwing open a window on a stuffy day.

"This fucks," she says. She starts to pass me my spoon, then withdraws her hand and eats another bite before giving it back.

I smile and dig in. Even half-melted, it's like eating a spoonful of bliss.

"I didn't mean to assume the worst. I'd understand if you were here in a vetting capacity, though."

Talon shakes her head. "You passed the only benchmarks I give a fuck about in that department. You're not white and you love my sister. She says you understand her and I believe that."

"I sense a *but*," I say warily.

She opens her mouth, then closes it, like the words she'd chosen are suddenly insufficient. "This isn't to scare you off by any means," she prefaces, "but I worry that you don't really know what you're getting into."

Uncertainly triggers a stream of adrenaline. Up until now, I thought knowing vampires and angels are real would be enough, but from the look on Talon's face, this may just be another instance of me being in denial.

She sets her empty ice cream cup aside and pulls her iPad from her purse, then opens up a Word document. "This is for you."

I drink my ice cream straight from the cup, then read:

> The shadows, the night, the darkness, etc., are some of the names for the world that consists of people who were once human but are not anymore. Each species has their own origins and their own endemic magic but they are now in a kind of confederation.
>
> These species include:
> -Vampires
> -Werewolves
> -Revenants
> -Mermaids (unconfirmed)

Vampires
-Created by my sister in the late 1400s.
-Originally intended to be biological warfare agents against the Ottoman Empire but are considered a failed experiment. They're essentially big sentient mosquitos these days. (She is "the" vampire but only shares some characteristics with them).
-Drink blood but still eat some human foods that are good for blood health e.g. Spinach, pomegranate, cayenne
-Run really fucking fast + are really fucking strong
-Levitate
-Master hypnotists
-Procreate by drinking your blood as you drink theirs
-Pretty exclusive species and don't go around randomly attacking people because more vampires = fewer humans and humans = food
-Allergic to holy stuff, silver, and sunlight
-Not allergic to garlic but not a good idea
-Have to be invited in
-Don't show up in pics or mirrors
-Scars get deleted when they turn
-Most ethnically diverse species

Werewolves
-Originally from Scandinavia
-Their queen was born in the 100s. She lives in Detroit.
-Eat raw flesh but prefer human hearts
-Run super fucking fast + are super fucking strong
-Can transform whenever but only reproduce during full moon. It's really involved so don't be scared of being attacked and turned in the middle of the night
-Allergic to chocolate and silver
-Not allergic to wolfsbane, still a bad idea
-Diverse globally, but most werewolves in America are Black

Revenants
-Created in a laboratory in Germany by one of
my sister's necromancer friends
-Like the kidz bop version of vampires
-Eat dead bodies, but prefer brains
-Run really fucking fast
-Allergic to silver and cold iron
-Regrow body parts
-Reproduce by feeding you your favorite dish
made with one of their own body parts. Very
ceremonial and romantic tbh
-Highest populations in France, Canada, and
New Orleans
-Z word is a slur

Mermaids
-TBD

"I put this together after your second date," Talon says.

Memories of that night tumble back—me standing in front of my apartment wishing I had the wherewithal to want something out loud, only to turn and see that Laura had disappeared.

"Did she say something about me?" I ask.

"Oh, yeah," she says, nodding. "She flew home and had a meltdown because she thought you were making her sick."

I gape. "*Sick?*"

Talon sighs a heavy, ruminating sigh. "She said something like, 'The aura she exudes has inspired a terrifying sensation of bodily starvation, and I have begun to produce fluids'," she says, adopting Laura's mannerisms seamlessly. "Then she stripped down on the spot to show me her underwear so I could diagnose her. I was in the shower at the time, mind you, squinting through the steam. I was like, 'Honey, I know it's been a while for you, but that's called getting wet.'"

My whole body heats up and disbelief puts me in a stranglehold.

"Yeah. She's not the brightest bat in the cave on the human front." Talon brushes her lip with her thumb, looking lost in thought. "Vampirism is hard enough, but when it's comorbid with cluelessness…anyway, I had to step in."

"You made me a cheat sheet so I wouldn't be scared of Laura?"

"Yes… and no." She looks away and back. "I don't know a lot of humans either, Oasis. This is as much for me as it is for her."

"Oh." For a moment, I'm looking in the mirror, feeling like the only person I have in my life is the one staring back at me. "Does this mean you won't get irritated if I ask a million questions?"

Talon pinches her lips, like she's trying not to smile.

"As far as I know, there's no forum for people who were raised by vampires. I'm *more* than happy to have you."

Quiet falls between us as the sun grazes the skyline. She proposes a walk to the Shakespeare Garden while the sun sets, and in the back of my head, I begin curating a playlist in homage to memories of this afternoon.

"Do the shadows scare you?" I ask.

"They're all I know," she says. "I have no idea what happened in 1897 and I feel like Laura will never tell me, but I *do* know that she and Mina had a psychic link. That's why we can see inside each other's minds."

More memories of me and Laura's first few dates make it to the forefront of my mind.

"She said you're always with her."

Talon looks away, gnawing her lip, still painting her palm with her braid. "Yeah."

"Is it a constant open line of communication?"

"More like a closed door to a secret room. All I have to do is knock," she says, twirling her braid like a lasso. "I couldn't control it when I was little, which is how Dracula found me, but then it got to the point where me and Laura used to have whole fights while sitting in absolute silence."

My eyes fall on the distant lake, the setting sun a strip of white on the waves. "What time is she waking up tomorrow?"

"I didn't get to ask her," Talon says. "Dracula gets fussy before bedtime, so I didn't bother asking him." Noticing my confused face, she asks, "Have you met him yet?"

I think back to the drawing of Vlad the Impaler hanging on my refrigerator. Laura said she has many faces, but for some reason, I assumed he was gone, and that Laura is his new permanent presentation.

"I guess not."

"I wouldn't worry about it," she says. "I assume meeting him is the human equivalent of seeing Laura's period stains on the bed for the first time."

I choke on nothing. She shrugs helplessly.

"What's he like?"

"Uhhh…" Talon exhales slowly into her fist. "You know how a cat sometimes sticks its paw in a glass of water, and then looks at it for a minute, and then knocks it over? He's like that—only cats have no real concept of right or wrong."

I hesitate. "So Laura and Dracula aren't the same?"

"They're the same. In the sense that ice is still water," she says. "Same memories, same powers, same general emotions. Different conduits."

"Oh," I say. It's all I have.

"I usually only see Dracula when it's bedtime, which is once a month, so I sometimes call him PMS," Talon continues. "He does the sleeping." She clasps her hands, frowning thoughtfully. "So you haven't met Darla either?"

"No," I say.

"Clara?"

I shake my head.

"Ava?"

"No."

"Valara? Luca? Raul? Al?"

I shake my head to each.

She puckers her lips.

"Have you met Carl?"

I stop short.

"*Carl?*"

Talon stops alongside me. She looks downright amused, evident in the dimples flickering beside her barely repressed smile. "Congratulations on your accidental polyamory."

"Thanks, I guess." I put both hands in my chest pocket like a kangaroo. We walk towards a plaque set low in a bed of clovers and mint:

What's in a name
That which we call a rose
By any other name would smell as sweet.
Romeo and Juliet, II, 2

When I look over at Talon, she's staring at the words, absently brushing her palm with the tip of her braid like she's painting the scene.

"Sometimes Dracula sticks around after he wakes up. He's more tolerable when he isn't cranky. But the older I get, the more fascinating I find him," Talon muses. "I imagine it must be disorienting for him, being raised in medieval times and then looking around at…this." She indicates a chip bag skittering along the pavement, then gestures to a flock of high schoolers sailing by on Lime scooters. "Laura's the face I asked for because I wanted a sister like Lilo from *Lilo and Stitch*, but I asked him once if he has so many other faces because he doesn't like his own."

"What did he say?" I ask.

"That if anyone recognized the face he was born with, he'd be put on trial for war crimes and genocide for all the impaling. But sometimes I wonder…" She sighs, then looks at me.

I probably look constipated from the effort of pacing myself with the nonstop questions, but it's hard when the conversation about my girlfriend suddenly became about someone else entirely.

"Has he hurt you before?"

"Never." She shakes her head. "But he's like all parental figures, I think. Sometimes they fuck you up without even meaning to," Talon says, steeped in deep thought. "If I fell off my bike in front of Laura, she'd give me a bandaid and a hug, but if I fell off my bike in front of Dracula, he'd go down to Toys R Us with his *kilijs* and threaten to build a better bike with their bones."

"And did he actually do it?" I ask uncertainly.

"With a bell and everything," she says, nodding. "One time, I found a kitten outside and took it home thinking I'd raise it, but it died a week later. I was hysterical," she says, shaking her head at the memory. "I put out Dracula's holy fire and dug him from his bed and cried in his lap. Then when my birthday came around, he gave me a box with this orange kitten curled up in the tissue paper. She was so still and so cold that I almost started crying because I thought it was dead too. Then her tail uncurled, and she stretched and blinked at me with these blood red eyes." Somehow, she both is and isn't smiling. "Now I have a cat who'll probably outlive me."

"Are you talking about Bird Bones? But she was in the sun," I say, vividly recalling her golden eyes in the sunlight.

"She got the bespoke vampire recipe so she can go in the sun. 'Cat goes in the sun with little Talon'," she says, adopting a heavy accent that I can only assume is Dracula's. "There was another time he and my brother took me to the zoo. It was the first time I ever saw him outside of the house," she says. "He turned into bats and went into the enclosure. We didn't see him for three days."

"I don't know if I should be laughing or running," I say, smiling despite myself.

"Don't run because of me," Talon says. "Do you have any idea how convenient it is when you're on the side of the road with a cop who has no body cam on, but your sister's a warlord who loves killing people? Sometimes all it takes is the eye thing and they're begging for their lives."

"Eye thing?" I mutter. "What eye thing?"

She grins. As I open my mouth to ask yet another question, she says, "I know I said I'd answer all your questions, and I will, but I'm even more fascinated by *you*."

I cross my arms. "I'm the least fascinating person you'll ever meet."

"Uh-huh. I doubt that," she says, amused. "Dracula loves fucked up things and fucked up people. But for all intents and purposes, we'll sub the words *fucked up* for *fascinating*."

I open my mouth to argue, then close it again, knowing full well I have no argument against what I accuse myself of being on a near daily basis.

"I'm not exempt, so don't think I'm here to make *you* feel fucked up."

"I don't need you for that," I say, at which she arches a brow. "I joined a cult, sold drugs, cut Bible verses all over my body, and had a heart attack."

"Bible verses? Oh yeah," Talon says succinctly. "You're his Holy Grail."

After a while, we come to a stop at a bench tucked between two beds of tulips. The red heads have begun to shutter closed.

"I didn't think I'd ever believe in magic again," I confess. "Literal or figurative."

Talon purses her lips. She looks left and right. Seeing no one, she snaps a tulip from the bed and gives it to me. "Someone as magical as you should never forget that magic is real." She crosses her arms, cupping her elbows. "Was it the cult?"

"Yeah." I brush the feathery tulip petals under my nose, wishing I had more to add.

Talon bites her lip and looks over at me like she's having an internal debate.

"What is it?" I ask.

"I'd *love* to show you something," she says, "but I'd hate to do the exact opposite of what I meant to and overwhelm you."

"Laura has what's left of my heart." I tuck the tulip in my overall pocket, leaving only the petals exposed. "Being overwhelmed won't change that."

She grins and soon, her iPad is back in the open. "I've never shown this to anyone, so this is exciting," she says, scrolling through her camera roll at the speed of light. She pulls up a video of a broadcast with KTVU stamped in the corner. The grainy palette and low resolution betray the age of the clip as she hits play.

"...as Oakland Police investigate what appears to be the triple homicide in the East Bay," the anchor says. An image of the three people populates the screen—two white men, who I assume are a father and middle-aged son, standing behind a white woman, who must be his mother. "Karen and Clyde Mercer, aged 60 and 67, and their son, 35-year-old Peter, were found in their yard near the Oakland-Berkeley border. Friends and neighbors say that the Mercers were devoted foster parents who provided homes for trafficked women and children. Their son Peter was a police officer with OPD. Viewers beware, as the following footage is graphic."

Graphic is an understatement for live broadcast TV.

It's one thing, seeing the human body contorted and bleeding like that when the eyes are X's, the limbs are single marker strokes, and the scene itself is a cartoon hillside. It's something else altogether, seeing three humans folded into pretzels and skewered on stakes, protruding from a sprawling, manicured front yard bound in yellow tape.

Talon stops the video there. "Oakland's famous for sex trafficking. I fell through the cracks three times with three different families before my sister caught me."

"Laura did that?" I ask.

"Dracula did it. Laura doesn't get blood on her hands," she says, like it's still a regular occurrence. She puts her iPad away. "He used to show me memories of him torturing and killing them whenever I had nightmares. Put me right to sleep." She smirks. "That's what I call magic."

Not long after, we embark on a quest for more Shakespeare quotes.

I wonder if I'd feel the same relish if Zeke died. I haven't forgotten that Laura admitted her intent to kill him, and I already professed my doubts that I'd feel anything at all if he died, let alone pleasure.

But then here's Talon, looking like someone just handed her a cookie. As we continue to wander on with no regard for the diffusing darkness of night, I start to wonder if that's what's missing—if the bloody death of the person who had helped break me would be the key to fixing myself for good.

sixteen

August 2, 2019

What sort of place had I come to, and among what kind of people?
What sort of grim adventure was it on which I had embarked?

sixteen

My illustrations of the Shire and Mount Doom were my favorite part of Full Cauldron's mini overhaul until the day before reopening, Kennedy's sister brought in a bunch of furniture that she was getting rid of—plush benches next to the comics, suede armchairs in the mystery section, a linen chaise in back with the kids' books.

My favorite is the black crushed velvet loveseat, shaped something like an octagon minus three sides, with a high back like a throne and arms like wings. The look on my face when I saw it in the nook of nineteenth century books prompted Kennedy's dad to run to Home Depot for a call bell for the register so that I can work from here and listen out for customers.

I've been sitting cross-legged in my new nest, wading through pricing a pile of Erle Stanley Gardner mysteries, working slower than usual because Laura is awake and here. She's wearing leopard print leggings and a black blouse with two gold bats linking the collar by a chain, hair piled up in a messy bun. As always, I can't stop looking at her.

I pick up a book, price it, close it, then take a minute or so to watch her flip through her Batman comic. Then I put it down and pick up another.

She smiles the first few times she notices, then frowns, then after a while, pouts over the edge of her comic. "Is there still dirt on my face?"

I shake my head, biting back a smile.

And so it goes, until Laura finishes her comic and turns the tables by staring at me, and staring at me, and staring at me while I pretend not to notice. She scoots closer to me—so close that our knees are touching, and I can feel her cold skin through my jeans. When this doesn't work, I see her in the corner of my eye leaning closer and closer and closer to me, until her nose is on my cheek. I turn my head to kiss her on the lips and keep pricing.

Laura groans. "What is this peculiar torment?"

"Who is Carl?"

Her eyes widen marginally. She scratches her temple thoughtfully, then grabs *The Phantom of the Opera* from the shelf behind us and opens it upside down, hiding her face behind it. A minute passes. She turns a page, but from right to left. Like she's actually reading it.

"What's the eye thing?" I ask.

She lowers the book an inch, so that only her brown irises and thick lashes are visible. "Which eye thing?"

"*There's more than one?*"

She grimaces. "My sister discussed me."

I poke her knee with my pencil. "What's the eye thing?"

I see the debate on her face and look around. We're alone in this corner of the store.

Laura hides her whole face again, then slowly lowers the book. The light inside hasn't changed, but her brown eyes seem to glint an otherworldly dark red. It's as if blood is the only thing inside of her, moving like her body's one massive vein.

I try and fail to not react: my lips part, and my heartbeat kicks up to a jog.

I nod.

She blinks, and her eyes are warm brown and sulking. Laura closes the book, crossing her arms as she draws her knees up to her chin. "I have mortified you beyond speech with my unholiness."

"No," I say, shaking my head as I pick up another book. "It just doesn't seem appropriate for me to be like, 'That's so cool.'"

A reluctant smile replaces her pout.

"So who's Carl?"

She ignores this. "I am happy that you and my sister were able to bond. Cypress has expressed interest in becoming acquainted with you as well."

Bits and pieces of passing Cypress-mentions resurface.

"What did he say?"

"'How come I ain't met your girl yet? What, you scared or

LACHELLE SEVILLE 217

sumn?"' Laura dictates with a southern accent as thick as my great-grandmother's. "And then I told him I would consult with you as to whether you would be interested in seeing his ugly face tonight."

"Tonight?"

"It is human happy hour at Hemaclysmic—a place for descendants of darkness." Laura rests her head on her knees. "Would you like to go?"

The answer is yes, but it feels like a lifetime's gone by since I fell asleep with her lying next to me, and each night I fell asleep without her was papered with visions of what we'd do when she woke up.

"I would like to," I begin, "but I actually…was kind of hoping…that you…" I fall silent and clear my throat. Laura watches me like whatever is about to come out of my mouth is fascinating beyond measure.

I clear my throat. "What I'm trying to ask is—"

"You want me to do the other eye thing." She shakes her head succinctly. "When circumstances arise, perhaps, but until then, you must make do with this."

She does the eye thing again, shuttering and revealing the sea of red under her skin.

"I'm not talking about the other eye thing," I say.

Laura blinks, so that her eyes are brown again, and frowns. "Do you want me to do the bat thing?"

"Eventually." I feel close to feverish with nervousness; I look left and right, but it's still just us in this corner of the store. "I'm obviously not very good at this, but I was hoping that tonight… and if not tonight then eventually…if not eventually, it's fine."

"*Aha.*" Understanding lights her eyes, and I almost heave a sigh of relief. "You are talking about the *other* other eye thing. No," she says, shaking her head, hands folded in her lap. "And it will take uncouth quantities of wine to alter my resolve."

Her words are resolute, but I see the flicker of a barely stifled smile on her lips, and I feel the familiar surge of bats in my stomach as she looks at me like I'm a nugget of gold in a rushing river.

"I want to meet your brother tonight, but I also want to have sex with you." I somehow get the words out without rushing, or omitting several, or looking away. "Just thought I'd put it out there."

"I, too, yearn for your flesh." She says it like it's an unfolding epiphany. "We will visit Cypress at Hemaclysmic and then we will have sex."

She lost me at the matter-of-fact admission to yearning. It's already playing on a loop in the corner of my mind where all things Laura-related rest, like flowers in a garden bed.

And so, with one question answered, I double back and ask, "So who's Carl?"

Laura scowls. Then she picks up *The Phantom of the Opera*, still upside down, and reads on.

*

I decide to look up Hemaclysmic on my phone while Laura lays next to me in bed, reading one of a stack of Batman volumes she bought this afternoon.

A club for vampires sounds like an *if you know, you know*, but no. According to Google, Hemaclysmic is "an underground gay night club featuring retro decorum and a modern menu," located just off the Hudson River in Hell's Kitchen.

Never not lit. Apple has a drink menu as long as the line to get in :P - 9 months ago.

I've worked here for years. Best bar in NYC hands down, super safe, all the regulars are really nice and management don't tolerate any b*llsh*t from heathens!!! - 1 year ago.

There's no mention of vampires, werewolves, or revenants in any of the reviews, and no pictures of the interior—just a street view of a shuttered dock in the alley behind a typical construction-plagued block.

"Hemaclysmic is a gay club?" I ask, setting my phone aside.

"Heterosexuals are an endangered species in the undead community." Laura leans back in bed so that the bats linking her collar sparkle in the light. "I know many teen vampires who became such so that they would live forever, rather than meet the Devil and be interrogated for homosexual acts."

Each word gives me more whiplash than the previous.

"*Teen vampires?* Are there no shadow laws against that?"

"Just as there are laws against adult humans terrifying youth into the shadows?" Laura says, eyes full of laughter. "If this was so, I would not be here to be loved by you, and there would be no vampires, teen or otherwise."

It's not my place to ache for people who felt so helpless that they switched species rather than find out for certain that God didn't want them. It's not my place, but I'm standing in it anyway.

"Do you pity us?" She asks.

"Do I look like I'm in any position to pity anyone?"

"No. You are one of us," she says. Then she opens her comic, reclines on her side, and continues to read, leaving me to ponder these soft words in the silence of my own mind.

Sunset brings a bundle of nerves over the sheer number of firsts ahead of me: my first time at a nightclub, my first time meeting Laura's brother, my first time having sex in...I don't know how long. My logical brain knows that Zeke restoring my virginity doesn't count, but when I search for memories Raymond, or the few guys I'd hooked up with in college, memories of my knees and palms chafing on office carpet override them all.

"I've never been to a nightclub," I say in a desperate attempt to derail this train of thought. "What should I wear?"

"If I dress you, it will be with you and I in mind." Laura dog-ears her comic and approaches my closet, opening one drawer then another, assessing the pieces she finds with a deep frown. She slips the bat chain around her collar over her lower lip and murmurs, "What should I take off of you tonight?"

If only I had something leopard print to match hers. Even thoughts of Zeke can't muzzle the animal in me, roaring for her.

For *it*.

A conduit—one of many.

"How much of you is you?" I ask.

Laura drapes a pair of black overalls over her arm, after deciding that the first pair were an upgrade, I had to get two more for my recovering wardrobe. She says,

"All of this is me." Then returns to the closet and slowly examines each of my plaid shirts, inspecting the sleeves and collars. She pulls one off the hanger and says, "Come to me, my Oasis."

I join her in front of the mirror, half-obscured by my laundry basket in the corner of the room. It's the first time that we've both stood in front of a mirror at the same time. She's right behind me, holding the overalls up to my chest, along with a blue, cream, and burgundy plaid flannel, but in the mirror, I'm alone.

"Tell me, Oasis," she says, hand trailing down my back as she steps away with the clothes, tiptoeing towards the closet again, "how much of you is you?"

"I don't think I have a me to begin with," I confess. "Sometimes I feel like I should be in your place—looking in the mirror, seeing nothing. But that's…"

I turn around and immediately regret my answer.

Laura's eyes are dark with otherworldly sorrow. Before I can backpedal, something grabs my lower peripheral vision: black mist unfurling between us. Her entire left hand is missing; the mist lingers around her wrist, which seems to be dissolving in real time. There's a bat on the floor, dragging itself across the carpet with its thumbs. Another one falls, and another.

I drop to the floor and stoop to gather them up. They're ice cold, soft as cotton, and limp as gelatin.

"It's not that bad," I insist. "I'm okay with it most of the time. Just—here." I try arranging the bats in the shape of a hand, which doesn't work in the slightest. They're lethargic in my palms and squeaking feebly. "*Angels.* Okay—everything's going to be okay."

Laura shakes her head slightly and widens her eyes.

In a blink, there are no bats in my hand—just her hand, palm-up and attached to her wrist.

"I am sorry," she says quietly.

"Don't be," I say, shaking my hands out to rid them of their anxious tremors. "This isn't how I wanted to see the bat thing."

"Nor how I imagined showcasing my favorite unholy privilege." Laura looks at me for a long, long while, eyes full of something I can't read. She turns back to the closet, swaps the first flannel for one patterned with forest green and navy blue.

I return to my bed.

"I am your girlfriend," she says, "and I am not okay with it. And because I know that there are times when actions speak louder than words, I will remind you that you have a you, as you reminded me that I have a heart, even if it is not in me."

I don't reply; I'm too thankful to see her hand in one piece.

Maybe one day I'll see myself the way she sees me.

The pile of bats that I still see in my mind's eye is enough of an incentive to try.

I glance at the bottom drawer of my nightstand. Before I can stop myself, I open the drawer for my lingerie and, when she turns around with my purple gingham flannel in hand, I hold up the pieces.

Her eyebrow twitches with intrigue.

She takes the lacy thong, then holds it up to the light and

squints. She stretches the elastic next to her ear, like she's at the farmer's market examining produce.

"Another time," she says, handing it back. "I will leave you to dress."

I watch her cross the room as I stuff the lingerie back where it came from.

"Laura?"

She turns with her hand on the doorknob.

"Oasis?"

"Do you trust me?"

Something in the air wilts. Laura looks to the window, the horizon a smudge of peach and indigo.

"Do you doubt my love for you?"

"You can't answer a question with a question. For that," I say, waiting for her eyes to return to me, "you have to answer both."

"I trust you. I am yours," she says to the view.

I don't doubt this. It's been less than a month of knowing her and loving her, but time no longer feels applicable to us. She's mine, and she was mine before either of us realized it.

"How much of you is mine?"

Her eyes snap back to me.

I hold her gaze for a long, laden moment, then get up and grab the clothes, making it clear that I'm about to change.

Laura opens the door and steps out, but not without looking back with eyes like fountains of blood.

My skin tingles as I strip. I button my flannel up to the neck and secure the straps of my overalls, then quickly tame my hair into a crown.

For the first time in a long time, I take a long, deliberate look in the mirror, at more than just my hair. All the parts of my body I once thought were sexy are buried under scar tissue and stretch marks from rapidly regaining weight post-Angelorum, but maybe I spoke too soon.

I don't hate what I see tonight.

*

The C train whisks us from South Harlem to Hell's Kitchen. My heart beats faster and faster with each stop that we pass. Before I know it, we're stepping off, weaving through the crowd of commuters. Once we're level with the street and walking towards the club, Laura links her arm through mine. We pass a bodega, a spot selling Jamaican patties, and a shuttered flower shop before rounding the corner. A long line snakes down the alley. Deep red light spills onto the sidewalk from within, broken by the shadow of a buff bouncer.

We bypass the line, but not before I get a good look at most of the people waiting to get in. There are people dressed as casually as me. Others sport dark makeup, spiked hair, tight patent leather clothes. More still are wearing stilettos, bright strapless dresses, and glittering makeup palettes. Just as diverse as the attire is the diversity of age—two women in fleece jackets and GoGo boots who look old enough to be the next Golden Girls; a cluster of middle-aged men wearing suspenders and bowling hats; a group of teenagers dressed like they just left the set of Michael Jackson's *Bad* music video.

The bouncer notices Laura and I approaching; he gestures for the person at the front of the line to step back and detaches the rope.

"Good evening, Master," he says.

"Good evening. Are you well?"

"Slow night tonight," he responds, despite the crowd behind us. "And who's this?"

"This is my girlfriend, Oasis," Laura says with a smile that warms my chest. "She is also my plus one."

"And a pretty plus one she is." He grins at me. "Make sure you order your Bloody Mary off the proper menu. Once you get a taste for the kind with platelets, there's no going back." He steps aside and ushers us in. "Enjoy yourselves, ladies."

Laura leads me down a long hall. Another bouncer's standing at the end, sporting a pair of black aviators. There's a sign on the door behind him:

NO SILVER
NO CRUCIFIXES
NO HOLY WATER
NO CONSECRATED IRON
NO BIBLES
NO BLOOD FEUDS
NO EXCEPTIONS!!!

Each stipulation has an illustration—a silver knife and chain, a flask of water, a wolf and vampire snarling at one another, all drawn in red backslash circles.

The second bouncer takes a deep sniff; he inhales for so long and with such volume that I almost expect him to scream at the end. Instead, he lifts the rope.

"Enjoy your night, Master and Oasis."

I'm practically shaking with excitement now.

A grid of stage lights hangs from the ceiling, swiveling in time to Donna Summer. The palette reminds me of a desert sunset—red, orange, gold, pale pink, all swiveling slowly over a three-, maybe four-story plunge, interspersed with massive spinning disco balls. Straight ahead, a crowded bar rests along the wall. I spot at least a dozen bartenders zipping back and forth. Behind them are more bottles than I've ever seen in one place. Between the racks are industrial chrome refrigerators; fog crawls from the doors when they open and shut.

Laura puts both elbows on the bar. "Apple," she calls over the music. I slide onto the stool beside her.

A minute later, someone responds to her call.

That someone is a tall woman with razor sharp cheekbones and salt and pepper hair trailing to her waist. She's wearing a bright red corset with skintight black leather pants, twirling a towel as she walks. A black eyepatch with a red apple stitched onto it covers her left eye.

"Master," Apple says delightedly. She leans over the bar and pecks Laura on both cheeks. She says something in Mandarin; Laura responds in fluent Mandarin, too.

No crash course from Talon could've prepared me for this. My eyes drift to one of the bartenders opening a refrigerator: inside are rows and rows of plastic pouches full of blood. The same bartender opens a second refrigerator closer to us. From afar, the tray she pulls out looks like it's full of olives, but as the red light bounces off them, I realize that they're white, and not green, and that those aren't pits, but irises. The bartender's nostrils widen, and she looks in my direction with a knowing smile and wink before tending to her patron.

"Apple, this is my girlfriend, Oasis," Laura says, gesturing to me.

Apple smiles and takes my hand. Her skin is ice cold, as are her lips when she kisses my knuckles. Her nose brushes my fingers as she inhales—without exhaling.

Laura clears her throat loudly.

"You really know how to pick your apples." Apple grins at

me. "Human happy hour is just getting started. Can I get you something?"

"Bartender's choice," I say.

"You got it. Master?"

"I am all set."

Apple smiles. "Finally."

I rotate on the stool so that my knees are pressed against Laura's hip.

"Master, huh?"

She scratches her jaw, eyes averted. "It is...my nickname."

I raise my eyebrow.

Apple returns with a golden cocktail. A wedge of green apple adorns the rim of the glass. She steps back and crosses her arms, lone eye narrowed with anticipation.

I take a sip; it tastes like pure apple juice.

"This is dangerously delicious. Thank you."

"Anything for Master's girlfriend," Apple says with a smile. "How did you two meet?"

"At my job," I say. "You?"

"Apple is the daughter of Ching Shih—another old friend, and the most hygienic pirate I ever knew," Laura says, smiling. "I attended little Apple's baby shower."

"We didn't *officially* meet until I was all grown up," Apple says nostalgically. "It was late '97, wasn't it?"

"1898. I returned to England to exact my revenge on Arthur Holmwood—"

"And I was on my way there to assassinate him. His father owed my old nest a debt after the second Opium War. Conniving old man went into hiding and thought dying would absolve him," Apple says sourly. "If the late Lord Godalming ever bothered to read the Bible he thumped so hard, he would've been familiar with the phrase 'the sins of the father'."

"I doubt he cared," Laura says dismissively. "Arthur had enough daddy issues to warrant a subscription."

Apple throws her head back and howls.

I can't tell if it's the single sip of liquor, but it feels like I'm having an out of body experience, listening to two undead women discuss events that unfolded in the nineteenth century.

"What were you exacting revenge for?" I ask.

The smile vanishes from Apple's red lips.

Laura doesn't answer. I feel her tense beside me and see the sudden glassiness in her eyes. There's an elephant at the bar, and I ushered it in.

"We should go," she says quietly.

"Don't be a stranger." Apple points at me. "If you're looking for a job, call me. One of my girls at the live bar just retired."

"That is *quite* enough of that," Laura says loudly. She grabs my hand and my drink and pulls me away from the bar.

"Don't be stingy, Master—bringing snacks into my club like this," Apple calls. "*Learn to share!*"

Laura doesn't respond. When we're alone, she sighs. "Forgive her appetite."

"I can't pretend it isn't flattering," I say. "But your menu is the only one I'm interested in being on tonight."

Her pace slows. She returns my martini and smiles sheepishly. With the disco music as loud as it is and the club still filling with patrons, it feels like we're in the eye of a brewing storm.

"I'm sorry if I brought up something painful," I say.

Laura stops walking and takes my free hand. "Do not be sorry, Oasis. We both have much to learn about one another." She gazes over the cavern-like dance floor. "Arthur Holmwood was a jester in the Van Helsing court. Lucy was set to marry him. Rather than respect her decision to join the shadows, he chose to interpret it as a slight on his ego, which resulted in her untimely death."

"Did you end up exacting your revenge?" I ask.

"I did not get the chance. Arthur apologized."

I gape. "Really?"

"He took a short trip on a running bowline knot and never returned," Laura says.

It takes a moment for the turn of phrase to sink in.

"He hung himself?"

"Actions speak louder than words." A dry smile pulls the corners of her lips. "I cannot pretend it did not disappoint me. It had been quite some time since I killed for sport."

I don't comment. I plan on fucking her tonight, and although I'm trying to put my penchant for denial in the rearview mirror, I'd rather be temporarily *not* cognizant of the fact that somewhere in there is a mass murderer.

"Where's your brother?" I ask.

"He is most likely in his usual haunt. Talon is here as well," she says, twining her fingers through mine. "Her shift at the live bar is almost over."

The staircase that she leads me up is as wide as a dance floor itself, with steps that are only an inch or two tall. There are people hanging out at tall tables set against the rails with drinks, and more tables spilling from dark, rounded lounges carved from the wall. Some of those lounges are obscured behind dark curtains; others look like clubs within the club. Everything and everyone's steeped in shadow, but I still see pairs of eyes on us. Some are tinted dark red. Some have a catlike yellowish-green glow. Some seem to flicker like candlelight in a draft.

The edges of the faraway, pit-like bottom floor are bathed in red light. They look like stages from above, but I don't see any poles. None of the people lined up seem to be throwing any money.

"What are they doing?"

Laura looks with me. "That is the live bar."

I squint; I can just see one of the seated persons beckoning to someone in a line. The two of them swap places. Then the person I assumed was a performer sits in the patron's lap and tilts their head to the side, exposing their neck.

Live bar.

"We are here," Laura says.

Here is another nook veiled by thick, purple velvet curtains, which Laura parts with a sweep of her arm. The cozy space looks like it was plucked from a gothic homemaker's magazine. There's an L-shaped velvet black couch against one wall and a matching couch adjacent, a liquor cabinet made of mahogany, and gold damask wallpaper. Less gothic is the enormous flatscreen television affixed to the wall, and the towering shelves of video games and consoles next to it. A dizzying game of Pac-Man dominates the screen, ghosts flying around the maze like bullets as the score ticks past two million.

Laura strides into the middle of the space, standing between the TV and a low, ornate golden table, blocking the view of whoever's sitting in front of it.

"Oasis, this is Cypress," she says, beaming.

"Master, move," Cypress mutters, leaning left and right, trying to look under hear arms as she spreads them like a kite. "Move, move, *move*."

I almost choke on my drink.

Laura and Talon's night-club owning brother is a lanky-limbed teenager with a head full of short dreads, a joystick in one hand, and a burning blunt in the other. His skin is lighter than both of theirs, and they have no features in common except that his eyes are brown, too.

The ghosts converge on Pac-Man at lighting speed, and the ball of yellow disappears with a series of chiptune bleeps.

Cypress heaves a groan.

"Beloved brother, here is my girlfriend," Laura says, satisfied, directing her arms at me like I'm a showcase prize.

He smacks his lips and waves his hands like he's shooing me away. "Don't nobody give a f—*sike*, naw. C'mere," he says, grinning; Laura nailed his southern accent to a T. He raises himself onto the couch behind him and pats the seat. "Come sit with me, Miss Oasis."

I oblige in a daze.

He drops the roach of his first blunt in the ashtray, then grabs a jar of weed and some Dutch wrappers from under the table.

"Anemic B positive, huh? Partial to B-neg myself," he says, looking over at me. "Polycythemia, if I'm feelin' gourmet."

I put my martini on the table and fold my hands in my lap, head spinning like a typhoon. "So this is your nightclub?"

"Mine and Apple's," Cypress says with a firm nod that shakes his dreads. He points to the blunt he's rolling. "Do you smoke?"

"It's been a while."

"Well, it ain't no pressure," he says while licking the tobacco leaf, "but sharing a fat one's my version of a handshake."

Laura sits next to me and puts her hand on the small of my back, as though to reassure me.

"Alrighty," I say.

"Alrighty," Cypress says with a bright smile. "Toto came hollerin' for you, Master."

Laura heaves a sighing groan. "Ásttora does not leave Detroit for fun, and *I* am here to have fun."

"That's your best friend, Master. You need a cell phone so you can stop leaving her hanging," Cypress says as he procures a lighter. "Adapt to survive."

"No," Laura says simply, leaning her head on my shoulder.

"I respect your decision, but it's not that hard to get used to," I say. "Also, internet addiction can't be a problem if you barely know how to use it."

"That, too. Don't be like me," Cypress warns. He sparks the blunt and pulls an ashtray towards himself. "You may not be able to see the scars that Tumblr left me with, but they're there."

"*Not* anymore." Between the two words, Talon yanks the curtains apart from the other side. She's wearing an all-black romper over a long-sleeved shirt, cuffs rolled up to her elbows, and poses like a burlesque dancer against the backdrop of swinging lights. She drops her arms and gasps. "And what are *you* doing here?"

"Just..." I look at Laura.

Laura looks at me. "Passing through," she says. "You should fetch an Uber, sister, and rejoin with us tomorrow."

"Can you fetch me a snack first?" Cypress asks through a hit of his blunt. "Got the munchies."

"Have you considered a tolerance break?" Talon asks as she crosses the room. Her face is paler than when I last saw her, like she's coming down with something.

"My blood stream moves too slow for that, sis," he says, exhaling smoke. "You'll be old and sere by the time I'm ready to smoke you out again."

Talon opens the refrigerator. Fog crawls out in plumes. She pulls out a drip bag of blood, along with a paper bag, drops the first in Cypress' lap, then nudges my drink aside and sits on the table in front of me and Laura. She unrolls the paper bag, revealing a can of Sprite with a cross drawn on the side in Sharpie and a rosary wrapped around it.

"Holy Sprite," she says, raising the can to me before downing it in four huge gulps. Then she scratches her neck delicately, right between the two circular scars. "Cy, Laura," she says through a belch, "close your eyes."

They obey, Cypress pulling his shirt up over his eyes, Laura hiding her face in her knees.

Talon pulls a small satin bag from her purse and withdraws her silver crucifix. She unclasps the chain and holds it out to me. "Do you mind?"

I take it in my hands; the links are cold and smooth. Once clasped, the silver sits just below the punctures, which, to my awe, grow fainter and fainter.

She tucks the cross deep into her shirt and covers the healing wounds. "All clear."

The vampires reemerge.

"I wish *someone* had told me you'd be here," Talon says with a huff. "I would've clocked out early."

"It's alright. Get some rest," I say, patting her knees.

"Y'all should skip the Uber and walk," Cypress says casually, looking from Talon to Laura and back. "Twenty minutes one way. Five minutes back for you, Master." He grins slyly at me. "Twenty-five minutes with your woman."

Laura gives him a look that I can't see. Her brother's eyes are playful, his lips twitching like he's trying not to laugh.

"Oasis, will you wait for me?" She asks. "It will be twenty-*four* minutes."

I lean close and kiss the back of her neck. "Go."

Talon hugs me, but the two sisters leave arm in arm through the curtains. The groove of a funk song thrums through the club.

"Pac-Man Vs.," Cypress says, passing me the blunt. He leaves my side for the shelves of consoles and searches. Whatever he's looking for seems to be high over his head. He reaches with one hand, then the other, then the other, then the other until I realize that he isn't reaching; he's climbing the shelves like a spider, barely touching the surfaces. He finds the console and hugs it to his chest, floating down like an umbrellaless Mary Poppins.

The shadows I prepared for are nothing like the ones I'm standing in. This darkness feels whimsical compared to the darkness I knew and left.

Cypress sees my face and smirks. He changes the setup and hands me the controller. The game begins. It's been years since I touched a console, but I find my footing quickly, commanding the ghosts around the maze like a general.

"Master's right," Cypress says a few minutes into the game. "You do have a pretty heartbeat. Hope it's alright to say."

"It is." My ghosts converge on him. "Thank you."

He smiles. "Anyway, I just wanted to look at you." He nibbles his thumbnail. "Master went out in the sun to see you, so I had to."

I grab his cold wrist, pull his hand away from his mouth. "Don't do that."

He frowns at the point of contact, but drops his hand nonetheless. "Hundred and twenty-two years, I ain't seen her so much as sniff in a human's direction. Next thing I know, she's wrapped up in black like a widow, sending the cat on missions to her Oasis."

Somehow, the memory of Bird Bones got swept to the wayside. Laura has a whole family, pet included.

"Cypress, how old are you?" I ask. The question has been burning a hole in my tongue since I set eyes on him.

"138," he says, grinning, "but I was two days away from seventeen when I left the mortal coil." This next round, his Pac-Man is more of a ghost than the ones I'm steering, stealthily sneaking offscreen and back.

"Is it invasive to ask how you died?" I venture.

"No." He smacks his lips slowly and reaches for his abandoned blunt, operating the joystick with one hand. "Lynch mob," he says through a mouthful of smoke.

It strikes once, then hits me in waves.

The age gap between me and Laura feels different. Her story is a cosmopolitan's; Cypress' story is mine.

I want to cry. Instead, I watch my game performance tank; I take the blunt and a long puff.

Cypress sets his controller on the table and turns to face me; he pushes his dreads up and binds them with an elastic band around his neck. We're alone and in silence, save the Pac-Man theme on repeat and the Gap Band muffled by the curtains.

"I got worried Talon might've scared you off after she told me she went to make sure you weren't white. I have a phobia," he says, wrinkling his nose.

Phobias are for spiders and elevators. What does it mean to be deathly afraid of something that already killed you?

I try and fail to summon speech—to carry on the conversation neatly.

Cypress leans close to me, brow furrowed. Then he trails an index finger up my cheek in the path of a fallen tear, like he's coaxing it back into my eye. I didn't realize it fell. I didn't anticipate the unzipping of this part of me.

"Angels be with me," I mutter, throat parched from smoking. I wipe my face with my sleeve. "I'm *so* sorry."

"That's one thing I don't miss."

I sniff. "What?"

He brushes his lip with his thumb, as though tempted to bite, but then drops his hands and sits on it while puffing.

"Feeling so short on time that I feel like I gotta apologize for feeling a feeling."

I scoff weakly. "You sound *just* like Laura."

"Or maybe Master sounds just like me." He raises a mischievous brow. "You ever been to Chevalier, Miss Oasis?"

"I haven't," I say, dabbing my runny nose. "Where's that?"

"It was my hometown, off the coast of Louisiana," he says, procuring the makings for another blunt despite the one we're smoking still being lit. "I ate it off the map. Well...*most* of it. Left all the kinfolk be. They changed the name." He sighs nostalgically. "Bit off more than I could chew, so Master bought all the milk bottles in a twenty-mile radius. Them leftovers lasted."

I stare. I stare and say nothing, because this is once again one of those times where nothing I have to say feels as reverent as it should.

"Bless your heart," Cypress says, like he can see it all over my face. "All I'm saying, Miss, is you got enough mourning to do over your own Jim Crow. I already got my eye for an eye. Master made sure of that."

"Why do you call her Master?" I ask as the urge to cry recedes, overtaken by fascination.

"Master is what *you* hear," he says, pointing with the blunt before passing it to me. "Vampires hear Master, or Master, or Master, or Master. Just depends on who she is at the time."

The expression on my face widens his smile.

"You're faring well in the shadows for a human," he says. "But then Kansas'll do that to a person."

I take a dizzying hit and hold it. "I'm not in the shadows," I say, exhaling a cloud of smoke. "I'm with Laura."

Cypress pulls a face, like he both agrees and disagrees.

"You're with Master," he says with the blunt between his lips, "but you're also with Master. Have you met her?"

My heart thrums like a kick drum in my ears.

"No."

"Then let me…" He takes a hit so deep that a centimeter of ash plummets onto the sofa. Then he exhales in my face. "… introduce y'all."

I squint.

Squinting is all I can do through eyes too swollen to open. Left for dead, still breathing, watching the backs of white people too spineless to end my life.

Time crawls, and though I will my heart to beat faster, to keep going, I know deep in my emptying veins that I'm dying.

The full moon shines down from the twilit sky.

My ears ring. My breaths stumble, faint, ragged. My body pleads for life; my heart pleads for the end.

Is it a sin to wish I'd hurry up and die? I'm in the middle of Foxtrail Fields, not a light in sight to signify civilization. Just me and the sugarcanes, still bent form a brush with a tropical storm. No one will find me. It's not suicide, really, to want to die, and to be in the arms of Death. I don't feel pain in Death's arms. It's like there was too much, and after passing the Rubicon, too much to be felt.

I can't move, but I can see the sky, the full moon a haloed blot through the film of blood over my eyes. At least I have it and the stars.

A snap, barely heard through the throbbing in my ears. Another, closer. Adrenaline alone rolls me over. I splutter into the dirt; I think my ribs are broken. I roll onto my back again, each movement a reed of pain. Pain congeals until it's too thick to wade through.

I hear distinct footsteps now, treading through the sugarcane.

Someone back to finish the work.

A silhouette eclipses the moon, pure shadow above me.

"Son of Van Helsing," comes a voice—honey sweet, but like a blizzard of flames. "For how long did you believe that I would not one day sniff you out?"

Van Helsing?

Does this have something to do with hell?

Is that where I'm going?

Is that where I am?

Through slits for eyes and the veil of night, I see a mulatto like me bending over my face, kinky hair in spirals under a straw hat. She's in Sunday stroll wear—a puffy-sleeved shirt with a high collar, a plain satin skirt that catches the moonlight. She takes a deep breath in but doesn't seem to breathe out.

"You are not the son I seek."

I don't know whose son I am. Mama and I would've been gone up north if I had a father who wanted a son. Instead, I have a mother too ashamed to tell me who he is, let alone seek him out for help. I wonder if she even knows who he is, or if he's a monster. I wonder if he'd care if he somehow finds out I died.

She looks moonward, and the rays refract in her brown irises as she frowns.

"Van Helsing, you filthy infidel. I feel even more justified in giving your wife the love you could not," she says to the sky, clicking her tongue. "Preacurvar. Dirty, dirty, dirty deadbeat."

Van Helsing? Deadbeat?

On the precipice of death is a cruel place to finally get the name of the man I've wanted to look in the eye my entire life and ask why he was gone.

The woman looks at me.

"You have been brutalized," she says.

She pauses, like she's waiting for me to respond, but I can't speak, can't blink—can barely breathe as my heart staggers on.

"I do not understand humans, son of Van Helsing. When I come from, you drank the blood you spilt while it was still warm," she laments. "And if *you could not drink any longer, you bathed in it. Modernity is depraved, I fear." She stoops next to me and unleashes her mane of hair, laying her hat over my chest. Her cold fingers singe and soothe my raw, bruised forehead as she smooths my hair back.*

Are you an angel? I try to ask but nothing comes out. Whoever she is, she's here for my dying moments, watching over me.

"Have you any last words or wants?" She asks, crouching closer, putting her ear right over my mouth. She smells like smoke and sugarcane, and like something I've never smelled before. "You are dying for nothing, and for this I will make your last wish my sabbatical before I resume the search for your brother, may the Devil rest his soul."

She's right.

I'm dying.

I'm dying for nothing.

Just because I don't want to be in this world doesn't mean I don't get to. Louisiana's in my bones, the ribs holding together everything I need.

This place wasn't the white man's anyway. They're the reason I never wanted to be here, the reason I'm dying for nothing, the reason I'm not sad to go.

Except I am sad.

Rage fuels each of my dying breaths. It wrings my voice from my throat in shattered gasps. "Kill...them...all."

The woman straightens up, silhouetted in the moonlight. She's right above me, but her shadow is nowhere to be seen on my body. She looks down, frowning at me like she misheard, and raises her arm to her mouth. Then comes a crackling sound, a pop, then a hiss—the sound of blood pouring from her wrist. When she lowers her arm, I see her canines pushing past her smiling lower lip, stained with her blood. Her eyes look stained with blood, too. They look like pools of it.

"You kill them all," she says softly, and puts her cold wrist on my mouth. Her blood trickles over my tongue. It tastes nothing like the rusty tang I taste when I lick a paper-cut or tilt my head the wrong way when my nose is bleeding. Her blood tastes sweet and tart and rich. Like ice cream melting in my mouth.

She must be an angel, or somehow attached to heaven.

Only the Lord could put blood this tasty in someone's veins.

I close my eyes, but still see stars. I feel her deep inhales as her lips skim my neck, feeling for the tenderest part of the vein.

I hear my own flesh pop as her fangs pierce my skin, like an asp's.

I open my eyes.

Cypress is holding out the blunt.

I'm breathing too erratically to trust myself with it, but I take it anyway. The muggy Louisiana night sloughs off me like a second skin. No breeze tumbling over the marsh, no mosquitoes or crickets scoring the twilight. Just the Namco Museum theme music and Parliament through the curtains. No sugarcane stalks or blurry blue sky, no woman kneeling over me. Just a slyly smiling Cypress.

"She saved you?" I ask hoarsely.

"*Saved* is a strong word, Miss Oasis. I'm still dead," Cypress says, scowling. "But it's a gift, even if it wasn't all for me."

"What do you mean?"

"Me and Talon are Master's revenge on the circus. Folks in her era liked to go for the bloodline—leaving folks with no heirs and watchin' 'em weep," Cypress says, stubbing the remnants of the blunt in an ashtray. "I reckon the only thing more twisted than killing someone's progeny is making sure they're ashamed of you."

I didn't anticipate seeing Laura in the shape of someone else so soon. I down the last of my martini.

"Wow." I have nothing else to offer through my most powerful bout of speechlessness tonight. "Sorry...I..."

Cypress shakes his head like it's nothing, grinning as he grinds more weed. "You're precious."

The teenager who's at least five times my age yet so adorable that I could fluff his dreads, thinks I'm precious.

"Likewise."

A mix of fluttering and squeaking fills my ears. I whirl around, surrounding my head with smoke as I exhale.

The cauldron of bats looks like a raveling, jet-black tornado. In the handful of seconds it takes to wipe the tears from my eyes, Laura's almost fully formed. She rubs her left arm so that a few fluffy heads smooth into her skin like lotion.

Cypress glances at his watch. "Twenty-four minutes came and went already?"

"As promised," Laura says. There's a bat fluttering above her head; it looks a little disoriented, as though it didn't get the memo about reassembly. Noticing this, she snatches it from midair and drops it in her blouse. "You waited for me."

I reach for her. Her cold hands wake a part of me that started to snooze while she was gone.

"I wasn't too rough with her, Master," Cypress says, pushing an escaped dread into the elastic. "Most of the laundry's still in the basket."

"Will you be needing your car, sweet Cypress?" Laura asks, though her eyes are on me.

"Nah. I need the exercise," he replies. "Take it easy Miss Oasis."

We leave him the way we found him, playing Pac-Man while puffing a fresh blunt.

"So that's the bat thing," I say above the music.

"It is indeed," Laura says. "I am not at my prime, however. Once I have eaten, there will be no stragglers to embarrass me."

The surreality of the purple room flakes away the further we get from it. Bluegrass now pours over the subterranean cove of a nightclub. We pass the bar, where Apple's whipping up something that involves juggling three shaker tins like pins.

"It's too bad. More humans should know about this place," I say as we pass the long line, full of fresh faces.

"Some are meant to," Laura says. "Like you."

I put my hands in my pocket as we stroll up the street. This flannel is barely a buffer between my skin and the cold. I'm in for colder still, though; I hope I don't make a fool of myself by shivering too much to do anything sexy.

"I know that we planned a convenient return to your apartment," Laura says as we near the corner, "but in the interest of trust, and to be sure that you know you have mine, I invite you to my home."

I come to a slow stop, licking my lips. Trying to play it cool while my heart flaps against my ribs. I take her hand in mine, watching as she bites her lip in anticipation. I wrap my arms around her. The feel of her icy skin on mine snuffs out the worst part of my brain—the *it's all too good to be true* lobe that is still somehow doubting that the person I'm holding is tangible.

"I accept."

Laura puts her chin on my shoulder and her hands behind my back, like we're about to slow dance. I've never encountered a smell like this—like fruit and fire and flowers all at once. For a fraction of a millisecond, I wish I was a vampire, too, so that I could breathe in forever and ever with no need to exhale.

*

Cypress drives a black Cadillac convertible, which Laura whips like a NASCAR driver, blasting past toll booths as we head north to her castle on an island in the Hudson. With a balmy breeze rolling off the water and the stars crammed between the mountaintops, I could easily forget that NYC is still in arms' reach.

Laura maneuvers off the highway, then makes a sharp left turn. The jagged walls of her castle serrate the cornflower sky, darkening the Hudson with its shadow. Smears of kudzu crawl up the broken brick walls. The Cadillac dips into a dark tunnel. A lullaby of a breeze combs through my hair as we whip through and emerge a minute later at the base of the hill on which the castle sits. She parks at the bottom of the stone steps fringed with string lights.

Tangles of wildflowers border the cobbled walkway through the untamed courtyard, overgrown with herbs. I catch whiffs of mint and lavender carrying thickly as we climb the steps.

The castle's tall double doors are made of dark wood, fortified with wrought iron hinges. They open without her touching them. The creaks echo in the wide, lofty hallway ahead as LED bulbs in the ceiling flicker on in succession, illuminating the exposed dark stone interior.

"I bid you welcome, my Oasis, to my house," Laura says.

When I look over, she's watching me marvel at the modern-medieval fusion of a home, smiling satisfactorily as we walk down the long, echoing hall.

"This is...so cool," I say.

"Come," she says, smiling. "There is a fireplace waiting for us."

Vaulted stone arches line the walls; it's too dark to see what lays beyond them. At the end of the hall, stairs spiral up and down. Moonlight through a stained-glass window bathes the stone floor in a bright scene—green hills, clustered homes, a wiggly tree, a church with no crosses on the spires. I recognize the signature opaque, detailed panes of authentic Tiffany-stained glass and on any other night I'd stand and stare, drinking in every detail, but tonight, I only have eyes for Laura.

"The Romanian Country," she says, slowing to a stop alongside me. Only my shadow follows us into the colorful light. "I cannot vouch for what it has become, but it was home, once."

"I've always thought of stained glass as a medium of nostalgia."

"Something I am prone to as of late." She reaches for me "A bad habit that I could not have exterminated without you."

I take her hand, let her pull me closer. "What did I do?"

"You showed concern for my lungs," she says with a soft smile. "I am excited to put them to use with you."

My blood chills, but my heart flames. I'm where I've wanted to be all day and night: in her arms. But as our bodies press together, I'm reminded of the fact that none of *my* organs are optional.

"Please tell me you have a bathroom."

"Through there," she says, gesturing to an archway several feet away. "I will wait for you."

I don't want to break away for this bodily function, but I manage it, trying to maintain a reasonable pace as I step into the sky-blue tiled bathroom. The light turns on automatically, illuminating shelves of combs and pomades, a claw foot tub obscured by a transparent goldfish shower curtain, and a wide stained-glass window depicting a golden-brown dragon curled up in a field of roses.

The last of my intoxication drains away as I empty my bladder and make use of the bidet attachment. I'm already so wet that there's a shadow of dampness on my overalls. I wash my hands with half a glance at my face.

Hand-in-hand, we climb the stairs, me trailing behind her. It gets warmer as we ascend. We emerge at another heavy door, which opens to a large, lofty room lit by a flickering fire. The stone walls are decorated with nothing but empty frames. Some are ornate and round, some plain and rectangular, some the size of my hand, others as tall as I am.

In the middle sits a canopy bed with drawn black curtains and gold sashes. The posts are carved in the slender likenesses of a hilly village. Next to the bed is a round bedside table, carved in the same fashion as the bed posts, with a pitcher, a bottle of wine, and two goblets.

Laura pulls the sash, parting the dark curtains, and sighs heavily.

The white comforter and pillowcases are all stained with blood.

Several big splotches are connected by droplets in varying sizes, like someone was stabbed or shot and tried to crawl away, only to be wounded again.

I cover my mouth in silence.

"I do apologize, Oasis," Laura says as she rubs her hand on one of the stains. "This blood is, like me, a facsimile."

Heart pounding, I follow in her footsteps. There's nothing on her hand. Up close, it's easier to tell that the blood stains are printed onto the comforter, and not stained. The semi-circular stained-glass window overlooking the bed doesn't depict a scene, or even a person. The panes are all ruby red and blob-shaped, another facsimile of dripping blood.

"I asked my ex-wife Justina to make this room fit for love-making," Laura says wearily.

"Including the décor?" I ask, looking around at the empty frames, which hang on every inch up to the ceiling.

"These are all the mirrors that I…Dracula," she says, pushing the bed curtains further apart, "have broken."

The palpitations die out, replaced with the familiar sensation of bats flapping in my stomach. I relate too much to be turned away. Even though the bed is stained with fake blood, it's here for us.

Laura moves to the other side of the bed. A five in one radio, cassette player, CD player, and record player sits atop the night-stand, complete with AUX cord plugged into an iPod classic.

"You have an iPod, but no phone?"

"Little Talon used to sit this above my bed when it was time to sleep." She scrolls through the iPod at lightning speed. "She put this album on repeat when it was released. It is my favorite."

The album in question is *I Am…Sasha Fierce.*

Somehow, I'm not surprised.

Laura closes her eyes and tilts her face towards the ceiling, like she's on the edge of breaking into song alongside Beyoncé. She sits at the foot of the bed, framed by the carved posts, and spreads her knees.

"Come to me, my Oasis."

Each step fans the flames of want in me, speeds up my heart until it feels like it might drill a hole through my chest.

Laura takes my waist in both hands and situates me between her legs, standing above her. She unbuttons my sleeve and runs her hand over my forearm, watching my face as the firelight dances in her eyes. She does the same with my other sleeve, wrapping my skin in goosebumps.

I put my hand on her shoulder, like touching her will tame the beast she's taunting.

She unsnaps my overalls, lets them fall around my hips like a skirt. She untucks my flannel and inhales. She inhales while push-ing it up, slowly revealing the landscape of bible verses and stretch marks on my stomach. She holds my waist, let's my shirt fall part-way onto her head as she puts her forehead between my breasts, head bowed like she's praying, still inhaling without letting out a breath.

The way she's holding me, getting me wet all over again, I'd snatch these clothes off and sit her right on my face if she didn't have her own journey mapped out already.

Laura stands and unbuttons my collar, then slowly works her way down, letting her fingers trail over my sternum.

"Carl is a scientist," she murmurs while pulling my flannel off my shoulders, tugging when it snags on my nipples, until it hangs off my wrists. "I invented a device to measure the speed and force of blood flow in the veins. I was in love with a human who spilled his own blood. I became an eager scientist—someone I hoped would show him the power of his blood and inspire him to keep it in his veins for me." She kisses my skin between words, leaving a column of cold that ends at my navel, where she inserts her nose, inhaling deeply, like she's trying to smell my insides through it. "I have been told," she says as she sits, lips brushing my happy trail, "that I am what you call a simp."

I breathe a laugh. "Good to know."

She tugs my flannel off my arms. She rolls my overalls down my thighs and pushes them down to my ankles, motioning for me to step out of them. I smell myself when I move, twice as wet as I was before, thirsting to touch and be touched.

"He was a hypochondriac—leeches, not razors, were his way," she continues as I straighten up. "Forty years, I spent fermenting his blood with love for me before he died at 67 without my ever having a taste—too devoted, he was, to his self-destruction," Laura says, feeling up my legs one at a time, surveying my skin with her fingers. She looks up at me as I comb my fingers gently through the flyaways on her forehead. I take down her bun and bury my fingers in her wild hair. "I have learned from those mistakes."

I swallow a moan building in my throat. "What mistakes?"

"I let him believe that his blood was something I desired. I did not properly convey that it was already mine," she says as her lips hover over my clit, torturing me with nearness. Her hands have been moving up and down my legs, grasping firmly in some places, gently massaging others. "I will not make this mistake with you." A kiss on my happy trail. "You are mine, Oasis." A kiss on my navel. "Not the angels'," she says, rising slowly, kissing my sternum, "nor the Lord's," she says, kissing my neck, "but mine." Her lips are on mine when she says, "Mine alone."

I put my hands on hers, stopping them in their tracks. "That goes both ways."

Her brown skin glows in the flickering flames. With no shadow cast by her own features, she could be an angel—an angel in the whimsical sense that predates all of this. Before Custodes Angelorum, and before the Devil, there was the guardian angel I silently thanked when my debit card swiped without declining, or when I got above a D on an assignment, or when I managed to make it across the street before the bus I was about to miss pulled off.

The guardian angel who caught me when I thought I'd slip through the cracks—when it seemed like no one would.

I sit in her place and lean back on my elbows, gazing up at her. "Fangs out."

A heavy frown darkens her sultry eyes. "Fangs out?"

I nod. "Let's see 'em."

She arches a brow. "You do realize that is the equivalent of taking out a spoon pre-coitus?"

"No, it's not," I retort.

"It is," she says with a hint of exasperation.

"Is not, and you know it." I cross my legs and arms, hiding the goods, and triggering a look of mild dismay. "You don't have to keep them out. I just wanna see."

Laura sighs and closes her mouth.

I hear a soft crackle. When she opens her mouth in a cheesy smile, her pearly white canines are longer, pointy tips poking her plump lower lip. Her smile wilts.

"I see there the disgust in your eyes," she says with the slightest of lisps, voice full of woe.

"You're so fucking adorable."

Laura gasps. "*I am an apex predator*," she lisps, "and—"

"*Shhh.*" I lean close, take her by the hips, and kiss her stomach through the fabric of her shirt.

I don't have her restraint or her patience.

I'm human and I'm starving.

I pull her leopard print leggings down. Underneath, a white thong covers the dark fuzz between her legs. Like my overalls, the fabric is damp when I feel with my fingertips. I run my fingers under the elastic while her hands rest at her sides, twitching like she wants to guide me.

I stand up again, unfasten the bat chain so that it dangles on her sternum, and unbutton her blouse. She isn't wearing anything underneath. Two gold bars pierce her nipples. I push them up, squish them in my hands, torturing myself alongside her.

A soft moan seeps from her throat; I look at her face, at her eyelids are fluttering, at her fangs sparkling in the firelight as she bites her lip. I toss her blouse aside, undo the clasp of her bralette, and clench it in my fist as I lean back.

I've been undressing her in my head since we met, body aching with want and wonder. I don't have to wonder anymore. Every corner of her body is a deadly blow to my repressed sexuality.

But I didn't expect to see scars—not on a vampire, and not on *the* vampire.

Laura has three dark, waxy scars in a column on her sternum.

"Are these recent?" I ask.

"This was my last mortal wound," she says, fingers in my hair. "The Devil gave me a scar to bear on all of my bodies."

I tap a finger on each scar, like I'm playing piano.

"Even the first one?"

"The first one is not a body," she says, pausing to retract her fangs. "It is a memory made flesh."

Something about the solemn undercurrent flicks the animal in me on the nose.

"I want to remember you."

For a moment she looks as windswept as when I asked if she was religious—like she's aboard a capsizing ship.

We're so close to one another that when I touch my breasts, I touch hers, too.

"You look lost," I say, cupping them in my hands.

Laura traces the compass rose with her fingertip, then she twists my nipple, rousing in me something carnal. I put my arm around her neck and kiss her. She grabs my ass, squeezing and rubbing and roaming. I pull her towards me by the waist, robbing us both of our balance and breath.

She's using those lungs now, straddled over me with her elbows beside my head, chest expanding against mine as she kisses my face, my neck, the dip of my collarbone. She grinds slowly, softly groans in my ear, pussy hovering over mine.

To think that I was almost too scared to want this—that I was scared I wouldn't know what I'm doing. To think that I ever worried that my scars would be at the forefront of my mind while her hand slides between our stomachs. To think that I ever thought her cold skin would do anything but make mine sing. She strokes my clit once, slides a finger inside of me and keeps it there. My body clenches; I hiss between my teeth, and somehow keep the beast in its cage.

I grab her wrists; she sits up and twines her fingers through mine, haloed in the firelight, eyes dazed and desirous.

"Sit on my face."

Laura bites her lip and nods, grinding like she's already there.

I drag myself from under her, crawl across the fake blood-stains until I'm at the head of the bed, reclining beneath the semi-circular window.

She crawls after me, then kneels at my feet, biting her lip as she rubs my shins. I see a question in her eyes; I hear it before her mouth is open.

"May I see your wings?"

I sit up, palms sinking into the mattress. I wish there was something I could say—that I could compare my wings to some-thing the way she compared her fangs to a spoon; something to soften the inhumanness. But there's nothing. Nothing to do but kneel with my back to her, gazing at the frosty red glass.

I want her to see them. I always have. I didn't want this to be the context, but then what other context could there have been? Not drunk, but still lubed up with an aphrodisiac, dying to bury my face in her pussy, too caught up in the nearness of her to give a fuck about the relics on my skin.

The fire flickers; Beyoncé belts *Halo,* a coincidence as amus-ing as it is goosebump-inducing. I feel the cold rolling off of her before I actually feel her fingertips. I try to track the movement, to paint a picture of the wings I only saw once, when Helena took a picture the day after to show me. Laura outlines the jagged feathers on my shoulder blades, the tips just above the small of my back.

The song ends, and Laura runs her hand down my spine.

"I have seen," she says softly.

I turn around again, so that my knees touch hers. I brace my-self to see a sea of sorrow in her eyes, but it isn't there. Instead, she looks like she had an epiphany, lips parted, fingers still in midair from where she traced my wings.

"I see you, Oasis," she says softly. "I see you."

I'm out of words to respond with, but it doesn't matter. She sees me. I stretch my legs out on either side of her, Laura straddles me, hands on my shoulders and covers my face with hungry kisses. I lean back slowly, gripping her thighs, squeezing her ass like clay.

Her pussy leaves a wet trail on my stomach as she heeds my coaxing. She holds onto the stone windowsill and settles above my face, hovering, close enough to smell but not touch; I don't have words for this musk between her legs, and I don't want them. All I want is her clit between my lips and my tongue unfurled inside her. I want to hear just how loud I can make the vampire scream.

She's looking down at me, biting her lip as she frowns.

"What's wrong?" I ask.

"What if I take the Lord's name in vain?" She asks, soft and uncertain.

"He'll get over it," I say, stroking her lips. "Heaven's above us, right? He's already over it."

For the briefest of movements, she looks utterly vexed, but then this assertion seems to suffice. Most of her face disappears from my sight as she sits on my face, pulling twin moans from our throats.

I lick her with my whole tongue, dampening my face from chin to nose. I do it again, teasing, relishing the snags in her breathing.

"So fucking wet," I murmur, adding volume to her voice. Another kiss before I use my fingers to expose her clit and put it in my mouth. I suck it gently, curiously, savoring the novelty of this feeling.

Her favorite Beyoncé album transitions to another, newer one, but right now, Laura's voice is the only music my ears have room for.

"Whose pussy is this?" I ask.

"Yours," Laura whispers.

I say it again: "Whose pussy is this?"

"*Este al tau*," she moans, straightening her spine, and pulls my hands up to her breasts. "*Sunt a ta.*"

She inhales deeply, grinds slowly in time with the movement of my tongue. She sighs my name, riling me up until it feels like I might come without even touching all the places it used to take. I hook my arms under her thighs as she moves her hips a little faster, moans a little louder. I feel her climbing higher and higher as her legs open wider for me, burying my face in her taste and her scent.

Her thighs tense. Each breath tumbles from her chest, and her mother tongue takes over. I hear my name in Romanian. Her body stiffens when she comes, still grinding, clit throbbing in my mouth.

"*Dumnezeul meu*," she groans, clutching the windowsill,

hunched over me. She swings her shaking leg over me and collapses at my side.

I sit up, climb over her leg so that I'm between her knees, elbows on top of them. "You've come a long way from thinking I was making you sick."

Laura scoffs, still breathing deeply, and closes her eyes. She feels for my hand and puts it on her chest where her heart would be.

"You have left me…spent like…a doubloon," she gasps.

"Take a breather," I say, kissing the spaces between scars. "I'm not done with you."

"And *I*," she murmurs, putting her cold hand between my legs, "have yet to begin."

Two knuckles around my clit, squeezing gently. One finger in, beckoning the beast in me out of her cage.

I bury my face between her neck and shoulder, where the bloodied pillows stifle my screams.

"This, I cannot have," Laura purrs. "I want to hear you." With her hands on my hips, she rolls me onto my back. She strokes between my legs, then raises her hand over my face so that I can see just how wet I am. Then she puts all four fingers in her mouth.

The verses on the body, the wings on my back; I never needed these to feel angelic. Laura looks like she's in heaven, digging her fingers in my pussy, then licking them like she just ate a plate of buffalo wings. When her eyes fall on me again, her fangs are out.

A laugh makes its way out of me through the moans because she's so adorable, so sexy, so mine.

She reminds me that I'm hers as she stretches out next to me, laughing softly in my ear, grinding on my leg as she strokes my pussy.

I'm hers to kiss, hers to love, hers to fuck until the fire dies and her iPod dies, too.

I'm not the angels', or the God whose name I wind up saying as she licks a trail down my stomach, fangs gently grazing my skin, but drawing none of the blood that'll soon be hers, too.

Hers, and hers alone.

seventeen

August 3, 2019

He must, indeed, have been that Voivode Dracula who won his name against the Turk, over the great river on the very frontier of Turkey-land. If it be so, then was he no common man; for in that time, and for centuries after, he was spoken of as the cleverest and the most cunning, as well as the bravest of the sons of the 'land beyond the forest.'

seventeen

I wake up warm and alone. Daylight through the stained-glass window washes the white of the blanket in red. I pour myself a goblet of water and gulp, then slip out of bed, unlatch a pane of red glass and peer out. Clouds blanket the sky. The murky river glistens to the left. To the right is a swath of dark green hills.

Ashes fill the fireplace. I don't remember when the night ended and sleep began. I kept going back for seconds and thirds, and now my whole body feels like I ran a marathon without stretching. My fingers touch fabric when I pat my head. Someone put a satin bonnet on my head.

Someone also left clothes folded at the foot of the bed—a long-sleeved Thrasher tee and a pair of joggers that are a little loose on me. Down the curved steps, I dip into the bathroom to pee and splash water on my face, searching for signs of activity and finding none.

I creep to the archway across from the bathroom and peer in. The room is rounded like a church apse. A mosaicked rose garden wraps around the vaulted ceiling, interrupted by different iterations of an orange cat.

Bird Bones.

Bird Bones spitting feathers on the ground; Bird Bones chasing a mouse; Bird Bones with a mouthful of rose petals; Bird Bones taking a nap in the thorny shade of a rosebush. Right beneath the mosaic is a cat tower as tall as me, the base clawed to threads.

The real Bird Bones is curled up at the top, one paw covering her face.

Her head is ice cold when my fingers graze the soft fur between her ears.

She uncurls with a chirping meow and stretches her legs. Her sleepy eyes land on me.

The golden eyes I remember are pure crimson, with black slits for irises.

She yawns and stretches again, first with her back arched, then with her stomach low. As she does this, the red drains from her eyes.

She leaps down and stretches yet again, then trots out of the room. I hurry after her down the long hallway into a sleek kitchen divided in two, with a stainless steel refrigerator on each side, separate sinks and stoves, two rectangular islands, and two stone countertops loaded with appliances. One side has a metal trash can beside the counter with a biohazard sign on it.

Cypress' silhouette falls across the second counter along with a motley palette of colors from the stained-glass window depicting a platter of fruits and vegetables.

"I hear ya, I hear ya," he's saying to Bird Bones meowing relentlessly at his feet. "Mornin', Miss Oasis."

"Morning." I join him at the counter with my back to the window, where he's dicing up what looks like dark red tofu. An empty plastic pouch next to the cutting board reads *Congealed AB Positive*.

Cypress lines a metal bowl up with the edge of the cutting board and uses the knife to scrape the gelatinous burgundy cubes into it. He sets it on the floor beneath the window, where the cat crouches low and digs in.

"Is that cat blood?" I ask, unsure of whether I even want an answer.

"Vampires can only drink human blood. Anything else may as well be Hi-C," Cypress says, dropping the pouch in the hazardous waste bin. "Master's around here somewhere."

"He's in his dungeon," comes Talon's voice. She veers in from the hallway with a rattling pill holder in one hand, a massive bottle of vitamins in the crook of her arm, and a bundle of mail in her fist. She's wearing a large t-shirt and leggings, and her long hair is in two kinky braids. She stoops to pet Bird Bones, then smiles up at me. "Good morning, Oasis."

"Morning. When did you get here?"

"Two minutes ago. I'm headed off to London for Semester in Stratford auditions this week." She sets the mail and pills on the counter. The bottle still has its foil, although the dents suggest that she tried piercing through with no success. "Cy, do you mind?"

"On it." Cypress' fangs dent his lower lip. He grabs the bottle and punctures the foil with one, then carefully distributes the pills in the holder while Talon shuffles through the mail.

"Why are you out of your coffin this early?" Talon asks.

"Waiting for Master to come and sign my permission slip," he lisps.

"You're in school?" I ask incredulously.

His fangs retract as he grins.

"I sometimes go when it's cloudy. I like to see what revisions they're making in history classes."

"He calls it going to the zoo," Talon provides.

"The humans are going to the Met today since summer school's almost out." Cypress glares at the floor. "Where is he?"

Talon puts her mail and her pills away.

"Just forge his signature."

"It's not an authentic human experience if I do that," he argues.

"You're already a vampire, Cy. You can't have any more authentic human experiences. And besides," she says, scowling, "humans forge signatures all the time."

While the two siblings debate the definition of authentically human, I peek at the mail Talon left on the counter. The topmost envelope reads *YOUR PERSONAL OFFER AWAITS*, addressed to *Vlad D. Tepes III*.

"*I'll* forge it," Talon says definitively, taking his pen and permission slip. "You're already late for class."

Cypress scratches Bird Bones between the ears while Talon reviews and signs the form. "Look up the exhibits and let me know if you want anything. You too, Miss Oasis."

I frown at the back of his head. "Anything like what?"

"I saw a jade comb from Japan last time I went," he says, shrugging. "Something like that?"

It takes me a moment to realize that he isn't talking about the gift shop.

"You steal from museums?"

"I steal from thieves," he says.

Talon folds the permission slip and slaps it into his waiting hand. "Surprise me."

"I'll surprise the both of you. *There* he go—just when I don't need him," Cypress says dryly. "I'll see y'all." He darts out of the room with an audible *whoosh*, legs moving faster than an Olympic sprinter's.

Maybe I haven't been as awake as I thought. It's all catching up to me now, like a tidal wave slapping back to the shore. Vampire cats, human zoos, casual museum robbery, and...*him*.

A gathering storm gains volume in the hall. The squeaking, fluttering sound intensifies, until the swarm of bats it belongs to sweeps in like a squall. They funnel into the shape of a man—a tall man with bronze skin, a sharp widow's peak, and high, clean-shaven cheeks. He's dressed all in Champion—Champion hoodie, Champion sweats, Champion high tops—leaning against the stone archway with his hands in his pockets. He bites the inside of his cheek and looks at Talon, then Bird Bones trotting towards him, then me.

Talon drops her phone in her purse and crosses her arms, glaring. The only sound is Bird Bones bathing at his feet. After a few moments, Talon strides over to him with her hand held out and a glare on her face.

His nostrils flare as he reaches into his pocket and unfolds a worn black wallet. Bills of all colors fan over the edge. His short nails are painted black, and there are rings on all of his fingers, including a golden bat wrapped around his index finger, like the one I've seen on Laura's hand. He folds a ten and a five into Talon's hand.

She shakes her head. "Fifty. *Five-zero*," she says, beckoning for more. "Plus, your hood is up. There's a fee for using all of it just to *not* show your hair off."

In silence, he tucks another two twenties between her fingers.

"*That's* more like it," Talon says, turning on her heel. "I'll text you, Oasis."

I hardly notice her leave.

"Okay," I say, half a minute too late. She's gone.

It's me, him—and Bird Bones, waiting for his attention.

I don't know what's on my face right now—if it's on a journey of its own, independent of my head, which is empty of all thoughts except one: Laura wasn't kidding when she said ugly isn't an option when preying on humans.

"I see you made it in one piece this time." I cross my arms and step closer. "Are you Carl?"

"No."

"Who are you?"

"I am Vlad Dracula," he says.

He has a thick accent and a quiet, deep voice—one that I can't help thinking would make an evocative singing voice.

"Should I call you Vlad or Dracula?"

"It matters not."

"Does that mean I can give you a nickname?"

He doesn't reply.

"I see," I say slowly. "It's nice to meet you either way."

Again, I wait, and again, he offers nothing.

"What are you up to?" I ask.

"Speaking," he says. "With you."

"Barely." I stand foot away from him, looking up into his dark-green eyes, searching for something familiar. "You're not very talkative, are you?"

"I suppose I am not."

"Are you shy?"

"I have been told I possess an unpleasant personality," he says, face unchanging.

"Oh."

Silence falls, and the staring match continues.

I put my hands in my pockets, too, and tilt my head to the side.

"Whose are you, Vlad Dracula?"

"Yours," he says in the same unaffected tone.

I nod. "Just checking."

His eyes, thus far caged and unreadable, glimmer with something like intrigue. "I am your baby?"

It takes a moment for me to realize what he's talking about; it hasn't really registered that this is the same person who was sitting on my face last night.

"Yes," I say. "So you haven't been doing anything today?"

"No."

"What do you usually do?"

He takes his hands from his pocket and crosses his arms. "I host the occasional dinner party."

For a moment, his answer makes no sense: he can't eat food. Then understanding dawns.

"Oh," I say. "That's it?"

"I do apologize for the emptiness of my existence before you," he says dully. "It is the unfortunate consequence of minding my business."

"I forgive you." My heart trips over itself as I move closer still. *The* vampire has a few pale scars on his original face—a tiny slash above his right eyebrow, another below his chin. A crescent gash near his temple looks a little red around the edges, like it's recent and in need of attention. I start to reach, then lower my hand when his eyes dart to it.

"What happened?"

He traces the curved wound with his thumb, like he forgot it was there, then stuffs his hands in his pockets again. "Jonathan Harker hit me in the face with a shovel. It will go away once I have fed. The rest will remain."

"Why?"

"This body is memory made flesh," he says, drawing more goosebumps to the surface of my skin.

Bird Bones meows once, long and loud.

He raises a curious eyebrow at her, then tugs his hood off as he crouches in front of her, revealing a headful of damp black curls, sending a whiff of citrus my way. Golden sleeping bats dangle from his earlobes. He stoops and picks up Bird Bones, who steps onto his shoulders, then disappears into his hood, head peeking out like a baby in a sling.

Then he looks at me, hands in his pockets once more, brow arched like he asked a question.

I take a step closer.

He takes a step away, angled towards the hall.

Another step towards him.

Another step away.

Like this is the closest I'll get to him.

I've been thinking about this moment in the back of my mind ever since I realized there was something to be in denial about, working hard to have no expectations because I know, fundamentally, that he and Laura are two different people, yet still cautiously asking myself just how different can they *really* be?

I hold out my hand and wait.

He and Bird Bones blink at me. He looks from my fingers to my face and back. The slow movements of his eyes bring vivid memories of Talon describing him as a cat who knows right from wrong.

I purse my lips, daring him to knock over the glass of water by taking another step without taking my hand. Slowly, he withdraws his left hand from his pocket, then rubs his fingertips with his thumb, like he's debating internally.

Is he?

Laura would've taken my hand by now.

He raises his left hand to his mouth. Then he bites off a sliver of his nail and spits it to the side.

I gasp. I march over to him, then grab his wrist, and force his hand away from his mouth.

He doesn't resist; he does, however, look at me like I threw a punch that missed.

"Don't do that," I scold. "It's bad for your teeth."

He takes my left hand with his right, cold be-ringed fingers slotted between mine, ample space between us as the disconcerted expression wears off his face. "The fighting hand must be free," he says quietly.

"Noted."

The walk continues.

"Not saying I had any expectations," I say, "but if I did, the head-to-toe Champion wouldn't have been one."

"There is no such brand as Vlad Dracula," he says. "I improvise."

I look him up and down. "People used to make fun of me and my brother for wearing it."

"List for me their names," he says with something like a smile. "No one loves making fun more than I."

We traverse the long hall until we're in the light of stained-glass Romania. Instead of going up like last night, he leads me down.

And down.

And down.

Lanterns with flickering pink flames hang overhead, throwing my shadow on the slick stones. The gently curved descent lasts at least five minutes before one of the lanterns illuminates a vaulted wooden door. It feels like we might be right above the Earth's core, but the pink lights spiral downward still.

He looks to me, brow arched, like he's asking if I'm ready.

My response is a similarly silent 'You tell me'.

He pushes the door open with one hand.

On the other side is pitch darkness. He feels along the adjacent wall, rings clicking on stone. A switch flips.

The interior lights up slowly, one flame flickering to life at a time, at varying heights and distances, until it's all visible—an enormous cavern with a crooked domed ceiling, and sloping walls covered in everything from closed doors, to cage-like bars, to stained glass windows, to hanging paintings, to drawn curtains. His dungeons looks like a beehive and a bat cave all at once.

Bird Bones leaps out of his hood and embarks on her own journey.

Dracula eases his fingers from mine and smooths his hair back, then tugs his hood up again.

"Get lost," he says, turning his back to me.

Whiplash robs me of speech.

"I will find you," he says as he walks away.

I scoff. "Thanks, babe."

I see his head turn as his silhouette shrinks, but he doesn't reply.

My head is spinning in so many directions that I already feel a little lost—so lost that I decide to obey and get lost for real among the doorways I can reach.

The first doorway I peek into is a fathomless wine cellar, crawling with mist.

The second is similarly cavelike, but with mountains of gold and jewels, like Smaug the dragon lives here. I guess in a sense a dragon *does* live here. I hold my breath and tiptoe in, then grab a handful of coins and squint. A small mound cascades over my bare toes when I try to replace it.

The next room looks like a natural history museum, with cases of skeletons and eggs in all sizes.

The next, a basement full of circular tables with glowing runes and grooves, and shelves of jars with everything from feathers to Skittles.

I step into an armory full of curved swords, daggers, and spears, then a room like a furniture emporium that sells nothing but ottomans. The one nearest to me has a sword in the middle of the cushion.

I poke my head into a room that looks like it's full of nothing but fumes and vapors. I pull my shirt up over my nose and squint. Beneath the miasma, frothing cauldrons sit on pink fire, and Cuisinart pans sizzle on retro stovetops.

My jaw drops when I come upon a walk-in closet the size of a coliseum. Shoe towers and racks of clothes, cases of jewelry as tall as the vaulted ceiling, all trickle down to a purple velvet bench. Dozens of garments are draped over and strewn around it. I reach for a glimmer of gold fabric—the jacket of a familiar tracksuit.

This doesn't look anything like an empty existence.

This looks like an existence so full that I can't even think straight. In fact, I feel disastrously close to dissociating as I exit the closet and enter a candle-lit reading room. There's a plush purple sofa, a dark table with several books open on it already, and only a few shelves.

Despite having her own apse, Bird Bones is fast asleep on top of an aged book that looks absolutely priceless. I click my tongue; she raises her head and blinks lazily. I peek at what she's sleeping on. "FRAN," "THE MO," and "UN-A" are all that's visible beneath her paws. Opposite, I see part of an inscription in skinny cursive. All I can make out is, *for your eyes only. With love and gratitude, Mary.*

I turn to the shelves for a look at the other titles.

I've heard of *Paradise Lost* and *Paradise Regained*; I'd even downloaded PDFs thinking I'd have the wherewithal to get through the ridiculously antiquated poetry. I've never heard of *Paradise Maintained*, though. It's thinner than the other two, bound in heavy brown leather. I pull it off the shelf and hold my breath as the stench of age creeps from the pages.

To the Prince of Darkness

Do give the other, older Prince of Darkness my best.

"Wow." I don't realize I've spoken aloud until Bird Bones returns a small meow.

I put Milton back. Moments later, my jaw drops.

In 1956, Billie Holiday inscribed a vinyl LP of *Lady Sings the Blues* with a ballpoint pen illustration of an upside-down bat and two words: *Next lifetime.*

My heart is thundering. I can't wrap my head around this much time, this long of a life full of this many people, this many experiences, this much raw history.

Another book catches my eye. It's all by itself on the top shelf, wrapped in layers of black cloth. Its position says that I should leave it be, but it occurs to me that in a place this big, if he wanted something hidden, he could do a lot better than this.

I stretch my arm all the way above my head, but it's still too high to reach, and the shelves are too full to use as footholds. As I debate a strategy, black mist crawls into the room, like storm clouds scuttling close to the earth. It gathers on the sofa and condenses into a man wearing all Champion.

He sits with his elbows on his knees, fingers steepled under his chin. "That of all things is not worth dying for."

I turn away from the shelf and put my hands in my pockets. "I didn't plan on dying."

"Nor did I," he says. "I have found you."

"Who says I'm done being lost?"

"I do."

I search for words and find none. I feel more lost than found in this cavernous room of rooms.

"Oaza," he says, reeling me in from the precipice.

"Who is Oaza?"

"You. And you are mine. Oaza mea," he says. "I will show you, Oaza mea, if it would please you."

My heart skips a beat. I shake my head. "I'm just being nosy."

He stands and joins me, mimicking my stance. "Me as well. I will show you."

I hold out my hand. He takes it slowly and I give the bound book a last glance and leave the little library with him.

"120," he says, pushing his hood down with his fighting hand.

My heartbeat.

Would hearing this have been as chilling if Laura had said it? Probably not. I'd compare him and her to Jekyll and Hyde if I'd read it; but then for all I know, that fictional dual persona may be in the same predicament as the vampire holding my hand—sitting in a dungeon nursing bitterness over being the central character of libel and slander repackaged as gothic fiction.

I stop walking, like standing still will still my thoughts too. When I look at his face, I have no thoughts at all—just a wordless question that burns my throat when I try to ask it.

"You fear me," he says quietly. To my horror, he loosens his fingers in mine.

I refuse and lock his hand in a vice grip. If I let go, there's no guarantee that I won't wash away, lost in the too-bigness of it all.

"I love you, even when I don't understand you," I say. "I just…" I gesture helplessly to him, then to the dungeon at large, then to him again.

He waits, expressionless.

"I just don't understand where I fit in," I finally say.

His brow wrinkles.

"You are breaking up with me?"

"No," I say, stunned.

"I am your summer fling?" He asks, frown deepening.

"*No*," I say, but the fact that this is his first concern makes me feel a little less buried alive. "You're mine, Vlad Dracula. I just don't understand why I'm yours."

"You do not yet understand yourself."

"Because there's nothing left of me to understand," I say.

"Do not say this, Oaza." His eyes sear through mine, familiar because Laura looked at me like this as her hand disintegrated into bats. He faces me, head bowed, eyes closed. When he opens them, there's no trace of green. Just pure white, like a cat's third eyelid stuck in a blink. Dark red tears well in his eyes. "I will cry."

"Don't cry," I breathe.

A tear of blood spills down his sharp cheekbone. By the time I convince my hand to wipe it away, it's gone, soaked into his skin like water in dry soil. He blinks, and his eyes are green again. "You are the mirror I could never break. Breathe."

I didn't realize I stopped.

Even if I don't understand what that means, I need all the proof the world has to offer that I'm more than just scars in the shape of a person.

I readjust my hand in his.

"Okay."

We walk on, nearing the vaulted door that had been next on my itinerary. A steady breeze gusts out, whipping his hair back like a Pantene commercial.

He points to a pair of Champion slides on the floor. They're too big for me, but I put them on anyway.

The vaulted, torch-lit room smells like a cow paddy, and looks like a cross between a medieval barn and a research lab. Tanks, pens, and cages of all sizes are set into the stone walls and dangling from the ceiling. Straw pokes out of some of them; grass and blankets from others. All around are soft hoots, purrs, chirps, clicks.

"Wait here for me." His hand deflates in mine, and he disappears in a swarm of black mist.

"Is that going to be a regular thing now?" I ask thin air.

Two-dozen black-eyed black rats swarm towards the Plexiglass window of their cage with the fluidity of a school of fish. A tailless kangaroo saunters out of the darkness and grips the iron bars of its cage, blinking. A squid in a massive tank of orange-tinted fluid swims rhythmically from one corner to the next, like a screensaver. A two headed cobra winds around a stick in its tank; it slithers towards the glass as I get closer, and I realize that the stick is a femur.

I'm not *here* anymore; my feet have been wandering. All of the cages I pass are occupied, and all of the animals within come forth to watch me, silent and observing, just like their keeper. In one dark corner, I see an inch of iron bars beneath a black curtain the size of a king size blanket. It's impossible to tiptoe in too-big slides, so I shuffle across the straw-strewn floor. I look left and right, then snag the curtain aside all the way. The pitch blackness inside makes it look more like a tunnel than a cage.

I hear a sound like a faraway stomp. The curtain rungs rattle. A sound like a violin. A fist of green light punches through the darkness. Hot air rolls out in waves, smelling of something brisk and minty. The circle of emerald light gets bigger and brighter, gaining speed, sounding so much like a tornado that I freeze. A mirage smears the flames firestorm rushes towards me, undercut by a screeching shriek.

My body won't move.

The green flames are as big as a tapestry when someone finally moves my body for me. He solidifies from a cyclone of bats between me and the cage and whirls me around so that I'm facing away from it, unable to move. Fire pours through the bars, whipping his hair into my face. The fire stretches a few feet past us before dying.

I somehow manage to stay upright as Dracula lets go and strides back to the bars. He scolds whatever's in the cage in Romanian and draws the curtain while it responds in short screeches, like it's talking back.

I slowly turn around, shaking and sweating.

Dracula is completely intact, crouched next to a wooden chest beside the cage, rifling in the contents. Moments later, he fishes out a piece of Wrigley's Spearmint gum as big as a briefcase, tears off the wrapper and balls it up in his fist, and slides it partway under the curtain. A black talon the size of his shoe peeks out, digs into the gum, and drags it out of sight, leaving sugar crystals in the crags.

I hardly see him approach, and jump when his cold fingers touch my shoulder, trailing down my arm until he's holding my hand.

"Is that a dragon?"

"I am nosy," he says, which both is and isn't an answer.

"You should put up signs," I say hoarsely, scowling. "Someone could get hurt."

"That is the general idea." His smile comes and goes like a wisp of smoke fading into the air. "I will not let harm befall you—here, or anywhere. Minty Fresh only wished to say hello."

We stop at a stall barred by half a wooden door. He unlatches it and leads me towards a smaller cage, which is attached to a deluxe hutch, with rooms and flaps and stairs for a small animal. The water bottle attached to the metal cage is full of dark red.

He lets go of me and stoops near the hutch, clicking his tongue. I hear straw rustling, accompanied by a small clucking noise. When he returns to me, he has a furry bundle of black and white in his arms.

A bunny.

An ice-cold bunny with a black coat that looks suspiciously like a cape and forms a widow's peak between her long white ears. Her eyes are red, her front teeth sharp and long.

He puts her in my arms with a smile that I don't have to second guess. "Bunnicula."

She sniffs my neck curiously, lingering near my jugular. I feel her ball of a tail wriggling in the crook of my arm and repress a shiver.

"Where did the blood come from?"

He bites his lip in silence, like he's hiding a smile.

Bunnicula ducks her head, turning herself into a ball in my arms, long ear pressed to my sternum. From above, I see her twitching nose and her blinking red eyes.

"She's mine, right?" I ask.

"As am I."

I kiss Bunnicula's head.

My stomach growls.

"I will feed you breakfast," he says. My heart sinks as he returns Bunnicula to her hutch.

I follow him, heavy with reluctance as I watch her hop curiously to the end of the cage, sniffing after us.

"When do I get to feed you?" I ask.

He frowns, heavy brow darkening his eyes. "You feed me. I must keep this face until sunset."

"When will I see you again?"

A strange look passes over his face—alarm, or confusion, or both. But like all his other expressions, it's gone so fast that I can't even be sure it was there.

He doesn't answer; I don't ask again.

"What about until then? Don't tell me to get lost," I warn.

We stop at yet another threshold that I haven't crossed. The floor on the other side is smooth cement. A row of floodlights illuminates the corrugated doors of storage units.

"*Who* is your realtor?" I wheeze.

"The Devil." He pulls a ring of keys from his pocket as he leads me up the hall.

We stop at unit 9 around a corner. On the other side is a sprawling maze of shelves and crates and stacks. Vinyl LPs and EPs, CD's, cassettes, 8-track tapes in cabinets, gathered around sofas and loveseats and equipment—a cassette deck next to a hammock, a phonograph next to a recliner, a Walkman on a daybed. Buoys of solitude in an ocean of music. I gape around, speechless, breathless, thoughtless.

"Get lost," he says, releasing my hand. "I will find you."

I don't need telling twice. My eyes fall on a mahogany record player near a plaid sofa, needle hovering above an Imogen Heap album.

Just when I thought I'd come to terms with the reality that I might not hear my mother's last words, this thing shows up to remind me that maybe I just haven't tried.

But this wasn't what he meant when he told me to get lost, and so for now, I dive into the shelves, and lose myself in something I know I can come back from.

prize (noun):

1. That which is taken from another; something captured; a thing seized by force, stratagem, or superior power.

2. (military, nautical) Anything captured by a belligerent using the rights of war; especially, property captured at sea in virtue of the rights of war, as a vessel.

3. Anything worth striving for; a valuable possession held or in prospect.

eighteen

August 26, 2019

It is too bad that men cannot be trusted unless they are watched.

eighteen

I had something of a crisis trying to figure out what to get Laura for our one-month anniversary. I kept asking myself what on earth I could add to the life of someone who has enough stuff to warrant an enchanted dungeon. The answer came to me in the form of a $2 Beanie Baby stumbled upon while thrifting for fresh plaid.

Batty the Bat has velcro strips on his wings, and so Laura's been wearing him like a bangle on her wrist, not taking him off for sex, for our walk to Central Park and back, or for another round of sex. Now his felt wingtips brush my temple as she fondles my ear, arm draped around my shoulders.

The thought of my brother putting Laura under the same microscope as my eating habits had me soaking in anxiety on and off since we made plans earlier this week, but with small talk in full swing, he looks more relaxed than I could've hoped for. We're sitting at a table overlooking the Statue of Liberty, shrouded in a night lit by a twinkling skyline, a thin veil of stars, and a waning silvery moon. Laura and I are on one side of the table—me in high denim jeans and my favorite purple flannel, her in black corduroy pants and a white silk blouse.

"What do you do for work, Laura?" He asks as she and I peruse menus.

I already know what I'm getting. With Laura here to sniff, I have no excuse not to eat this time.

"I dabble in the sciences," she answers with a smile.

"Which ones?"

"Animal, mortuary, brain," Laura says, gesticulating casually. "Whichever the moment calls for."

Mirage raises his eyebrows. "Did you go to school for all of those?"

"I did not attend school. I was educated by the Ott—"

I pull my flannel over my face to cover a fake sneeze.

"Bless you," Mirage says.

Laura rubs between my shoulders. "Bless you, beloved. As I was saying I was educated…in modern day Turkey," she says, catching on. "From there I became an apprentice."

"Turkey? That's awesome. Where are you from?"

"Wallachia."

"Like Vlad the Impaler?" Mirage laughs.

Laura puts her hands in her lap and smiles widely, canines sparkling in the candlelight. "Like Vlad the Impaler."

"Is there anything else you'd like besides this?" He asks, indicating the bottle of Merlot in the middle of the table.

"I'll have the spinach, kale, and arugula salad," Laura says, stroking Batty. "Braised, please."

"Alright. Oasis?"

"The usual."

He smiles at me, and I smile back.

Once he's gone, I let out a breath I didn't realize I was holding. To my surprise, Laura exhales alongside me.

"Are you tired?" I ask.

"I am taxed, yes. I will be sleeping tomorrow until Tuesday," she says, looking away.

I do the math in my head and instantly wish I hadn't. "Eight days?"

Laura pinches her lips and reaches for her wineglass. She drains it in a gulp and pours some more in silence.

My heart beats faster, until I can barely swallow. "Does this have anything to do with you being hungry?"

"The connection is negligible," Laura says.

"Eight days without you isn't," I say. A chill steals over me, coating me in fear. "Is me cherishing my blood the real reason you haven't had any of it?"

Her nostrils flare, pouting delicately. "You need not worry about your blood as it relates to my health."

My heart stammers. "What does that mean?"

"I will be wholly honest with you, *iubirea mea*," she says, rotating her glass by the stem, unblinking eyes on mine. "I do not trust your brother. I do not trust most men, but I do not trust him for the way he has made you feel."

"The way I see him isn't who he is," I say, thrown. "Don't let me make a bad impression."

"Mirage made his own impression with his blood. It smells sweet," she says, smacking her lips after a hearty sip. "Liars taste sweet. I find them cloying on the tongue."

I narrow my eyes, searching for traces of a lie that I know I won't find. She wouldn't lie about this—making up scents to drive a rift between me and my brother, knowing I can count all the people who love me on one hand.

"What could he be lying about?" I ask, more to myself than her.

"I will unlock his mind and peruse…" Laura raises her menu and unfolds it in front of her face so that only I can see her eyes morph from static brown to swirling red "…if it would please you."

I almost say that that's cheating, like this is a guessing game with a victor and a prize. "Not this time."

The eye thing stops. She lowers the menu.

The last thing I want to do is overreact and make myself look as insane as Mirage used to make me feel, but there's a short list of things he could be lying to me about, and all of them make me feel insane independent of his influence.

I don't know how much time passes with me staring at the river before Laura slams down the last of the wine like a shot of liquor.

"Will you wait outside for me?" I ask. Best case scenario, we lose an hour of our one month anniversary to a false alarm. Worst case…

Laura shrugs into her sweater just as Mirage appears with two plates.

"Mirage, you must forgive me," she says with a wistful glance at her braised greens. "Although it smells both delicious and safe to eat, I cannot partake in this luxury tonight."

"Aw," Mirage says, crestfallen. "Don't be a stranger." He sets the plates down and extends a hand that she doesn't hesitate to shake. "*Wow* your hand is cold. Are you sure you don't want some tea to go?"

"I have known nothing but warmth since I met your sister.

I will see you quite soon, beloved," Laura says, readjusting Batty's wings around her wrist as she gets to her feet. "I love you with all that I am."

"I love you, too."

I don't watch her go.

Instead, I watch my brother sit across from me with Laura's food. Chicken tenders, sliced and steaming, greens, and mashed potatoes are once again on my plate.

"She seems cool," he says.

I spear a sixth of a tender on my fork and put the whole scalding chunk in my mouth. "I'm sorry she couldn't stay. I think you'd really like her."

"I'm happy for you," Mirage says, watching as I blow on a forkful of mashed potatoes and shovel it down.

"This is *delicious*," I say. It's also the only barrier between me and making a scene. With my mouth full of food, I can't ask straight up if he's told me any lies lately. "Any word on the BBQ joint?"

"Still scouting locations. I feel like I can't go any further without a name for it, though."

"Too bad we weren't triplets."

"Can you imagine?" Mirage scoffs.

"Mom would've had to pick different names, unless she named one of us Desert—I mean *Desert*," I say, pronouncing it first as a verb, then a noun. "Which one of us do you think it would've been?"

If Mirage hears my attempt at passive aggression, he doesn't entertain it.

"Why not the one who doesn't already have a name?"

"Because the one who doesn't have a name isn't here to judge whether they actually fit that name," I reply, still eating at the speed of light. "I'm definitely not an oasis. Are you a mirage?"

"I don't think so," Mirage says slowly, pushing leaves across his plate.

After months and months of glaring at me for not doing the same, he's staring at me instead of eating.

"Why wouldn't you be an oasis?" He asks.

"Why would you desert an oasis? You wouldn't," I say, answering my own question. I scrape together the remains of my food, which I forced down so fast that I'll be lucky if I don't projectile vomit on the elevator. "Ergo, I must not be one."

Mirage swallows hard. He lays his fork down and gulps half his glass of water. "Oasis, what's wrong with you?"

"Nothing," I say sharply. Then, realizing that my voice is climbing towards a problematic volume, I try to reel it back in and approach this like the level older sister I once was.

"Nothing feels wrong until I'm with you."

Our gazes lock.

"I'm sorry you feel that way," Mirage says.

The ice in his eyes knocks the wind out of me. I can't approach this like the level older sister I was once because that's not what I am to him anymore. Three years apart scrubbed that Oasis away—three years where our only contact was the occasional *how are you* text, or calls on our birthday, because holidays stopped mattering after our mother died.

But no amount of time will change the fact that I can stare him down like prey and squeeze lies out of him like toothpaste from a tube.

The car keys. The last few Capri Suns. The 3DS we used to share.

Nothing he's ever hidden from me has stayed that way for long once I had something to suspect.

"Tell me what you're hiding," I say, "or I swear on Mom's ashes I'll flip this table over."

"How can you swear on Mom's ashes when you lost them?" He asks, like he had the words lined up long before this conversation.

I wipe my mouth with my napkin and fold it on my empty plate. "Whenever you deflect with shit like this, it's usually because I'm on the right track. Tell me."

Mirage looks at me with wide eyes, like I brandished a weapon.

"Are you being serious right now?"

"Are you gonna tell me of your own volition, or am I gonna have to…?" I bump the table with my knee so that it shakes, sending ripples through our untouched glasses of water.

"*Don't*," he hisses.

I bump it again with both knees, relishing now, because even if he isn't hiding anything, that's one too many times that Mom has surfaced in his repertoire of guilt tactics.

"Oasis, *stop*," Mirage hisses, flattening his hands on the table. "Helena tried to get in touch with you, okay?"

Slowly, the chaotic mirth drains out of me, taking with it all cohesive thoughts, leaving just her name echoing in my empty head.

"What?"

"Helena found me on Google and asked to see you."

"When?" I demand.

Mirage glances at a patron walking past us towards the bathroom and gives them a small, embarrassed smile.

"Last week."

"Were you ever going to tell me?"

Mirage holds my gaze. "No."

A half-laugh of disbelief makes its way out of me, but nothing is funny. "*Do you have any idea how much she meant to me?*"

"I don't care," Mirage seethes. "*Look* at what those people made you do."

Something in me snaps, like a thread over a candle. Flipping the table isn't enough.

"Look?" I repeat. "That's what you want? You want me to look?" I stand up and tug my flannel off, so that he and everyone else can see the semi-sheer tank top that had been meant for Laura's eyes only. "*You* look, Mirage. You look at me," I say loudly, drawing more attention, "and you tell me how come this isn't punishment enough. *Tell me why you get to play God with my life.*"

His jaw drops.

Good.

"Oasis—"

"*Don't,*" I cut across. "I can't keep making excuses for you. How can you say you have nightmares about me dying when you make it so hard to be alive?"

Mirage flinches.

I see the hurt in his eyes, but it's too late: the dragon is out of her cage.

"I'm proud of you...for this." I gesture at him, the table, the restaurant at large full of staring patrons. "But I didn't survive a heart attack just for you to break my heart every time I'm with you." I lick my lips, all too aware of how nauseous I am, of how close I am to crying, of how long my arms have been out of my sleeves. "Take care of *this* Oasis, Mirage. I'm done."

My eyes glaze with tears. The last I see of my brother's face is a stark turn of the tables: him gaping at me over a full plate of food while I storm away from an empty one, speeding past patrons reading menus with *my* name on the top.

I'm shaking and out of breath by the time I get to the bathroom, struggling to get my arms back in my sleeves. I'm crying by the time I get into a stall, tears and sobs having snuck up and yanked me in a headlock.

I hear the familiar rushing, squeaking sound of a torrent of bats, and I feel Laura's arms around me, her cheek against mine, her lips on my ear.

"I just don't get it," I say, my voice in a million pieces. "Is it really that hard to love me?"

She lets go and holds me at arm's length, gaping at me like I drove a knife into her back. "In all my years, nothing has been easier. You must understand this."

I wish I did. I wish I could stop feeling like everyone I know secretly wishes they didn't know me. That one day everyone, including Laura, will realize I'm a lost cause.

"I come from a time when love came second to dynasty," Laura continues. "You live in a gentler era. Betrayal from a brother must sting differently when power is not the motive." She unrolls a fistful of tissue and uses it to blot my face. "Blood is a powerful tonic, but it is not always family. Knowing this may help you and your brother, should you choose to mend what has become of your bond."

I take a few deep breaths until I can do so without feeling like I'll sob.

With her hand, she wipes away a few tears that escaped the tissue. "I am sorry to have facilitated this pain. I desperately wanted to trust him."

"Me too." I get my arms in my sleeves at last and lean against the stall door with my back to it. "I'm sorry we didn't get to celebrate us."

"The night has not yet begun," she says with a coy smile. "You and I are scholars in the discipline of entertaining ourselves on short notice."

My head hurts, my throat hurts, my heart hurts from where my brother ripped it open, but some appetites are impossible to kill.

Laura licks her lips, deepening her dimples, and pulls off her cardigan.

"If I asked you to fuck me like you will not see me in eight days, what would you do?"

I reach for her hand, tug her into my arms. "I'd fuck you like I'll never see you again in my life."

A sharp smile, a deep inhale. She kisses me, lips journeying from my face to my neck. Having sex in the bathroom outside of my brother's restaurant is a new level of off the rails, but it's one I don't mind reaching if it means that for now, I forget what came before.

Laura stops kissing me.

When I open my eyes, hers are closed. She's holding her stomach, pinching the bridge of her nose.

Just as quickly as it drained, adrenaline is back in my veins.

"What is it?"

She makes a noise in her throat, but doesn't speak. Then she whirls on her heel, drops to her knees, and vomits, clutching the porcelain toilet rim with both hands.

It flushes automatically, but not before I see the purplish red tint swirling in the water.

My body quivers as I lower myself next to her.

"Baby, look at me. What's wrong?"

The gloss is gone from her lips, replaced with a sheen of dark red. She opens her mouth as though to speak, then grabs the toilet and heaves up all her wine.

I reach above my head for more tissue as she slumps into me.

"Laura, are you okay?" I ask, shaking so badly that the words hardly make it out.

"I am okay," Laura says feebly, wiping her mouth on her wrist. She uses the toilet and my arm to pull herself to her feet. "Once you have reconciled with Mirage, you must ask him why he served me spoiled wine."

"The wine did this to you?"

"Nothing else could have. It is the only thing I have consumed," she says, holding onto both my arms, gaping at the toilet.

"Could that be part of the problem?" I ask.

She looks me up and down, scowling, and shrugs back into her cardigan. "There is no problem," she says. "We will celebrate us, and then I will sleep, and then I will return to you."

Laura starts to open the door, but I grab her hand, putting Batty in a stranglehold, and force her to face me.

"Laura, you are the *only* stable thing in my life right now. You can't get sick," I say, dangerously close to crying all over again. "I was your human before I was your girlfriend. Why won't you drink my blood?"

"I will," she says, a quiet rasp. "In time."

"Puking your vampire Soylent equivalent seems like a pretty

appropriate time." I look around the stall, as if the steel walls or tiled floor will back me up. My eyes return to her face. "Do *you* think I'm broken, too?"

Her jaw drops. "I have seen you, Oasis. Your heart has weathered maelstroms." She cups my face, shaking her head, looking as close to tears as I feel. "Do not let it beat askance for me."

"Laura—"

She puts her forehead against mine.

"Please. I am your baby," she says softly, rending my heart. "Please take me home to be with you, that I may afterwards rest and return to your arms."

I want to press—to push until the truth oozes out like pus from a pimple. Instead, I kiss her nose.

"You're my baby," I murmur. "Let's go."

Leaving the stall with my arm around her shoulders feels like a mistake, but I've already thrown down once tonight with someone who was hiding something, and Laura isn't Mirage.

Things with him have felt like a lost cause ever since I woke up shackled to a bed, but Laura isn't a lost cause. She's *the* cause—the first person on my mind when I wake up, the last to leave it when I go to sleep. We've been together for a month, and now the only life I can imagine without her is the one that made me sometimes wish the defibrillator had malfunctioned.

ragnarok

August 27, 2019

Whilst they played wits against me—against me who commanded nations, and intrigued for them, and fought for them, hundreds of years before they were born—I was countermining them.

ragnarok

Years ago, the shadow gripped Bird Bones tight and raised her from the bowels of New Jersey, where she oversaw an ungrateful batch of humans who did not appreciate her compassionate reign—or so the shadow said as it carried her to its dungeon with promises that the birthday girl would take kindlier to her presence.

It was right.

Bird Bones is the fifth pillar in the family comprised of a human, a vampire, a vampire witch, and *the* vampire—the shadow, currently stretched out on a sofa in its dungeon while she kneads its chest, trying her best to provide it some comfort as its friend sits in an adjacent armchair with a clipboard and a pen.

"Is this the first time?"

"No," the shadow replies.

She marks something on its page. "When was the first time?"

"July twenty-fifth."

"And the last?"

"Before I slept."

Another few marks.

"When did you last sleep?"

"I awoke on the third," says the shadow. "I sleep at sunset today."

A series of marks, and a frown on her freckled face. "Are you feeling disoriented?"

"At times."

"Moody?"

"Less and less."

The shadow's friend sighs. She looks like a human on the surface—a medium-built woman with rippling muscular arms, wide curvy hips, and shrewd green eyes. She rakes a hand through the mane of kinky red hair from which she gets her name—the red wolf, though through Bird Bones' feline eyes, *the lime-green wolf* would be a better fit for the only dog she respects.

"What do you think?" Asks the shadow.

The red wolf sighs gravely and turns the clipboard around, revealing an illustration of a flying fox bat with balls so big they don't fit on the page.

"I'm afraid it's terminal, Vlad."

The shadow heaves a spluttering sigh and covers its eyes with its many-ringed fingers.

"C'mon, Bats. We both know what's wrong with you," the red wolf says, balling up the drawing and tossing it in the shadow's direction.

It bounces off the shadow's head; Bird Bones sits up on its chest, debating. Then she leaps down to investigate.

The shadow sits up, pouting. "Return to me, beloved."

Bird Bones doesn't abide. She can't until this ball of paper understands the reach of her wrath. She swats it across the stone floor, where it settles against the leg of the red wolf's chair.

"I don't understand you, creature," the red wolf says, nibbling her pen. "Why are you doing this to yourself?"

"Why am I consulting a Viking puppy for vampire health issues?" The shadow asks darkly. "This is a good question."

"You *have* a human," the red wolf continues, as if the shadow never spoke. "Apparently one who doesn't mind this ugly face."

The shadow slides off the sofa and paces away, leaving Bird Bones to guard the ball of paper from beneath.

The red wolf bares her canines, adorned with filigreed gold grill, a low growl rising in her throat. "Your Ragnarok is coming."

"I believe in no hell but the one I will not see," says the shadow.

"Ragnarok isn't hell. It's Revelations." The red wolf pulls out her phone. "It's right under your nose—or would be if you weren't so stubborn." She sighs and pockets the device. "I can't believe you found a human who tolerates you not having a phone."

The shadow strolls to the bookshelf, gazing up at a bound black book. It rubs its lip, sets its teeth to bite its thumbnail, then drops its hand and turns its back to the book.

"Why haven't you tucked in yet?" She asks with less humor and more concern. "You can tell me."

The shadow remains silent.

"Is it because of that train of humans you ran through? The ones from that book you keep burning?" The red wolf presses with a vexed frown. "Nathaniel...Amelia...and...Lola?"

"Jonathan, Mina, and Lucy," the shadow corrects quietly.

"I don't understand what you were doing in that part of Europe anyway," the red wolf says, baffled. "Once you're west of Czechia and south of Sweden, you may as well be in Niflheim."

"They were writing good books and dressing nicely in that century," the shadow says with a sour scowl. "I could resurrect and destroy Van Helsing again and again until the end of the world and it would not recompense me for all the outfits I lost when he destroyed my castle."

"I bet. That man really hated you," the red wolf remarks. "Was the sex with his wife worth it?"

Again, the shadow is silent, but a small smile comes and goes.

"You and your milfs," the red wolf mutters. "Anyway, I need you back in battle shape, Voivode. We have a common enemy collaborating with an enemy that's exclusively yours," she says with another growl that makes the shadow cross its arms.

Bird Bones swats the ball of paper. It ricochets off the red wolf's boot, skittering out of reach.

The shadow scoops it up, clicks its tongue to lure her from hiding as it resumes its spot on the sofa. She obliges and curls up on its empty chest.

"I put a nose on the uh...Van Helsing Institute...for you," says the red wolf, barely repressing hysterical laughter. "They've been using your retail therapy to try and find you."

"Oasis told me of this," the shadow says. "It has been a thing of the past since the day I decided to love her."

"Maybe, but she couldn't have told you that they just hired a freelance hypnotist. Hers could be next in the pile of *bookish bodies*," the red wolf taunts, canines sparkling.

Bird Bones stirs as the shadow stiffens beneath her, raising its head slightly.

"Jacob must have lost his patience," she continues. "Now someone we both despise is doing what he used to, which is run around New York following the trail of empty shelves, trying to hypnotize innocent cashiers into describing you—except our favorite freelancer is using this job offer to sate its appetite."

The shadow rubs its face, groaning through its fingers.

"*Parasite*," it seethes. "Will 1897 haunt me for the rest of eternity?"

"That's the nature of memory, Bats." The red wolf heaves a sigh of its own. "I should have killed it when I had the chance. This is what happens when you treat revenge like a meal with courses."

"No matter what it seems, it is never too late to send a soul to hell," the shadow says, scratching Bird Bones under her chin. After a moment, it says, "I am unwell, Ásttora."

"Really? I had no idea." The red wolf gets to its feet, hands tucked in its pockets. "Does your family know?"

"No."

"Your girlfriend?"

The shadow says nothing.

"Wow," the red wolf whispers. "Damn near six hundred years old and you still care if a human thinks you're a monster?"

"She knows I am one," the shadow says laconically, looking to the ceiling. "It does not mean she should bear witness just yet."

The red wolf looks to Bird Bones, confused and pleading.

"That's fucking delusional. Drink her fucking blood, you stupid bat."

The shadow is silent for a long time, massaging the stubble on its chin with one hand, scratching Bird Bones with the other.

"Will you watch over her while I sleep?"

"Yeah, but if the parasite strikes, I'm striking back," the red wolf says simply.

"But you will be sure," the shadow says, fire creeping into its voice, "that no harm befalls her?"

"I won't let her sustain any damage she can't walk away from. You've been hangry for too fucking long," the red wolf says, round nose wrinkled. "I'm ready for Oasis to deliver me from that. Just go to sleep, wake up, and drink your girl before you get so sick that you have to call the friend who can actually diagnose you." She raises a provocative brow. "The one with wings?"

The shadow cradles Bird Bones in its arms so as not to jostle her when it sits up, jaw set, eyes flaming.

"It will not come to that." It releases her and dissolves into a cauldron of bats that takes off towards the door. But the cauldron of bats partially congeals in midair just before the threshold, and the shadow falls to the floor as though rained down from a cloud.

"*Odin's eye*," the red wolf gasps. She rushes to the shadow's side as scattered bats crawl back to its form. "Are you okay? How many paws am I holding up?" She asks, holding up none.

The shadow groans and rolls onto its back, intact, but immobile.

The red wolf scoffs in disbelief. "You're only doing this so I'll dig the old dirt out of your bed and put the new dirt in."

"I am not," the shadow moans as Bird Bones sniffs its face. "I am ill."

"Whatever," the red wolf says, already on its way out the door. "Come on."

Bird Bones meows and leaps down to investigate.

The shadow turns to her and winks before peeling itself off the floor to follow, scooping her up along the way.

nineteen

Listen to them—the children of the night. What music they make!

nineteen

By the time day five of Laura's eight-day sleep rolls around, I'm feeling way more in tune with the turbulent grey sky than I have in a long time. It's past noon, and I'm working hard to push the clouds out of *my* metaphorical sky before our candidate shows up at 12:30 for his paid trial shift, which Kennedy and I both agreed is less disrespectful than an unpaid interview.

The plan is to have him help with online orders so that he can have an idea of where stuff is before we open tomorrow. The problem is that we're already out of bubble mailers, the latest box of unpriced books is still unopened, and the register computer has been updating all morning.

"I'm about to say fuck this," Kennedy says, jiggling the mouse. Even the swirling cursor is frozen.

"Tell you what—if August can talk the computer into working, we hire him, no questions asked."

Kennedy shakes his head, alarmed. "It's your call on whether we hire the guy, but we can*not* set the bar that low."

"You're right," I sigh. I'm starting to wish there was no bar to set. I don't think I have the capacity for more change, including another face to see on a regular basis, but who am I to gatekeep someone's employment?

After another ten minutes of groaning and lip smacking at the computer, Kennedy gives up and retreats to the office. At least I had the forethought to print some of the shipping labels yesterday. I tuck them into the pages of the books that have no mailers, then focus on taping labels to the mailers we *do* have.

Usually, tasks like this lubricate the spaces between thoughts where anxiety festers, but the definition of *usual* changed when I let Laura into my life, and anxiety is much too small a word for the pit in my heart. I wonder if she can hear it—if the pain of knowing that she's hiding something from me has a rhythm of its own.

Someone knocks hard on the door, rattling the window. I jump and drop the tape while attempting to cut a piece. It plummets with a tearing sound and rolls away.

I groan and step over the unfurling adhesive disaster. I open the door without peeking through the signs.

The pale young man on the other side of the threshold is wearing all black—black acid wash jeans, a black Darth Vader hoodie, black Converse. His light brown hair is cropped short. Grey eyes glitter beneath his fine brows.

"Hello," he says with a smile. "I'm August."

The breeze is too sharp for my sleeves, but his smile is so familiar that all I can do is frown.

"I'm here for my first shift. I hope."

"Yes, you are." I step aside and close the door after him. "Sorry. I'm Oasis. I thought I recognized you for a second."

"You do," August says as he pulls back his hood. "I'm probably filed away as *guy who can't read a Closed sign.*"

The memory rises slowly from its grave.

"Actually, I had you filed under *creep.*"

He inhales sharply and gives me a chagrined smile. "Here's my chance to set the record straight."

"Better make it count." I lead him past the register and point up the hallway. "The office is on the right. I'll be up here when you're done doing logistical stuff with Kennedy."

"Yes, ma'am."

I narrow my eyes at his back when he walks away. I remember our first meeting with crystal clarity now, but for some reason, that doesn't feel right. I feel like I've seen him somewhere else. But I have five hours to remember where.

In the meantime, I evaluate the damage left by the rogue tape. It stuck to two mailers and their labels, my pencil, the counter, the back of the display case, the leg of my stool, and a foot of hardwood before ending its journey beside an unopened box of books.

I shake my head and set to work peeling the tape off its victims. I hear the office door open as I strip part of my pencil of its yellow while freeing it.

"...show you how to use the register and everything," Kennedy's saying. "She's got a system going back here, so if you have any questions, ask her."

He and August appear at the end of the hallway, August removing his jacket while Kennedy shrugs into his own.

"Where are you going?" I ask.

"Home. I'm gonna play some more *Castlevania*. You two don't need me here," he says, zipping his jacket up to his chin. "August is the perfect fit."

I look at August, who looks away bashfully. For a moment, I'm speechless: I could've sworn Kennedy said that was up to *me* to determine.

"Are you sure you need to leave? I'm not an expert on everything," I say pointedly.

"August is a fast learner," Kennedy says, bright as a star. "You'll figure it out together."

"See ya," August says, waving as Kennedy opens the door and disappears up the street.

All I can do is stare.

Even if I don't get the final say in August's employment, how could he leave me alone with some guy neither of us knows?

"Alright, boss. What's next?"

That's a good question.

"Well...usually we just..." My stomach growls.

August inhales sharply. "Maybe we should pause training so you can eat. I can order food if you want," he says. "Whatever fuels my redemption."

I look around and scoff. One of the worst parts of dissociating is recognizing it for what it is and not being able to stop it. The things I see on a near daily basis all look foreign and incomprehensible—all because Kennedy left me alone with this guy. It's hard not to stare, because not knowing where I remember his face from is as unsettling as being alone with him.

"Do you mind walking to the store with me?" I ask. "We need more mailers anyway."

"Okay," August says. He waits for me to put a beanie over my braids and a second, heavier plaid jacket over my everyday flannel.

Outside, he tilts his head skyward, grey eyes the same color as the clouds overhead. Sundays are the deadest I ever see this corner of Manhattan. The gelato spot up the block has only a few patrons; across the street, a Black woman with a salt and pepper bob looks like she's relaxing in the grass with the Humane Society's entire canine roster. They're laying down in an orderly fashion while she smokes a joint and chats on the phone.

A lithe copper-red poodle with a black handkerchief around its long neck catches my eye. Unlike the other dogs, who are either gazing at their owner, looking left and right at pedestrians, or lazing with their eyes closed, this one is staring right at me.

"Are you a dog person?" August asks.

"They're sweet," I say. "Are you?"

August shakes his head. "I got attacked by one when I was younger. I'd outlaw them if I could."

"Don't say that too loud in public," I warn.

He snickers. "The public should think twice about assuming everyone wants to pet their ugly dog."

I try not to laugh, but I can't help recalling Talon glaring at a dog when we went to Central Park. By the time we're on our way back with a bag of supplies and, in my case, a honey bun and an Arizona, I'm feeling a little guilty for being so affronted that Kennedy left us alone.

We take a different route back, down a street full of brownstones teeming with activity.

"Are you from New York?" I ask.

"The Netherlands," he says. "But I've lived in America most of my life. I spent a lot of time in Michigan."

"Did you like it?"

"I loved it. Detroit was an amazing place once," August says wistfully. "The Dutch were mistaken to give up their attempts at a colony there."

I eat more of my honey bun to keep from commenting.

"Where are you from?" He asks.

"Kansas."

"Capital of prohibition. Nice," he says, grinning. "What brought you this way?"

"It's a long story. Basically, I…" I trail off.

August's eyes are fixed on the direction we came from, his nostrils flared wide.

Seconds tick by. I tense too.

"What's wrong?"

"I…"

Two teenagers round the corner—one with a fistful of CDs and the other with a leash in each hand. Two black Rottweilers trot side-by-side on one dual leash; a pit bull with a vibrant crimson coat strains the other.

The teens stop at a brownstone to speak to the residents; I catch the words *mixtape* and *SoundCloud*. They pass over a CD and continue up the block in our direction. The Rottweilers are allowing themselves to be petted, but the pit bull's neon green eyes are on us.

"Is that for me?" I ask as they approach, eliciting dual beaming grins.

"Anything for a lady rocking plaid on plaid. Check it." The one nearest whisks a CD off the top of his stack like a poker dealer. "J Dilla meets John Carpenter."

"Wow." I look closely at the artwork. The D in the title, *Devin's Night*, is in blackletter font. "I can't wait to listen."

He grins. "I'm on SoundCloud, too," he says, indicating the link on the sleeve. "And BandCamp, if you tryna get ya boy to NYU."

"You bet. August, do you...?"

But August isn't next to me anymore; he's halfway up the block, watching warily.

"I forgot he gets nervous around dogs," I say.

"Your friend Gus is missing out. Cinnamon's a sweetie pie," the kid says. "'Cept when it comes to waking everybody in the building up when the mailman's tryna keep it lowkey. Ain't that right, Cin?"

Cinnamon looks over her shoulder, as though sheepish.

"Thank you," I say, waving the CD. "I can't wait to listen."

"Cinnamon—c'mon, girl."

Her canines bare; a snarl creeps from her throat, but her green eyes aren't on me. If I didn't know better, I'd say she was glaring at August up the street, like she overheard him saying how he really feels about dogs.

I drop the CD in the bag of supplies and hurry up the street after him.

"Sorry. I can never say no to new music."

"I understand," he says quietly.

A fresh wave of guilt follows me all the way back to Full Cauldron. Once we're inside, I make my way behind the register and try to mentally recalibrate.

At least the computer finally restarted.

"Alright—I think I know what's first," I say through my last bite of honeybun, but the space in front of the counter is empty. I ball the wrapper up in my fist and stuff it in the trash. "Where'd you go?"

"Here," August says, still out of view. He strolls from the pathway of shelves leading to the fantasy section and holds up a copy of *The Hobbit*. "Your signs sold me on this."

I grin, though I'm mostly relieved to see that he doesn't seem upset about the dog encounter. I nudge the trash can aside and beckon for him to join me. "Let's get you register trained so you can learn to do some selling of your own."

August scratches the back of his head, wincing. "I'm claustrophobic."

"Sorry," I say, hurrying out. "I promise I'm not doing this on purpose."

"It's alright. It's a Sunday," he says as we swap places, me in front of the counter, him behind it. "I'm sure you'd rather be with your girl."

I almost forgot I used Laura as a rebuff when we first met. "That's usually the case."

"Where did you meet?" August asks, too pleasant and inquisitive for me to feel as ruffled as I do.

"We met here," I say.

"Bookstore romance, huh? Some people have all the luck." He jiggles the mouse, clearing the word-of-the-day screensaver.

"Password is alucard," I say, somewhat bitterly. Just because August isn't *that* bad to be around doesn't mean Kennedy's off the hook for choosing *Castlevania* over helping me train him. "All lowercase."

August inputs the password and hits enter. The error noise booms from the tiny speakers. He tries again with the same result.

"Is caps lock on?" I ask.

"No," he says, frowning at the keyboard. He tries a third and fourth time.

I start to join him, then think better of it and put my elbows on the counter, nudging the monitor so that I can see. There's only six characters in the password box.

"You might be spelling it wrong," I say, pointing.

"You said Master, right? How many ways can you spell that?"

"I…" I didn't say master. I didn't say anything close to master. I blink a few times. Each millisecond of darkness behind my eyelids twitches back the curtains of reality. I back away from the counter; I try to put my heartbeat in check right away, which is as useful as trying to catch fog in my fingertips.

August takes his hands off the keyboard and clicks his tongue softly. He chews the inside of his lip, eyes hard as steel. He puts his hands in his pockets and sidles from behind the register.

I whirl and lunge for the door, stumbling back when my hand collides with a solid wall of cold.

He came out of nowhere—just a whir of sound and blurry black. Now he stands between me and the only way out.

"Jacob Seward says hello. I told him I'd keep it clean this time, but you're not making it—"

I cut him off by raising my fingers in the sign of the cross.

August hisses and shuts his eyes as smoke seeps from between his eyelids. He opens his mouth in a frothing snarl, cowering against the door like he's in the path of jetting firehose.

I back away a few steps, then turn on my heel and run for the office.

Kennedy's Catholic.

Reluctantly Catholic, but Catholic enough to keep a rosary in the office; I've seen him nibbling on it while doing payroll, swinging it around on his fingertip like a lasso.

I slam and lock the door and turn on the lights. The desk is a mess of paperwork, merchandise catalogs, ARCs, books in need of repair. My body's shaking so badly that my search only makes it messier.

"Come on, Oasis," August says from the hallway. "Can't it just be the two of us for a little while longer? My daddy's posse is nowhere near as fun as I am."

He laughs, full of mirth.

I ignore him, rifling through the desk drawer, sifting through paperclips, rubber bands, box cutters, loose change.

"I smell that," August says in a sing-song voice.

My chest is heaving when I look down at my hands. There's a slice in the middle of my left index finger and a bloodstain on a broken box cutter with an exposed blade.

I'm bleeding too profusely to hold my fingers up without wincing, but this isn't how I will die. My heart didn't make it through cardiac arrest just to stop pumping at the hands of some random vampire. I grab a thick Sharpie and a stack of index cards, then tear the cap off the marker with my teeth, holding my breath to tamp the fumes. I draw cross after cross, building a deck while

August monologues. Three quarters of the way through the index cards, my finger is too slick with blood to hold the marker. I let it fall from my writing hand and hold the cards in my right, curved like I'm about to shuffle.

I ease the door open a little, showing an inch of my face and body.

"It's alright," August says. He's standing in the middle of the hallway, blocking my view of the *Star Wars* display straight ahead. "Over a hundred years a vampire, and I'll never get tired of playing with my f—"

I wrench the office door open all the way, raise my right hand, and let the deck of crucifixes fly out like playing cards at a casino.

It works.

He closes his smoking grey eyes and flails against the wall, giving me room to run past him, and around the corner.

The clever idea falls to tatters when I get to the door.

It's blocked.

Between me running into Kennedy's office and back out, August moved the racks of comics.

There's no way out.

"Unfortunately, we're on someone else's schedule," he hisses, gripping my shoulder, pushing me to my knees when I try to fight back.

I try to kick; reach over my shoulder and grab a fistful of comics to hit him in the head with. He grabs my hands roughly and pins them to the floor.

"Where's Master been getting his fix? Here?" He asks, tracing my jugular. His hand travels down, hovering over my stomach, like he's about to reach between my legs. "Or here? Either way, *he's being greedy*," he whispers.

Somehow, I draw enough saliva in my dry mouth to spit in his face. "Go to hell."

August's grip tightens, but he doesn't wipe it off. "Look at me," he growls with his face close to mine.

It feels like my heart's never beat this fast in my life.

I'm going to die.

Are you listening to my heart, Dracula?

I'm going to die.

August's fangs are still exposed, glinting in the lights above. His sparkling eyes find mine. His pupils widen as though someone pushed a button, leaving a rim of grey iris.

"You'd rather be with me, Oasis. You'd rather be mine."

My pulse slows. "That's not true."

"It's true. You want to be with me, Oasis," he says; his pupils shrink to pinpricks, then bloom again, darker than black. "You want to be mine."

"No." I know who I want to be with. I know whose I am.

"You should be with me, Oasis," August says, a soft plea. Again, his pupils shrink; again they bloom, this time breaking through his irises like the yolk of an egg, painting his eyeballs in darkness. "You should be mine."

I don't think I should, but I'm not sure. The only sure thing is him, standing in front of me, a bright face in a dark world.

"You're with me now, Oasis. You're mine," August says.

"I'm yours?"

"You always were," he says, stroking my cheek. "And you always will be."

"And I always will be," I whisper, holding his hand in place.

He wipes his face with his shirt and smiles.

I sit on the floor while August puts the comic rack back in place. Then he pulls me to my feet, straightening my flannel.

All I can do is watch, smiling.

I'm with him.

I'm his.

He raises my left hand to his face, frowning. I wince as he stretches out my finger. Fresh blood oozes from the cut. Streaks of it have dried on my palm and knuckles.

"Does it hurt?" August asks.

"A little," I murmur.

"Don't worry." He opens his mouth and licks my hand, dragging his tongue around and between my fingers, suckling the slice in my finger.

I don't stop him.

I'm his.

Wisps of blue peek between the clouds.

The sun is still hidden, but August is the only light I need.

"Where are we going?" I ask.

"Somewhere you'll love," he says, wrapping his arm around my shoulders. "Close your eyes, okay? We'll be there when you wake up."

I don't ask questions.

I close my eyes and let my head sink into his chest.

I'm his.

I always have been.

*

When I open my eyes, I'm not in Full Cauldron. Memories of my exit from the store knock around my skull as I sit bolt upright, breathing hard.

I'm alone in a windowless square room, laying on an unadorned rectangular bed with a tube of fluorescent light humming overhead. I'm fully clothed and unrestrained, rendering my initial fear—that I'm once again institutionalized—null and void. But the absence of handcuffs doesn't change the fact that I'm alone in a windowless square room, with nothing but a steel door to suggest a world beyond this place.

There are scratches on the wall to my right, close to the bed—HEL and the start of a P.

My heart thuds as I search my pants and flannels. I don't have my phone. I don't know where I am, and no one else will, either.

My cut finger throbs when I grab the door handle, pushing and pulling with no results.

I step back from it, fighting to stay calm as I backtrack through my memories. August's face and voice fill me with disgust, but he isn't the one I need to worry about: *Jacob Seward said hello*.

The door opens and my pounding heart pounds even harder.

Dr. Seward stands on the other side. He's wearing a plain black t-shirt and blue jeans, and his beard looks recently trimmed. "Good afternoon, Oasis. I'm sorry this is how we have to meet again."

He isn't alone.

I count five other heads behind him, all peering in like they're at the zoo. A sixth sidles into view behind them: August.

My fight or flight instinct malfunctions, overridden by fury. I march closer and make the sign of the cross. "*You nasty piece of shit.*"

His fangs crackle into view and smoke issues from his eyes.

Dr. Seward blocks August from sight.

I stumble back to avoid a collision, glaring. "What am I doing here?"

"I think you know the answer to that," he says matter-of-factly. "You're here to help us."

"And who's *us?*" I demand, glaring at his silent companions.

"This is Oliver Morris and his son, Brian," he says, gesturing to the two men on the left. "This is Ella Holmwood and her husband, Drew."

A middle-aged blonde woman nods while her husband, a black-haired man with glasses, puts his arm around her.

"And this is my sister Heather Seward," Dr. Seward finishes.

She waves her fingers unenthusiastically.

I look from one unfamiliar face to the next. I recognize their surnames thanks to Laura and Talon, but the novelty of meeting the descendants of fictional characters wore off at the second Van Helsing.

"Are you people supposed to matter to me?"

"We're descended from the men and woman who brought Dracula to his knees in 1897," says Oliver. "And we're the ones who're gonna kill him dead for good."

"The sentient search dog says you outed yourself with the sign of the cross," says Brian. Both him and Oliver have heavy Texan accents.

"Just because I know vampires are real doesn't mean I know the vampire you're looking for," I say, laying the exasperation on thickly.

"*These are not the vamps you're looking for,*" August mocks from the hallway.

Oliver grabs him by the neck of his hoodie. "Keep inching towards uselessness, Van Helsing," he sneers. "I'll rip your head off and barbecue your bones myself."

Dr. Seward throws August an additional dark look, vanishing his smile. Then he turns back to me. "We know that Count Dracula has been living in New York for at *least* fifteen years. We have FedEx shipping manifests documenting oversized shipments from multiple landscaping companies in Târgoviste to a nonexistent address in Fishkill," he says. "We know he's been buying copies of *Dracula* in bulk at bookstores across New York. We have point-of-sale records going back to 2004," he adds, as Heather brandishes a manila folder.

She holds it out for me to take, but I back up, out of reach.

"We have footage showing *no one* being on the customer side of the register during no less than fifteen transactions at Borders, Barnes and Noble, and the Strand," Dr. Seward continues tightly.

The dots begin to connect.

I'm not the first person they've interrogated. He asked August to keep it clean this time because the other times…weren't.

Back in Central Park, the passing notion of a bookstore serial killer had been just that—a passing notion. Now the bookstore serial killer is watching me with vile grey eyes.

"This institute was founded for the sole purpose of investigating *every* supposed *coincidence* affiliated with the monster known as Dracula," he says. "Is it a coincidence that the day before I paid a visit to your store, the pattern lapsed?"

If I'd placated Dr. Seward to begin with instead of snapping, I might not be here now. I almost feel nostalgic for those few days where I wondered whether he was a roleplayer, but no: His obsession is generational *and* well-funded enough to moonlight as a police investigation.

"If I knew Dracula, why would I tell you anything about him?"

"Because he has an extensive suite of mind powers—ones that make hypnosis and possession look like assault and battery," Dr. Seward says while the rest of the VHI look on. "He can put tastes on your tongue, and sounds in your ears, and memories in your mind. He can change your dreams and rewrite what's in your heart. He can inflict the torments of an army with a single thought."

"He could have you right under his spell," Oliver says. "Same as Lucy Westenra all those years back."

"She underwent a great trauma just shy of her twentieth birthday. Count Dracula corrupted her, body and soul," Dr. Seward says gravely.

As he says this, the Morrises back out of the crowd, giving August room to sidle closer. They're all packed too tightly together in and around the doorway for me to even consider ramming my way through.

"Dr. Van Helsing encouraged her to journal, but Count Dracula shared a psychic link with her," Dr. Seward says. "Much of what she wrote in her delirium was destroyed when he possessed her fingertips. She died a slow, painful death, fraught with psychosis."

Several moments pass during which my brain struggles to attach meanings to the words.

"Corrupted?" I repeat.

"He finds broken people and shapes them in his image," Dr. Seward says, more earnestly than before, seeming emboldened by whatever's on my face. "I see no reason for you to be next."

Broken.

The word I sometimes see hovering above my head like a thought bubble whenever I glimpse my reflection.

It might not be too late to lie my way out of this.

But that word—*broken*—makes me want to act broken too; to give the world a reason to strap me down and jam a needle full of sedative into my thigh.

"You seem like a smart woman, Oasis," Heather Seward says, like she's slinging out the good cop routine. "Help us end him. Tell us where he is."

I emerge from the corner of my mind swathed in rage. "I can't wait to tell him how many of you there are," I say, looking from one to the next. "It's been a long time since he killed for sport."

August laughs. "She's funny."

"Van Helsing, make yourself useful or I will put you down right here," Dr. Seward seethes.

In a split second, August is right on front of me, grabbing my arms too fast for me to react. My ass hits the bed again. He grips my shoulders and pushes me back so forcefully that the air leaves my lungs.

I close my eyes tightly so that I can't see his.

"I'm just the muscle now, sadly," he whispers, lips hovering near my forehead. "Can't I get just one more look of those pretty brown eyes?"

"Move it, mosquito," Brian snaps as heavy footsteps resound in the hallway.

"Hypnosis is a dying art," Dr. Seward says. He sounds further away, but I don't open my eyes to see where he is. "Abraham Van Helsing knew this."

Maybe if I close them tight enough, I'll realize that I'm still at Full Cauldron nursing a hunger headache, because this—this can't be real.

"He realized that if possession was the method of the monster, it should also be the method of the man hunting him," Dr. Seward says. "He also wanted to be certain that Lucy's death wasn't in vain, and so he took samples of her blood as the scaffolding for a possession serum that's been in development for over a century."

My eyes open. My heart surges into my throat.

August isn't the only one standing over me, blocking the hiccupping light.

The Morrises are both there in doctor's coats, one holding a syringe, one holding a vial of viscous red fluid.

"Wait," I say, voice fragmented with the fear I've been ignoring out of spite. I try to sit up, to look Dr. Seward in the eye, but I can barely lift my head, and can't see anything but the hill of my chest rising and falling. "You don't have to do this."

"We didn't want to," Brian says as he pierces vial with syringe. "Ain't that right, Jake?"

"We hoped the sound of your heartbeat in distress may have pulled the beast out of hiding," Dr. Seward confirms. "It was a long shot, expecting such a creature to be capable of affection."

August blocks the light with his entire head, pink lips pursed in a mocking puppy-eyed look.

"Hear that? Maybe he just doesn't love you."

My mouth stays glued shut.

He loves me.

He loves me because Laura loves me.

I kick and squirm as multiple sets of hands hold my limbs and head in place. A needle pierces the crook of my arm. My heart throbs as the fluid enters my veins.

Laura loves me.

Knowing this is like knowing my own name, which is…

I don't know what my name is, or anything that came before this.

The needle comes out, the fight leaves my body, and the importance of my escaping this place disappears.

They all let go.

I sit up and gaze around.

This is someone else's body now; all I am doing is holding onto it.

"Remember not to use her name," Oliver warns.

"Look at me," Dr. Seward orders.

I do.

"Tell me if you know Count Dracula."

"I…" I falter. There's something wrong here. This *is* my body—reluctantly mine at times, but mine nonetheless. I grit my teeth and keep my eyes squeezed shut. "I don't know…"

"The first vampire," he says. "Do you know him?"

"*I don't know him.*" My eyes open, and I'm once again gone from myself, aching to cry. "But I want to."

An awed smile spreads over his mouth. "Have you fed him?"

His face blurs through my tears. I'd rip my heart out right now if I had the means. I don't remember who he is, but the hole in my soul where he belongs throbs like a snapped bone.

"She's resisting," Oliver says, vexed.

"He says...I will." I lick my quivering lips. "*He doesn't trust me,*" I whisper.

"Where is he?" Dr. Seward asks.

"Asleep in the earth."

"She's an artist," says August. "Make her draw his face."

"Let's take her upstairs."

"Not with the level of emotion she's showing," Brian says, throwing out a hand to keep Drew in place. "This stuff ain't like mind-to-mind possession. Without someone on the other end of the link, she'll break off if we press too hard."

"Prep a second dose," Dr. Seward instructs. "Get her some paper."

Their voices swim above my pulse. It feels like I'm bound in chains, trapped in my body, unfeeling but for the need to sob. I blink away tears as Heather hands over a paper with several printed screenshots from a bookstore's security camera footage. One shows a young man passing a stack of books over the register; the next frame, the books are gone, and he's waving at the door, which is closed. In the next frame, it's opening, and in the next, closed once more, like a ghost walked through it.

She puts a pen in my right hand.

I keep staring at the frames.

I know who's on the other side of the register.

She was no ghost.

I was the ghost when we met, falling at breakneck speed before she caught me.

Heather flips the paper over in my hand, disappearing the frames.

I sob. I was so close to remembering.

"Draw Dracula," Dr. Seward commands.

I stare at the paper and pen. Why do I know that name? Why do I feel so wounded?

"She's left-handed, dumbasses," August advises.

Heather switches the paper and pen in my hands.

"Draw Dracula," Dr. Seward repeats.

"Give her a fucking clipboard or something," August sneers. "You humans are so lame."

"Shut up, Van Helsing," Heather says as she puts the folder under the paper.

Another name attached to a face that I can't recall.

One connected to Dracula, who I can't remember, but am certain I love.

But how can it be love if remembering is so hard and so painful?

"Maybe he just doesn't love me," I whisper.

"What did she say?" Ella asks.

Dr. Seward starts towards me.

"Don't touch her. Just give her a moment."

I turn around in bed with my back to them so that none of their faces can interfere with the strain of recalling.

Big green eyes peer at me from the recesses of memory. Dracula's?

Is this his heavy, surly brow? His long, arched nose?

His face emerges from the fog like the sun through parting clouds. I put the paper blank side up, first outlining his eyes, nose, and mouth, and then shading some of his cheeks in blue ink. I don't realize how hard I'm crying until tears splatter on his forehead. I shade around them with the ballpoint pen.

I take another paper out, draw Dracula's face again—a side profile. Another from an angle. Another from straight ahead. Another from slightly below.

"Realistically, how much can we do with drawings?" Ella asks under her breath.

"What, you've never seen *Enemy of the State*? Or the news?" August snickers. "The feds have tracked down protesters based off pictures of cleavage. If you can't find *one* Master based off pictures of his face, then you all should just close up shop."

"Depends how good the drawings are, really," Drew comments, like he's watching a spectator sport. "How many is she drawing, anyway?"

I'm at twenty-two.

Twenty-three ballpoint pen portraits on the backs of FedEx logs, cash register receipts, and security footage frames.

If time is still real, I can't feel it.

The only thing I feel is an elusive, impenetrable lack.

Twenty-four and counting.

And still not enough.

"Stop," Dr. Seward commands.

I drop the pen as I finish portrait number thirty-six. I flex my aching fingers and gather the drawings in a stack.

Something isn't right.

This is his face, but it isn't all of it.

There's something else off the page—something I can't see. Another face, maybe. Or something bigger. Something unfathomable. Unknowable. Unshowable.

"Show us," Dr. Seward says.

I turn around, holding the pictures to my chest.. "He's mine."

"*Show us*," Ella hisses.

I shake my head, wrinkling the pages as I press them to my heart.

"He's *mine*."

He advances.

"Jacob, don't touch her," Oliver warns.

Dr. Seward ignores him and bends over me. His hand lashes out too fast to evade as he tries to snatch the bottommost drawing from the stack in my arms.

The paper rips, leaving me with everything below the tip of my Dracula's nose.

Dr. Seward turns the other half around and shrieks. His body goes rigid, like a cartoon electrocution.

Pink flames erupt between his hands and shoot towards the ceiling. Tendrils whip around the room, drawing more shouts from his fellow kidnappers. A thin rope of flame lashes out sideways. It snaps me in the chest above my fingers, rinsing my heart of the serum's hold.

I remember why it's beating so fast.

I remember who I am, where I am, why I'm here.

I look at the stack in my arms, floored through the fear because you'd never know from looking that this is the first time I've ever attempted to draw in ballpoint pen.

The pink fire dies.

Dr. Seward rounds on me, clutching his arm. Red welts snake up his sleeve.

He opens his mouth.

I throw half the stack at the disjointed front of Dracula hunters.

The hellfire swells and whips like a jellyfish swimming towards the seabed, drawing screams from its immobilized victims. The room fills with it, each page fueling the leviathan of pink.

Somehow, I'm not paralyzed with them. To me, these unfurling flames are a breeze.

I steel my whole body and bolt, ignoring their screams as I wedge between Drew and the doorway.

August's fingertips swipe the air behind me. Smoke seeps through his eyelids as he sniffs for me, fangs out. The hem of his sleeve is gone; his arm is embers.

I throw the rest of the drawings. Flamingo pink fire explodes in midair.

August's shrieks echo after me as I make my escape down a long, dark hall. I feel blank from the overload of adrenaline; like all I am is two running legs and a hammering heart. I run past doors like the one to the room I was in. I run and run, waiting for a break in the monotonous layout of door after windowless door.

I reach a staircase. I'm wheezing, yet force myself to run up, unable to fathom anything but the next few footfalls. I can't hear anything but my own heart—can't tell if there's anyone after me, or if the flames freed me. The stairs terminate at a door with a circular window. My finger splits open again when I wrench the door handle and hurl myself over the threshold.

I'm in a lofty lobby, with a curved nook like a receptionist area and empty rows of chairs sprawled in front of it, seats pooled with dirt and dust. Empty hallways stretch left and right, walls covered in chipped white paint. The whole place smells like a basement—damp, mildewed, desiccated.

Leaves and paint chips crunch underfoot as I revolve on the spot. A window high above a pair of steel double doors frames a sky full of grey clouds. If this was a hospital, it isn't anymore, and the VHI's goings-on below are all hidden in plain sight.

My chest aches as I run for the double doors and slam down both bars. They open, but only a sliver: a thick chain on the other side binds the handles. I see another set of double doors beyond. These are transparent and one of them has no glass left in the metal frame. Through one of the taut steel links lies green and nothing but. Green ivy crawls up the walkway. Overgrown green grass bends in the breeze.

I turn back to the lobby.

There must be another way out.

But now that I'm at a standstill, the thought of moving again makes me want to sink to my knees. The last doctor I saw told me that he never would've known my heart had failed if I hadn't told him. Maybe after what I put it through, I can't ask it to take me further than this.

A ticking sound meets my ears from the other side of the doors, but as I turn around to try and open them again, I hear a slam.

"That was a neat trick, Oasis," August yells, "but the fun's over now."

I can hear his fangs marring his words, but I hear something else, too: the ticking sound recurs, coupled with a sniffling, snuffling.

"Where are you, Oasis?"

Desperation mounts in my chest. I push the doors again, begging the chain on the other side to disintegrate. I can't stop hyperventilating.

August's hands are like cold vices on my shoulders as he drags me away from the doors and whirls me around. The pink flames left black welts on his face and arms. His glaring grey eyes find mine. He wrenches my hand from my side so that both of us can see my bleeding finger.

"I thought I cleaned that up for you," he growls. "You should learn to take better care of yourself."

I start to cry. All I want is to go home.

I hear more footsteps over my tears as the door opens and shuts, opens and shuts, opens and shuts again and again. I see faces over August's shoulder, but can't make out any of them.

"Get another dose prepped," says Brian, breathing hard. "Van Helsing, bring her over here."

"*At-at-at.*" August moves so that he's behind me. He grabs my hair, forcing my head to the side, and sniffs up and down my neck. "Van Helsing *this*. Mosquito *that*—like I don't know who the vampire hunters' next target is once you've caught Master," he hisses, taking a small step back. Amusement fills his voice when he says, "At least my dad had a reason to be obsessed with the guy. Has he fucked any of *your* wives lately?"

I hold by breath to stop crying, but all I end up doing is choking.

"*Shhhhh.* I won't let them put anything else in you," he whispers. "I'm sorry I brought you here, Oasis, but it's just you and me from now on."

"God damn it, Van Helsing," Dr. Seward shouts. "Bring her back, or so help me…" He trails off.

The cold of August's lips leaves my neck as he turns to look at the doors behind us.

I strain to hear over my own frantic breaths.

It's the ticking sound again.

August sniffs, inhaling for nearly half a minute.

"What is it, Van Helsing?" Ella asks.

"I don't know," he mutters. He seems to have forgotten that he was kidnapping me out of spite.

His discomfort invigorates me, but he's still holding my injured hand, making it impossible to cross my way out of his grip.

The snuffling gets louder, more plentiful, followed by panting and whining. When I twist for a glimpse, I see a shadow under the door.

The whining intensifies as ticking turns to scratching. The animal on the other side brays. The lone sound turns into a hair-raising chorus of howls.

"Werewolves," August hisses, backing away from the door, taking me with him. "*Fuck.*"

"Ain't no such thing," Brian snaps. "Quit fucking around and give us the girl."

"Is too a such thing," says a woman's matter-of-fact voice on the other side.

Another round of short, soft howls rises like tide.

I strain to see Dr. Seward and the others: one by one, they're pulling out guns, pointing them at the doors. My heart kicks into overdrive.

"Is that you I smell, Van Helsing, you filthy fucking parasite?" The woman calls playfully. "*Eeeeeee-hee-hee-hee!*"

A growl rises in August's throat, rumbling in my ears.

"The plan was to put you down on the spot, but since you took food off your master's plate..." She heaves a theatrical regretful sigh. "You know I have to take you to him."

August lets go of me and turns on his heel, sprinting back the way we came too fast for me to make out his legs. Simultaneously, a gunshot cracks through the air.

I scream and duck, but the shot didn't come from inside.

The doors fling open. The chain falls with a hollow *ding*. A dozen wolves run past me, all different colors, all taller than my waist, some as tall as my shoulders.

They stream after August, splitting the VHI like a bowling ball. I cower on the spot as bullets start firing, seemingly with no effect on the wolves, who all disappear down the stairs and halls.

A woman with a loosely tamed mane of red Afro steps through the open doors, clutching a pistol of her own in a black leather glove clad hand. Between her shrewd, sharp green eyes, the tattoo of a D in blackletter font beneath her jaw, and the studded collar around her neck, she looks like she probably beats people up for a living.

She looks somewhere in her twenties, wearing a dark green t-shirt that reads *Wayne State School of Medicine.* She looks at me as though to address me, but stops beside me instead. I look over my shoulder to see what she's looking at.

Ella, Heather, and Drew are all brandishing silver crucifixes while the Morrises and Dr. Seward aim their guns at her.

The stranger looks from one to the next, seeming unimpressed.

"Your crosses won't save you from me. Fenrir eats gods like yours for breakfast and shits them out on the sidewalk…" she raises her gun and pulls the trigger, shooting a third eye into Ella's forehead. "…For humans like you to step in."

Drew moves to catch her body, but the stranger is faster, shooting him in the temple. They both collapse in unison. In the blink of an eye, she advances on the bodies and snatches the silver crucifixes up, examining them in her gloved hand.

Dr. Seward starts to run, but she wrenches him back by the arm.

"You're—"

He fires a shot at her face; I scream yet again, but there's no blood, no splatter of flesh and brains.

The bullet goes into her open mouth mid-speech and doesn't come out.

She glowers at him, unscathed. "You're the only one making it out alive for certain," she says. "Dracula's been so *moody* this past century and a half. A good hunt will cheer him up—fresh air and all." I hear the bullet clicking between her teeth like a jawbreaker before she spits it in his face, eliciting a horrified shudder. "Right, Doc?"

She lets go roughly, shoving him to the floor, and watches him scramble through the doors, tripping on the broken chain, a snide smile on her face.

"I'd save the rest of you for him, but we came all the way from Detroit for this," the woman says, returning her attention to Heather and the Morrises. She points to each of them, Heather gaping at the Holmwoods' bodies, Brian with his gun drawn, Oliver standing in a puddle of his own urine. "I hope there's enough to go around."

Almost as one, they run; Heather vaults up one hall, and the father-son duo sprint down the other, Oliver leaning on his son for support.

"That's right. Get those hearts *pumping*," the woman yells, chuckling to herself. "Odin's eye," she says upon turning back to me. "You're on the floor."

I didn't realize I'd sunk to my knees until her shadow falls over me.

She crouches in front of me, unspeaking, and fastens a crucifix around my neck.

"Thank—"

She cuts me off by grabbing the neck of my shirt from behind.

I yelp as she drags me through the filth towards the doors, legs trailing helplessly.

"I'm here to rescue you, but I promised the pups we'd get a few licks in before I gave that piece of shit over to your girlfriend." She stops at the threshold and lets me fall flat on my back.

I open my mouth, but she holds up a finger before I can speak. Then comes a waterfall of screams—Oliver, then Brian, then Heather, all spilling agonized shouts from different directions. A symphony of snapping growls and snarls accompanies the patchwork of screams.

The woman nods her satisfaction.

"This could take a long minute, so just…" She wrinkles her freckled nose and makes a shooing gesture. "Go relax, unwind, breathe. You're safe now."

"I…" I can't argue. The threats have been categorically eliminated.

"You're Oasis Johnson. I'm Tora," she says. "Sit tight while we treat ourselves to some torture. If you need me, just holler. I'll find you."

Then she turns around, leaving me to gape at her back. She bends down next to the Holmwoods' bodies, removing her glove one finger at a time, and punches through Ella's ribcage like drywall.

My stomach seizes with horror.

Tora peels Ella's sternum off like a Band-Aid, then pulls her heart from her chest with a squishing, slippery sound.

She looks over her shoulder, frowning.

"We can split it."

I shake my head, dazed.

She shrugs. "Suit yourself."

I roll over and stagger to my feet. My legs are numb from being dragged across the floor, but I somehow make it to the doors. The last I see of Tora is her biting into Ella's dripping heart like a pear.

I limp through the broken glass doors.

A grey and breezy afternoon greets me. A sign carved into stone above the doors reads *J. Seward Sanitarium.* The sprawling gothic exterior reminds me of every boarding school I ever pictured in middle school, reading books about catty white teenagers with trust funds and Ferraris.

The lawn is a jungle of crabgrass, the brick walkway lined with stone benches overgrown with fingers of ivy. A thin river flows straight ahead, perpendicular to the front of the building. Remnants of a stone bridge jut from the water.

Am I still in New York? How did I even get here? Was I carried, or hypnotized into walking?

Maybe Tora is right.

I should take this opportunity to relax, cherish how alive I am. I guess a dual-purpose rescue-revenge is better than no rescue at all. How better to avoid my imminent breakdown than by walking through the courtyard of an abandoned sanitarium?

I drag my feet through the grass as I head towards the gently coursing river. Trees bow over the water on the other side, forming canopies on the bank. There's nothing but green across the water—no roads or homes visible through the trees, no rooftops or skyscrapers above.

I wonder what'll happen to this place now that its owners are mostly dead—unless there are others out there nursing vendettas against a monster they haven't met personally.

A glint across the river catches my eye—a glassy interruption in the curtain of green. It's a vaulted greenhouse, half-buried in the foliage.

I squint at it. Then, almost involuntarily, I look at the riverbank. The water looks slow and shallow enough to cross with no real hassle, the rocks large enough to step on.

Given what just happened, I should probably sit my ass down somewhere until the werewolves have had their long minute of revenge, but I'm desperate to understand everything about the awfulness I've been dragged into—to see just how deep this all goes.

I descend the gently sloping bank. The grass thins and turns to mud. Holding my breath, I step onto the first mossy stone I see jutting out of the water, then hop to the next. Somehow, I make it to the other side with nothing but another dizzying dose of adrenaline. I climb the bank, kicking through the brambles and brush.

The greenhouse casts a chilly shadow. The gilded wrought iron archway screams Victorian; the original Seward could have founded this place immediately after *Dracula* was published.

The outermost glass door hangs off its hinges. A pair of benches sit on either side of the atrium within. Past them, the innermost door is intact and closed, threshold buried under dead leaves and broken branches.

Warm air pours out, like the place is sighing with relief. A marble fountain sits at the crossroads of the two main walkways, bone dry and full of dirt. More benches line the soil beds. The trees are the only plants left standing, unruly branches punching through some of the panes. Vines crawl along the frames and through the broken glass like green creeks.

There are no signs—nothing to indicate which plants have lost their lives to neglect. As I walk towards the barren fountain, despite all that's happened today, all I can think of is how nice it would be to come here with Laura.

She's my favorite part of every day and the star of my daydreams on the days I don't see her.

She found me.

So why do I feel so lost?

A door juts out at the very back of the greenhouse, situated under another gilded archway, affixed to a small room with stone walls and a burnished metal sign: "GARDENER'S SHED — NO PATIENTS ALLOWED." Instead of a deadbolt, the door has a combination lock so old that the numbers are Roman numerals.

"Amateurs," I mutter as I kick the leaves aside.

I flatten my right hand on the metal. With my ear to the door, I twist the dial, straining to hear the three prize-winning clicks.

The shed exhales a damp, musty scent. I see packets of seeds, cans of fertilizer and partially obscured behind a rack of rusted tools, yet another door.

This one doesn't have a lock: all it takes is a nudge of the rack and a tug of the handle before I'm staring down a dungeon-esque flight of stairs that seem to go on forever before disappearing into a puddle of darkness.

As a Black person, I should know better than to go down random stone staircases, yet here I am, stooping next to a dust-coated box of white stick candles and another full of matches. I fumble and drop two of them in the hunt for a flame.

The descent isn't as deep as I thought, and the candle ends up being unnecessary: it illuminates a lever adjacent to the doorway that takes all my strength to flip with one hand.

The huge space looks wholly incongruent with the greenhouse concealing it. Heavy duty spotlights overhead showcase portions of what looks like the world's biggest and most disorganized basement, sunk two flights of metal stairs below the threshold like a mine.

My heart races as I descend the clanging steps.

All there is...is *stuff*.

Clusters and piles of it, loosely segregated by function. I see a warehouse worth of furniture—chaises, benches, tall chairs. Caches of weapons and shields sit along the walls, guarded by suits of armor. From afar I spot an iron maiden and several guillotines among them. Most of the collection seems to be made of clothes. Some hang off retail-style racks, but the bulk of the garments are piled onto even more furniture, on the backs of animal statues, in mounds on the floor.

A ring of filing cabinets and wardrobes not far from the stairs suggest that someone started to tame this dust-covered chaos. Cardboard boxes full of documents are lined up next to and on top of them. Dust plumes rise underfoot as I examine the label on one: "*Sheet Music,*" typed in mono-space font on yellowing paper, affixed to the metal with shiny scotch tape.

A blocky analog radio plugged into the wall sits atop another labeled "*Correspondence.*" I turn it on, straining to hear words through the twisting static: "*...not looking good for the Mets despite two consecutive wins against the Phillies last month...*"

Whoever had been listening to the radio left their garbage on the filing cabinet. I blow out my candle and exchange it for a dust-coated McDonald's bag, squinting at the unfamiliar logo of an anthropomorphic hamburger wearing a chef hat and pinstripe pants. According to the faint ticket inside, this order was placed back when burgers were fifteen cents.

I find a brand-new box of acid-free archival folders beneath the trash. I open the top drawer and pull out the first one I see.

Inside is a yellowed piece of parchment, wrinkled and torn at the edges. Most of the calligraphic handwriting is nonsense to me, except for the signature, which makes my heart skip a beat: I've seen it before, inscribed at the bottom of a drawing on my refrigerator.

A typewritten letter is stapled to the front of the folder:

```
        Acquisitions Committee, the Met
                                Cloisters
    99 Margaret Corbin Dr, New York,
                              NY 10040

September 29, 1955

To whom it may concern:

My name is Dr. Jonah Seward of the
Verge Historical Institute. I have
recently inherited a great number of
artifacts spanning many centuries
from my father, Dr. John Seward,
who operated J. Seward Sanitarium.
These artifacts include clothing
and garments, housewares, weapon-
ry, architectural remains, books
and other publications, and histor-
ical correspondence. It is my be-
lief that many of these items may be
welcome additions to your collec-
tion. Since I believe your time to
be valuable, I am carefully enclos-
ing an authentic letter exchanged
between Vlad Dracula and Matthias
Corvinus for your consideration in
the hopes it will intrigue you to
meet and discuss.
```

I stop reading and skim some of the other folders, leaving dusty fingerprints on the cardstock. All the medieval documents bear similar letters to curators at museums across the world, including the Transylvanian History Museum. Some of the letters correspond to items in the wardrobe—Elizabethan Gamache boots, an eighteenth-century French silk suit, a Victorian velvet evening gown, a pair of late-nineteenth century Levi Strauss denim overalls.

All the wonderment leaves my body, quickly replaced with nauseating anger.

How dare they pawn my girlfriend's stuff?

I remove the stiff indigo overalls from the wardrobe and drape them over my arm, surveying the maze of items. Now that I have some idea of how deep this all goes, the newest most pressing question is: how much of this can I carry?

Moreover, how *fast* can I look for all the things Laura ever mentioned? My head hurts, my feet hurt, my body feels like it was thrown in a food processor and reassembled; I'm hungry, thirsty, musty, and tired, and for Tora, the rediscovery of some of her friend's lost possessions would probably lengthen our stay here.

The thought inspires me to sprint to the clothes and start grabbing stuff off the racks—shawls, tunics, some of the basques I remember Laura talking about. I plunge through some of the piles, freeing items whose names and eras I couldn't even guess.

As my gaze falls on an armoire full of mismatched shoes and handbags, I realize that it won't matter how fast I collect things, since Tora will notice me having gone from empty-handed to staggering under the weight of so many clothes.

This pressing fact doesn't stop me from depositing my finds on an evening gown with a train as big as a quilt so that I can sift through a pile of purses. I manage to extricate several from the tangle of straps and decorative fringe. Cool metal grazes my fingertips when I free a perfectly round black satin reticule. An ornate bat brooch is pinned over the embroidered design of a moon hanging over mountains, with tiny pearls for stars.

No time constraint will ever be pressing enough for me to surmount the insatiable curiosity centric to my girlfriend. I don't know for sure who Laura was in the 1890s, but whoever it was, they probably carried this. I loosen the drawstrings and tilt the reticule into the blaring spotlight. There's nothing inside. The lining is pure black, but the shade of black doesn't match the shiny fabric. I stick my hand in—and in, and in, and in, until my whole arm is gone, and the purse looks like a decorative covering for my shoulder stump.

I pull my arm out. I turn the bag upside down and give it a shake. Then comes a distant sound like the jostling of a full book bag. I look around as the sound gets louder, but I'm still alone, the dust undisturbed except for my footprints. It's coming from the reticule, volume increasing steadily. Seconds later, dozens of sheathed swords and knives tumble into the pile of handbags, narrowly missing my knees, some with their handles quivering, some still lodged in the fabric.

I crawl back, heart racing at warp speed, and grab one of the swords—or try to. It's so heavy that my arm almost pops out of the socket. I go for a smaller knife with Arabic writing on the hilt and drop it in the bag, which I then hold up to my ear. The faint clatter comes half a minute later.

I get up, breathing like I just ran for my life all over again and leave the reticule on the floor, then drag a floral carpet bag ten times its size from the pile and angle it above the opening. The carpet bag twists and contorts, like someone's trying to wring it out. I let go; it funnels into the reticule as fluidly as water.

My sense of wonder is back, and it's almost impossible to maintain the same grab-and-go approach. I pack my scores, then throw in the knives and swords that I can lift. I work my way through the clothes with no methodology. All of this is to ensure a smile is the first thing on Laura's face when she wakes up. And although not all these clothes are her size, some of the lacier, racier numbers are things I'd like to see her in.

Actually, there probably won't be much smiling when she wakes up. Being in here, I could easily forget that a few flights of stairs and a river separate me from the place that'll certainly spice up my future nightmares with the memories it holds.

I hustle to an area full of shelves and crates that seem devoted to domestic miscellany, with everything from candles, to stuffed animals, to incandescent light bulbs. After tossing in a few spearheads, I find a huge copper plate engraved with a dragon emblem and use it to carry an ebony teapot, a stack of colorful ceramic saucers, and a gravy dish shaped like a swan.

I haven't put any glass in the bag yet; there's a chance I'll accidentally destroy Laura's priceless dishes and give her a reason to frown instead. Maybe that wouldn't be such a bad thing.

I could smash these plates to pieces and present them to her; show her how I feel instead of wasting time talking. After all, my life is too short for that.

I set the plate down on an ornate end table, reticule swinging off my wrist, and turn to an array of shelves holding nothing but boxes—jewelry boxes, cardboard boxes, cigar boxes, metal lock-boxes, boxes with seemingly arbitrary labels, boxes with sigils on the tops, boxes that seem to have no way of being opened.

I don't know the difference between an alder wood box and any other wood box, so I pluck all the ones that look coronet sized from the shelves, plus a few tins with bats and skies engraved on the sides. I stack them all on the plate and drop the scores in the bag, not bothering to listen for crashes as I close it on my wrist.

I put my face in my hands, uncaring of the filth, blocking the whole place from sight.

Plundering relics of Laura's other lifetimes won't fix the hole she ripped in my heart by not being awake and therefore able to stop this. It won't change the fact that I wouldn't be here if she had let me feed her.

I blink tears from my eyes and keep moving. I speed up my scavenging and finish with the filing cabinets, dumping as many folders as I can into the cardboard boxes and dropping those in the reticule.

Maybe seeing Laura's excitement will alleviate the dead feeling stealing over me as I climb the stairs and pull the lever, plunging the mine full of spoils from Castle Dracula into darkness.

I emerge to a greenhouse riddled with blades of sunlight. With my dignity in the toilet for the day, I find a rusty pail in the gardener's shed and squat over it to pee, then slosh it at one of the barren soil beds, stoking a hair-raising sensation of déjà vu from my descent into Custodes Angelorum.

Tightening the reticule straps over my shoulder so that it's hidden under my armpit beneath two layers of flannel, I leave the unkempt haven of a greenhouse behind—a generous helping of calm before the storm.

The skies have cleared, but clouds gather in my chest as I cross the river, pausing in the sanitarium's shadow to splash water on my face. It must be late afternoon.

I peer into the empty lobby, glaring at the trail in the dust formed by my ass when Tora dragged me to the doors, hating August that much more for being so awful that his torture must go on for this long.

Sighing, I remove the thinner of my flannels, then find the thickest, softest patch of grass in the lawn to curl up on and rest my eyes.

*

"Can you still walk?" Comes an alarmed voice.

I jump and roll over, fingers tangled in the grass. I see Tora's black boots first, then her fitted black cargo pants and t-shirt. She could be Black Kim Possible, if not for the bloodstains splattered on her knees, shins, and freckled face.

"Yeah," I say hoarsely, though as I get to my feet, I realize that this may be a lie. I have no idea how long I was out, but it was long enough for my legs to finally realize just how much they've been through.

"Good," Tora says with an approving nod. She walks towards the riverbank, then kneels beside the water and puts her whole face in, shaking her head vigorously.

Fascination flits beneath the surface of my wired exhaustion, barely felt. A pack of werewolves just saved my life, and I don't have the headspace to be curious.

"I have eaten a heart and slaked my thirst for revenge," she says when she returns. "We can take the Bifröst to your home."

I look around for a car or a road, finding none. "The what?"

"Bifröst. The burning rainbow path from Midgard to Asgard," she says, frowning, like I should know. "You can't tell Dracula, though. I've been telling him for centuries that Heimdallr doesn't allow passengers."

I have no idea what she's talking about.

This world just keeps getting bigger, and I keep feeling smaller. Like there'll always be more to wonder than to know about the person I love most.

"I won't," I say.

Tora tilts her head back and calls, "Heimdallr..."

The rest of her words are lost on me, spoken in a language that sounds like it calls for some serious tongue acrobatics. I brace myself for yet another assault on my adrenal glands, but nothing happens, except for Tora frowning at me.

"There's no need for cowering. Heimdallr's a gentle god," she says. "He likes humans."

"You spoke to a god?"

"Yeah. Christians do all the time, don't they?" She asks, smirking. "Personally, I don't understand monotheism. You've only got one god, and if he's boring, who the fuck do you talk to? Like, if Baldr was the only god, I'd probably just kill myself, but I think

Christians go to hell for that, don't they? Do you just become atheist?"

"I'm...not sure." The only thing I'm sure of right now is that I'm within spitting distance of dissociative breakdown.

"Oh well." Tora grabs my wrist.

I don't protest. In fact, it's a welcome gesture. Despite all my efforts, I'm losing track of myself. Who knows what'll happen if she lets go?

I start to wonder if she's playing some kind of sick joke, implying I belong in the sanitarium by leading me back towards it. A moment later, I realize that we aren't walking towards the doors. I blink hard to make sure my eyes are still working.

We come up on a street-level subway entrance in the middle of the walkway. My name is on the sign where a train line designation would be.

Tora leads me down the stairs. My nose expects creosote and stale station air, my ears the din of commuters. Instead, I hear a breeze as we fold through the turnstiles. The platform overlooks a sea of clouds too dense to see the world beneath. A wide rainbow, glittering and opaque, arcs towards the concrete in real time, as though painted horizontally by a giant brush. The quilt of stars is as bright as daylight and throws our shadows crookedly behind us.

A dark blot in the distance grows larger as bright red drips off the rainbow and onto the platform in viscous puddles, like the light is being soldered to the concrete.

"Your feet must hurt," Tora says as the blot enlarges. "Gulltoppr will lend his."

An ebony horse with a rippling mane of gold strands gallops towards us over the rainbow, fitted with a golden saddle and reins.

I get the urge to cry, seeing something so sublime and beautiful out of nowhere.

The horse ducks his head under Tora's outstretched hand, neighing gently. The eyes under his sweeping lashes are as gold as his mane and tail. Tora pats Gulltoppr's side; he drops down on his rump, sitting like a dog.

I climb into the saddle and tuck my sore feet in the stirrups.

He rises with a neigh, mane rippling like liquid sunshine.

"He thinks you have excellent form," Tora says as she takes the reins. "Do you ride?"

"I'm from the Great Plains," I say. "Everyone there knows how to ride."

"This is true in Asgard as well," she says. "It should be standard practice through all the Nine Realms, once Midgardians break the automobile habit."

Gulltoppr's hooves clack on the bridge like it's made of cobbled stone. The red transitions to orange; at one point, Tora's hair seems to blend seamlessly with the shade underfoot. My eyes catch onto colors that I'd kill to blend on my own, and I find myself repressing the urge to leap down and peel them off to take with me.

"Are you a god?" I ask.

"I'm their dog. I was a gift to Thor from Fenrir during post-Ragnarok reconstruction," Tora says with a smile that shows all her bright white teeth.

"Thor like the movie?"

Tora shrugs. "I don't think he's seen it to like or dislike it. Anyway," she says, "the gods are just like humans, in that they also wish they knew what their pets are thinking. Ergo, he asked Loki to give me the power of speech. Turns out I talk too much. Call Midgard my backyard."

I gawk. I wasn't prepared to meet anyone else whose reality is founded in what I believed to be fictional.

"Thanks again for saving me. I couldn't have asked for a better rescue party."

"You had it under control," Tora says.

"You wouldn't be saying that if you'd seen me," I say, curtailing a scoff.

"I did see you. You saw me, too." She frowns up at me. "Didn't you recognize me?"

I rack my brain, sifting through the horrible events of the day for a glimpse of her.

Then I squint at the top of her head.

Her face isn't familiar, but that shade of vibrant red is.

"Were you that poodle? And the pit bull with that kid?"

"Don't let Devin hear you call him a kid," she warns. "He's 309."

"But you still saw me getting kidnapped," I say bluntly. "And you let it happen?"

"Yes," Tora says, fixing me with a disconcerted scowl. "And now because of you, the parasite know as August Van Helsing will be kibble for Garmr in Hel, and when he's answered to the goddess Hel for his crimes, your Devil will have a turn. Thank you, Oasis."

It's hard to hold onto any sense of betrayal while being thanked, and harder still while learning that the battle against August Van Helsing started way before he kidnapped me. It's also hard to feel anything but serenity, surrounded by this many colors and clouds. Tora and Gulltoppr are both walking up the gentle incline, but it doesn't feel like we're going towards anything. At this point, I don't mind.

"Since you seem pretty familiar with August, can I ask you how the son of a vampire hunter turn into a vampire who then helps hunt down *the* vampire?" I ask.

"Not much to say, really. His dad was more interested in getting revenge on Dracula than raising him properly. August was the Victorian equivalent of an incel before Lucy bit him for trying to rape her on her deathbed," she says, arching a brow when I gasp silently. "Unfortunately for the rest of us, she didn't kill him, and Van Helsing couldn't bring himself to. But since August is a Van Helsing, these past few generations of Sewards have regarded him as the tragically vampirized son of the world's greatest vampire hunter, sympathetic to their crusade against Dracula and his underworld. Decade after decade, they'd ask for his help sniffing out the big bad vampire, and he wouldn't deliver. You'd think after over a century of not finding Dracula, they'd have realized that all they've been doing is feeding their pet mosquito. Which is partly my fault," she adds with a sigh. "Should've killed him when I had the chance."

"What did he do to you and your pack?" I ask, as full of curiosity as I am disgust.

"When American slavery ended, some slave-owners pretended otherwise and kept their whips and slaves for decades after. The parasite freelanced for them—catching runaways in exchange for a meal," Tora says, voice like acid. She looks up at me. "Adds a whole new layer of yuck to his kidnapping you, doesn't it? I don't see Dracula letting him die anytime soon." Gulltoppr shakes his head; his braying almost sounds like wry laughter.

My stomach churns.

It didn't occur to me that August could be any worse of a being than what I'd already experienced, or that I could feel any luckier than I already do for having made it out alive.

"I've been tracking him on and off for decades," she continues in a milder tone. "He started working with those inept vampire hunters again a year ago."

"Did Dracula know?" I ask.

Tora tightens the reins in her fist, eyes fixed straight ahead. The lack of immediate response hollows out my chest.

"I told him last week that the parasite was in the picture. He asked me to watch out for you while he slept, and I told him I wouldn't let you sustain any damage you couldn't walk away from." She frowns up at me. "You can still walk, right?"

I take my feet from the stirrups and roll my ankles.

She nods her approval.

"Do you know why he's sleeping so much?" I ask.

Tora looks away and back, away and back, frown deepening each time.

"Odin's *eye*, you humans are adorable," she mutters. "He's sick, okay? Your girlfriend is sick."

My heart drops, even though I'd already put that much together.

"How bad is it?"

Tora shrugs.

She clutches the reins in one hand and with the other combs her fingers through Gulltoppr's mane. "At first it was just headaches and lethargy."

"When was that?"

"Not too long ago. Somewhere around 1967," Tora says, shrugging slightly. "Next thing I know, he's falling out of the air mid-bat and puking wine so hard it comes out of his nose. He can't even *levitate* anymore," she says, abandoning all hesitation in her bewilderment. "Târgoviste is about to have a dirt shortage from how much he's been sleeping. And before you ask," she says as I open my mouth, "*yes*, I do know what's wrong. It's called malnourishment."

"Why won't he just drink my blood?" I demand, firing off the next question in the queue.

Gulltoppr tosses his head, like he's asking the same thing.

Tora drops her hand and scowls at us both.

"I assume it's because of Lucy Westenra. I don't blame him on that front." She sighs heavily, shaking her head at the horizon as the arch in the bridge declines. "Imagine having a drink of someone only for them to turn around and say *sike, I'd rather be a vampire*."

I bite down on my lip to keep from asking yet another question, but the tactic doesn't work for long. "Does he not trust me?"

"Dracula is one of my best friends. He doesn't trust anybody," she says. "I assume that's what all the faces are for. They trust on his behalf."

I don't just lose my train of thought; it careens off the tracks and explodes one car at a time.

"None of his faces has ever had a girlfriend, though. I don't doubt that he loves you. Neither should you," Tora says, as if she can hear my heart sinking, shattering the Bifröst and plummeting through the clouds down to Midgard, or Asgard, or whatever -gard is under us.

The Bifröst reminds me of certain parts of the Kansas River—the kind of colorful quiet that doesn't let dark thoughts quicken into spirals. I don't want to be heartbroken right now.

I take a fistful of Gulltoppr's mane gently and detangle the strands with my fingertips. I catch a glimpse of his golden eye, like he's trying to investigate, but he doesn't shake my hand away.

Thus, I spend the rest of the peaceful journey braiding loosely, ignoring the decline in the bridge and the passage of yellow and green underfoot.

The Bifröst terminates at a pair of familiar skinny doors: my fire escape, with a violet threshold where the grates would be. The sun slanted through the curtains suggests the golden hour.

Tora snags the reins, guiding Gulltoppr to a stop. She gives me her hands and helps me down.

Now that they're under my weight, my legs feel like lead, gelatin, and like they spent some time in the Iron Maiden, all at once.

"You'll have to finish these one day," Tora says, running her fingers through the four braids I completed. "All the horses in Asgard will be turning their heads."

Gulltoppr tosses his head, neighing his agreement.

"Take care of yourself, Oasis," Tora says as she opens the door. "If you don't, Heimdallr will tell me." She pulls me into a hug so tight and so warm that for a hairsbreadth of a second, I forget how filthy and musty I am and hug her back.

She mounts Gulltoppr herself. He swishes his golden tail and kicks his front legs in the air, neighing, then gallops back the way we came.

If only the other end of the Bifröst led to somewhere other than *there*. I'd keep these doors open forever, gazing at the back half of the Roy G. Biv acronym, where violet bleeds to indigo, and indigo climbs into blue, and bluish teal forms the apex of the bridge. Closing the door is like changing slides: Bifröst one moment, alley the next. Fluffy grey strokes mar the darkening blue sky, with a strip of sunlight like the rind of an orange curled around the horizon.

My apartment feels utterly foreign, my furniture and food like they belong to someone else.

I keep the light off in my room and peel off my flannel, dropping it on the floor, pull the sweat-dampened reticule from under my armpit and put it on my bed.

I can't bring myself to do anything else, like I'm a shaken bottle of pop, liable to boil over if I unscrew the cap by doing any of the things I was desperate to do on the way here.

I can't even imagine what Full Cauldron looks like. My haven is in ruins, and the only person who might be able to make any of this better is asleep.

I'm not sure Laura could make this better, though. I feel too dead to cry, rifling through memories of the day like I'm looking down at them from a panopticon. The sky bruises dark blue, and I continue to stand like I just got here.

Someone knocks and I don't even jump.

Another knock as I shuffle through the darkness. I flip on the kitchen light and open the door so that less than half my face is visible. My hand slips off the doorknob; the door opens all the way on its own.

Vlad Dracula strands before me in an ensemble of head-to-toe Champion, hands stuffed in his hoodie pockets as he leans against the wall, a mirror of the first and only time we met.

Only this Vlad Dracula is pasty pale, long hair up in a bedraggled bun, irises coated in a hazy blue film, dilated pupils asymmetrical and blob-like. The brightest part of his face is the curved red shovel wound, crusted with dirt, like it happened on the way over. Dirt dusts the hollows of his cheeks and the fine hairs of his temples.

If Tora hadn't told me herself just how ill he is, I would've had no doubts anyway.

He looks worse than ill.

He looks like the corpse that he's technically been this whole time.

"I have come to apologize with all that I am," he says, soft and hoarse, lips and tongue tinged dark blue. "May I come in?"

"I forgive you," I breathe.

"I have not yet begun to apologize." He blinks, slow and

sluggish. "Your heartbeat is my silence, and I heard it fade out of reach, but could not move to grasp it. I should have been there."

Suddenly, I'd rather talk about anything but that. "You were asleep. I can't be upset with you for being tired."

"But you are."

I want to lie. I don't want to be upset with him when he's in this shape, but I didn't want most of this day to begin with.

"I love you even when I don't understand you," I say. "And I don't understand why you'd rather go to sleep for a week than let me feed you."

"You feed me," he says, deep voice crackling mid-sentence.

"*No*, I haven't. If that was the case, none of this would be happening." The floodgates open on all the desperation I've been trying to drown since I saw Laura on her knees. "They pumped me with a serum made from Lucy's blood. Before that, August Van Helsing licked my blood off my hand. I was hypnotized, but I could still feel under the surface. He was disgusting."

"He will pay for his assault on your being," Dracula says, quiet and seething.

"That doesn't matter to me right now. Is it because of Lucy?" I ask, crossing my arms. "If so, I'll tell you right now I don't want to be a vampire. I need these scars more than I hate them."

His silence only exasperates me further; I get the urge to shut the door and go scream into a pillow.

"They were going to kill me to get to you," I say, exasperated. "Does that not sound familiar?"

More silence. A fly zips up the hall and lands on his forehead. It hops across his face, settling on his open left eye, where it rubs its tiny fists together, fully obscuring his milky iris.

"I see what losing her did to you, except with me, there's no book to burn," I continue quietly. "But I guess if you haven't tasted me, there's nothing to miss anyway."

His eyes darken as he straightens to his full height, stirring the fly into flight.

"You would accuse me of wasting your time?"

"You're the only reason time even *means* anything anymore,"

"And you do not believe this to be true for me?" He asks sharply.

"How can it?" I demand. "You're standing here with this scar on your face that I could help heal, and you just won't let me. And I don't understand why."

He grazes the wound with his pallid fingertips. Flecks of dirt tumble into the folds of his hoodie, and the musky scent of AXE body spray drifts over when he moves. "You believe I am ugly?"

"*No.*" I feel tears on the way, creeping around my throat like a strangling hand. "Why won't you let me feed you?"

"You feed me with all that you are," he says, deepening the hole in my heart. "And I love you with all that I am." His voice snags, betraying exasperation that I never would've gleaned from his face. "I love you such that I..."

"That you what?" I press.

He closes his blue lips, tucking the rest away.

I wait, and wait, and wait. I wait so long that the fly returns with friends; they surround the shovel wound like a pig trough.

"I love you too, but no. You can't come in," I say, fighting to keep my eyes on his face. "I think I need some space." I clear my throat, hold my breath for a moment. "I can't watch you make yourself sick and if you love me, you won't ask me to."

"There is no *if.* You have invited me in," he says quietly. "No matter the face, I may come and go as I please."

Tears fall as I look up into his eyes, too cloudy with his sleep for me to see the green beneath. "But you won't."

The silence stings.

This is supposed to be goodbye, but I can't bring myself to say it.

"May I hold you once before I leave you?" He asks.

I want to sob, but I know how it goes when I've been trying to hold it in for this long. If I open my mouth, I'll never stop crying. I nod and step out so that we're toe-to-toe.

He puts his arms around me, squeezes tightly.

Hugging him feels like standing in a burst of spring rain—the kind that bracketed hot, humid days in Kansas with icy sheets and made me want to run around in nothing but my skin. I remember doing so once when I was nine and feeling weightless; I remember my mother being torn between awe and chastisement because I had no remorse about how good it felt to be naked in the backyard in the rain.

He rubs a circle between my shoulder blades.

I tighten my arms around him, press my ear to his empty, silent chest.

He smells like blood and wine under the AXE, undercut with the sickly-sweet scent of putrid flesh. It sticks in my nose and throat, but I swallow my instinctual repulsion. I'd wrap myself in a blanket of this if I could—take it with me to unfold in the aftermath of this moment.

The saccharine smell sharpens. Then it's all I can smell. It tickles my eyes, too, still stinging with the need to cry. A crackling sound replaces the silence; it sounds like it's coming from the space between us.

I open my eyes.

Smoke spirals upward from where our bodies meet. Pink flames chew a hole beneath the C logo on his hoodie. The fist-sized fire is at the height of my collarbone, unfelt by me. The arms of the crucifix Tora put around my neck poke above the neck of my t-shirt.

The hellfire dies, but Dracula continues to smolder at the heart, the smoke too dark and thick to see the flesh beneath. When I look up, his eyes are pure white and rimmed with red.

I choke on a sob. "Baby, no—"

He explodes into bats, like his skin was nothing but a balloon containing the cauldron. They flock up the hall, squeaking amongst themselves. Something else remains, excluded from his disintegration. It spins on the ground at my feet as the squeaking quiets.

It's an iPhone.

I pick it up and retreat into my apartment, wiping my face with my arm as the tears fall freely. It's a newer model than mine and looks brand new. It has no password, and the wallpaper and app arrangements are the defaults.

Apple Music is the only app that's open. He has a single playlist titled with the beating heart emoji. So far, there are only two songs, both by Billie Holiday: *All of Me* and *Body and Soul*.

Walking to my bedroom feels like walking on broken glass. All the aftercare I've been fantasizing about—showering, eating, crying—falls to the bottom of my to do list. I put the playlist on and set the phone on my nightstand. I lay down without brushing my teeth or washing my face.

Sleep comes in a rush.

Just before my eyelids turn to lead, I fumble for the crucifix and throw it into the darkness in the general direction of the trash.

September 2, 2019

In the moonlight opposite me were three young women, ladies by their dress and manner. I thought at the time that I must be dreaming when I saw them, for, though the moonlight was behind them, they threw no shadow on the floor.

twenty

My stomach wakes me, growling at the advanced stage of hunger that makes me feel like I might throw up. I bolt out of bed, tripping over my disheveled blankets, bumping into the table on my way to the kitchen. I scarf down two bananas, some leftover pasta, and a few pieces of waxy salami that should probably be going in the trash instead. Then I gulp water straight from the faucet.

Autopilot pulls me through every task I ignored for sleep. I strip down and stuff my filthy clothes in the laundry basket, along with the linens I slept on. When that's done, I take a shower, keeping it under half an hour—just enough time to wash my body and hair, but not enough time to formulate any shower thoughts. I put on clean leggings and a t-shirt and finally check the time on my laptop: 2:22 AM.

I could laugh at the irony.

If the angels weren't with me then, they certainly aren't now. I feel as lost as was when I first turned to them, only this time, my life is stable in all the ways it wasn't back then.

With sleep out of the question, I decide to watch *An Unexpected Journey* on my bare mattress. I glance occasionally at the nightstand, looking for a phone that isn't there. I can't stop picturing Full Cauldron in tatters, blood and comics all over the place, office like the victim of a robbery from my desperate search for a vampire deterrent.

This could cost me Kennedy. His mother's lifeblood left in my hands for one Sunday and it wound up destroyed. Does he know that he was most likely hypnotized? Is it my place to tell him?

I leave the movie on as background noise and distract myself with laundry, once again endlessly thankful for in-unit laundry, a must-have for rewiring dissociative episodes into opportunities for self-care.

The round black reticule tumbles from the sheets as I billow them out. I wonder how much of the wardrobe it contains is machine washable, and there's no use lying to myself about the fact that maybe one or two things I yanked from the cache are for *me* to sample. But I threw so much in that I'll probably forfeit my deposit if I turn the bag upside down to peruse.

I detangle a thong from a pair of jeans and toss them in separate piles, unsuccessfully stomping out nagging memories of a satin black corset and a pair of velvet boots embroidered with daisies.

I dump my towels and sheets in the washing machine and start the cycle. Then I kneel at my bedside with the reticule, loosen the strings, and peer into the blackness for a glimpse of the haul. I stick my hand in up to my elbow, probing thin air as on-screen, Bilbo prepares his dinner. I remember a teapot just like his among the things I dumped carelessly into the bag. It was almost the same shade of green, decorated with ducks and wheat.

My fingers touch something. Looking inside, all I see is my arm cut off at the elbow, but I feel cold, curved porcelain graze my palm. A handle hooks over my lax fingertips. When I pull my arm out, I'm holding the exact teapot I was picturing, intact and somehow in my hand.

Carefully, I put it on the floor and reach in again, working off a hunch.

I remember liberating a Levi's denim jacket from 1880 that had been offered to the Victoria and Albert Museum. One moment, it's an image in my head; the next, it's in my hand, shedding dust on my mattress. A fleeting memory of a leaf-patterned silk dress with a domed skirt leads to me getting to my feet to pull the garment out with both hands.

Everything I recall, no matter how vaguely, finds its way to me.

Could I get away with setting some of my girlfriend's things aside for my viewing pleasure? We haven't even made up yet and I'm already thinking about kissing and beyond.

I shove my hand in, summoning a lacy white basque and bloomers, and a pair of satin purple slippers.

This outfit assumes that Laura is the one I'll be making up

with. What if it's him? Does he have any interest in kissing, let alone beyond?

A shirt with ruffled sleeves comes to mind, then flies into my hand. The overalls look his size, as do a pair of black leather boots that fold under the knee. The whole outfit looks like it was put together for someone who works mornings on a pirate ship and nights in a coal mine.

I make separate piles at first, then consolidate, leaving it up to whoever I see to mix and match from the selection.

Separate or together, both outfits are missing a cherry on top. What could be sexier than a crown?

Or in this case, a red coronet.

I picture one of the wooden boxes and pull it out once it sails into my hand. Inside is a mini writing desk, complete with stationary and a bottle of ink. A smaller, darker box holds a pair of golden opera glasses and a frilly folding fan. One by one, I strain to remember which boxes I grabbed, and one by one, I'm disappointed by their contents.

After a few more failed attempts to summon the coronet, I Google *alder box*, hoping it might jog my memory in case I saw it and forgot. Once I see it online, I faintly remember a similarly colored box plucked from between a flour tin and a fractured vase. I picture it, and it flies into my hands.

I line it up with the edge of my bed and remove the lid. A piece of paper falls out, folded into quarters and frayed at the edges, elegant cursive faint with age. I stand up for better lighting and read:

Master,

If you are reading this, then I have been taken from you, if not by Seward's straitjacket and threats of hypnosis, or by Van Helsing's garlic flowers, then by your oldest friend the Devil, from whom I have confiscated this trophy. I must confess to skepticism when you said I had the power of an army of witches, and that the gift of night would leave me with no equal. On the second count, I disagree, for the woman powerful enough to go to hell and back to retrieve her friend's heart finds an equal in the woman powerful enough to give the Devil her heart to begin with. Now it is within your reach, to give as you please.

Your friend,

Lucy Westenra

My fingers quake as I nudge the lid off the box again. The red and pink lump nestled in black satin certainly *looks* like a heart. It could be a life-sized sculpture of a heart, carved and painted with near laser precision, with a thin lacquer over the…

It beats.

The letter flutters from my hand and lands on my laptop keyboard.

The heart contracts and expands rhythmically, kneading the satin like soft knuckles. When I raise the box to my ears, I hear the valves opening and shutting, sounding as it would while nestled between two lungs behind a sternum.

I count ten beats in fifteen seconds, which is forty beats in a minute, which is, according to the internet, the resting BPM of an athlete's heart.

My own heart is sprinting so fast that it hurts.

What if I never see its owner again?

I can't go back to that empty life, when I was too shy to befriend my coworker and too lonely to call my brother out for treating me the way he does.

The heart's soft thumping seems to speed up, too, like it's syncing with mine.

Forty to sixty.

Sixty to ninety.

Ninety to one-twenty.

One-twenty to one-forty.

I lose track as it pumps faster and faster, ticking like a bomb.

Rapping on the fire escape doors quickens my pulse again.

Only one person knocks at the fire escape.

Did he hear his heart in addition to mine?

Has he come to collect it?

Because that's not happening.

I put the lid on and tuck it under my pillow, then rearrange the clothing piles so that the things I don't own are hidden. After yanking a random flannel off its hanger, I hurry to the dining room and throw the doors open.

Cypress is squatting on the rail like a grasshopper, beaming from the darkness, dreads gathered on top of his head in a bouquet.

"Mornin', Miss Oasis."

"Good morning," I breathe. "What are you doing here?"

He raises something slung across his body and tosses it.

It's my purse, wallet, phone, and keys all tucked safely inside.

"I took some selfies if you wanna take a peek," he says, a pointed, playful suggestion.

I unlock my phone and open my camera roll.

The selfies are devoid of his face. All I see is the extremely familiar backgrounds at absurd angles: comic racks and aisles of shelves, the front counter and register, the disorganized back office. It's Full Cauldron as it should be, cleansed of August's violence.

"You did this?"

"Some of it. Your Irish friend came back while I was on my way out. He felt guilty for leaving you all alone with my brother, but he couldn't explain why he did it," Cypress says, grabbing the rail, leaning back like a gymnast. "I reminded him that he went home because the new guy didn't show up, but it was all good because your girlfriend's enthusiastic little brother was there to pick up the slack. He'll be alright."

"Cypress, I...*your* brother?" I repeat.

"Long lost for lack of trying."

I knew I recognized August from somewhere else.

If only I'd made the connection sooner.

"What's going to happen to him?"

"I already happened to him." Cypress tugs something off the rail and unfolds it.

Squinting, I can just make out the edges of Darth Vader's helmet and cape on front of a black hoodie, which is almost in shreds.

"What he did to you was rude, so I killed what was left of him." He puckers his lips, wrinkling his freckled nose. "Master has plenty of toys in his chest."

A chill sweeps over me. I swipe through photos of the store again. "I can't believe you did this for me."

"Most of the time when I hear a human talk, all I can think of is how much better it would sound choking on its own blood." Cypress leaps off the rail. The grate thunks under his sneakers. "But it's like I said: you're precious."

I join him on the fire escape, bare feet stinging from the cold grate. Dark clouds shroud the twilit horizon.

"How's Dracula?"

"Eh. Truth is he's been sick for decades. It's just easier to notice sometimes than others." He unties his dreads so that they flop over his eyes and ears like a mushroom cap. "One time, he got stuck in his first form. Had to drink a whole vineyard and sleep for two months just to put another face on. All the wine and sleep in the world can't replace human blood."

Anguish fills my heart at the thought of my girlfriend

being gone for two months, which is longer than the span of our relationship.

"Must be hard to see him like this as the human girlfriend—short lifespan and all," Cypress continues with a pensive pout. "But you can't force someone to eat—vampire or human."

He's right.

I of all people should know.

"But he's immortal," Cypress says cheerfully. "He'll be alright eventually, even if it's not within your lifetime."

I suck my teeth and manage to pull off something like a smile. "Thanks, Cypress."

"Any time. I should get on with my grocery shopping," he says, binding his locks again. "Sun'll be knocking on the sky before long."

"Grocery shopping?"

When he opens his mouth to speak, his fangs glisten in the dining room light.

"Sleep tight, Miss Oasis," he lisps.

Then he climbs onto the rail and leaps off, somersaulting in mid-air like an Olympic champion, and lands silently across the alley. He smiles up at me and waves before taking off around the corner as a blur.

I savor the breeze for a few minutes, mind a maelstrom of relief and confusion, then return to my room to listen to my girl-friend's heart.

twenty-one

<u>**Talon Tepes**</u>

Hey you ♡

         Hey ♥ How are you?

The web of our life is of a mingled yarn, good and ill together

         I assume this means you're having fun?

Tis neither here nor there

Jk I sure am!!! I'm sad I only have a day left, but I think I locked in my spot at the globe

I heard what happened. How are you?

         Eh (ʻ⌣ʻ)

         Did Laura tell you?

Cy did. The psychic link is "offline." Tina says it's mal-nutrition, but whatever it is, it's sparing my sister from being yelled at

Anyway I won't bring all that

back up unless you want to
talk about it.

No need to yell at her. I think
I did enough damage. Not
sure what's left to say either,
but I appreciate it. I just wish I
didn't feel like Dracula doesn't
trust me. It's not like I can love
Laura in isolation.

I can't believe this is your life
(̄ ∧ ̄*)

I understand completely

Not to be all "you can't fix
him" but Dracula isn't normal. He's been set in his ways
for centuries. Trust issues
are the least of his concerns

Maybe, but they're at the top of
the list for me right now. That's
my girl

Well in that case, what are
you up to today?

I'm gonna try installing box
braids for the first time

Why do you do your hair
yourself?

I mean is it quality time alone
with yourself or is it mostly
for protective purposes?

Hm...both, I think. Why?

Justina wants to meet you.
She also does my hair when
I'm in a rush and I'm sure
she'd be happy to do yours.

She's also the perfect person

to talk about this with. She's
known Dracula longer than
anyone except the Devil

        I did hurt my finger running
        from August and can foresee
        braiding being a pain in the ass
        (×﹏×)

        And I suppose I've met every-
        one in your immediate family
        but her. Is she a vampire?

Yeah and a witch. I'll send her
your #

Heads up: she likes to play
games

        She can certainly try.

        *

Justina Szilágyi-Drăculești

Szia Oázis (´♡﹏♡`)

        Hey Tina! (∩﹏∩) How are
        you?

Disgusted! (´ ∀ `)╯ ～ ♡

I'm cat sitting while Voivode
Dracula sleeps. Hideous
creatures. I would much,
much rather behold you

        Bring her over here! I haven't
        seen my bunny since I met her
        and I need a cute fix
        ฅ(•ㅅ•🍬)ฅ

Before I can follow up by asking what time she's free, a knock
resounds from the front door. I'm still sitting on the toilet while
wrapped in a towel, blow dryer balanced on the sink. I slather on
lotion at top speed, then dress in a long-sleeved t-shirt and sweats.
I've never met a love interest's cx before, since Raymond and

I were practically kids when we first got together, so I try to swallow my nerves as I open the door. The person on the other side takes my breath away: Laura, dressed in high-waisted jeans and a tight t-shirt featuring a Rubik's cube with only the red, white, and green sides showing. She beams at me, Bird Bones tucked complacently under her arm, Popeyes bag dangling off her wrist.

"No dream of mine could do your face justice," she says. "Will you marry me?"

My first instinct—to pull her into my arms and kiss her whole face—doesn't arise.

That's not Laura—not with that defined shadow falling across the threshold, stretching towards where I am, rippling like a disturbed pond while she stands still.

"Didn't you miss me, my love?" She asks.

I narrow my eyes. "Laura doesn't use contractions."

"*Dracula*," the imposter mutters darkly. Her pout looks so much like Laura's that I almost lean close to double check, but her shadow moves before I can, independently of the being it's attached to. It peels from the floor, a solid wall of darkness, and shields her from sight. Then it lowers like a curtain, revealing a tall, rosy-cheeked woman looking down at me.

"*Beautiful* Oasis." Her honey brown eyes drift from the threshold to my face. "You are… *beautiful*." She steps closer, dropping her voice. "We could be constellations," she whispers, shadow scintillating like a disturbed pond. "They'll see our stars in the sky and yearn for a glimpse of our light in their empty lives."

I crack my knuckles, lost for speech.

"Your life is a canvas, Oasis," she murmurs. "Will you let me come in and paint my love all over you?"

I find my voice at last. "I'm in a relationship, so no. Are you Tina?"

"Yes," she says. "Will you marry me?"

"No," I reply. "Come in."

Tina purses her plump red lips. She takes a step, then another, until she and Bird Bones are both firmly inside, standing in front of me. "Here is the disgusting feline," she says, raising Bird Bones, who has nothing but contentment and adoration in her golden eyes. Tina drops her unceremoniously, causing her tail to twitch irritably as she stalks towards the dining room. "This is from Voivode Dracula," she says, raising the Popeyes bag.

I take it in silence, feeling worse than hypocritical.

I've been ignoring my growling stomach all day.

"I already bought hair," I say, pointing to the packs that I purchased from the beauty supply store this morning, arranged on the table with several combs and pomades. "And I—"

Tina's hand darts out, cinching around my wrist. She tugs my sleeve up to my elbow, twisting my hand left and right as she examines my scars.

"When I come from, scars were the language of battle." Her hand travels up my arm without touching my skin, raising shivers from my bones. "The alphabet of war."

I ease my hand from her grip. "I haven't been to war."

"Then why do I smell it on you?" She asks, pulling out a chair, gesturing for me to sit.

She perches on the chair across from me and opens the bag, dark hair rippling with every movement. She pulls out the two boxes—one for each of us—plus two cans of Sprite with a bodega receipt clinging to the condensation of one.

"You fear for Voivode Dracula's health," she says.

"Yes," I mumble.

"You love Voivode Dracula?"

"Yes," I say, louder. "I do."

Tina nods pensively. "Then let me ask you this," she says. "Will you marry me?"

I scowl. "No."

"It was worth a shot," she sighs. "If I were stingier, I would tell you some of the worst things he's ever done so that you would flee his arms for mine." She cracks open a Sprite and sips. "Next lifetime."

I open my can. "Since when do vampires drink pop?"

"It's not for me." Tina breaks a biscuit in half, brow raised. "My brides get hungry too," she says. Simultaneously, something dark crawls into my vision, rising from the floor and over the table legs like a swelling river. Her shadow moves like a being of its own, bending without light's influence. It rises above her head, hiding her behind a curtain of darkness. When it falls, she's gone, and a dark-haired, dainty Japanese woman sits in her place, wearing her loose clothes, holding the same biscuit in her hands. She says something don't understand, then takes a huge bite.

Her shadow lifts, too, then drops with a silent splash.

A tall woman with dark ebony skin and a bald head sits in the chair now, tilting it back on two legs, munching a mouthful of biscuit. "*Mmm*-mm-*mm*."

Again, their shared shadow lifts, and again it plops back to the floor at the feet of a paper-thin blonde woman with green eyes and stubble on her sharp jaw. "I *love* this century's food," she says thickly. She swaps the biscuit for a wing. "Salt is my new religion."

Her shadow rises like a curtain, then hits the floor again, writhing and rippling.

Tina smiles at the look on my face.

"This could be us, Oasis. You drink blood for me, and I eat food for you—for *eternity*," she says, a loud whisper.

"I'd rather eat *with* you than *for* you," I reply, tipping pepper into my mashed potatoes. "Aren't you having a good time?"

"I suppose I'm having a good time," she sighs, bested.

We finish eating in near silence, except for Bird Bones bathing near the fire escape.

Tina clears the table afterward, then examines my supplies like an appraiser.

"Were you testing my loyalty?" I ask.

"On behalf of Voivode Dracula? A-*hah!*" She laughs, throwing her head back. "His very existence is a test on the world."

"I never got the chance to ask you about the decor for our lovemaking," I say. "Was *that* a test?"

"Alas, I was at the bottom of the stairs, waiting for you to flee in fear and come into my arms." She sighs listlessly. "I fled when the lovemaking began but resolved to try again."

Lost for a reply, I grab my laptop off my desk and open it on the table.

"Do you want to watch a movie?"

"I'll show you what I want to watch." She takes the laptop for herself and turns the screen out of sight.

Just when I start to implement a rated-G rule, she puts it back. She's logged into her YouTube account, and all her liked videos have to do with Rubik's cubes—Rubik's cube algorithm explanations, Rubik's cube tournaments, reviews of Rubik's cubes designed for competitions, of Rubik's cubes greater than three-by-three, of Rubik's cubes that aren't even cubes.

The first video she navigates to is of an AI trying to solve a 100-by-100 cube.

"I take it you're a fan of Rubik's cubes."

"Ernő Rubik is a great Hungarian inventor. His cube is the highlight of modernity," Tina says proudly. "Second to salt and saturated fats." She moves behind my chair and combs her cold fingers through my blow-dried hair.

"Talon warned me that you like to play games," I say, watching the morsels of color line up onscreen.

"Voivode Dracula plays enough games with your heart. But then he learned from the finest," she sighs. I feel her cold lips next to my ear when she whispers, *"The serpent."*

I glance at my right arm, where I sliced Psalm 91:13 on my wrist like the time: *You will tread on the lion, next the cobra; you will trample the great lion and the serpent.* A relic from a time when the Devil was an angel to aspire against, and not the angel who took my girlfriend's heart out.

Tina dumps all the alligator clips on the table, then whisks open a pack of hair and begins to separate it for braiding. Another pack rustles and another.

I glance over my shoulder.

She isn't alone.

The three brides I saw eating are all standing around her, opening the other packs, patiently separating the hair and lining it up along the backs of the chairs. They're all standing at the edge of Justina's rippling, writhing shadow, like they're wading in dark water.

"Voivode Dracula trusts no one if he can help it," Justina says, gently turning my head to start the first braid. "He is cruel, conniving, paranoid, manipulative, volatile, spiteful, vindictive, vengeful, and blood-thirsty."

Each adjective makes my eyebrows raise a little higher, until my forehead is sore.

"And he wore his outside clothes to bed when he was human," she concludes. Then she drops her voice. "But you should see under the faulds."

"See what?" I ask.

"Monster cock." She smirks and lets go of my head. "Very fat," she says, indicating length and girth with her hands and the comb.

It takes everything not to cover my face with my hands. It's convoluted enough, discussing my shapeshifting girlfriend with her ex-wife, but objectifying her default form with her ex-wife feels like a level of irreverent I never thought obtainable.

"Always made me curious," Tina continues, "but I'm a lesbian."

"What about Jonathan?"

"Ayaka's appetite was to blame for our involvement with

Jonathan Harker and John S*ssseward*," she hisses. Then she says in a milder tone, "She liked their accents. Didn't you, baby love?"

A soft laugh near my ear makes me jump. A second pair of hands touches my head; in the corner of my eye, I see the thin, porcelain arms of the bride who must be Ayaka braiding on the other side of my head.

I try to look at her, but another pair of hands repositions my head.

"Voivode Dracula will never die. He'll never break," Tina says. "He will simply accrue damage and never work through it because he died at twenty-four, before the human brain is fully developed. That's really the long and short of it."

I flex my fingers, causing the half-healed gash on my index finger to sting. "I guess that's insightful."

YouTube interrupts the AI's progress with an advertisement for itself. I feel hands and more hands on my head, all of them cold, parting my hair and braiding it at lightning speed. The finished braids fall on my back and shoulders too fast for me to gauge how much of my head is left.

Tina strolls in front of me, lips pursed, seeming lost in thought as she pulls her necklace from under her shirt: a Rubik's cube keychain dangles from a black leather string. She kisses it like a rosary.

"I'm to blame, to some extent, for his recent stupidity. I may or may not have ruined his previous meal," she says, now twisting it absently, "when I accidentally convinced his beloved Lucy Westenra to become a vampire."

My skin crawls, but I breathe through it, stopping my heart from racing before it starts. "You did?"

She shrugs noncommittally. "She asked me if I thought she was ugly, and with honesty being my best policy, of course I said yes."

My eyes widen.

"I also told her vampires can't be ugly because otherwise they'd never attract prey. And sure, *I* thought she was ugly, but I didn't think she'd actually ask," she says, brow scrunched like she's still confused.

I watch her face pass through various shades of vexation, unsure of how to feel, or if I even feel. The gulf between me and Laura feels so wide that everything but the solution to us is for the birds.

Tina leaves for the kitchen, shadow stretching like the light is moving and not her. One at a time, pairs of hands leave my head. I blink hard several times as the brides they belong to drain from the room, pouring into her shadow as she fills a clear glass bowl with water. She returns with one hand on the side of the bowl, one hand on the base. As she walks, bubbles begin to rise from the bottom. Steam wafts over the rim. It's the two of us and the first three brides I met, each holding a small towel and a fistful of my braids to dip in the hot water.

"Where did the others go?" I ask. "I didn't get to thank them."

"I'll let them know," Tina says, smiling. "Of course, you could tell them yourself if you became my bride."

I sigh and lean my head back over the chair. "I'm in a committed relationship, Tina. I'm sorry."

She stands over me, arching a brow. "Me too," she pouts.

Her brides dip my hair, sealing the braids, and roll them dry.

To my left, a towel flumps to the floor—then to the right, then behind me.

The brides are gone.

Tina's shadow ripples in a puddle on the floor. She takes my hands, pulls me towards the bathroom.

The face I see in the steam-stained mirror is a stranger's.

For once, she's looking at herself and not away.

For another, she likes what she sees.

My reflection is alone. It looks like my edges are laying themselves when in fact, Justina has a comb and edge control in her hands.

She circles me like a sculptor, moving from one side of the sink to the other. When she looks at me, her canines are longer, sharpened to fine, dainty points that dimple her lip when she smiles.

A moment later, she's frowning, too—smiling and frowning, like I just told her the most out of pocket thing she's ever heard in her long life.

"Voivode Dracula has ears for his prey above all others," she says, lisping, "and none for himself. He listens to your heart to be sure you live on."

"I know," I say, guilt-ridden.

"Why do you listen to his?"

My blood runs cold.

My damp braids swing over my shoulders as I look in the direction of my room.

"*Shhhhh*," Tina whispers. She puts a finger to her lips even though I haven't spoken. "I'll help you with this game," she says, nodding.

"I don't know what you're talking about," I lie, unconvincing even to myself.

"You have told Laura why you hesitate to eat, yet she has not told you the same. I don't believe our Victorian era antics are to blame."

"Meaning?"

"Lucy's loss was tragic, but she was only his friend. Not his food," she says, dark eyes half-closed and on me. "Old habits die slow deaths, Oasis, and Vlad Dracula is *old*. Let me show you my theory as to the nature of his fast."

In the corner of my eye, I see something dark swarming across the bathroom floor. A tide of black crawls from under the tub, washing over the tiles like water over the banks of the river. It creeps up the walls, swallowing the mirror, spreading up the frosted window like a tint.

The last I see of Tina before she slips out of sight is the comb in her hand and the Rubik's cube pressed to her lips.

I'm alone in a darkness so dark that it feels like I'm nowhere at all.

I'm not afraid.

None of the palpitations from before the darkness carried over to where I am now.

"My wife Justina wished to dine with us," comes Tina's voice, but dramatically deeper, like she's impersonating someone. "I would say no to *God* before I said no to her."

The curtain of black drops, and I'm standing in a drafty square room, fuzzy teal towel completely at odds with the medieval furnishings around me.

A long, wide wooden table sits in the depressed middle. On one side sits Tina in a midnight-colored dress and furs, coronet perched on her silken black hair, and Vlad Dracula—deceptively older, adorned in dark red, with a thick, curly mustache and stubble, and his coronet snug over a head full of tumbling brown curls.

Opposite them sit two men, both wearing colorful, draped clothes and huge white turbans. A bard in black furs plays a sitar-like instrument in the corner near the fire.

None of them seem to notice me standing near the wall beneath two curved swords and a bronze shield with a dragon on it. I cross my arms and step closer to the table. There are guards stationed at the wide doorway—four of them in furs and armor, hands on the hilts of their swords. More are stationed around the room, flanking the enormous fireplace.

"Voivoda Dracula, congratulations on your marriage."

I squint.

One of the men sitting across from them spoke, but in Tina's voice—deeper, and with a different accent.

"Thanks, Mr. Ottoman," says Tina herself. She looks to Dracula, who takes her free hand and kisses her knuckles, green eyes aglow, like he can't believe his luck. She smiles at his touch. "And you haven't asked, but I can tell you want to know, so *yes*. He's hung."

The man laughs, but his laugh is Tina's laugh.

Tina's head turns, and her eyes fall on me.

"Beautiful Oasis," she says, smiling. "You found your way."

A second Tina remains seated like a glitch as she rises and walks around the table to meet me under a lit torch. I take her outstretched hand and let her lead me down the cold stone steps.

"When are we?" I ask.

"1475. Budapest. Voivode Dracula is nearly a vampire. He still eats human food to keep up appearances." Tina pulls off her coronet and runs her fingers through her hair while the other her listens to her husband speaking. "This memory is fuzzy."

"Is that why you're paraphrasing?" I ask.

A smile plays on her lips.

"...*war*," the man is saying with Justina's voice. "War war war *war* war war. Hungary, Ottoman, Hungary, Ottoman war war war war. *War*, war war, Hungary, Wallachia, Transylvania, Ottoman, war, war, war, war. War war war war." He and his companion point at the table while she repeats these words with different inflections. "War war war war. *War* war war."

As he continues to argue his one-worded point, a troupe of servants walks in with empty plates and goblets on bronze carts.

"Sir, my dick is *far* too big for religious conflicts—I mean, you really *must* be fucking with me right now," Dracula says, rapping his ringed knuckles on the wood. "Have you any other horrible ideas to present before we eat?"

The Justina at my side laughs quietly as she guides me closer for a better view of the table. In comes the food on more carts—platters of vegetables and lamb, steaming loaves of bread.

Dracula watches the food being served with a look I recognize all too well—the shrewd eye monitoring the journey of each morsel onto his plate.

"Leave these carbs for me," he says to the bread cutter, who nods and leaves the stone pan next to his plate.

A bottle of wine makes its way from the cart to a servant with a bucket of hot water. After a few minutes, the servant removes the bottle and presents it to Dracula, who uncorks it and sniffs with flared nostrils. He fills his goblet and raises it in a toast to his visitors.

The Tina at his side touches his arm, pulling the goblet away from his face. "Forgive me, but I have lost one husband already, and you have many, many, *many* haters. It's not that I don't trust you, Mr. Ottoman," she says, gesturing humbly, "but I would prefer that someone first drink from Voivode Dracula's cup."

"Why would we, his political enemies, tamper with his wine?" The man's companion demands. "Do what you must, but you have lost your *mind* if you believed we would make an attempt on the Voivode's life."

"I believe you, I believe you, but my wife Justina deserves peace of mind," Dracula says, beckoning at no one in particular. "Bring me some loser to taste this wine."

A servant comes forth to take his goblet and carries it off to the side.

The Tina holding my hand looks to the open doors as the sound of heavy footsteps pours in.

Two armed guards drag a third person into the room—a black-haired young man, bound and gagged too tightly to move or speak. They stop to the left of the table, adjacent to Vlad Dracula, and wait with the unmoving hostage.

"One of his little lovers," whispers the Tina at my side, light with laughter.

I hear a kick drum pounding steadily amidst the lute notes, playing a broody tune as the torches flicker in the draft.

"This was my heartbeat back when I had one," she says, hushed like we're at the movies.

Dracula gestures for the guards to remove the gag, eyes fixed on the Ottoman visitor, who's staring ashen faced at the welts around the hostage's mouth.

Tina watches herself hold onto Dracula's arm as a guard forces his wine down the captive's throat. He gags and convulses, thrashing limply in their hands.

"A prince should protect his bed as aggressively as he protects his borders," Dracula says, except his voice isn't Tina's; it's the one I recognize, weathered with artificial age, but still as deep and measured as the man who came to ask my forgiveness. "*This*," he says, gesturing to the spluttering, choking hostage, "is why my wife follows me everywhere but onto the battlefield."

The visitor's companion keeps him from getting to his feet. He balls his hand in a fist, like he doesn't know whether to throw a punch or scream.

Dracula motions for the return of his goblet. He sniffs deeply, putting the rim right under his long nose.

"You could have made my wife a widow," he says curtly.

Another sharp gesture with his ringed hand, and the guards drag the captive to the edge of the table.

Dracula stands to his full height and steps away from his ornate chair. He pulls a dagger from his boot, jams it under the lover's Adam's apple, and twists it like a spigot. Then he holds his goblet beneath the fountain of blood that pours from his throat.

He takes a mighty sniff of his goblet, then a small sip, and smacks his lips as he sits back down to his arrangement of sliced bread.

"You may not be the Devil," the visitor says in a thundering voice that must have been his own, "but to the Devil you will answer."

The Voivode dips a slice of bread in his goblet and takes an enormous bite, face the epitome of ecstasy. Slowly, the age slips away, until he looks as young as the Vlad Dracula I know, too.

"*I already do.*"

His deep laugh echoes in my ears as the scene strips away.

I'm back in the bathroom again.

I didn't feel much in Tina's head, besides curiosity, but back in the real world, I can barely hear my thoughts beneath my heartbeat.

"The goings-on of those Victorian clowns have little to do with the wayward beast's refusal to eat," Justina says, laughing softly. "Time is a desert when you have nothing but. You must remind him."

"Remind him that he's immortal?" I breathe. "I think he knows."

"Remind him that you are his Oasis. Your blood is his reason, your heartbeat his lullaby." She pouts. "You should be mine, you know."

A small smile breaks through the rush.

"Maybe next lifetime."

Tina sighs and rolls her eyes. "You're only saying this because you know I won't have one."

September 3, 2019

Do you know where you are going, and what you are going to?

twenty-two

Mirage

Here's Helena's number. I'm sorry I brought up mom. And I'm sorry for ruining your one month anniversary. Does Laura hate me?

No. She's rooting for your recovery. Not everyone bounces back from being a jackass ٩(˘ ᵕ˘)

What's the treatment for that

Therapy (ﾉ◕ヮ◕)ﾉ*:･ﾟ✧

Seriously?

So when you tell ME to go to therapy, it's a suggestion, but when I say it, it's 'seriously'? Okay then ง(⁎˃̵ ⁎)ว

Okay well maybe I'm just not ready to cry in front of a stranger

I'll give you something to cry about: https://youtu.be/ Elc1ntXuWPY

Too far sis :(

<u>Helena</u>

Hey Helena it's Oasis
(°‿°♡)

**Aaaaah! You and those emo-
jis still haha**

**What are you doing later? I'm
out of class at 2:30.**

Where do you go to school?

Parsons

Oh that's so cool! I'm off at 3 if
you wanna stop by my job and
leave together.

Alright (≧‿≦) ♡

*

It took me a couple of hours to stop staring at the back of Kennedy's head, waiting for him to finally recollect the day he left me here with a stranger, but the only time he mentioned August was to express his relief over him not showing up.

Looks like my haven is too powerful to be tainted.

"Do you want me out here, or do you want me to hide in the office?" Kennedy asks seriously.

"I don't think hiding is necessary."

I flip the door sign to closed, then set to work straightening the comics while he balances the register. I sort of wish he'd come with me, but I don't say this aloud, because he probably would.

"My only concern is that she isn't here on her own behalf."

He frowns, mouthing numbers to himself as he counts the nickels.

"You mean you're worried she's here to try take you back?"

"I'm more worried she'll succeed," I admit.

"Which I get. Cult susceptibility is almost always situational, though. If anything, you'd be trying to deprogram her—assuming she isn't telling the truth." Kennedy whisks the dollar bills from their slot. "Have you told Laura?"

"I..."

Haven't seen Laura in over a week.

Haven't seen the face beneath hers since he left with a flaming hole in his chest.

Would be an absolute wreck if I didn't have his beating heart on my nightstand to monitor.

"I'm going to. We're kind of taking a break."

His jaw drops. "What happened? Actually, you don't have to talk about it right now," he says, saving me the trouble of crafting a lie on the spot. He fills out the deposit sheet and finishes signing the form, then seals the deposit envelope and sets it aside, giving me his full attention. "Do you need a hug?"

"Yes," I confess.

Kennedy flattens his hands on the counter and, with unprecedented agility, leaps onto it. He stands to his full height beside the register, grinning at my shock, then steps off, landing next to me with a floor-rattling thud and spreads his arms.

I shake my head and throw mine around him, squeezing hard enough to snap him at the rib cage.

He wheezes, then does the same, until we're both squeezing and wheezing, my ear on his cheek.

"I'm so happy you chose to participate in capitalism here of all places," he says hoarsely.

"Me too," I manage.

We let go in unison, each breathing like we went jogging.

"Well, I'll be in the gothic nook with this," he says, waving a copy of *The Hobbit*—the same one August feigned interest in and abandoned at the counter. "Yanno, I've given this book about ten tries already, but those cute little hobbit feet you drew may have sold me once and for all."

"Just the feet?" I ask. "Not the dragon or the wizard?"

"Just the feet," he says as he walks away.

Alone, I lean on the counter, staring at the edges of his shoe print on the glass.

Cypress unearthed the copy of *Frankenstein* I set aside for purchase and forgot. I open the book and fall upon a random line: *I bitterly feel the want of a friend.*

What a coincidence.

If I wasn't sold before, I am now.

"Can I take this copy of *Frankenstein* and pay for it tomorrow?" I call.

"Only if you come in ready to be quizzed on the first five chapters," Kennedy calls back.

My phone buzzes just as I flip to the opening pages.

I yell goodbye and step out into the warm, quiet afternoon.

I look left.

I see her soft green eyes before I see the rest of her face.

The last time I saw her, we were both gaunt as banshees, and too high to hold a conversation. Now, her cheeks are round and rosy, her body at least three times fuller beneath a long-sleeved blue V-neck and tight black jeans.

"Oasis?"

All my doubts slough away. I run and throw my arms around her, yanking into a back-breaking hug, bouncing on the balls of my feet. She's real, she's here, and she's healthy. Her weight gain is enough to dash the paranoia I had about her being here on behalf of the Angelorum: Zeke would never keep her in reach at this size.

"I'm so fucking happy to see you," she squeals in my ear.

"Me, too."

Pedestrians pass us by; the traffic light changes twice. A lifetime seems to come and go before we break apart.

I turn instinctively towards Central Park several blocks away.

Helena falls into step with me. "Sorry it took me so long to reach out. I was scared that...I was scared."

I thumb the pages of *Frankenstein*, glowering at the pavement. "I'll be having a serious conversation with my brother about boundaries," I say. "The last one was just me yelling."

"I don't blame him," she says, slinging her purse onto her other shoulder. "And this was before he spoke to me anyway. By then I'd already resigned to the idea that you hated me, so I ended up just thanking him for letting me know you were alive."

The sun gleams through a swelling strip of airplane exhaust, turning flyaway strands of dark hair into threads of gold around her face. I'd be overflowing with heartbreak over her words if I wasn't so grateful to see her.

"You're always in my thoughts," I say.

She smiles. "You, too."

A hunger headache winks in my temple. I survey both sides of the block, looking for somewhere to eat. It's time I put the days of starving myself firmly in the rearview mirror—if not for me, then for the person who can hear my vital signs from fifty miles away.

I spot a Hungarian pastry shop across the street, and though my only exposure to Hungarian anything is a several-centuries-old vampire witch, it'll have to do.

"I have to eat something. Are you hungry?"

"I ate on campus," Helena says, gathering her dark hair in a fist. "I used to have trouble eating food other people made. It broke my dad's heart."

"That's where I've been," I say, bittersweet. "My girlfriend has been helping me recover."

Helena arches a brow as we cross the street. "What?" I ask.

She shrugs nonchalantly. "I always wondered if you went that way."

"I didn't know for sure until I met her." I bite my lip, banging the crosswalk button with my fist. "I had my suspicions when I met you."

Helena looks away with a dimpled smile. She looks as beautiful amid the urban sprawl as she did in the verdant woods of Blessed Falls. "I was so scared you'd hate me for leaving you at the hospital," she says as we cross the street. "Then when I got out, I was scared you'd hate me for preaching the Angelorum in the first place."

"Life was so easy when I had no control over it," I confess. "But you gave me a blessing. *I* was scared that you'd never get that blessing yourself. When did you leave?"

"December. I was in the hospital regaining weight and deprogramming for weeks. My aunt pulled a lot of strings to get my application read at Parsons so long after the deadline. I got my blessings—twice over now that I'm here with you." Helena slows to a stop outside the pastry shop, fiddling with a lock of her hair. "Things were so fucked up when I left. I still haven't said a word to anyone. I've been beating around the bush with my therapist, but now that I'm with you…" She bites her lip, green eyes a plea. "Oasis, can we talk about that shit?"

"Helena," I say, taking her hand in both of mine, "I am *dying* to talk about that shit."

She grins. "I'll wait here, then."

I leave the pastry shop with three staff recommendations—a Hungarian donut, a Romanian cake with a plum in the middle, and Turkish baklava. I take small bites of each in rotation, mollifying my appetite.

Fifteen minutes later finds us under one of the towering elms in Central Park, looking out at an afternoon full of joggers and high school students.

Helena talks while I eat, starting with what happened after Philly. "I understand now why it was hard to feel truly close to anyone in Custodes Angelorum, but you were closer to me than anyone. Then you were gone, and I only had Zeke to talk to in any way other than passing."

"I always suspected we were the only people who were actually friends with one another," I remark.

"He does that on purpose, so that when someone does something he doesn't like, he can turn around and insist that he's spent more time with them than anyone and can see the evil in their heart," she says, curdled with disgust. "He tried to make you a martyr. The angels kept accusing me of ruining *your* path to divinity by taking you to the hospital. They were calling me jealous and disloyal, but then Zeke said he understood that I'd gotten so attached to you because you were everything I wasn't."

"Fuck him," I seethe.

"I did."

My jaw drops. Crumbs of baklava fall from my open mouth.

"Not real fucking," Helena clarifies. "Rape fucking." She gathers her hair above her head, then takes my hand and puts my fingers down the back of her shirt so that I can feel the smooth, rigid scar tissue from a thick cut on her shoulder. "I got my wings two weeks after you were gone."

I can feel the shards of my broken heart shifting as I probe the scar I on her back. I pull my hand away, speechless.

Helena lets her hair cascade down again. "I think you leaving scared him. He took away our phones and all the car keys over the next few months. He started assigning penance monitors to snitch on people who didn't cut deep enough to bleed. Oasis, he started *hitting* people with his stupid bibles," she says, lowering her voice even though we're alone. "He called everything he did an endurance test. It was like being in prison, except every awful thing got rebranded into a divine improvement tactic."

A cloud passes over the sun, plunging us in a chill.

"I got kicked out of the Psalms because I went up to one-oh-four. It was like the end of an eclipse," Helena continues. "The sun was out, and I started looking at everything around me for the first time. I hadn't even realized that Danielle was gone."

"She left?" I ask through a mouthful of pastry.

Helena nods. "Then Zeke boxed up her stuff and put it in his office. She came back for it, found me and said she wanted to talk to me about the food," Helena says, chewing the inside of her cheek. "She went to see Zeke about her stuff, and I never saw her again. When I asked him, he said he hadn't seen her at all."

I stuff the last of the plum pastry in my mouth, using the flavor as a buffer between my spirit and this news. Hearing all this, I wish I'd bought a dozen more. "I'm happy you left when you did."

"I am, too. I'm just ashamed of how long it took," Helena says. Then her voice cracks. "I think Octavio is dead."

"*What?*"

"He had a seizure. Probably from all the...everything," she says, lifting the neck of her shirt to blot her eyes. "Zeke and the guardians took him in the house to revive him, and he never came back out. They said they stabilized him and an ambulance came overnight when we were all asleep, but after the way Zeke reacted to me taking you to the hospital, I know that's not true."

The sun peeks through the clouds again, but I still feel cold. I only have a few memories of Octavio, which is more than I have of everyone besides Helena and Zeke himself, but helping a stranger move is an indisputable attribute of a good Samaritan, and I remembered that every time I saw him.

"Clarice told me to stop crying about him because it was clouding the air and making it hard for Zeke to hear the angels," Helena says, glowering as she wipes a frustrated tear from her eye. "They were trying for a baby. She'd just had a miscarriage when I left. She's half the reason I left."

"She probably would've been mine, too, if I hadn't almost died," I say dryly. "What happened?"

"I asked her if she didn't think a baby's crying would cloud whatever angel radio Zeke tunes into. Then I said maybe he put something in her food to make her miscarry the way she and the other guardians put stuff in our food."

"*You didn't,*" I gasp.

"I was just talking shit, but the look on her face said I'd hit the jackpot I wasn't going for," Helena says with a helpless shrug. "A week later, I got Nineteen-Sixteened."

"You got *what?*"

"For context," Helena prefaces, "Zeke added the book of John to his bible. On 8/18/18, he left a copy on everyone's pillow with a notecard saying the angels were getting anxious, and that they suggested an exercise to '*help*'," she says, adding drastic air quotes, "vessels who aren't vesseling. A Nineteen-Sixteen is a barefoot walk of shame from the mines to the falls—shirtless, so everyone can see your wings, which is supposed to be the vessel equivalent of Jesus carrying his cross. John 19:16."

"And *everyone* walks *two miles*?" I repeat.

"Zeke bound my hands and assigned people to hold the ropes. At the end, he asked me if I thought I deserved my wings, or if I should know what it feels like to fall. I said I deserved them. The angels didn't agree."

My heart numbs with horror. "Did he push you into the waterfall, too?"

She nods.

"And everyone *let him?*"

"I let him push everyone else who got Nineteen-Sixteened," Helena says, face flushed with shame. "I left about a month later—on foot. I *walked* to Philadelphia with no phone, no jacket, and no food."

My desserts have been working miracles through this conversation, but they're gone now, and I feel the full force of her words with no sweet treat to soften them. "I'm sorry, Helena."

Helena shakes her head forcefully, like she's clearing out the memories.

"Oasis, this is *me* saying sorry. To you *and* to me. It feels like I went to war and back, but I feel so much stronger just seeing you. Plus, I left with my weed plant and she's still thriving. You should check her out sometime." She lays on her back, hair fanned above her head like a nimbus. "Thank you for letting me tell you all this."

"Thank you for telling me," I say.

"I considered telling the police, too," she says.

"So did I," I confess. "But if white supremacists and school shooters watch the news and learn from one another, I'm sure cult leaders do the same."

"Yeah," Helena agrees quietly. "I just wish I could stop feeling like I left everyone else to die."

"Danielle probably felt the same," I say. Guilt, rage, and horror all battle for the spotlight in my heart. "Besides, Zeke would probably try and convince everyone we're tainted if we tried to talk anyone into leaving."

"They wouldn't need him for that," she says. "People were always jealous of you for being so close to him. They thought you threw away the good life. Suddenly Zeke's affection was a hot commodity."

I lay beside her, combing my fingers through my braids. "Were you ever jealous?"

"Nah." Helena interlocks her fingers on her stomach, grinning. "I was too busy wondering which way you went."

twenty-three

Laura's finished playlist clocks in at two hours and two minutes. Now it's onto the sleep playlist, which I now know wouldn't be for her, but for Dracula.

This complicates things.

Tangerine Dream set the stage for hers, but for his, I hear the tinkle of a glockenspiel over a buzzy bass, and soft swirly synths rising through it like ghosts from graves.

These are the opening sounds of one of Noctivagrants' earlier songs, recorded and pressed before I was born, but as easily recalled as a radio hit.

None of their music is available for streaming. They have no Wikipedia page, and their only digital mention is on an indie music forum, in which someone asked whether any of their music is online. Six others chimed in with the same question, but the thread locked years ago with no answers.

I've been through this research cycle before, each time convincing myself that I did my due diligence before resigning to regret. Not this time.

It's hardly five o'clock when I finish washing the dishes and putting away leftover fried chicken. There's plenty of time to revisit my abandoned markers or blow Kennedy away by reading the first five chapters of *Frankenstein*, but between Helena and my playlists, my mind is on one track only.

Nevertheless, I pack up my purse for a solo trip back to Central Park, layering my flannel over a black hoodie. I put Laura's phone in my pocket in case mine dies and head out, *Frankenstein* in hand. I walk in the wrong direction for several blocks, on a semi-deliberate path towards the gas station, where I pay for a pack of Twinkies and a holographic pocketknife.

It's only after I've gotten on the 1 train towards 86th that I inwardly admit it: I'm not going to Central Park.

I needed to see Helena. After seeing her, I can finally admit to myself that part of why I never planned a trip back to Blessed Falls. If she was there and I couldn't talk her into leaving with me, it would've been as bad as leaving empty-handed.

Now that Helena's a text message away, there's just one person left to liberate from the jaws of Custodes Angelorum, and she can't walk out on her own.

I read a few pages of *Frankenstein* in the Enterprise lobby, waiting for my rental to be washed and inspected.

After a year of being a pedestrian and nothing but, the most stressful part of driving is traffic. I never noticed from the street just how many serial tailgaters call this place home. By the fifth honk over my not blasting through the light the millisecond it turns green, I'm ready to burst through the HR-V's sunroof and scream.

Past Newark, there's hardly any westbound traffic. I relax and put on a playlist of Noctivagrants' contemporaries and inspirations— Télépopmusik, Faithless, Massive Attack, Four Tet. I can hear the points where I'd start blending some of their songs together if I were a DJ. These points keep my hands on the wheel, my foot on the gas, and my heart too occupied to hear my brain's alarms throughout the drive to Blessed Falls.

The sun is a peach-colored blur behind a thick patch of clouds by the time I see the town's wooden welcome sign: *Come to Blessed Falls! Angels will catch you.*

Waves of lush grass ripple like an emerald sea. Nostalgia fogs my head as I drive past Blessed River, Holy Creek, and Sacred Hills. It's even more beautiful now that I can see it without a film of drugs and starvation clouding my vision. The commune is on the northwest edge of town, skirting the mines that swallowed the first iteration of Blessed Falls.

I park half a mile away on the shoulder of the only road leading towards it. I don't risk playing any music while I wait for curfew. Music keeps me sane, and the sane thing to do would be putting the car in reverse. Instead, I loop a ten-minute voice memo of my girlfriend's beating heart. Mine is most likely out of echolocating range, which I try not to think about.

I have no plan.

Plans require forethought, and forethought is another part of what kept me away for so long.

Laura offered to come here with me, but I need to do this alone. For one, every building in this commune was a chapel at some point, and who knows what that could do to her? For another, I'm not ready for her to see what my life was before her. For her to feel the same unplaceable abjection I felt while walking down the road for the first time.

I made my bed.

It's time to lay in it.

9:19 curfew comes and goes. I leave the car unlocked and set off on the ten-minute walk down the dirt road.

From the vantage point of gone, the chapels fashioned into dormitories, crammed with enough people to be a small college campus, look alien, if not downright inhumane. It feels like the crosses above them are watching me.

Sunset leaves a gold lacquer over the treetops, hemming a deep blue sky. It's empty out, but dim light shines through some of the curtains, and figures move back and forth. The Guardians' house sits at the end of the dirt road, with a facade of chipped white paint and a shingled roof. The only lights are upstairs.

I sneak behind the penance chapel through the untrimmed grass. Ivy hugs the brick beneath the stained-glass saints gazing inward. I can just make out the edges of the exorcism chapel beneath the oaks, and the crest of the hill that rolls down to the mines.

The porch attached to Zeke's office comes into view. I remember nights when he suspended curfew so that some of us could smoke and trip with him—the inner circle I never realized I was a part of because I felt close to him alone.

I creep up the porch steps and work at picking the lock with my gas station knife. When the deadbolt gives, I slip the blade between the doorknob and the wall, and press.

The door creaks lightly. I freeze, but there's no sound.

Zeke's office is unoccupied. It's exactly the same as it was every time I came in feeling lost or lonely, down to the tray of blank index cards. Sometimes, I still feel like he's watching me, conferring with the angels about what he should write on them.

I didn't factor my feelings into the non-plan.

Somehow, I foolishly assumed I'd step calmly into the same room in which I had my back mutilated, my body violated, and my future ripped away, placed in the hands of angels who weren't there. Memories of all the horrible things I did to myself nip at my heels like hounds, but being in here reminds me that no matter how responsible I am for myself, my anger is misplaced. Zeke saw I had no will and no way, and so he gave me one, using divine purpose to play God with my life.

I point the flashlight on Laura's phone at the stained-glass doors. Two grey angels kneel before one another, separated by black handles.

I wondered about this room, but never asked. These stained-glass angels guarding it helped me maintain the illusion that this was all sacred. I pry them apart with the knife, then swap it for Laura's phone.

I anticipated the vaguely organized possessions of former vessels in a few sparse piles, or on a table, gathering dust like relics in an attic. What Zeke has going on in here looks like an evidence storage room. Shelves wrap around the square walls, all with ample space to hold just over a dozen labeled, lidded cardboard boxes.

I move close to one. It's labeled in Zeke's curt penmanship on a 'Hello my name is' sticker:

Don - Kokabel

Next to that is a cross, or a dagger.

I compare it to the box next to it.

Andrea - Yeqon

No dagger.

I've never heard of these people.

The light falls on a wood patterned box, labeled with a daggerless, familiar name.

Helena — Sariel

Sariel is a fallen angel.

A Watcher in the Book of Enoch.

I move on, heart thundering when I see a box with my name.

Oasis - Semyaza

Semyaza is another Watcher in the Book of Enoch, an angel who helped lead the rebellion in heaven. I have no dagger, either. In all my time here, never did I consider that I might end up the vessel of a fallen angel. I was always going to be Gabriel.

I don't have time to be curious about Zeke's psychopathy. I open the lid of my box and shine light on the contents.

Tears sting my eyes and fall fast.

The Noctivagrants' album that I need for Dracula's playlist

is right on top, with a dark film photo of the Kansas River at night for the cover art. The next has a blurry picture of me and Mirage's sandbox in the backyard, also at night. The third album is the motherlode I came here for, in every sense of the word.

The band chose a picture of me, Mirage, and Mom at the county fair as the sleeve for her pressed ashes. In it, we're somewhere between 3 and 4. I'm in her left arm, and he's in her right. We're stuffing cotton candy in her Afro, and she isn't stopping us.

I step out of the terror and into the light.

There's nothing to fear while holding this.

Seeing her smile one more time was worth this panic.

I forgot all about the folded Billie Holiday sweatshirt I left, and the hyper-coordinated black and green plaid pants, black and blue plaid flannel button up, and black and purple gingham high-top sneakers from what I considered to be my Midwestern version of an emo phase.

Most of these clothes are for a skinnier, sicklier Oasis—leggings that wouldn't fit over my arms, let alone my thighs, shirts so small that their only use would be drying my hair.

The records are supposed to be my priority, but since the whole box is here, I may as well. I close the lid, then ease it off the shelf. Unprepared for the weight, I elbow a box beside it before stabilizing. From within comes a hollow clacking sound.

I glance at the label.

Hello my name is
Danielle - Azazel

The hairs on the back of my neck prickle upright. Another fallen angel. Another dagger.

I nudge the lid up. A well-loved sketchbook slants over something round. I pull it towards me, balancing my box on my hip, then move the sketchbook off it. All the possessions in the box are hidden under a pile of bleached bones. A skull with no teeth sits on a folded beanie. The phalanges and metacarpals colliding must have made the rattling sound. They surround individual ribs and a spear-like sternum, all in disarray like toys in a chest.

There are verse numbers carved in the bones.

I don't take more than a glimpse. I back away, nearly dropping my box as I stumble towards the door.

Danielle went into Zeke's office and never came out. Clearly, she wasn't the first. That could have been me if my heart had given out hours earlier.

Just a boxful of bones in an office.

There's a long drive ahead to break down about this. Sprinting out with no regard for the noise I make sounds like just as bright of an idea—as bright as can be with such a stupid parent idea, but before I can move, the aged floor creaks in the chapel hallway, outside the other door to Zeke's office, which soon eases open.

I don't have time to close the doors to the closet of bones when the light turns on.

I see a familiar shadow fall into over the desk and freeze, feeling every drop of petrified disgust that I said I'd save for later.

Zeke approaches from the right and opens the door all the way. The surprise on his face doesn't last long. His eyes home in on me standing in the dark, box in hand. His physical appearance hasn't changed, but I see him through a grotesque filter now, every feature of his face growing more hideous by the second.

"The angels said you would return," he says.

I don't reply. I'm too close to vomiting for speech.

His gaze goes past me to Danielle's box, lid halfway off.

"Oasis, what have you done?" He asks, but his voice sounds empty—devoid of any real gravity, or shock, or anger.

A million furious, wry retorts run through my mind, none stronger than the urge to flick the pocketknife out and stick it between his ribs. Thoughts of violence smother all common sense, like a tsunami devouring the coast. My own thirst for bloodshed scares me more than he does. It prompts me to stride through the angel doors.

Zeke swipes for me, but I duck to the side, ramming the back door open with my shoulder.

"Come back here, Oasis."

I take the porch steps down two at a time. Stars twinkle in the cobalt blue sky, more plentiful here than in New York—beautiful, even as I power walk out of the chapel. I walk quickly through the grass, eyes on the road as I weave my way back to it. I focus on putting one foot in front of the other, trying my damnedest to ignore him screaming my name.

Something hard hits me between the shoulders, knocking the wind out of me. I stumble but manage to keep a hold of the box. I keep walking, but look over my shoulder to see what it is. I can just make out Zeke walking quickly away from the chapel holding something in his arms. The corner of a white book juts from the grass behind me.

Zeke's bible.

He lobs another with a grunt. It skims the tip of my nose on its way past my head, bringing tears to my eyes.

I run.

More bibles glance off my arms and legs, and more screams bounce off my eardrums. I reach the gravelly road, Nikes kicking up dust and rocks. Left and right, chapel curtains sweep aside as lights flicker on. I don't stop to absorb the faces peering out at me and Zeke.

"*I stand in the presence of God,*" he yells, hurling another, "*and I have been sent to speak to you and to tell you this good news.*"

Luke 1:19.

The verse featured most prevalently on my body.

"I GAVE YOU YOUR LIFE, OASIS," Zeke screams.

It takes everything and more not to turn around and challenge this.

Years of painting myself with a razor. Years of starving. Years gone.

I see the Honda grille as I pass the last house, hugging the box tighter when it slips against my torso.

I don't look back to see if he's gaining ground. As far as I'm concerned, he isn't there. I'm alone, running because I want to, not for dear life.

He isn't there, screaming my name or my verse.

He isn't there.

He isn't there.

He isn't there.

Yet I hear his footsteps getting louder, his breath coming in gasps too short to squeeze words out. It doesn't matter. The car is here, hood still warm when I crash gratefully into it. I stumble along, breathing hard, and wrench the back door handle. The door doesn't open. Instead, my elbow cracks painfully, and I drop the box.

I wrench the driver's door with the same result.

The doors I know I left unlocked, locked automatically.

So much for forethought.

It feels stupid to fumble around for the keys rather than keep running—to dig my quaking hand in my pocket like the final girl in a horror film.

Zeke is close enough that he could hit me with a bible if he had any left.

My fingers find the clicker. The interior lights flick on.

I wrench open the door, slamming Zeke in the face and chest as he gains ground on me. I pull it back and slam it on him again, using the time it takes him to regain his balance to grab the box and throw it at the passenger seat.

A hand grips my left shin.

I kick hard, clinging to the steering wheel, struggling to pull myself in, slam the brake pedal with my right foot, and press the start button all at once.

The door opens all the way, then slams on my left foot.

I feel a pop and scream. The horn blares under the heel of my palm as I try to grab my ankle.

Fingers tangle in my braids and yank my head back.

The force makes me choke. Tears and stars chop my vision to pieces.

Zeke drags me out of the car scrambling and screaming. My ankle throbs and sears. My fingertips blister trying to hold onto the center console, the seat, the door handle.

I fall facedown, sending splinters through my ribcage, and inhale a lungful of dust. Laura's phone skids out of my pocket as I struggle to shield my face. I can't reach for it, can't reach for my own phone to let someone know how badly I fucked up, coming here alone, barely armed.

Zeke rolls me over. The knife slips out of my chest pocket and clangs on the road near my head. The car's interior lights illuminate the blue shadows under his eyes, which look hollow and unfamiliar.

This isn't the Zeke I knew. This one is a different, more desperate breed of monster.

Or maybe he was this all along, and I didn't, or couldn't, or wouldn't see it.

I kick at his torso and groin, sending white hot pain through my ankle. He takes my shoulders in his hands, pinning me to the dirt road.

"Prove to me that you deserve the life I gave you," he pants in my face, shaking me like my father would when I couldn't stop crying as a child. Then he raises me a few inches and slams me on the ground.

Everything muffles and dims. I'm losing the battle to stay conscious, my body a minefield of aches and pains.

He didn't give me life.

My mother did.

I know Mom would rather I let her ashes crumble in the middle of nowhere than risk my soul by coming back, but she can't understand what it's like being in a world without her. She'll never feel the pain of slowly forgetting her voice.

I hear the door slam and feel Zeke's arms under me. Each throb of my head feels like a thunderclap. I beg myself to stay awake, to fight as hard and cleverly this time as I did when a vampire and his handlers tried using me to get to my girlfriend. But there's no cavalry of werewolves on the hunt for me or my captors, and the space I asked for fills with darkness that soon claims me for its own.

bunnicula

Bunnicula doesn't remember much before the shadow. She can faintly recall taking glamour shots for PetFinder, but nothing more. After that came the dungeon, and the creature that converted her from adorable prey to adorable prey with fangs. The shadow stripped her of her hunger for hay, and left her with an appetite for human blood and carrots.

The shadow crept into her head, softly telling her that she was a gift for Oasis. Oasis.

The first and only warmth Bunnicula has felt in her new life as a vampire bunny.

The past few days have been her first out of the hutch, where she has so far enjoyed several Spicy Hot V8 and O-negative smoothies and engaged in curious sniffing with Bird Bones, the sunset-colored cat with an appetite for human blood and the occasional mouse.

Mostly, she's been with the shadow, which had stuffed its sweatpants pockets full of carrots and vials of blood so that Bunnicula would be cozy on their journey through the infinite storage unit containing the annals of music. The shadow spoke to her as it listened to certain songs, telling Bunnicula that they reminded it of Oasis' heartbeat at this or that moment in their relationship.

She will return to us, the shadow said whenever she asked about the soft thumping sound that filled her floppy ears and the lavender smell that tickled her nose—two of few things that had survived her twenty-minute short term memory. *We are hers.*

Tonight, at the behest of its brother, the shadow left the house. It put on its most recent face, Laura, and searched its fathomless closet for an outfit, carrying Bunnicula in the crook of its arm. Recent though their acquaintanceship may be, Bunnicula perceived quite easily that the immiserated shadow would've preferred to stay in its dungeon seeing and speak to no one except Bunnicula and the other occupants of its menagerie. In the end, it put on yet another Champion sweatsuit, but in pink, fitted for Laura's smaller figure.

"Did you *have* to bring the bunny, Master?" Asks Cypress, laying on his back on the floor, console controller balanced on his stomach.

The shadow, cradling a glass of wine, glances at Bunnicula on the other end of the couch.

Bunnicula hops daintily across the cushions, sniffing its pocket for carrots. The shadow scoops her into its lap and pulls one from its Champion fanny pack by the leaves.

"She will return to us," it says, stroking Bunnicula's cheek.

"Yeah, but not tonight," Cypress says, not looking away from his video game, which involves an elf burdened with bow and arrow running over a hillside gathering flowers. "You're gonna overstimulate that poor thing."

On the contrary, Bunnicula enjoys the muffled music beyond this niche of the club, the sounds of wasted vampires and other nightly creatures enjoying one another's company *without* a bunch of humans running around funking up the place with their tantalizing scents.

"Who's to say you're ready to see her, Laura?" Asks Tina, the vampire witch eating fettuccine alfredo in the corner. "Apologies often require explanations, and even *I* see no reasonable explanation as to why you would let your food molder."

"Oasis ain't *moldering*. You're being dramatic, T," Cypress chides. "Master, I think what she's trying to say is that you're bringing stress into the life of your human for what *seems* like no good reason."

"I'm saying this in *addition* to the other thing," Tina corrects. "One more incident along these lines and I'll have no choice but to claim the blood and love of Oasis. She will marry me, and she won't ever have to *return* to me because she'll never leave."

The shadow opens its mouth, fangs glinting, and hisses mightily.

Tina drops the forkful of pasta she'd been about to eat and returns the gesture.

Upon hearing Oasis' name, Bunnicula points her mind to the shadow in search of answers. Why is she gone, where did she go, when is she coming back?

She will return to us, the shadow replies again, resolute. *We are hers.*

"I hope it wasn't something I said," says the Norse puppy Tora, currently let loose off her Asgardian leash. She adds battlements to a castle of cards on the squat table near Tina.

Nearly everyone the shadow holds dear is here with it while it broods, yet it seems no less inclined to stop doing so.

"How's she supposed to return to you when you don't have a phone?" Asks Cypress.

"She has a phone. You have a phone," Tora says, frowning. "I paid a thousand dollars for that phone and gave it to you when you woke up."

The shadow sucks its teeth in silence.

"*Odin's eye, Bats.* I had to borrow money from Uncle Loki," Tora says, disgruntled. "You better not have lost it."

"I left it somewhere safe," the shadow says. Its attention sways in the direction of its sister tearing the curtains apart.

Talon enters with a suitcase and duffel in tow. Exhausted bags rest under her eyes and her heavy frown morphs when she sees Bunnicula in her sister's lap. "Who is this?" She asks, closing the curtains behind herself.

"A gift," the shadow says, stroking Bunnicula's head. "Bunnicula awaits the return of Oasis with me."

Talon's scowl deepens drastically.

"Well, while *you* were here awaiting *her,* *I* was awaiting at the airport for you to pick me up." She glowers exasperatedly. "I can't believe you'd let your health get to the point where you can't even talk to *me,*" she says, dragging her suitcase in, stopping short of the shadow. "I paid sixty dollars for an Uber here."

"I am sorry," it says, sipping, both testy and ashamed. "It will not be this way for much longer. She will return to us."

"How can she return to you if you don't have your phone?" Cypress points out.

"It is in a safe place."

"Is this place safe?" Talon demands, one hand on her hip, the other brandishing her own phone.

The shadow observes the screen.

Bunnicula, unable to decipher the light, feels colder than cold beneath her cape of black fur as the shadow swells with darkness.

"Oasis has gone in search of her mother's voice," the shadow says.

"Don't tell me that's where the cult is," Talon says, ashen-faced.

Cypress pauses his game. "What kind of cult? Hubbard or Jones?"

"Does it matter? She could be in danger."

"They are misled by a false prophet. It claims to speak with angels," the shadow says pensively.

Bunnicula, having nibbled her carrot down to the leaves, looks around for something to wash it down with, but there are no upside-down bottles of blood in sight, like in her hutch. She informs the shadow of her thirst, with no immediate response.

"Now what?" Tora asks, now constructing a drawbridge of cards for the castle.

"Isn't it obvious?" Tina drops her fork in her bowl. "I must journey to Pennsylvania to rescue Oasis and propose to her."

The shadow finishes its wine in several gulps, then rises.

"Woah, woah, *woah*," Cypress says, dropping the controller, getting to his feet. "Master, wait."

The shadow whirls around, eyes blazing as it cradles Bunnicula in one arm.

"How many people are in this cult?" Asks Cypress. "Enough for a snack? Enough for a meal? Enough for a party?"

"Are you *seriously* thinking of drinking a bunch of cult victims?" Talon demands.

"I thought about dressing my salad with the cashier at Sweetgreen today," he says, frowning at her. "Since when do you question the food chain?"

"Since Oasis has been through enough," she says, throwing up her hands.

There's her name again—the only sound Bunnicula really cares to discern from the mouths of these bipeds.

"It's a cult, T," Cypress argues. "Nobody'll miss 'em. It's the closest we can get to ethical consumption."

Thirsty for blood, the bunny's patience is nearing depletion. With a series of irate clucks, she asks the shadow yet again where Oasis is.

"You are right, sister. Oasis has been through much," it says quietly. "Which is why, brother, I will leave you and Apple to host this party."

"Three revs, two vamps, and a wolf per head—that's eighteen-hundred invites," the dread-headed teen says excitedly. "This could be like Singapore '43 all over again."

"Guess I'll meet you there, Bats," Tora says, cracking her spine.

"And I'll beat you there, Laura," Tina says, smiling, waving at the shadow. "Oasis will flee you and grow old with me."

The shadow continues through the curtains without responding. It carries Bunnicula through the sea of light and sound, then out of the club, taking long, purposeful strides down the street. It walks quickly from Hell's Kitchen to Times Square, Bunnicula in the crook of its arm. Before long, it reaches its destination and tugs open the door.

A human in striped black and white smiles at the shadow.

"Welcome to Foot Locker. Can I help you find something?"

twenty-four

The darkness doesn't last long. I'm in Zeke's arms, leaden limbs dangling as he carries me. My head is pounding, lolling, and drowsy. Through tears, I see just how far into the commune I am again, the Honda a bleary pinprick up the road.

The car isn't that far away. If I cared about myself, the distance between me and it would be an inch.

Or so would say the man holding me like a baby.

I concentrate on this gross fact—that I'm in his arms—and use it to force myself to move. I roll over and fall at his feet, screaming when my ankle splinters. I can't run like this. I can't drive like this. I can't fight like this.

But I can't die like this, either.

I was nothing but bones for Zeke once. I refuse to be bones in a box, left to gather dust among other bone-filled boxes.

I can't do that to my girlfriend.

I know what it's like, holding out for something that feels safe to eat.

Laura waited 122 years for me. True, I can't force her to eat, but I can't be the reason she goes back to starving.

My ears ring as I look left and right. Curfew is long past, but the open doors of nearby chapels frame the silhouettes of onlookers. As I struggle to my feet, I have to wonder how regular of a thing this is to inspire no movement, or if Zeke has gone from angel whisperer to divine disciplinarian.

I scream—no, and let go, and get off—but the onlookers look on.

Would I have done that? Would I have watched him beat someone past the point of being able to scream for help, and done nothing to stop it?

Zeke grabs my braids again and yanks like he's reeling me in, cricking my neck with a pop. The stab of pain soaks all the fight from me. He carries me back along the bible-strewn path to the guardians' house. Back in his office, he dumps me in the chair across from his.

I can barely sit upright. I didn't realize the extent to which Hollywood lies about the durability of the human body when it comes to taking a beating. I feel closer to the grave now than I did a year ago on my deathbed.

Zeke sits across from me like it's 2015 again, and I'm too lost to realize that I don't belong here. He turns on his desk lamp, casting a sterile glow on his index cards and the remaining bibles on his desk.

"I'm sorry. I didn't want to hurt you physically, but the angels gave me license to," he says, still breathing hard. "You're too far removed from their will."

As my vision stabilizes, so does his face. Dirt smudges his cheeks. Locks of hair fall over his manic eyes. I've been calling him a monster for months, and now more than ever, he looks the part.

"You mean from *your* will," I croak.

"I gave you what you wanted: a purpose. A life worth living," Zeke says, frowning pensively, like I'm right where he wanted me all along.

Anger broils in me; it feels like the only fuel I have left in my tank. "You used me as a template for your chessboard of angels. How many wings have you given now?"

A sneer tightens his lips. "Helena's whispers, I assume. Your fall from grace enabled hers. I lost both of you that day."

"Don't say her name," I spit hoarsely. "You played God with our lives."

"You had an archangel depending on you," Zeke hisses, knuckles whitening as he laces his fingers tightly. "I *wish* you were within the reach of salvation for what you've become."

"You don't know what I've be…"

I stop talking.

This is what he wants.

If only my body was fit to fight my way out of this. The only defeat I'd accept from him is knocking him out of his sky, making sure he has no more chances to mount the clouds. I stand; the pain in my ankle makes me gasp. I hobble to the door behind. Zeke doesn't move to stop me.

The deadbolt hasn't been touched, but the door refuses to open.

I throw my whole body against it. It opens a centimeter, then slams, as though someone's on the other side, back pressed against it. I press again, harder. Again it shuts, this time with a small grunt.

I look over my shoulder at the other door and see a shadow on the floor on the other side of it.

We aren't alone. Someone answered my cries for help, but in Zeke's favor.

Hysteria dizzies me, but I don't sit back down again.

"What is this?" I demand. "Ezekiel, what more can you take from me?"

"There won't be any taking. Converse to a restoration, the angels demand reclamations for vessels who sow without reaping." He opens his desk drawer, triggering formless déjà vu. I recognize the familiar red and white packaging of a plastic box of single-edge razors from the hardware store. "*And the angels who did not keep their positions of authority but abandoned their proper dwelling. These he has kept in darkness, bound with everlasting chains for judgment on the great Day.*"

"You're insane," I say, lost for anything else.

"You were the paradigm vessel, but the wings on your back will serve you no more," he says, flicking open the lid of the box. "It's time to return them."

I swallow a mouthful of vomit as déjà vu drags my restoration from the recesses of memory. Time smeared away most of the event itself, but I remember the deadness in my core that made it possible to survive his touch from start to finish.

The Zeke of then and the Zeke of now seem to reach for me at the same time. I tip the chair over and try to run at the closed door again, but my foot won't hold my weight, and I hit the ground face-down, knocking the wind from my chest.

Zeke stomps on my back. Sharp pain shoots through my chest on both sides. With his other foot, he steps on my scrambling right hand. I hear a crunch and feel too much pain to take inventory. A sob turns into choking.

The sleeves of my flannel leave my arms, which stretch above my back as Zeke pins me to the ground with a knee between my shoulders. He sinks his shin deeper into my spine until I can't move to stop him from tearing my shirt apart, hacking the fabric with his razor.

Black blots my eyes as my shirt leaves my body, exposing me to the draft.

I can't breathe, can't suck in air or push it out.

"This is your warning, Ezekiel, to lift any hand you have laid on my beloved."

The deep voice trickles into my mind from far away, muffled by distance, my heartbeat, my choking gasps.

"I smell your stench. I hear your foul heart. If you have harmed Oasis…"

Dracula's threat hangs in the air like fog.

Zeke stands up. "What did you do, Oasis?"

I roll over, gasping, carpet chafing the bare skin of my back. I try to scream, to let him know that I'm here, that I'm done taking space, that I want to go home and wake up from this.

Zeke glares down at me with a frenetic film over his eyes. He grabs a bible off his desk, bends over, and hits me across the face.

"What—did—you—do?" He asks, striking me with each word.

My body is too heavy to move, my brain on the cusp of darkening.

"False prophet, if you have brought harm to my Oasis, you will answer for it before God through his favorite, the Devil," Dracula says. Supernatural volume propels his voice through the air. *"I will send you to hell in tatters."*

"False prophet?" Zeke spits.

A hair-raising, semi-familiar screech swells over the commune, drawing scattered screams.

I taste blood on my tongue and choke on a trickle of it, chuckling.

Zeke towers over me, too far above for me to see the fury on his face, but I hear it in his quaking voice: "Who is that?"

The walls rattle with his voice and the air trembles with another sonorous screech.

"WHERE IS SHE?" Dracula roars, like rolling thunder. *"WHERE IS MY OASIS?"*

"Who did you bring here?" Zeke demands.

I can't tell whether I even have a voice when I push the words out: "My baby."

He lets out a feral shriek. His shoe hits my temple as he kicks me in the head and grabs my shoulders again, slamming me on the ground several times in a row. The bible strikes my face again and again. Somewhere amid the blows, I lose hold of the light and careen into darkness once more.

get your girl

Bunnicula peeks out at Blessed Falls from the fleecy interior of the shadow's hoodie pocket. She's the tiniest component of the compact cavalry deployed on foot to Blessed Falls, with the largest being the dragon, Minty Fresh, circling overhead. The bunny sees the commune of chapels as clearly as dawn. The crosses adorning them make her squint and bare her fangs, until Tora shoots them off with her gun, rousing screams from the occupants.

The shadow turns its head left and right, following the sound of Oasis' heart. It comes upon a chapel with peeling white paint.

A human flits around the back and darts into the dark maze of pint-sized churches.

"Nothing guilty about the speed of that exit *whatsoever*," Tina remarks.

"I'll snatch him," Cypress calls, laughing up the road. Then he yells to the guests waiting in the Pennsylvanian woods: "*Everybody please hang back until Master gets his business straightened out. Thank you for your patience.*"

The shadow pays them no mind though, focused only on one sound—one heartbeat. It walks around the rear of the tallest chapel, kicking through the underbrush, and reaches a porch. It climbs the steps and, finding the door ajar, opens it all the way.

The simplistic, utilitarian room is nearly empty. There's a desk, a chair on either side of it, and a lamp throwing fuzzy LED light onto the walls and floor.

The shadow remains at the threshold, staring at a figure sprawled on the floor.

Bunnicula peers around the wall of fabric, long ears pressed together in the cozy pouch, made less cozy by the rage rolling off the shadow in silent, seismic waves.

It crouches beside Oasis, pushing back some of her braids. Bunnicula disembarks from its pocket to see the full scope of damage.

Oasis' face is bruised and dirt-stained, her scarred arms splayed, her chin and left cheek scraped like she was dragged somewhere. Her braids are tangled with leaves, her exposed ankle swollen and purple. Her shirt is torn in back, the two halves spread beneath her like wings.

Bunnicula wriggles from the shadow's grip and hops the length of Oasis' body, one ear roving gently over the side of her rib cage like a metal detector. She stops when she hears a slowly beating heart.

The shadow puts both of its hands on Oasis' bruised, swollen face, endeavoring to soothe the injuries.

The door opens, and the shadows of Tina and Tora fall over the threshold.

"Odin's eye," Tora says softly.

Tina kneels beside the shadow, sweeping her dark hair over her shoulder. Her hands hover above Oasis' forehead and neck, palms aglow. She examines her arms and chest, gently traveling down her torso and each leg without touching them.

"Two fingers broken, a fractured rib, a sprained ankle, a dislocated shoulder, and a concussion," she lists. She sticks out her lower lip, pouting. "And look at her beautiful face."

The shadow adjusts its hands on Oasis' face, unspeaking.

Bunnicula shuffles closer to her neck to investigate a gash on her jaw. The blood caked around it smells tangy and tantalizing, but Bunnicula refrains from sipping.

The door opens again. Something sails over Bunnicula's head like a satellite in the sky. It crashes into the wall, leaving a concave dent in the wood.

Looking over Oasis's sprawled arm, Bunnicula discerns the shape of a person on the floor in a heap.

"Got him, Master," Cypress says.

"Volume, Cy," Tina whispers, crossing her arms.

"Whoops." Cypress joins the trio of bipeds. "Oh no." His face falls. "What happened to Miss Oasis?"

The shadow looks over its shoulder at the lump of a human, still in an unconscious pile near the wall.

"Dracula," Tora says sharply. "Get your girl." She raises an eyebrow at the shadow, who turns back, nostrils flared, eyes bright red.

Tina cups Oasis' chin, turning her head so that she faces the ceiling.

Still crouching, the shadow relocates Bunnicula to its shoulder, then presses its thumb to the middle of Oasis' forehead and incants in the whispers of witches. Her first breath is a sharp wheeze, followed by a gurgling groan. From above, Bunnicula sees her bruised eyes flutter open and her blood-stained lips part. Blood vessels have broken in one of her eyes, marooning her brown iris in a lake of red. They flick frantically from face to face.

"Oaza, can you hear me?" The shadow asks.

Her gaze returns to it and Bunnicula balanced on its shoulder.

Bunnicula remembers the awe on Oasis' face when they first met, the warm look in her eye when she first took her in her arms.

That look is gone, replaced with fear of the rawest degree.

"Who...?" She stops to gather her breath and, seeming unable to, wheezes and gags.

Tora kneels at her head. "Oasis, do you remember me?"

Oasis gasps wordlessly. She tries to clutch her chest, but quickly stops with a groan. "Who—?"

The effort of trying to speak seems to push her past her limit. Her words deteriorate into strangled sobs and screams.

"Oaza, please—you must calm down," the shadow attempts.

She doesn't. She begs to know who they are, where she is, to be taken home. She tries to reach for the shadow with both her injured and uninjured hands, pleading with it because it hurts so much.

The shadow puts a hand on her forehead. It whispers again and Oasis falls unconscious mid-sob, tears mingling with the blood on her face.

"That's a relief," Tora says, getting to her feet.

"Toto, she was screaming bloody murder," says Cypress.

"She's got some sort of post-traumatic amnesia, which means she has a traumatic brain injury, which means it's a relief she woke up at all," Tora says.

The shadow gazes down with blazing green eyes, hands clasped loosely between its knees.

Cypress' face goes from dismayed to intrigued. "So she won't remember this?"

"Anterograde amnesia is most common in PTA cases, so it's possible she won't—"

"Thanks, Toto," he interrupts, grinning. Then he kisses his fingertips and presses them to Oasis' forehead gently. "Feel better, Miss Oasis."

He's gone soon after, throwing open the door, yelling into the night: *"FANGS OUT, PINKIES UP!"*

A mob of vampires responds: *"THAT'S THE WAY WE LIKE TO SUCK."*

Music erupts: someone brought speakers.

The fur on Bunnicula's back raises as screams rise from all sides, like flames under one of the shadow's bubbling cauldrons. Only in its dungeon has she heard this many sounds of torment.

The night traveled far for this feast.

Tina strolls to the door, too. Formless figures rise from her shadow. Each clarifies slowly into a person-shaped shadow tethered to hers as she opens the door after Cypress. Soon, a handful of her brides saunter around her, giddy and simpering, fangs sparkling.

"You know what I like, beloveds. *Only* the strongest. *Only* the most beautiful," Tina purrs to her brides. She kisses each of them on the lips, then ushers them from the room and out into the screams. "Feast for me, feast for me, *feast for me.*"

Tora joins her at the door and puts two fingers between her lips. Her whistle pierces the night.

"Soup's on, puppies!"

Amidst the responding howls, she turns to the shadow, still crouched on the floor.

Tina shrugs.

"Well, I'm here. May as well look for new brides, yes? I have accepted that neither of you will be mine."

"Sorry, Justina. I'm on the human diet, same as your ex," Tora says sadly. "Dracula, I'll grab a bite and meet you at hers."

The two women exit, so that only Bunnicula and the shadow remain with Oasis.

It cups her face with its palm in silence. Then it grasps her right shoulder and raises her partway off the floor, peering between her back and the carpet. Darkness passes over its face as it reaches for something sharp, flat, and shiny.

"Oh my God," the lump of a human in the corner groans.

The shadow's face turns to fire. It recites:

"But there were also false prophets among the people, just as there will be false teachers among you. They will secretly introduce destructive heresies, even denying the sovereign Lord who bought them—bringing swift destruction on themselves. Many will follow their depraved conduct and will bring the way of truth into disrepute. In their greed these teachers will exploit you with fabricated stories. Their condemnation has long been hanging over them, and their destruction has not been sleeping."

The human groans again, louder.

"To reach across the table onto another man's plate," the shadow seethes, rising. "There is nothing so base. Nothing so animal. Nothing so…monstrous." It towers over the human, seeming taller than the room itself. "You disgust me."

"Who the hell—"

"Hell will be a mercy after I have finished with you," the shadow hisses. "If you had crossed me in my youth, I would have shoved a spear through your brain and left you at the gates like a flag."

Movement, another tight groan as the human tries to get to its feet.

Bunnicula hears the crunch of bone as it steps on the human, eliciting shrieks that make her bare her fangs.

"You will not die tonight. My revenge is chronic. I spread it over centuries. *Time is on my side, and the Devil is my sponsor.*"

The false prophet whimpers, stammering insults and pleas alike.

"I will show you darknesses like no other. I will paint every corner of your mind the color of fear until you wish you had never been given form." The shadow's voice climbs above the false prophet's screams, soon interspersed with gags. It squeezes the razor in its fist, glaring with red eyes, then stoops beside the false prophet. "You do not need this tongue, false prophet. Your days of speaking have concluded. From now on, you will listen only."

Bunnicula, whose interest in the shadow's methods of torture pale to her interest in Oasis, wriggles under the torn fabric of her torn shirt. She hears formless gasps and gags, presumably the sound of the false prophet choking on its own blood.

"And this is the pathetic member you used to violate my Oasis. You have no further need for this as well," the shadow says, quiet and disgusted. "When I come from, to rape another man's wife was to tamper with the bearer of his bloodline and threaten the sanctity of his dynasty. But I am my own dynasty and *Oaza mea* is not my wife," it says curtly. "She is my life. *My* vessel. To spill her blood is to spill mine." Its voice climbs to a tremendous roar, and the room quakes with its wrath. *"How dare you encroach my kingdom from the shadow of the Lord?"*

Bunnicula flattens her ears as the false prophet's squelching screams eclipse those of the humans' outside.

She ventures deeper breath Oasis' torn shirt, muffling the false prophet's cries. She sniffs along her bare skin, then nuzzles into the pit of her splayed arm, and savors the sound of her pumping heart.

The shadow finishes its preliminary torture soon after, and Bunnicula peeks out in time to see it hauling the bleeding, moaning human to the porch. It summons Minty Fresh to escort the false prophet back to the dungeon, then returns to crouch beside Oasis. It extends a bloodied hand as it watches Oasis' chest rise and fall.

Bunnicula had nearly forgotten her appetite. She hops closer and quickly laps up the warm blood puddled in the shadow's palm and coating its fingertips. Once its hand is clean, the shadow gathers Oasis in its arms and carries her out of the chapel, Bunnicula nestled securely in its pocket. Soon after, she sees wisps of green, and hears a grumbling roar overhead as Minty Fresh lands to recover her prisoner.

?????

You must not shrink. You are nearest and dearest and all the world to me; our souls are knit into one, for all life and all time.

twenty-five

My eyelids take forever to part, my arms eons to connect to my brain and push the covers off my body. Pain stabs my side. All of me hurts. My leaden head throbs when I look around the unfamiliar room. Laundry in the corner, a window framing dark blue straight ahead, a nightstand with two phones on it and a mug of water.

I start to grab the water and wince. Two fingers on my right hand are in casts. My ankle is wrapped and elevated.

Everything but the pain is fuzzy.

Why am I in so much pain?

Movement.

A silhouette in the doorway.

A tall, dark-haired man enters the room. Gold bats sway from his earlobes. He kind of looks like one, with his big green eyes and long nose. He also looks tired and torn. A curved wound slices his sharp cheekbone.

Something must have happened to us.

He sits beside me at the edge of the bed, taking my hand when I reach. His feels like a fistful of snow, made even colder by the rings on all his fingers. "Oaza, you are awake. How are you feeling?"

"Like I got into a fight with an orc and lost. Are you alright?" I ask hoarsely. Every fiber of my face hurts from the effort of speech. "Where's Ray?"

"He is not here." He pauses. "He was safe when you last saw him."

"What happened?" I ask.

"I should be asking that of you," he says, gazing raptly at me. "Do you remember me?"

"Of course I do," I lie. I glance at the letters on his grey hoodie, the only clue I have to go by. "You're Champion."

He licks his bright red lips, and for a moment, I fear the worst: that I'm wrong. That I don't remember him, or anyone, or anything.

"I am Vlad Dracula," he says quietly.

"I'll remember that," I say, pulling his hand closer.

My head hurts. My body hurts.

Why am I in so much pain?

Everything but the pain is fuzzy, like it's all I've known, and all I'll ever know.

The man holding my hand has a cut on his face. He looks tired and fraught.

"What happened to us?" I ask.

His thumb twitches over my knuckles. His green eyes seem to cloud. "I am uncertain," he says. "I believe I have failed you."

I look at my hands in his.

How could he have failed me?

I don't even know him.

Maybe he's a doctor.

I look around, but see no medical equipment. Just a window, some laundry, and a man holding my hands, watching me with green eyes guarded under a dark brow.

He looks wan with worry.

There's a bright red wound on his cheek.

Something must have happened, but of the two of us, I'm the one who seems to have taken the most damage.

"Did I do something?" I ask.

He looks uncertain, or afraid.

It must've been bad, but when I reach for memories of before, I find nothing.

"You were maimed in pursuit of your mother's ashes," he says quietly.

My mother.

The last I heard from my mother, she was headed to the doctor's office.

Finally going to see someone about those migraines.

She should've been back by now.

"Where is she?" I ask.

The unfamiliar man lets go of my hands. "I will return."

I don't want him to leave. I don't know who he is or who I am, but he does.

In his absence, I stare around the barely-furnished, unembellished room. It looks like someone stays here, but not like anyone lives here.

Movement in the corner of my eye.

I see someone in the doorway—a man with broad shoulders and green eyes, holding something square.

He puts it in my hands. Only then do I notice that two of my fingers are broken.

I try to focus on the record and not the cut on his face.

Were we in an accident?

There's a woman on the front of this vinyl cover. A Black woman with a huge Afro, holding two toddlers adorning her hair in cotton candy.

Goodnight, Lyn, reads the title in chunky white font.

"Thank you," I say, smiling. "I can't wait to listen."

The stranger sits beside me, stroking his lip with his thumb, watching me with a helpless look that I don't understand. "Do you know who she is?"

"My mom," I say. She hasn't shown me this album before. There's no track list on the back—just another picture of the two babies sitting in the grass, eating an elephant ear. "If you want, I can ask her to sign it."

He licks his lips slowly. "Do you know who I am?"

"Of course I do," I say, glancing at the text on his hoodie. "You're Champion."

*

Champion helps me to the bathroom, then elevates my ankle and gives me a book to read in bed: *Frankenstein*. I keep having to go back and reread entire paragraphs that wind up making no sense because the page before slipped from memory.

This would all be so much easier if I admitted to myself that I'm just not cut out for school right now. Maybe if I took some time off, reading might be an opportunity to enjoy myself instead of an opportunity to fail at something else.

Someone knocks on the door, which is slightly ajar. She has kinky red hair in a ponytail down her back, and freckles on her nose and cheeks. She sits at my bedside with a chair, smiling like she knows me.

"Hello," she says. "Do you know my name?"

I don't remember her face. Her t-shirt says *Wayne State Warriors*, which means nothing to me.

"No," I say, closing my book.

"I'm Tora. I saw you a few days ago. You went and got amnesia since then," she says, clasping her hands in her lap. "I'm going to ask you some questions to get an idea of how severe it is, alright?"

"Alright," I echo.

"What is your name?"

"Oaza," I say, parroting a whisper of a memory.

"When were you born?"

"I...don't remember," I answer quietly, startled by the wall of black between the question and the answer.

"Do you know where you are or how you got here?"

I look around the plain room, trying to find a foothold in the unfamiliarity. "No."

"Have you ever lived in New York?"

"No."

"Have you ever had a girlfriend?"

"I wish," I mutter.

This makes her smile briefly. "Tell me what you *do* remember," she says. "What you did yesterday, what you're doing today and tomorrow."

I clear my throat as a surge of anxious nerves makes my head throb. "I'm pretty sure I went to class, then to work, then home," I say, not because I distinctly remember, but because that's all I ever do, a dismal routine that I couldn't forget if I tried.

"Where do you work and go to school?"

"Popeye's," I reply. "I go to University of Pennsylvania."

Although with my grades, that probably won't be the case for long.

"That's impressive," the woman remarks. "Are you in touch with your parents?"

"Dad, no," I say, curtailing bitterness. "My mom is dead."

"I'm sorry to hear that," she says sympathetically. "When did she pass?"

"I...don't remember." I grit my teeth, chest knotted with mourning as dissociation looms. "Time hasn't made sense since."

"I promise you it will again," the woman says.

She continues to ask questions, most of which I forget after answering. At the end, she says, "Your name is Oasis Eleanora Johnson. You were born July 13, 1997. It's Wednesday, September 4, 2019. You live in New York City, and this is your apartment. You're here because Dracula found you in Blessed Falls, Pennsylvania. You were badly injured."

Each word makes less sense than the one before.

"I...haven't read *Dracula*," I reply, hoping it's in the vicinity of the right thing to say.

"Vlad Dracula is a person," she says. "He's out there sitting at the table."

I frown. "Is Champion still here?"

Tora seems to hesitate. "I'll go and check," she says. "Is the name Laura familiar to you?"

I rack my brain, foraging through the fuzz and the ache. "She's the girl from *Carmilla*," I say, which is both the only book I've read for class this semester, and the only thing that makes sense since in a conversation about *Dracula*.

After a few more questions, she stands, and I pick up the book in my lap—*Frankenstein*.

"Thank you for this," I say, raising it.

"You're welcome," the woman says, and leaves.

a cruel place

Bird Bones originally intended to swing by Manhattan to check on Bunnicula, having gone several hours without seeing her sinister widow's peak poking out from behind the furniture legs. A darkening blue sky vaulted over her long trek from home to the heartbeat's apartment, where her nose told her the vampire bunny awaited.

The shadow awaited too, and was there when she sprang from alley to fire escape, then climbed the rusty metal stairs. It carried her over the threshold to join a somewhat disgruntled Bunnicula on the kitchen floor.

The shadow now sits alone at a table while the red wolf speaks with Oasis. Soon, the red wolf exits the room and joins the slouching shadow at the table.

"You said the amnesia was acute, yet she does not remember me," the shadow says, cutting Bird Bones off mid-greeting. She meows irately at its rudeness.

"It's good to see you, too, Birdie," the red wolf says. Then she points forcefully at the shadow. "I *told* you your Ragnarok was coming. If only you'd learned a lighter kind of magic on your romp with the Devil. You could use that big brain of yours to heal hers." She crosses her arms and stands over the shadow, vexed. "The things you could do if you weren't who you are."

"*What is happening to her?*" The shadow demands.

"Odin's eye, Vlad. That man tried to *bash her head in*. Deep down, she probably *wants* to forget," the red wolf says. "She's not wholly incoherent. Just confused—and lucky for you, she's not panicking. Look in your playpen for an example of how much worse of a state she could be in, as far as brain injuries go."

Bird Bones flattens her ears as the shadow rankles like a dragon.

Tired of their droning, she investigates a door, slightly ajar. She hears a familiar sound within—Oasis' heart, pumping steadily.

Oasis herself is standing behind the door, just visible, face a motley of bruises, one eye swollen. She holds a book to her chest, peering unseen at the shadow and its companion.

"What about Laura?" The red wolf asks. "There's no guarantee, but seeing her face might stir something."

"I am stuck with this face." The shadow runs a hand through its hair, glowering. "I believe my attempt to transform gave me a hernia."

"Ah. Malnourishment?"

It says nothing.

"Well, this is *very* helpful for the vampire medical text I'm composing. It's called *Vlad's Anatomy*."

"Gray was the doctor," the shadow mutters. "We were friends."

She shrugs. "It's my book. I'll title it what I want."

A pause.

"I should have believed her when she said she loved me," says the shadow. "Instead, I let her marinate until she lost faith in me."

Bird Bones, crouched behind the counter, sees part of Oasis' blackened brown eye through the door. She's turning over the book in her hand, listening anxiously.

"I can't imagine needing someone the way that you do, but *you* chose the human diet. Give her a few days to unscramble. Impatience and regret don't suit you," the red wolf says, patting its back. "On the bright side, she thinks your name is Champion and once again has no idea she's in a relationship with a mass-murdering sentient bat colony. And at least your cage has a new occupant, right?"

"Assuming Minty Fresh did not eat it," the shadow says darkly.

The heartbeat steps away from the door, back into her room.

Robbed of the only interesting sight in the joint, Bird Bones joins with the shadow, twining around its outstretched leg, waiting for its affection. She catches sight of Bunnicula's widow's peak, the rabbit's red eyes betraying a dark brain brewing with schemes to catch and nibble her tail.

"I'll drop the bunny off at yours," the red wolf says. "Do you want me to make your bed for you before I head back to Detroit?"

"I would like that very much, but I have not checked the status of the shipment, and I will not leave Oaza in this state," says the shadow. It leans forth in its chair and scoops Bird Bones from the floor. "I have a favor to ask of you, kitty cat."

Bird Bones balances on its shoulder, feeling, as always, on top of the universe from her vantage point beside its head.

*

FedEx is a cruel place. The distribution center is a microcosm of chaos—boxes abound, yet none of them are open for lounging, and most of them are on conveyor belts, moving too fast to be clawed. In the bellies of dungeon-like trucks, humans toil, slick with perspiration, breathing like they're running for their lives.

Bird Bones can smell the soil of Wallachia from a mile away after years spent witnessing it being carted into the house and down to the shadow's dungeon.

The shadow owes her big time.

Her sharp nose latches onto the stark, sweet aroma from several trucks away.

She gallops to the end of the dock, ducking under one trailer, then the next until she's at the end of the facility, peeking in where a truck just pulled off. She tightens her haunches, then leaps into the cacophony.

This is feline hell—noise everywhere, humans soaked in sweat and misery. The wooden crates of Romanian earth are on a pallet labeled NEXT DAY OVERSIZED.

The crates aren't alone.

A human in a bright vest with a walkie talkie stands with another in all black with a beard, a badge, and a crucifix.

Bird Bones' hiss goes unnoticed in the folds of warehouse noise. She creeps back until she can't see the man with the crucifix anymore, then watches the exchange while crouched behind a broken crock pot, which sits abandoned beneath a motionless conveyor belt.

"…can't let you take or open these without proper identification," says the vest. "I'm sorry. That's just policy."

"I understand," the crucifix says humbly. "Is it alright if I make a few phone calls?"

"Go right ahead." The vest consults a clipboard, then tunes into its walkie talkie. "*Copy.*" It looks to the crucifix. "I'll be back in just a minute."

"Take your time."

The vest leaves.

The crucifix promptly puts its phone away. It takes a flat silver box from its inside pocket, burnished with a plain cross, and opens it. Through the palette of warehouse stenches—chemicals, cardboard, rubber, sweat, tears—the cloying smell of sacramental wafers rises like fire.

The crucifix casts a glance over its shoulder; the vest is engrossed in conversation with another vest. One by one, the crucifix pushes the razor-thin wafers between the planks like tokens in a slot machine. It walks the length of the two stacked boxes, wedging wafers in the wood, forming something like a holy bubble to contain its next move: a vial of oils that, when unstoppered, reeks of roses and myrrh. The man with the crucifix empties it on top, pouring the oil in the shape of a cross in two swift motions.

The vest is gone, called away by an overflowing chute, presently spilling packages over the slide.

The crucifix strikes a match and drops it on the box.

Bird Bones can just see the tips of the flames dancing at the height of the crucifix's chin.

These are holy fires, the smoke from which makes her fur stand up and her eyes water.

The flames stay contained to the shape of the cross, but Bird Bones can see the true extent of the damage. The vitality curdles out of the earth and dissipates like fog.

The crucifix takes a flask of holy water from its hip and douses the fire.

The boxes look no different, but the earth is no longer the subtle sweet of the shadow's home. It has all the convalescence of broken glass.

Bird Bones has seen enough. She sprints from the facility but walks most of the way back, not at all thrilled to tell the shadow, already so hungry for sleep, that it will not be doing so any time soon.

twenty-six

A dozen pages into *Frankenstein*, I crawl out of bed, wincing, and hobble to the window. My head pounds. The room sways. I clutch the sill to stay standing. The sky is deep blue. I don't recognize the skyline outside, but I'm clearly not in Kansas anymore.

Now is not the time to panic.

I see two phones on the nightstand. One has scratches on the screen and a picture of an upside-down bat as the wallpaper. The other has a picture of Legolas and says *Passcode required to use Face ID*. Both look ten times more sophisticated and expensive than my iPhone 4. I hope I didn't lose it.

According to the phones, it's just after 10 o'clock at night. For how long have I been holding my bladder to avoid putting that book down?

I put the phones down too, and venture to the door. From here, I see part of a table and a strip of a dark kitchen. Whoever lives here is lucky enough to have in-unit laundry just outside the bathroom. I can't help pausing to look at the dining room on my way to it. The open fire escape can't be up to code, seeming more like a balcony than a means to safety.

The open doors frame an unfamiliar silhouette, but I have to pee too badly to investigate.

The bathroom is as plain as the bedroom, with a dark blue towel draped over the rim of a claw foot tub, and a wide frosted window overlooking it. Colorful bottles of shampoo and jars of conditioner line the sill.

I'm scared to look in the mirror above the sink. Based on

how much my body hurts, I can't be a pretty sight. Worse, I don't know how I got this way, or how I got here, or where here could possibly be.

Someone knocks softly.

"Oaza, are you alright?" Comes a deep voice.

"That depends," I say warily. "Who are you?"

"I am Vlad Dracula," he says.

I frown at the door. "Like the book?"

"Not quite," he says. "You should not be on your feet."

He's right, whoever he is. I can easily imagine myself toppling from putting weight on my foot while trying to sit on the toilet.

"You can come in," I say.

The door opens.

The man crossing the threshold has long, dark hair and eyes like pale emeralds. He's clad in a plain black hoodie and sweats. The sheen of his locks and the haircare products on the windowsill say this apartment is his. I recognize him, albeit vaguely, from the cut on his face: whatever happened, had happened to us both.

He lifts the toilet lid for me in silence. His hands are cold through the sleeves of the pink hoodie I'm wearing. I hold onto him and pull down my matching sweats.

A soft gasp escapes me as I sit on the toilet. The sound of me peeing fades behind a dull ring as I behold the mosaic of scars on my thighs.

Bible verses.

The same one over and over: Luke 1:19.

They look old, warped by stretch marks and cellulite.

I look up at the man in front of the towel rack across from me. Would he know who did this to me? I finish peeing, but don't move to wipe or stand. Shadows of more scars wind down my shins, like my whole body is covered in a verse I don't know.

"Do you know who did this to me?" I ask, unsure of whether I can stomach the answer.

"Yes," he says, quieter. "It pains me to remind you of its existence. It fed on your blood for some time and tried again last night."

"It fed?" I repeat with an uncomfortable laugh. "Was it a vampire or something?"

"Worse. A false prophet," he says. "I yearn for your return so that I can show you what remains of it."

I wipe, frowning. Maybe he's just as out of it as I am. "I'd like to wash my hands in the kitchen, please," I say. "Mirrors are off the table until I figure out what's going on."

"I have a disdain for them myself," he remarks as he helps me to my feet. "I am here with you. Nothing else is going on."

I wish I could believe that. I can't read his face or tone. He's a mystery, but I'm short on people to trust and reasons not to panic.

"Did we already go to the hospital?"

"Ásttora cared for you," he says, like I should know who that is. "She wrapped your ankle and fingers and gave you ibuprofen for the pain."

"And she couldn't give you some stitches?" I ask, surveying the cut on his face. "That looks deep."

"It will heal once I have eaten."

I gaze around his apartment as he leads me to the kitchen, noting the lack of décor and scant furniture besides a desk and table—nowhere to lounge or recline, like he just moved in, or doesn't spend much time here.

"How many organs did you sell to get laundry in unit?" I ask, eyeing the setup on the way to the sink.

"I have no organs worth purchasing."

"Don't be silly. And don't be stingy, either," I scold. "I'm looking for a place, and I'm not about to lower my standards."

"And I would never ask that of you." He provides squares of paper towel and stands beside me while I wash my hands.

"Do you remember what city you are in?"

"Philadelphia," I say warily. "Are you sure you're alright?"

"We are in Manhattan. And I will be when you are," he says. "What is your name?"

"Uh-oh," I say, barely refraining from rolling my eyes. I dry my hands and scrunch the wet paper towel in my fist. "I think it's a little late in the game to ask that."

"It cannot be too late. You have amnesia," Champion says quietly. "I must be sure that you remember me and for this you must remember yourself."

I could laugh. Amnesia is one hell of a card to pull to justify forgetting my name after we...

I don't know what we did. I don't know who he is, how he got here, why he's still here. All I have to go on is the fact that I'm not scared of him, which could simply be a byproduct of brain damage.

"Okay," I say. "So did we...?"

He stares at me, not at all catching my drift.

"Did we hook up?" I ask frankly.

"We have long since graduated from that," Champion says.

Me and him?

"You must be fed," he says before I can ask anything else.

This feels abrupt, but I suppose if someone I cared about was marooned on an island of amnesia, I'd be short on words, too.

*

Champion gives me a book to read at the table while he cooks.

Whatever it is smells so good that I can hardly focus on the first page of *Frankenstein*. Instead, I watch him move around the kitchen, wearing black latex gloves like he does this for a living.

Which reminds me, I should text Mirage to see if tonight's an easier work night than the last few have been. His boss had better pray I never set foot in that restaurant when he's running back of house.

I leave the book on the table and limp to Champion's bedroom. There are two phones on the nightstand, but neither of them is mine. One is off, and the other has Legolas from *Lord of the Rings* as the wallpaper.

Maybe I do have a type.

It's almost midnight; he has an unread text from someone named Kennedy.

I hobble back to the dining room and sit at the table, opposite his open book.

Champion turns off the stove and leaves the kitchen. He only has one bowl, one spoon, and one glass of water in his gloved hands. He puts them in front of me and sits opposite me, frowning at his book.

The colorful soup he made has meatballs and sour cream in the center, garnished with green and red vegetables.

I dig in. Chewing really showcases the soreness in all my face muscles, but the soup is too delicious to stop.

"What's this?"

"Ciorbă de perisoare," he says.

"Why aren't you eating?"

"I do not consume meat."

"Oh. Well, thank you for going out of your comfort zone," I say.

"My comfort zone is wherever you are," he says. "What is your name?"

"Oaza," I answer.

"What is my name?"

"Champion." I eat some more soup, frowning. "It's my turn to ask questions. Why do you have two phones?" I ask before he can ask something else. "Are you a drug dealer?"

"I have one phone, obtained for you alone." His face doesn't look insulted, but it feels like I've touched something tender without meaning to. "What is your next question?"

"Uh…" I fish for something more innocuous and glance at *Frankenstein*. "Is that your favorite book?"

"It would be very close to my heart, were my heart still within me." He puckers his lips, flipping idly through the pages. "Mary was generous in her portrayal of Victor. But then I only gave her the lighter details. Just enough to ensure she championed over Lord Byron," he murmurs, slouching away from the table.

"Huh. Maybe I'll buy a copy for myself," I say.

"We will go to Full Cauldron when you are stronger."

"What's that?"

"You work there," Champion says. "You said it is where you first saw my heart."

Broth spills out of my spoon as it slackens in my hand.

No it's not.

There are more holes in my memory than substance, more gone than left, but I know in my heart that isn't true.

I saw it somewhere else—when, where, or how, I couldn't say.

I'm trying not to panic, but having this non-memory, yet not knowing where I am or where I began, feels like the end unto itself.

I finish eating in uncertain silence.

Champion takes on the dishes while I struggle to read the first chapter of *Frankenstein* through tired eyes. I make it a few pages before closing the book, diverting my attention to my host.

I try to jog my own memory with facts to clear the confusion—my name is Oaza, it's a spring night in Philly, and I'm screwed if I don't come up with a study strategy. If only sadness could be factored into the whole satisfactory academic progress thing. I'd have better grades if I had less of that. Champion flicks the kitchen light out, drying his hands on his hoodie.

"Is it alright if I spend the night?" I ask. "I don't mind getting a Lyft if you have to be up early."

"This is your apartment, Oaza," Champion says, reaching for me. "In fact, it is I who was not welcome here."

I lean heavily on him as he guides us towards the bedroom. "Why wouldn't you be welcome in my apartment?" I ask. "We just met."

"You needed space from me," he says.

My heartbeat quickens. "Why?"

He'd been about to lower me to the bed, but I cling to his elbows, sort of sitting in midair. Not panicking may be the best course of action, but it's hard to keep that up when I don't understand what he is to me.

My gaze sticks to the red slice on his cheek.

"Did you give up on me, too?" I ask quietly.

His brow creases deeply. "Oaza, I do not ever leave a meal unfinished."

I return his frown.

"You have to start a meal to not leave it unfinished."

Champion's eyes widen as he sits me down, gaping at me like I slapped him.

"What? I didn't see you eat anything," I say. "You shouldn't go to bed hungry."

"You feed me," he says quietly, "with all that you are." He leaves the room, which turns into a wordless echo chamber of his voice once he's gone.

*

It's almost one in the morning when Champion washes my face, going the extra mile with a bowl of hot water and a washcloth in the bedroom so that I won't have to face the bathroom mirror. His many rings are piled on the nightstand next to a bottle of face scrub.

I sit on the edge of the bed, hands between my thighs, marveling at the temperature contrast between the water and his cold hands.

"No offense, but you should consider taking iron pills," I say, warped by his fingers patting my face dry. "My roommate gets a senior discount on supplements."

"It is 2019, Oaza." He rubs moisturizer onto my cheeks and forehead, then delicately under my bruised eyes. "Your roommate is gone."

"It's hard to use past tense with her, but I know she's gone," I say, even though it doesn't feel like it. She's gone, and I was lucky to ever have known her. "If she were here, she'd stop me," I sigh. "But if she were here, I wouldn't be in this position in the first place."

Champion sets the bowl of water on the floor. He continues to crouch in front of me, fingers laced under his chin. "Which position?"

I shrug, reluctant to say it aloud and be told categorically how bad of an idea it would be. "I saved a Craigslist post for a 'co-op/commune'," I say, adding air quotes. "I told someone else, and they said that's code for cult. Now I can't unhear it."

Champion sighs silently.

"What?"

"I bask in cruelty and torment, Oaza. It now seems," he says, standing, "that I am being given a taste of my own medicine."

I open my mouth to speak, but something on the floor catches my attention. Rather, something *not* on the floor.

I see my shadow thrown by the lamp.

I don't see his.

"You don't seem very cruel to me," I say, eyes still glued to the hardwood.

"Because I am a simp for you," Champion says plainly, and leaves.

I lay down, blankets drawn up to my chin, gazing out at the dark Philly skyline.

I thought I'd be more terrified moving to this city, but maybe this is proof that things *can* change for the better.

After a while, Champion returns.

I peek at him through heavy eyelids.

"Goodnight, Oaza," he says.

"Goodnight," I say uncertainly.

He turns out the lamp.

The door closes, and I'm alone.

Something feels off. I can feel the holes in my head where memories used to be; there's too much empty space for me to remember where he belongs. Still, I assumed he would be coming to bed with me, and the fact that he isn't is terrifying. What if we aren't connected in the way I assumed?

The harder I try to steer my brain towards sleep, the harder it is to shake this feeling of disorientation.

Is he upset with me because of the accident?

If only I could remember what I did well enough to apologize for it.

Maybe I should've been saying sorry instead of goodnight.

After a while, I slide out of bed and leave the room, leaning heavily on the doorknob. It's dark in the dining room, except where the dim glow of the city night filters in through the fire escape.

I see the outline of Champion's shoulders as he sits on the rail, like a cricket preparing to launch from one grass blade to the next. Cursing my ankle, I limp through the darkness to the table and nearly fall over it trying to keep my balance.

Champion climbs down and turns on the lamp above his desk. "Oaza, you must be careful." He sets a notebook down among his art supplies, then comes to me. "You are not tired?"

"I am," I say uncertainly. "Aren't you?"

He looks taken aback, and for a moment, I wonder if I have it all even more wrong than I thought. "I do not make a point of advertising it."

"Do I look like a customer to you?" I ask, raising my eyebrows.

"I…cannot say," Champion says, looking even more lost.

"That's because you're tired. I'm not the poster child for good grades right now, but I think homework should wait," I say, jutting my chin at the notebook.

He stuffs his hands in his pockets, eyes on me. "Do you know who I am?"

"I don't," I confess. "But I know you're sleepy. I'm sleepy, too. We should…"

Champion's green eyes drift to his bedroom door. "Oaza, I cannot sleep in a bed—" He stops abruptly and clears his throat. "I cannot sleep in a bed with my hair like this. It must be bonneted."

I hold out my hand. "Then let's bonnet."

Champion nests his fingers in mine, rings like ice between my knuckles.

He procures two black satin bonnets for us from the bathroom and secures the adjustable enclosure on his, then helps me tie up my braids.

By the time my head hits the pillow, I can barely keep my eyes open, but I do, and continue to watch Champion even after he turns out the lamp. I hear his rings on the nightstand and feel his weight dip the mattress. Even with my eyes closed, I can see his face—long nose, big brooding green eyes, red lips.

I can't see anything else, though, when I dig for evidence of him from before tonight.

Did we hook up?

I must have seen him on campus before and thirsted in passing before whichever app we met on enabled me to make the approach I never would've made in real life.

Was it Tinder? OkCupid?

I open my eyes and raise onto my elbow.

I have to squint to see his silhouette. It looks like he's propped up, too.

"Are you watching me sleep?" I whisper.

"Yes," he whispers back.

"How long have you been able to see in the dark?" I snicker.

"Five hundred and twenty-four..." He clears his throat. "Seconds. Which is close to nine minutes and therefore not long at all, really."

"Weirdo. You're lucky you're a math whiz and I'm in the market for a tutor. Otherwise, I'd be flying out of here," I mumble sleepily. "Goodnight, Champ."

"Goodnight, Oaza mea."

I sink into the pillows again and reach for him, intent on being the big spoon, but he's still propped up, probably lost in thought. I shimmy closer and put my head on his chest, but sink into sleep before I can encourage him to do the same.

twenty-seven

*If you had gone to the bottom of the deep blue sea, I would have followed
you there, too.*

A woman's voice snakes through my brain like a river rushing
after rain.

Your life is too short for me to waste your time.

A cold hand in mine, brown eyes sharp as spears.

You reminded me that I have lungs. And a heart.

A glimpse of the moon, dotted with specks of black.

I would give it to you if I could reach.

*

I sit bolt upright in bed, breathing hard.

My head feels heavy and sore, but the pain concerns me less
than the dreams draining from it. There was a woman, but the
daylight pressing in seems to push her features out. I reach for her
voice and grasp silence.

It's for the better.

I don't even know what time it is and my whole body is hot
and buzzing like a live wire. Having wet dreams about someone
while in someone else's bed is a new tier of thirsty. Still, I can't help
trying to summon more of the dream as I reach for the nightstand.
There's a text from someone named Kennedy. Is he the guy from
my English lit class? Whoever he is, he sent a screenshot of a blue
dot northwest of Philly—somewhere called Blessed Falls.

??? Wyd?

> I think you may have sent this
> to the wrong person.

I divert my feeble attention to a text from Mirage:

> **I know you're still upset with
> me, but I need a chaperone
> to It: Chapter 2, so what can
> I supplement my apology
> with? Desperate enough to
> make cookies btw**

I don't know how to respond; I have no idea what he's talking about. But who am I to say no to cookies?

> Surprise me.

I heave a sigh and toss my phone aside in search of my bag. I don't know why I'm in such a hurry. All my manager's gonna do is send me home, but I've called out so many times this semester that I should at least show my face, so they'll see firsthand that I'm injured—and maybe even feel a little sympathy.

I can't believe I'm about to walk to the bus stop on a twisted ankle to stay in good standing at a job that pays me $7.25 an hour. But I won't be walking anywhere if I can't find my bag, so I make my way to the dining room. The scents drifting to it from the kitchen are making me reconsider my exit—eggs, biscuits, sausage.

Champion is at the stove, still with his bonnet on, holding a wooden spoon congealed with eggs. He looks up, and for a moment, I can't think around the feeling that I know him from elsewhere. Like we were in the middle of another moment before course correcting to this one.

I shake my head.

My brain'll say anything to keep me here.

"Good morning, Oaza mea," Champion says without looking up. "I am preparing for you biscuits and gravy, from your homeland Kansas."

I walk slowly to the table to watch, straddling indecision. I should regretfully decline and hope that doesn't ruin whatever's unfolding between us, but I'm equally tempted to forget I even have a job and just roll with this.

"I do love biscuits and gravy. Thank you." I peek at all four chairs, then turn around to look at his desk. There's no sign of my bag.

I must have left it at home. Sighing, I sit and prop my foot up on an empty chair.

Champion turns off the stove. The oven door opens and shuts. A moment later, he joins me with a single plate.

The eggs are as fluffy as clouds, and the biscuits and gravy look like they were torn from a country recipe book.

"Thank you," I say as he puts it in front of my clasped hands. "You're not hungry?"

"Not for this," he says, sitting across from me. "What is my name?"

"Champion."

"What is your name?"

I start to remark on how bold it is to think making me breakfast makes up for not knowing my name this whole time, but I realize that I don't know my name off the top of my head, either.

"Oaza Mea," I say after a moment.

"When were you born?"

"July thirteenth," I say.

"Year?"

"1997." I scowl and pick up my fork. "Are you trying to look at my birth chart?"

"If it would please you," says Champion. "Where are you now?"

That's a good question. A quick frisk of my brain turns up no clues on how I got to his place, let alone where it is.

"I don't know, but I do know that I have to get going soon," I say regretfully.

I take a bite of biscuit and feel even more regret. This isn't the type of breakfast you eat before limping into Popeye's. It's the preface to a day of self-care—something I haven't practiced since my ex-boyfriend was there to keep me accountable.

"Do you by any chance have a plain burgundy t-shirt?" I ask. "I don't think I brought my uniform."

Champion removes his bonnet. His long, curly black hair tumbles down over his shoulders, perfect as a painting.

"You do not work for Popeye any longer, Oaza. His hold on

you is severed," he says, tossing the bonnet in the air like pizza dough.

I scoff. True, my head is so fuzzy that I don't even remember coming over last night, but the depression and dread inherent to working in fast food transcends reality.

"You work at Full Cauldron," he says. "I have already spoken with your employer regarding your ailment to ensure that you will not be penalized."

I hesitate.

Full Cauldron.

I look over my shoulder at the fire escape, which is closed, curtains drawn and throttling the sunlight.

In some untraceable memory, the doors are open, and there's someone on the other side, waiting. Waiting for me to descend those stairs. Waiting to catch me at the bottom of the rusty ladder. Waiting to love me.

"Fine," I say, barely there. "But if I get fired, you're picking up my Netflix tab."

"If you are fired, then the one responsible will be the Job to my God," he says.

"I'm not religious, but I *think* I hear the sentiment," I say. "You'd be speaking my language if you said you'd make them the Witch-king of Angmar to your Éowyn."

Champion puts his elbows on the table, knitting his fingers together. One of his rings is a golden bat, wings spread like it's giving his knuckle a hug. "I must view these Ring Lord films with you," he says decisively. "Perhaps there is something to be learned from this Éowyn—techniques that I have not implemented."

"I think *you* would be teaching *her*," I say as I scrape together the remains of my breakfast. "She's a terrible cook."

*

Like the epitome of his name, Champion washed my pink sweatsuit. We'd match if his wasn't heather grey—and if he wasn't wearing a ski mask, tinted black Ray-Ban aviators, and motorcycle gloves. I lean heavily on his arm as we disembark from the elevator of his apartment building and broach the sunny day. This part of the city feels like it was copy pasted from another metropolis—one with shorter streets and taller buildings. It almost doesn't look like Philly at all.

I look up and down the street, feeling inexplicably windswept. Between school, work, friendlessness, and a bank account that's constantly hovering at E, it feels like it'll be years before I see everything that this city has to offer.

But it's hard to feel my usual woe with Champion at my side, even if he is dressed like he's about to commit strong-arm robbery.

"Is this what you usually wear when you go to bookstores?" I ask.

"In a manner of speaking. I do not usually present this face in civilized situations."

"I don't see why," I say, frowning. "As long as it's not self-esteem issues."

He turns his head, presumably looking at me through those dark lenses.

"You believe me to have a pleasant face?" He asks.

"Well, yeah," I say, frowning as we come upon a crosswalk. "Otherwise, I wouldn't have…"

Had sex with him? Did we have sex?

I can't remember.

Maybe we decided to be friends instead.

But a decision like that requires having met in the first place, and when I search for our genesis, all I see is the red scar on his cheek.

My eyes travel from his covered face to his name emblazoned on his hoodie, down to his shoes with blue Cs on the sides. My shadow stretches towards the curb, parallel to the streetlight, utterly alone, like I'm leaning on thin air. The crosswalk light beeps. I try to recalibrate my train of thought as we cross the street, but it's like the conductor leapt off.

"I just hope they have what I'm looking for," I say.

*

It's been a minute since I was surrounded by books in a context other than cramming at the library.

Full Cauldron makes me wish I had the time, money, and attention span to justify a splurge. To the left is a glass counter, with mugs and folded hoodies in the display case and buckets of buttons and pins beside the register. We pause beside a cluster of comic racks so that Champion can remove his gloves, glasses, and ski mask.

He gives me his right hand.

I shiver and scowl. "I like all the rings, but I think they're messing with your circulation, Champ. Your fingers are freezing. Not that I'm complaining," I add quickly.

"I do not feel my cold," Champion says. "Only your warmth."

I run my tongue over a split in my lip, lost for words.

We straggle towards the shelves. The place definitely looked smaller on the outside.

As we pass as bookshelf full of *Star Trek* novelizations, I notice a young man making his way up the hall from an office.

"I can't believe you work here," I say as the two of us approach the register. "This place is so cool."

"You are the one who is employed here, Oaza," Champion says, eying the cover of a Batman omnibus. "This is where we first collided."

"If you say so," I say wryly. "Let's see if *he* knows where *Frankenstein* is since you conveniently aren't employed here."

Champion obliges, and the two of us approach the register.

"Excuse me—ope. Never mind," I say, interrupting myself. The tray of hand-illustrated directories answers half my question. "These are nice. Did you draw them?" I ask Champion.

"You drew them, Oaza," he says. "Kennedy can confirm this."

Champion gestures to the employee, who'd sat down on a stool next to a box of books, but swiftly gets up again. Kennedy has green eyes and dark hair, and a t-shirt with a dancing shamrock on it.

"How are you feeling?" He asks.

I look over my shoulder to see who he might be talking to, thoroughly confused by the amount of concern in his voice.

"Have we met before?"

His face passes from shocked to devastated in seconds flat.

"Oaza, this is Kennedy," Champion says. "You work here with him."

I blink at the register, the comics, the posters.

"No I don't," I say.

"What makes you think you don't work here?" Asks Kennedy, somewhere between wary and disappointed. Then he scowls at Champion. "More importantly, what makes you think *he* does work here?"

"First of all, how would I know? My guess is because he's cosplaying Batman, but you're the one who hired him."

"Cosplaying Batman?" Champion mumbles, gaping at me. "What is the meaning of this?"

I ignore him.

"Second of all, as much as I'd like to work at Nerds 'R Us, I can't afford to work somewhere that doesn't feed me during my shift," I say, "and I don't see a fryer in here. So if we're done with this weirdness, I'm pretty sure we came here for something."

I instantly regret my honesty. He looks to Champion, whose face is unreadable. A silent conversation seems to flow between their green eyes, Champion's obscured by his profile, his coworker's darkened by his brow.

"Am I forgetting something?" I ask, even though I know I am. I can barely remember the words that just came out of my mouth, let alone what they were in response to. "I can fill out an application if it makes you feel better," I say, which seems to scatter the tension.

"If you ask me, you deserve a break from remembering," says Champion's co-worker, whose name I've already lost. He beams. "Welcome to Full Cauldron. You said you're looking for *Frankenstein*?"

"Yes, please," I say, smiling back. "I'd hate to put Champion to work on his day off."

"Are you kidding? Champion *loves* working here. In fact," he says, stepping past his box of books, "he loves it so much that I'm sure he won't mind keeping lookout while I take you to find Frankie myself."

Champion's nostrils flare as his coworker joins us and offers me his arm. He looks reluctant to let me go, standing stock still like a cat ready to pounce.

"Take care of her, Kennedy," he says quietly, releasing my arm.

"Oh don't worry, Champ. I'd hate for anything to happen to my livestock," Kennedy says rather pointedly. He guides me through the shelves towards the back of the store.

"How are you feeling?"

"Well, I'm not at work today, so I have no real complaints," I say.

He laughs. "Where do you work?"

"Popeye's."

It's hard not to pull a face just thinking about how badly I don't want to work there.

Full Cauldron isn't crowded at all, which I like. There wasn't even a hint of a line, whereas Popeye's usually has a line before the store is even fully open.

A shelf adorned with colorful hand-drawn signs catches my eye. I recognize Smaug the dragon, Bilbo with his walking stick, and Shadowfax the horse.

"Which one of you drew these?" I ask, full of both awe and envy.

"Oh, *man*," he laughs.

"What?"

"I've never been around someone with this kind of amnesia before," he says, face torn between a smile and a frown. "You're hilarious."

My first instinct is to refute the amnesia claim, but I can't even remember his name. I laugh instead. He comes to a stop at a corner of the store that's decorated with Halloween store spider webs and pictures of gas lamps. A crushed black velvet loveseat sits against the wall between two shelves.

I, too, yearn for your flesh.

I stand still, but Champion's coworker keeps walking, and I almost topple.

He catches me before I can fall, eyes wide and alert. "Are you okay?"

I recover my physical balance quickly, but my brain still feels askew. When I blink, I see red eyes blinking over the top of an open book. I hear a voice, too—my own, asking a playful question, receiving no answer.

"Does someone named Carl work here?" I ask uncertainly.

"No," he says.

"Oh."

"*Frankenstein* is right here," he says, tapping a brand new paperback. "But I think you should consider getting *this* one. He touches the spine of the next book—a jacket-less, clothbound dual volume containing both *Frankenstein* and *Dracula*. "Double the fun."

I pull it off the shelf and turn it over in my hands.

"So who is Champion to you?" He asks.

"He's your coworker," I say, scowling. "Maybe you should ask him."

"Wow," he says softly, but he's smiling. "Oasis has truly left the building. I really wish my mom was alive right now. I mean, I always do," he clarifies, "but right now especially."

"Why?"

"You know how parents sometimes accuse you of not lis-tening to them? Well, you're a real live clinical example of words going in one ear and out the other. Everything I've said to you has been like throwing half-cooked spaghetti noodles at the wall and watching them fall off," he says.

"I'll take that as a compliment," I reply, frowning vaguely.

"It is," he says. "And of course I'd also want her to meet you when you actually know who I am, but this takes precedent."

For a long, long time, mentions of death, moms, and dead moms have felt virtually incapacitating, but here and now, I feel both honored and amused—amused enough to laugh alongside him.

Moments later, I feel an ominous pinch in my stomach. I lean on his arm again, trying my best not to let the pain and dread show on my face.

"Do you have a restroom?"

"This way," he says.

He leads me past a shelf of manga to a small bathroom scent-ed with apple cinnamon Glade. I'd been fully prepared to wad up some tissue, but thankfully, the woven basket full of tampons and pads next to the toilet is the first thing I see.

"TMI, but more places need to take a leaf out of your book," I say.

"I'll be sure to let the person who put them there know how appreciated she is," he says.

I shut the door and hurry to the toilet as fast as I can, still hoping for a false alarm.

The universe doesn't deliver. Although my thong isn't stained, I feel blood flow out before I start to pee. But more horrifying than the start of my period are these scars on my thighs: Luke 1:19 over and over, slashed up and down my legs.

Some have gotten faint.

Others have darkened.

What happened?

They can't be recent, but maybe they're connected to the holes in my memory. I steady my shaking fingers well enough to insert a tampon and resolve not to panic while washing my hands.

Outside the door, Champion's coworker lends me his arm again. My pulse calms as we make our way back to the front of the store.

By the time I see Champions' face, I forget what set my heart racing in the first place. He's standing behind the register now, ringing up a teenaged girl with a stack of V.C. Andrews novels.

"Your change will be six U.S. dollars and two pennies." He tears her receipt off the register and slides it across the glass like a detective pushing a folder of evidence towards a suspect. "Here is proof of this exchange."

"Thanks," she says, before joining her friends at the door.

I step up next. "So this is what you look like in your element."

"I am in *your* element, Oaza," Champion says. "This is…" he trails away, gaze fixed on the book I just set in front of him.

"Isn't this great, Champ?" His coworker says, rapping the cover with his knuckles. "She came in for one classic, and now she gets to leave with *two*."

Champion sucks his teeth, glaring at the book like it uttered fighting words. After a moment, he pulls it towards himself and gingerly checks the inside cover. He inputs the price, then opens his own wallet and pays.

He and his coworker switch places. I tuck the book under my arm, then grab hold of his.

"It was nice meeting you," I say to his coworker.

"You, too." He sits on his stool and reaches for a book. "I expect to see you back here to fill out an application."

Outside, I take a few deep breaths, trying my best to surmount my confusion. This doesn't look like Philadelphia in the slightest.

"Oaza, I think it would be unwise for you to read this book," Champion says as he puts on his ensemble of sun-deterring accessories.

I frown at the book under my arm. "But I'm already reading it. Aren't I?"

"I am referring to the inferior half of the volume."

We pause at the crosswalk.

I squint at the spine of my book, having forgotten that I got more than what I was looking for. "You don't like *Dracula*?"

"Oaza…" He gazes at me through the slits of his ski mask. "That book made me an even more dangerous being than I already was. Your condition is proof of such."

I have no clue what to say. It's not like I can deny my alleged condition when I'm just barely keeping up, operating on groundless faith that I can only hope is instinct in disguise.

"Prove it again," I say.

"What?"

"I can't remember anything, Champion, let alone you being dangerous. So prove you're a danger to me now," I say, "and I won't read…" I pause to double check the title. "*Dracula*."

"No," he says without hesitating.

"Then no."

The signal prompts us to cross, but he doesn't move and neither do I. A cloud passes over the sun, chilling my skin.

My stomach growls audibly, cutting short the silent discourse.

"You must be fed," Champion says quietly.

Before I can respond he puts an arm around my waist, bends his knees, and picks me up, balancing the book in my lap. I blush as he crosses the street in silence, carrying me like my own personal Prince Charming—or in this case, my Champion.

*

Rather than have me hobble around the grocery store alongside him, Champion leaves me at his apartment.

For a while, I occupy myself by reading *Dracula*, which is first in the dual tome. Or trying to.

It's strange being in Champion's apartment without him.

Strange being anywhere without him.

Like he's the glue holding it all together.

How can that be if we just met?

Did we just meet?

I can't remember the details of the accident we were in, but I have a feeling I'd be much worse for wear if it wasn't for him. If only I could remember what happened and when; that would determine the appropriateness of my desire to be close to him.

I close the book and leave it in bed, debating just how far I'm willing to go for nosiness. Not far enough to go through his closet. *Definitely* not far enough to peek into his nightstand. I walk unsteadily out of the room.

His desk is loaded with markers and pencils, plus a jar of dry paintbrushes and a sketchbook.

His worn notebook is there too, open facedown, balanced on the corner nearest the fire escape.

On the one hand, going through someone's personal notebook might be just as bad as going through their closet. On the other hand, if it was *really* that sensitive, it would probably be else-where, and it would most certainly be closed.

Instead, it's open to a page titled *Chapter 8*. He's a writer.

The cover has no title for the work-in-progress.

I skim the chapter.

Skimming turns to reading, and soon I can't stop reading.

It doesn't feel like a fictional work in progress either. It feels real, like a memoir.

Worse, I know that verse—Luke 1:19.

Where have I read Luke 1:19?

I read all the way through chapter nine, in which Champion discovers that he may be the only one with wings in his cult.

My heart throbs in my chest, choked with anger and sadness. Is this why I have yet to see him without his hoodie on? Or why I have yet to see him eat?

I flip through the blank pages that comprise chapter ten and stumble upon something that doesn't seem to be part of the narrative. I gasp quietly.

It's a list of songs under the word *Laura*, with tiny bats and hearts drawn in the margins. Champion has killer music taste—I'll give him that much. But no matter how desperate I am for companionship in this town, I refuse to be complicit in infidelity of any degree. I won't partake in causing Laura pain, whoever she is.

Maybe it's an old playlist. I should ask to be sure before I extricate myself from whatever this is. But then I'd have to admit to picking this thing up to begin with. I return to the page it was originally open to and put it back, then pick up my own book and resume reading *Dracula* in bed.

*

After a dinner of fried pork chops and mashed potatoes, Champion gathers markers and a sketchbook off his desk. I can't help glancing at his notebook.

Maybe I should just keep my mouth shut. Find out about it and Laura, whoever she is, later. He tears two pages out and lets the markers roll loosely between us, choosing a dark green one for himself. For a while, I watch the sky beyond the fire escape slip through various shades of blue. The Philadelphia skyline looks so different from here, but I've had few opportunities to see it well enough to recall how it looks from home.

"Oaza mea," Champion says. "You are distracted."

"Distracted by the fact that I can barely draw a straight line," I say wryly. "I'm a terrible artist, Champ. No type of amnesia will push that from memory."

He looks up from his drawing, which so far consists of a green ellipse.

"You remember your amnesia?"

"I remember you telling me I have amnesia." I frown at the table. "But I am feeling sort of...unmoored...to be honest. Like I'm just rolling with the tide." After saying that aloud, it's impossible not to think inwardly of the wrongness lacquered over everything I see.

The sky looks wrong. My pink clothes look wrong. This whole apartment, down to the chair beneath me, feels wrong. I know I'm injured, but how did it happen? Running for the bus? Pulling pop syrup off the shelf at work? Studying too hard?

The only thing that doesn't feel out of place is Champion.

It must be the cut on his face—the fact that whatever happened, had happened to us both.

I must have done something.

I pick up a pencil and start drawing the first thing that comes to mind: his face. Presently, he's biting his lip in concentration, filling in the ellipse with delicate lines.

"I don't think I've seen you laugh or smile yet," I comment.

"Would it please you to know that I smiled at you last night?" He asks. "The lights were out, and you were fast asleep."

"It does please me." I haven't butchered his nose in my drawing, and so move on to his mouth. "I have a confession."

"And you offer it to me freely?" Champion asks, glancing at me.

"Yeah. I'd want someone to do the same for me. I, uh..." I lick my lips, heart running a marathon in my ribcage. "I read some of your journal. Only the last two chapters," I say in a half-hearted attempt to diminish the severity of my invasiveness. "But still."

I look up from my drawing to the real Champion watching me, chin in hand, brow creased slightly.

"I just wanted to apologize," I continue. "And I know we just met and all..." I stop to clear my throat, all too aware of how awkward I'm making this. "What I'm trying to say is that I see you. And if you ever want to talk...I mean, I don't have a whole lot of people around for testimonials, but I think I'm a good listener."

"Oaza, that is not my story," Champion says quietly. "It is yours."

I frown. "Why would you say something like that?"

His green eyes look briefly and inexplicably anguished. "It is yours. I wish I could shield you from it," he says. "But I hunger for you, and so you will remember it, as you must remember me. Remember that I love you, and that you love me."

I narrow my eyes to slits. He must be playing games.

Trying to bury the evidence while it's in plain sight.

"If that's the case, who's Laura?" I ask casually. "Because I sure don't know her."

His eyebrows shoot up to his forehead. "What do you mean?"

"I saw the playlist you're making for her."

Champion gets to his feet, unspeaking. I peek at his drawing on the table. It's the outside of Bag End, bright green door shrouded in grass and greenery. My eyes widen at the elaborate detail, and when I look at the back of his broad shoulders, all I can think is how much it'll suck if this tall artsy guy who fell into my life out of nowhere has a girlfriend.

He sits back down, notebook in hand, eyes engulfed in broody darkness.

Maybe Laura isn't who I first assumed.

"Feel free to ignore everything I just said if I'm in the process of embarrassing myself," I say, resuming sketching his face.

"You have not embarrassed yourself. I, however, am guilty of that and more," he murmurs, scowling deeply at the list of songs. "I have made a near-fatal error in judgment, Oaza mea."

I pause drawing yet again, the better to absorb what he's saying. "How so?"

"This is your unit of measurement," Champion says, sounding far away. "The metric of your love."

"Playlisting? Yeah," I say. "But what does Laura have to do with that?"

"You love her."

I open my mouth to deny this, but the words don't make it out. The name feels different now I take his notebook and scan the list.

It's possible that this is my handwriting.

But how?

"Laura isn't your girlfriend?" I ask him.

"No."

I turn a page and frown even harder. "Who is Dracula, then?" I ask, arching a brow. I flip the notebook around, brandishing it in his face. "Is this a *platonic* sleepy time playlist?"

Champion reclaims his notebook. Alarm widens his eyes, but it doesn't look like the alarm of someone caught cheating. For all I know, I'm just taking him on a painful trip down memory lane, bringing up people long gone from his life.

"I am Vlad Dracula, Oaza. And you…you love me for all that I am, with all that you are." Champion closes the notebook and switches from a green marker to a grey one, gazing at me all the while. "I am sorry that I doubted you. I would pray to God that you love me still, if it would please you."

I look left and right, like I'll find some other Oaza. His words make no sense when directed at me.

I haven't loved anyone since Raymond. I was scared of it then—scared of what love would mean without high school and parents keeping the other components of our lives in line.

Maybe that fear lifted when I met Champion, and those words made their way out of me before the accident. The curved slash on his face has yet to scab over.

"This is mine?" I ask uncertainly.

"You shared it as part of your disclaimer to me," Champion says.

I pick it up, go back to the beginning, and read through with no furtiveness, spotting mentions of Mirage, Raymond, and Aurora, and of the verse I saw stamped on my legs in the form of scars. Visuals flash as I read some of the later passages, like I'm squinting through a smudged peephole at a dark hallway of hazy memories. A girl's green eyes smiling at me. A churning waterfall grabbing me in a fist. A stained-glass angel gazing down at me, sunlight pressing through the panes of his robes as I skimmed blood from my veins to make room for his divinity in my body.

If this was my life, I'd be tempted to pretend otherwise by any means. But that temptation would probably buckle beneath the need to share—to air out the unspeakable horrors of the past as a long-winded disclaimer, just like he said

As I close the notebook and look to Champion again, I realize definitively that there is no 'if'.

His eyes are helpless, tinged with sorrow.

Mercifully detached and hazy as it feels, I remember that this is my story.

Why did I let him read it?

"So, this is mine," I say as casually as I can. "But you can't expect me to believe your name is actually Dracula."

"It is a term of endearment," Champion says defensively. "My name is Vlad."

"Well, you don't look like a Vlad."

"Then what do I look like, Oaza, arbiter of names?" He asks.

"You look like a Champion."

With that, I get to my feet slowly and head towards the bathroom, closing the door just in time for a viscous cramp to cleave through my abdomen—so painful that I double over, gritting my teeth until it feels like my jaw might snap. Pain ripples through my temples as I search the medicine cabinet, frowning at the bruises on my face. I don't have time to ponder their hazy origins. Instead, I look beneath the sink for a tampon. The box is so dusty that I have to speed-wash my hands just to change.

Irritatingly enough, there's hardly any blood on the one I just pulled out—though I suppose as far as health goes, I should be celebrating that there's any at all.

My last period was in February, which makes this the third this year. But between not having blood stains on my mattress and the rising cost of tampons, menstruation's one thing I wasn't too sorry to see get lost in the annals of Custodes Angelorum. How could I have forgotten the place that took the blood from my veins, stopped my heart from beating, and left me barren?

I return to the dining room, sitting across from Champion while he twirls his pencil between his fingertips.

"Are you alright?" He asks.

The honest answer is no. It's June, and I've been living off a loan that Mirage jokingly calls reparations, insisting I don't pay him back like that'll make up for how I got from point A to point B. Deprogramming is a lonely task, but it feels like I should be secure in my distance from Custodes Angelorum before I get close to someone else. Yet these past few months, hardly a day's passed wherein I haven't declared to myself that I'd start taking more initiative in the realm of getting my back blown out.

At long last, I have a specimen.

Why'd my period have to show up at the same time as him?

"Yes," I say anyway.

"When were you born?"

"I'm a Cancer sun," I say. "You?"

He purses his lips.

"I am an Aquarius."

"Good to know."

"Do you know where you are now?"

"I'm, uh…I'm here. Talking to you." I point a green marker at him, smiling. "*Champ*."

His brows knit in a deep valley over suspicious green eyes. "Do you remember me now?"

"How could I forget you? You're the only customer I've gone on a date with," I say, detailing the sky with several blue markers.

Champion puts his pencil down. "When did we meet?"

I start to say something snippy, but the cut on his face reminds me that we were in an accident. He's probably just as scrambled as I am.

"You came into Full Cauldron wearing a ski mask and motorcycle gloves. You have a sun allergy," I say slowly, waiting for a glimpse of recognition in his eye. "You said you were burning copies of *Dracula*."

Nothing seems to register. Then,

"You have begun to merge memories of me with memories of me, forming an entirely novel me," he says after a moment, somewhere between awed and vexed. "The inner workings of your concussed mind would be a fascinating long-term study, were you not still lost to me."

I wasn't lost before, but I am now.

How bad was our accident?

"Are you sure you're okay?" I ask with forced calm. "Maybe we should go to the hospital. You could have head trauma."

"This need not be," Champion says, returning to himself. "I remain silent so that I may cherish your voice without hearing the din of my own."

"You have a wonderful voice," I say, frowning, but still relieved. "You could start the baritone takeover I've been waiting for."

"I prefer this to show business." He caps his marker. "It would please me to glimpse your artistry."

I look down at my drawing of Bag End, suddenly self-conscious. Markers are darker than watercolors, more stubborn on the page, but somehow, I think I pulled it off. I take the leap and hold it up. He leans across the table, lips pursed like an appraiser. "This is quite good, Oaza," he murmurs approvingly. "Quite good."

I grin.

"Your turn."

Champion holds up a self-portrait. He hasn't drawn his eyes yet, but the likeness is flooring.

If my jaw wasn't so sore, I'd let it drop.

"You didn't even look in the mirror. Now that's just unfair," I say, sulking as I pick up a brown marker for Bilbo's bench. "Save some talent for the rest of us."

*

I thought I'd be a lot more nervous letting someone cook for me after Custodes Angelorum, but when Champion leaves the table and starts cooking of his own accord, I neither question nor stop him.

Instead, I continue reading *Dracula* at the table with my laptop open and Google at the ready, so that the abundance of unfamiliar and antiquated terms won't hinder me on top of the concussion, the origins of which still elude me.

"What are you making?" I ask.

"Goulash," he says. "From Hungary."

"Funny. Jonathan Harker just ate Hungarian food, too," I say, glancing at my recent Google search for 'paprika hendl'. "Actually, let me stop. I forgot you don't like this book."

"It would be just as apt to say that the book does not like me," Champion says darkly.

I read on, opening tab after tab to stay afloat in the slow-moving narrative. After some time, I flip forward to see just how much further before I get to *Frankenstein*. It looks like *Dracula* takes up over half the book.

I sigh and keep at it, reading on even though I feel my attention span thinning. After a while, I start skimming outright, blasting through a whopping eighteen chapters in pursuit of an interesting plot point.

It's a relief when Champion comes over with a flat bowl of what looks like gourmet beef stew.

I push my laptop back as he sets it in front of me. As I open my mouth to thank him, I notice something on my laptop. The screen itself went dark; it's the reflection that makes me frown.

I see my face—my bruised eye and busted lip, further indicators of the amnesia accusation's merit.

But I don't see Champion.

He's right behind me, placing a spoon and fork next to the bowl, but I'm alone on the dark, glossy screen.

I close it and try not to stare too hard at the back of his head when he steps away. He sits across from me, chin in his hands.

"You're not hungry?" I ask.

"Not for this," he says.

I can't read his eyes or face, and wonder momentarily if I'm setting myself up for a repeat of Custodes Angelorum by allowing myself to be fed. Granted, he and Zeke couldn't be more dissimilar. Zeke was always on the hunt for ways to sprinkle his profound wisdom into every conversation; no day in that cult went without a profound revelation of some kind. Champion, on the other hand, seems to speak only when spoken to. Moreover, he seems to do more watching than speaking.

I'm too hungry to overthink eating right now. As I dig in, I fixate on the table. Everything atop it—the bowl, my laptop, the closed book next to it—has a dark shadow wedged between it and the wood. Champion, with his elbows planted firmly on the surface, doesn't seem to have one. Like an optical illusion in the shape of a man.

He clears his throat, and for a moment, I worry that my thoughts were somehow audible.

"Are you enjoying *Dracula?*" He asks instead.

"I'm not *not* enjoying it," I say vaguely. "I like the descriptions of the settings and stuff, but Jonathan seems kind of racist to me—all the comments about Count Dracula's nose. And then there's the part where Lucy says she can't blame Desdemona for being seduced by a Black man."

His eyebrows raise in surprise.

"I had dog-eared the page so I wouldn't forget, but I guess racism transcends brain damage."

Champion pulls the book towards himself and skims the page in question.

"I hope it would please you to know that if such a statement was made in reality, I was unaware," he says, frowning lightly. "As for myself, I do not put store in color. You all bleed red."

"And what do you bleed?"

"I do not bleed unless I am in the mood. If you were to pry open the wound on my face, it would appear as another orifice."

"Note to self: don't open Champion's face wound," I mutter.

He closes the book and returns it to its place beside my laptop. Each of his movements enhances the illusion that he's shadowless.

How hard did I hit my head?

It feels too late to be scared of him, but it's not every day that someone simply has no shadow, and if it wasn't for the fact that I could never cook anything this delicious on my own, I'd accuse myself of hallucinating his existence altogether.

I finish eating and go back to reading while he does the dishes.

In addition to frustration over the disinteresting plot, I feel an inexplicable weight in my gut reading Dr. Seward's diary entries. I skim faster, like I'm running away from them, reading less than half the sentences to completion. It isn't until I get to September 30 in the narrative that Dr. Van Helsing finally offers up something worth reading: vampire characteristics.

...he eat not as others. Even friend Jonathan, who lived with him for weeks, did never see him to eat, never! He throws no shadow; he make in the mirror no reflect, as again Jonathan observe. He has the strength of many of his hand—witness again Jonathan when he shut the door against the wolfs, and when he help him from the diligence too. He can transform himself to wolf, as we gather from the ship arrival in Whitby, when he tear open the dog; he can be as bat...

I look up, frowning at Champion in the kitchen. His hood is down, his hair up in a floppy bun. The golden bats dangling from his earlobes swing with his movements. He's wearing dish gloves, but I remember a bat ring being on his ice cold hand, which felt, as Jonathan wrote, *more like the hand of a dead than a living man.*

My laptop isn't a mirror, but he still had no reflection. And then there's the fact that even now, folding the gloves over the sink, flipping out the kitchen light to join me, he seems to have no shadow.

The scars on my body are proof that I've believed in crazier things than vampires, and now that I'm almost a year out of Custodes Angelorum, I can admit to missing believing in something more magical than myself, but this representation of vampires is problematic at best.

It would certainly explain why Champion doesn't like *Dracula*.

It doesn't explain why *she* doesn't.

"You appear deep in thought," Champion says, sitting across from me once more.

I start to lie, because whatever I have with him feels too precious and promising to contaminate with thoughts of what could have been with someone else. Then again, it would be a disservice to myself to shy away from my attraction to women now that I have free reign over my own life.

"This woman came into the store today and bought all our copies of *Dracula*. She was wearing this gold tracksuit, and she…" I trail away, struggling to recall her face and voice. "She was beautiful. I wish I hadn't been too shy to get her number. I didn't even ask her name." I heave a sigh laden with regret. "Anyway. Just putting it out there. Transparency and whatnot."

"She and I are the same essence, Oaza," Champion says, brow creased. "You need not be transparent."

"I can keep it to myself next time if you'd prefer." I work to keep my voice steady, even though my heart is pounding like a jackhammer. "It's been a while since I entered the dating scene."

Champion licks his lips slowly.

"Champion?" I ask after several minutes of silence.

His green eyes flit to me. "Oaza?"

"Are you a vampire?"

"Yes," he says, letting his hair down.

I nod, chewing the inside of my cheek. "Can I see your fangs?"

He fixes me with a look of mild surprise, then sucks his teeth and bares them without smiling. Two sharp, pearly white fangs have replaced his canines, denting his lower lip.

"That's it?" I ask.

"There can only be two fangs," Champion says with something of a lisp. "Otherwise, the integrity of veins will suffer. I am a vampire, not a barracuda."

I stifle a giggle. "You're so cute. You look like a kitten."

"I am not cute," he says, deadpanning.

"Have you seen yourself in the mirror?" I snicker.

His eyebrows shoot back up, practically grazing his hairline.

I cover my mouth. "Whoops," I say through my fingers. "Guess not."

*

By nightfall, I'm exhausted. I don't remember what I did today to justify such an empty head, but I'm not complaining. Instead, I'm watching *Desolation of Smaug* with Champion. We're side-by-side in my bed, a foot and a half apart, with my laptop balanced on a pillow between our outstretched legs and the lamplight dimmed.

Typically, this is my favorite way to bond when I'm too tired to talk, but right now, I'm not too tired.

I'm just too busy thinking about the vampire beside me.

About where we began, where we are, where we're going.

When I look over at him, his nostrils are flared, and his green eyes are fixed on Smaug's piles of gold and jewels.

"You don't like the movie?" I ask.

"I am somewhat disgusted by this dragon's lack of a system for organizing his spoils," Champion says, massaging his temples. "At least put them into separate rooms."

I snicker, but soon fall silent.

I've been telling myself to wait until I'm stable in life and unquestionably sane to want someone, but the wound on his face and the bruises on mine are a reminder that just because I'm not going to die in a suicide cult doesn't mean that the life I have ahead of me is safe from being cut short.

But then something occurs to me, and I realize I should be certain that the art of seduction has an audience in him before I attempt it.

I hit the space bar and sit up straight to look Champion in the face. "Can vampires have sex?"

A consternated frown passes over his features. "Generally speaking, yes."

"Don't you need a bloodstream?"

"I am the bloodstream," Champion says. He taps the space bar again and focuses on the screen, though the frown remains. He crosses his arms and ankles. Then, to my horror, he nibbles his thumbnail.

"Don't do that," I say, grabbing his wrist, forcing his hand down onto the bed. "It's bad for your teeth."

He doesn't look my way or respond, but he doesn't take his hand away, either.

The movie plays on, but my attention is shot: all I can think about are the cold fingers laced between mine. How they'd feel without the rings, and elsewhere on my body.

Soon, the credits are rolling. I let go of his hand, shut my laptop, and slide it under the bed, frowning when it hits the corner of a pale wooden box. I'm too preoccupied trying to wrangle my primal urges into submission to see what it is.

I swing my legs over the edge of the bed. My confidence in

my ability to walk unaided winds up being premature, and I nearly crash into the closet door after accidentally putting weight on my injured foot.

Champion is next to me in a flash, steadying me with a cold hand.

I regain my balance physically, but my head keeps spinning.

A dull throb in my abdomen reminds me that my period is most likely responsible for my horny levels going off the charts. The why of it all doesn't help when I can't remember anything about the vampire in my crosshairs. I know we met at work, and that we went on a date, but I don't remember inviting him in, and I'm not sure why he's still here. The accident must have been during or after our date.

Whatever happened, it was bad enough to leave a scar on a vampire's face.

No wonder I can't remember anything.

Did we have sex?

Amnesia aside, I feel like I'd remember having sex with a vampire.

It's been so long since I felt touchable that I'm certain I'd remember his touch.

"Where was to be your destination?" He asks.

"Bathroom." I need a cold shower, ibuprofen, and sleep.

But as he helps me out of my bedroom, I start to feel like what I need has nothing to do with hygiene, cramps, or exhaustion. I get the feeling it has nothing to do with sex either, which is odd, because once that train of thought leaves the tracks, depression over the unlikelihood of me getting laid is usually the only thing that can stop it.

"Okay, just—wait." I stop walking. "Time out."

Champion stops, too, frowning as he holds onto my arms.

I let go of him and hobble to the table, then lean on the edge of it, neglecting the soreness in my broken fingers as I grip the wood.

"I'm confused."

"It is the amnesia. I will clarify," Champion says.

"Did we have sex?" I ask.

"Yes."

"Oh." I clasp my hands, blinking rapidly at the floor as I mull over an answer I wasn't actually prepared to receive. "Before the accident?"

"Oaza, we had no accident. We have been fucking profusely since August."

I start to point out that it's the middle of June, but the air coming in through the open window is calm and cool, not heavy with humidity.

I search for memories of him and find nothing but a cache of jealousy.

I'm jealous of myself—of the me I don't remember being; the me who supposedly fucked a vampire.

"If it would aid your memory, I wear a different face with you," Champion says quietly.

"Like a shapeshifter?" I ask.

"Yes. You like for me to sit on your face."

My breath hitches, chest burning with curiosity. "Can you prove that?"

Champion puts his hands in his pockets. "No. I am ill."

I cross my arms, struggling to make sense of the conundrum through a head full of butterflies.

"What kind of illness can you have?"

"If a vampire does not feed, it will simply die," Champion says. "But I am the first vampire, and I will be the last. I am eternal, and so I am ill."

My heart pounds harder, because even though conceptually, vampire malnutrition makes perfect sense, it also seems like a joke.

But Champion isn't smiling, and neither am I.

"Why haven't you fed?" I ask. "Is it because you're here?"

"It is because you are not."

"Champion, I'm standing right in front of you," I say, dizzy.

"And because of me, you do not even know who I am. I will feed when you remember me," he says categorically.

"What are you waiting on me for?" I demand. "I can take care of myself for an hour, or however long it takes for you to go out there and…"

I don't know how to finish. My only real exposure to vampirism is a black-and-white soap opera.

"I am not some gluttonous mosquito," Champion says before I find words, brow furrowed over stormy green eyes, "and I would starve for eternity before I sank to consuming blood that I did not ferment with love for me." He takes a small step closer, biting his lip. "*You* are my prey. I will drink of you when you remember that you love me, and then I will be nourished."

I don't know what's more disorienting right now: being told that I already know and love someone I just met, or being told that the me I don't remember being loves that someone enough to let them drink my blood.

Only one fundamental fact remains like scaffolding: he's hungry.

"Why wait?" I repeat.

"You must remember that you love me."

"Champion, you're the only thing that makes sense," I say tersely, which deepens his frown. "I can't remember what I was doing an hour ago, or what I had for breakfast—"

"Biscuits and gravy," he interrupts quietly.

"That *you* probably made. Didn't you?"

Champion remains silent.

I pinch the bridge of my nose, straining to recollect everything he's ever said to me.

"Do you still doubt me?" I ask.

"No," he says.

"Will you feed now?"

More silence.

I bite the inside of my cheek, hoping that none of the frustration in my spirit is showing on my face.

Is this how Mirage feels whenever I pass on the food he cooks at his restaurant? Like he could shake me by the shoulders until the irrationality leaves my brain? Like he could scream and cry and curse until the veil over my eyes lifts, and I realize that starved is no way to live?

"You should not be on your feet this long," Champion says, like we're done here.

"You're *absolutely* right." I hoist myself onto the table, leaning back on my hands. "How old are you, Champ?"

He puts his hands in his pockets. "588."

I purse my lips. "You were around for slavery?"

"There has been more than one instance of slavery in my lifetime," he says. "I assume you are referring to the one that placed you here to be loved by me."

A shiver caresses my spine.

"My great grandma was born on a plantation. Her grandma had been a slave," I say. "Then Kansas joined the union, and suddenly, she didn't have to pick through master's scraps to feed herself and her children. She swore none of them would ever go to bed hungry again." I sit up straight, hands on my knees. *"It's plenty to eat, now. Ain't no reason for you to go to bed hungry,"* I say, echoing my great grandma, my grandma, and my mother all at once. "You think because you're a vampire, you're the exception? In *my* house? A-tuh."

Champion clasps his hands, standing before me like a contestant in a talent show, mouth set in an unreadable line. "What are you implying?"

"I'm implying that you need to relax," I say, somewhat hypocritically.

I'm not relaxed just yet.

In fact, I feel light-headed with adrenaline as I untie my pink sweatpants.

"What are you doing?" He asks, sounding as guarded as he does intrigued.

"We're gonna fuck." I push the waistband down to my thighs, wriggling until all my scars are in plain sight, and nothing at all is between my bare ass and the table. "We do that profusely, right?"

"It would be unwise for us to have sex while you suffer from a traumatic brain injury," Champion says, watching without intervening.

"Do you want to have sex at all?" I ask, hoping that the confidence I never have didn't make its debut at the wrong time. "Because if you do, then I don't want to wait to remember how it feels to be loved by you."

His hands break apart, like he's contemplating reaching.

"You said I already love you, and I don't doubt you."

Champion flexes his fingers, nostrils flared. Then he twists off the bat ring and clenches it in his fist. "It has been some time since I used this face to the end you are proposing."

"Likewise," I say, spreading my legs.

Another ring leaves his index finger as he takes a slow but sure step towards the table, nibbling his lip.

"What is my name?" He asks, close enough to see every shard of green in his irises.

"Champion." I slide my index finger under the band of my thong, clicking my tongue, subtly feeling for my tampon string. Somehow, I keep a straight face as the wad of cotton exits my body.

"What is your name?" He asks, now within smelling distance.

I steel my body against a tide of chills.

"You're gonna say it soon enough."

Champion stops at my knees. He smells like something tart, something sweet, something fiery, something sylvan. He could touch my legs if he wanted; spread them wider like I want. But his measured tread reminds me of every cat I've ever known, who watched me while my arm got sore from reaching, aloof about wanting my attention.

"I must confess that I was not ready for you the first time we met," he says.

"And you think you are now?" I ask deviously.

The night exhales through the fire escape, fluttering strands of his hair past his shoulders.

"I only have one more question." I loop my tampon string around my finger and pull it out all the way, then hold it up. I see it dangling in the corner of my eye, slick and burgundy. "Does this have any nutritional value?"

Champion's eyes widen; for a moment, he merely looks surprised.

His pupils dilate, swelling to the size of his irises. The thin rings of green break, and the black of his pupils spills out like yolk from an eggshell. He tilts his head to the side, eyes like ebony orbs.

I look down, following what seems to be the path of his gaze. There's already blood pooled on the table between my legs, soaking into my thong.

A soft, creaking snarl meets my ears, and when I look up, his lips are parted, fangs glinting. Dark veins snake from the depths of his hoodie, swelling over his temples, climbing beneath his widow's peak.

I hold my breath. A voice deep in the back of my mind asks if I really understand what I've done, bleeding in front of a vampire. But that voice is nowhere near as loud as the awed silence for the me I can't remember—the me who found this creature and made it mine.

"I'm not your prey, Champ. I'm your prize," I say, swinging my tampon like a toy mouse. "*Come and get me.*"

The sound issuing from his throat gets louder and rhythmic, like inhales and exhales. He steps closer, each movement preternaturally sharp and tight, like there's a beast inside clawing to the surface of him.

"Have a seat," I instruct, nudging the nearest chair with my foot.

Champion lowers himself rigidly, nostrils flaring. He takes the rest of his rings off in two fluid swipes; some roll off the table when he drops them on either side of me. He seems to be watching the tampon, swinging like a pendulum in the breeze beyond the fire escape.

I let go of the string.

His hand flashes out, snatching it from mid-air. His chest heaves and a strained, guttural sound comes from his throat as he bites down on his lip, closing his blackened eyes.

When he opens his hand, the tampon is pure white and compact, like he absorbed my blood through his palm.

My lips part.

How did it feel the first time I truly realized he isn't human? Did I ever?

For a moment, I was jealous of the me beyond memory—the me who somehow summoned the comfort and confidence to fuck someone profusely.

Not so much anymore.

Maybe it was meant to be this way—two different me's for two different faces.

I reclaim the tampon, which looks like it just came out of the wrapper, and let it roll across the table. Then I take his hand and put it firmly on my left thigh. He does the same with the other, slowly, tenderly. His nostrils are the only part of his body in motion as he continues breathing rapidly, like he's scared I'll run away before he can get close enough to taste me.

I beckon with a finger and comb my fingers through his widow's peak. His hair feels cold and fluid, like satiny strands of ice.

He bends closer, fingers squeezing my thighs. Then he tilts his head up, black eyes refracting every shard of light in the room.

"Be careful with those fangs," I say, leaning back on my elbows.

Champion scoots his chair right up to the table and tugs my thong all the way off, flinging it over his shoulder. His nose and mouth disappear beneath the shadow of my stomach. Cold wafts off his face like the inverse of steam as his breathing intensifies. I hear the subtle squeaking of his tongue on the table and somehow refrain from inching forward so that it's touching me instead. If I didn't have an agenda, I'd shove his face right into my pussy, wrap my whole body around his head and shoulders like a shawl.

A moan builds in my throat as his tongue glides over me, cold and wet. He goes deeper, breathing jagged, head ducking under my hand as I ravel locks of his hair in my fingers. The bridge of his nose grazes my clit. His tongue slithers even deeper inside of me, twisting like a serpent, pulsing like a heartbeat, doing things I can't even visualize.

Once the first gasp is out of me, I can't swallow the rest. I lay back on the table, drowning in the song sewn from our sounds.

Everything I can't remember doesn't matter because I know I've never felt anything like this—never felt a tongue go so deep or writhe like a creature of its own. This isn't about me, or him, individually: it's about the fortress made of us, where hunger comes to die. Here, the walls are full of my moans and his growling groans; here, starvation doesn't stand a chance.

The chair scrapes on the floor, and I open my eyes in time to see Champion rising, breathing deeply, tongue reeling back into his mouth like measuring tape.

My eyes widen.

Faint stubble shadows his cheeks, but the gash is gone. The only red on his face is from me, smeared over his chin and nose. The black of his pupils spools back into his green irises as he gets to his feet, still holding onto my thighs. Then, standing over me, he wipes his mouth, disappearing the blood from my period so thoroughly that it's as if his palm was a washcloth.

I raise my eyebrows. "So the fangs are just...?"

"Cute," Champion finishes with a smile to showcase them. He flattens his hands on either side of me, grinning. "I did not say grace, Oaza, you distracted me so."

"And you're *smiling?* You're like a whole new vampire," I say, still breathing fast.

"*Oaza mea who art on this table, hallowed be thy name...*" He leans in, pressing his forehead against mine, breathing in, and in, and in. "*Thy pussy warm,*" he says, exhaling, drenching me in goosebumps, "*thy will be done, here, now.*"

I wrap my legs around him, ignoring the pang in my ankle, and lick his smiling lips.

"*Soothe on this night my appetite,*" he says as I gather the hem of his hoodie and pull, "*and forgive me my trespasses...*" He snatches it off and presses my hands to his bare chest. "*...for they are abundant.*"

He's wearing nothing underneath. I pause while reaching for the back of his neck and hold onto his shoulder instead.

There's a column of three scars on his sternum, and more in

addition to it scattered across his body—pale gashes, dark burns; wide, jagged, straight lines, amorphous blobs. The one that looks most intense stretches from shoulder to shoulder like the neck of a sleeveless shirt.

"What happened?" I breathe.

"The Middle Ages." He grabs my thighs again, fingers nearly evenly spread across a column of scars on my thigh, like notes on a scale. "*Lead me not into starvation, but deliver me from hunger, for thine is the kingdom,*" he says, hair trailing in my face as he sniffs the top of my head, "*and the power,*" he says, cold nose grazing my temple and jaw, "*and the glory, for ever, and ever, and ever, and ever…*"

He keeps murmuring this as he pulls me into his arms. My mouth is too busy for me to say grace myself, face buried in his neck, kissing and biting, salivating at both ends. But as he steps into the light of my bedroom, I see something on his shoulder blades from above—something red and raised, like a scar.

Champion lowers me onto the bed and pulls back, chewing his lip, then leans in to kiss me, one knee between my legs.

"Wait." I put my hand between our mouths, heart hurtling against my ribs. "Turn around."

His smile slips, and his glittering green eyes darken.

"Show me," I say softly, stroking his temple where the vanished wound had been. "Please?"

Champion stands up, towering over me, then turns around and kneels, so that I'm looking at his back from above.

Wings.

They're wider than mine, raw, red, and rugged, burned on his skin rather than carved. Each has three curved lines and a sharp thumb, like the wings of a bat—or like the wings of the Devil.

"Thank you," I say. I have nothing else.

Champion turns around again, still kneeling in front of me, massaging my legs. "Thank you."

I reach for his waist, tugging the strings of his waistband. "Thank *you*," I say, brushing my nose with his.

He steps out of his sweats and sighs through his nostrils. "I believe it is *I* who should be thanking *you*."

I look him up and down, grinning.

A real live undead naked vampire in my bedroom.

"That's really not necessary, but—" I clear my throat as a sweat breaks around my neck "—you have my thanks."

Champion pulls my hoodie off, folds it neatly and, as I shimmy back onto the bed, puts it under my injured ankle. Then he reaches for his phone on the nightstand.

I can't stop smiling, can't stop thinking about how it took mild brain damage for me to stop feeling like a hostage to my trauma, a martyr without a cause. Billie Holiday's familiar lush voice fills the room. Is the sudden déjà vu from her? I haven't heard this song in years, but I feel something sharp and sore in my heart.

The heavy feeling lifts as Champion kneels between my legs, kissing the tops of my knees, my thighs, my breasts; I could easily forget each and every one of the scars on my body with his hands roaming over them. I feel his dick on my stomach, cold and hard and, like most of him, unlike anything I've ever felt.

For a while, we're just this: lips and fingers and skin and want. Impatience surges through me as he kisses my collarbone and neck, fiery and consuming. He stretches out so that we're chest to chest, his legs slotted through mine. I wrap both arms and a leg around him, kissing every inch of skin that my lips can reach, arching my back.

All the filthy things I haven't done in years are on my mind, and I want to see just how many I can execute with this vampire tonight. I reach between our bodies, feeling for the smooth tip of his dick.

"It will be cold," he says sheepishly.

I plant a kiss on his bicep, right next to my head. "Not for long."

Despite the disclaimer, I end up giggling as he enters me, his moans undercut with deep laughs. I hope I remember us like this—his cold lips on mine, my breath on his scarred collarbone, his voice crashing in my eardrums. His moans sound different now—not the growling groans of starvation, but the softer sounds of a different breed of hunger.

"*Come to me*," he whispers in my ear, gripping my hips while we're chest to chest, stroking so good I could cry. "*Come to me, Oaza mea.*"

I almost do.

Almost.

I stop at the edge, grip his shoulders, and roll us over, showing my ankle none of the same consideration he did when laying me down.

"Mm. What maneuvers are you planning to execute?" Champion asks, hands clasped under his head.

"Starts with a six," I say, arching a brow.

He rolls his hips, still very much inside of me.

"If the next two numbers are also sixes, I have been there," he says drolly, tapping his shoulders, "and done that."

I slide off his torso, then sit on top of him again and smirk over my shoulder. In silence, I sink low, gripping the slick shaft of his dick. I kiss the tip, teasing with my lips. It's my turn to grip his thighs, to run my tongue over him. My turn to put him in my mouth like a Bomb Pop.

His voice muffles as he buries his face between my legs again, and after some time, I have to choose between sucking and screaming.

"*So wet,*" Champion murmurs, tonguing my clit like a caramel. "*So warm,*" he moans, two fingers deep. "*Come back to me,*" he whispers, bringing me closer and closer to the edge. "*My Oasis.*"

It feels like I'm floating—like the wings on my back are unfolding, taking me to the heights I thought I'd go before I got them.

Only somehow, with my forehead on his abs and the blankets bunched in my hand, I keep going higher, until I'm all I can hear, and he's all I can feel. The orgasm hits me like a ballistic, sends me soaring. By the time I touch back down, my throat is raw, my body deflated, my chest sore from heaving.

"*Dumnezeule,*" Champion whispers.

Somehow, I manage to roll over, breathing hard, legs like lead.

He sits up on his elbows. His face and neck are dripping wet, and the grey sheet under his shoulders is the color of charcoal, like someone threw a bucket of water at him.

"What happened?" I ask hoarsely.

"The Great Flood." Champion licks his lips. His tongue keeps revolving, lengthening right in front of me, until he's licking his whole face dry. It furls back into his mouth, leaving me speechless.

He reaches for me; I lay in his arm, unable to avoid the puddle I left on the pillow.

"*All the springs of the great deep burst forth and the floodgates of the heavens were opened,*" he says, "*and roaming the desert known as time, I found my Oasis.*"

"*And wandering the battlefield known as life,*" I murmur, stroking his jaw with my fingertips, "*I found my Champion.*"

"Amen," Champion says.

"Amen."

twenty-eight

September 7, 2019

I am longing to be with you, and by the sea, where we can talk to-gether freely and build our castles in the air.

twenty-eight

I wake up with a dry mouth, a heavy head, and limbs so sore it's like I spent my dreams in a boxing ring. I roll over, squeezing my eyelids shut, desperate to postpone my entry into the waking world.

In the darkness, a humming voice reaches my ears—quiet, but familiar. The song is familiar too. The harder I try to steer myself back to sleep, the harder it gets not to hum along.

By the time I give in and open my eyes, Beyoncé's *Sweet Dreams* is planted firmly in my skull. Sunlight paints the closed curtains gold. The square of muted light warms my bare legs; one of my ankles is wrapped in an ace bandage.

A woman's face and figure clarify beside me—a woman with dark skin and a black bonnet on her head, brown eyes half-lidded as she watches me rouse.

Sleep sloughs away with a gasp. Pain pinches my chest and two of my fingers when I try to push myself up.

"Careful, beloved," she says, smoothing the pillow. "What is your name?"

My heart skips a beat.

"Oasis. Why?"

"Do you recognize me?"

"Of course I do," I croak. "I miss you."

"What is my name?" She asks.

Fear steals over me, and the last of my tiredness drains away as I sit up on my elbow.

"Which one?"

Laura smiles and slides a little closer to me. "This one."

"Laura. I miss you," I say again. It's the only piece of reality that makes sense right now. "When did you get here?"

"A few days ago."

"*Days?*"

"Do you know what day it is?"

"No," I admit. I rub my eyes, an awkward feat given my broken fingers. "Wednesday?"

"It is Saturday. You have had amnesia," she says.

I blink several times, then roll my eyes. "Yeah, right."

"I will cure you of your disbelief." Laura puts her hand on my shoulder. "Lie with me, beloved."

I heed her touch and lay back down, frowning as she pulls the sheet over us.

We're both naked.

I spot a few lime-colored bruises on my shins. Beyond the random injuries, much of my body is covered in hickeys, scattered over my stomach and chest almost as abundantly as my scars. I squint at my left breast, then grab it to better examine a faint bite mark.

Whoever left it has a mouth bigger than Laura's.

"Did I...?"

"Did you...?" she asks, brow arched.

Cheat on my girlfriend?

Where would I have even found the opportunity, or the gumption?

I don't remember going on a bender, but I wouldn't put it past myself to have needed some type of cushion after seeing Helena, even if it felt cathartic at first.

"What is the last thing you remember?" Laura asks.

"I was gonna go to Central Park again," I say slowly.

"And then?"

"I..." After several minutes of fruitlessly frisking my memories, I purse my lips. All my life, amnesia's been nothing but a plot device that I can't watch without breaking into stressed-out hives, but here I am with my body nowhere near as intact as it was when I parted ways with Helena, and no explanation for how that happened.

"What happened?" I ask.

"After cross-referencing with Kennedy, my theory is that your quality time with Helena inspired you to return to Blessed

Falls—without me," Laura adds pointedly, batting her eyelashes. "We arrived in time to find you mangled on the floor. Ezekiel had bludgeoned you with a bible."

My heart thumps a manic rhythm, but I can't summon any evidence against her theory.

After a moment, I stop trying.

I'm in no rush to remember Zeke making another effort to break me.

"Who's 'we'?"

"Myself, Ásttora, Justina, Cypress, and Bunnicula comprised the search party. As to who comprised the dinner party, I cannot say," she says. "You were my only concern, and so I did not stay. I am told it was one for the books."

My heart sinks, and sinks, and sinks, until I can hardly feel its aching beats.

As far as I'm concerned, I was just with Helena, discussing Custodes Angelorum with abject curiosity and firm detachment. I was supposed to spend the rest of my life wondering what became of the place; I wasn't supposed to influence its fate.

But even if I don't remember what came after seeing Helena, I remember what I felt while I was with her: like there was one person left to free from Zeke's clutches. Like there was no point in waiting to find her.

"Are any of the vessels alive?" I ask quietly.

"Some of the wolves left with...doggie bags," Laura says evasively.

Unable to reason myself out of it, I burst into tears.

Laura clicks her tongue softly. She peels the blanket back and pulls me into her arms, stroking the nape of my neck, trailing her nose along my forehead. "Why do you cry, Oasis?" She asks, leaving a crown of tender kisses beneath the elastic of my bonnet.

"How can you ask that?" I say, feeble and incredulous. "If I hadn't gone, they'd still have the chance to leave. Why should I be the only one who gets to walk away?"

"You did not walk away, Oasis. I carried you," Laura says. She sets her jaw, one hand resting on my cheek. "And if you had not been unconscious, I would have turned back to slaughter everyone who heard you scream and did not move to keep you safe."

I wipe my face on the blanket.

Our eyes stay locked as I regain control of my breathing.

Then in a blink, hers go from brown to pure white, ringed

with dark red. Her face crumples, and a long wail comes from her throat. Tears of blood spill down her cheeks, soaking into her brown skin as more follow.

I start crying all over again, and pull her into my arms.

The conversation devolves into wordless sobs as we hold onto one another. But as always in her arms, I could easily forget that anything but us exists.

"Twice in one week, your heartbeat left my ears," Laura says, sobs fading to sniffles. "I am sorry I breached the space, but I could not leave until you remembered me."

"I took all the space I needed. If you hadn't batted off again, I would've called you back." I kiss her knuckles, still struggling to wrap my mind around the void in my memories. "I love you so much."

"And I, you." Tears of blood fade from her cheeks as she sits up. "If I could die for you, I would not hesitate."

Sitting up makes it impossible to overlook the tenderness between my legs. In fact, it's impossible to overlook what looks and feels like the aftermath of getting my brains fucked out.

I open my mouth, then close it when I spot a pink hoodie, and a larger grey hoodie with matching sweatpants strewn in a trail out the door. There are two phones on the nightstand. On a hunch, I reach across her lap for hers: it's just past noon, and the music app is paused on *Body and Soul* by Billie Holiday.

"Did we have sex?" I ask.

"I made a modest effort to deter you, seeing as you were traumatically concussed, but you were incredibly hormonal and I was...*touch-starved*," she says, like she only just realized. "We made love for nearly nine hours. You have been asleep a mere five."

"*Nine hours?*" I choke.

Laura watches my face with a curious half-smile, like she can hear all the questions in my head and is just as eager for answers.

"Unholy abomination though I may be, I am blessed to have so many bodies for you to touch—if it would please you."

My face flames, and for a wild moment, I'm jealous of the me who somehow met and seduced Vlad Dracula.

"*Nine hours?*" I say again.

"After you fed me, we began as missionaries. Soon after, you sucked my dick and squirted on my face," Laura says, stroking the space between two trident scars. "And then when it seemed like you were ready for sleep, you changed your mind and opened the drawer, and proceeded to fuck me in the ass." She smiles, content and nostalgic. Then she keeps going: "And then you suggested we shower, and so we made love in the tub. And then when we left the tub…"

I clutch my heart while she continues to describe what sounds like the most sexually adventurous night I've ever had. I'm unsure of whether I should even run the risk of accidentally arousing myself by trying to remember.

"It has been quite some time since I kept on that face for the pleasure of it," Laura concludes with a sigh. "I thanked you then, but I thank you again now."

"You're welcome, but…" I probe my neck, but it's one of few parts of my body that doesn't feel like it went to war and back. "What do you mean 'after I fed you'?"

"You had your period," she says. "It was how you coaxed me to the table."

My eyes widen. I throw the blankets back all the way, exposing us both. There's no bloodstain beneath me.

"Had, in the past tense." Laura bites her lip, watching me critically. "Would it please you to know that I cleaned my plate?"

"It does please me," I say, feeling a million miles away.

A wisp of déjà vu rises from the black, like I've said these exact words before.

Laura's still watching me, bonnet slightly askew, gnawing her lip rhythmically.

I take her shoulder, leaning to the side, and survey her back. From here, I see bare brown skin, but from another vantage point way in the back of my brain, I see red slashes in the shape of wings on broader shoulders, burned atop other scars.

The memory's there and gone faster than a blink.

"I love you, such that I would show you my wings, too," she says quietly. She puts her hand on top of mine, and for the first time, I realize that her fingers are warmer. "I am sorry that I doubted your love for me."

"Tora said you have so many faces because you don't trust anyone," I say. "Is that true?"

Laura breathes a laugh. "I have so many faces because one size does not fit all—for humans and garments alike," she says. "You are the first to try on more than one of me."

My cheeks warm. I kiss the back of her hand, then crawl over her carefully and perch on the edge of the mattress.

"Where are you going?" Laura asks, sitting beside me.

"Nowhere." I squint under the bed and move my laptop aside, reaching for the alder box. Even now, it feels too precious to pick up.

She tilts her head to the side, recognition faint in her eyes.

I balance the box on my thighs and open it.

The pumping heart within is at sixty BPM according to my ears—sixty and climbing.

Laura gapes at her heart as it beats faster and faster.

"Where did you find this?"

"Lucy found it," I say as my own heart races alongside hers. "There's a letter somewhere."

Laura reaches.

I scoot further away, tightening my grip as I close the lid. "Excuse you," I scoff. "This is mine."

"Why can I not touch my own heart?" She asks, signature pout in place.

"Because," I say, narrowing my eyes. "I strongly suspect you might throw it at the wall just to see what happens."

She opens her mouth, then closes it and sucks her teeth, clearly defeated.

"That's what I thought."

"Between this and your amnesiac antics, I have never been so thoroughly humbled in all my centuries. You are, very truly," Laura says, getting to her feet, "a prize for a champion."

I put the box in her place and curl up in bed as she puts on her too-big grey hoodie.

"Did I get more than just an ass whooping in Blessed Falls?"

"Your mother is safe from Ezekiel's clutches," she says, muffled. Her bonnet emerges, and she pulls the hoodie down to the middle of her thighs. "He is not safe from mine. It would please me to show you what has become of him, but Talon has attuned me to the art of the trigger warning." She sits beside me again, loosely tucking me in. "When we reach his cell, you will see that his penis and tongue have been severed and swapped."

I haven't the faintest what to say. Zeke is the last person I want to think about or discuss, but I'm also morbidly curious to see my girlfriend's handiwork firsthand.

"Thank you," I say.

"No, no, my beloved Oasis," Laura says, smiling. "Thank *you*."

*

I hadn't really noticed how naked my apartment is until Kennedy stepped over the threshold, and I realized that I only have three places to sit—some chairs, my bed, or the floor.

It's easier to ignore the barrenness from the fire escape, where he and I have opted to sit with our legs dangling over the grate while Laura makes soup and sandwiches in the kitchen.

"Well, thanks for not firing me over those no-call, no-shows," I say, after reviewing our brief text exchange during my amnesia spell. The screenshot of my blue dot in Blessed Falls looks more surreal every time I pull it up, but there's a rental receipt from Enterprise in my inbox to authenticate it. "I hope I didn't scare you too bad."

"You did." Kennedy crosses his ankles, fingers curled around the bars as he gazes out over the alley. "But then I met your girlfriend, and uh…he scared me a lot more."

"He…?" I swallow, winded and whiplashed. "What do you mean?"

"Your girlfriend, Vlad Dracula, came in and said that, uh…" He scratches his head, glancing over his shoulder. "He said that you'd been mauled by a false prophet, who'd been swallowed by his dragon, Minty Fresh, who would then shit the false prophet out in his dungeon." He sips from his bottle of guava kombucha and smacks his lips. "Then he did this thing with his eyes," he says, wincing slightly, "and said if I fired you, he'd make me the Job to his God. Then he wrote down specific verses on a receipt, and uh…" He clears his throat. "Yeah."

I cover my mouth, mortified. "I am so…"

"Sorry? Try *slick*," Kennedy says, half-grinning, half-grimacing. "You really had me fooled. Thanks to you, I know vampires are real. What better way to find out than being threatened by the most famous one?"

I look into the kitchen, where Laura's stirring a pot of soup, headphones fixed over her ears while she listens to the playlist I made.

"Oasis, I promise you—all I am is impressed." Kennedy sips more kombucha, then tucks the bottle between his knees. "I mean, what choice do I have with your girlfriend being who she is?"

"I haven't even checked the news to see if Blessed Falls…" I trail away. "I'm not ready for the guilt to catch up to me," I confess.

"I wish the supernatural food chain was enough, but it still feels like my fault." I fold my hands in my lap, eyeing a rat skulking between two trash cans across the alley. "Should I tell Helena?"

"I wouldn't," he says, mouth twisted in a sympathetic frown. "Survivor's guilt is real, but your heart is heavy enough, and it's not your fault a monster loves you. Self-admitted monster. Lord knows I'm not talking shit," he adds, raising his hands innocently when I scowl. "And maybe *I'm* a monster myself for thinking this, but I couldn't care less about who or how many strangers got eaten if it means you made it out alive."

The guilt doesn't abate, but this does make me feel better, like opening an umbrella during a storm. Besides, he's right about my heart. Between the VHI and Custodes Angelorum, I'm wondering if I should check in with a cardiologist to make sure everything is still in order.

Soon, Laura calls us into the dining room, having prepared tomato soup and sourdough grilled cheese for us, and a glass of dark red wine for herself. She waits until I'm seated to sit beside me, while Kennedy sits across.

As I glance beneath the table to elevate my foot on the fourth chair, I glimpse something pure white under it and narrow my eyes.

A snow-white tampon.

"Thank you for cooking, Laura," Kennedy says. "In high school, I always imagined a slight reversal of roles when it came to hypotheticals about feeding and vampires."

"I have chosen the well from which I draw my drink," Laura says. She notices the path of my gaze and smiles. "And I have chosen wisely."

LAURA
31 songs, 2 hours, 250.1 MB

	Name	Time	Album	Artist
1	Hello	4:17	I Am... Sasha Fierce (Deluxe Version)	Beyoncé
2	Catch You	2:39	Catch You - Single	BACKWHEN
3	Bottom of the Deep Blue Sea	3:52	Loner	MISSIO
4	I Want More, Part 1	2:49	No Roots	Faithless
5	I Want More, Part 2	3:11	No Roots	Faithless
6	I'm Making Eyes At You	4:29	Partie Traumatic	Black Kids
7	Burn Them Down	3:00	Sicklove Paradise	Kamandi
8	Vamp	4:52	The Last Resort	Trentemøller
9	Bloodsport	5:24	Bloodsport	Sneaker Pimps
10	Underwater (feat. Tina Malia)	6:31	Wildstyle	Bassnectar
11	Monster	4:48	Patterns EP	Sorsari
12	Bleed Together	5:05	Bleed Together - Single	Matt Lange
13	Girlfriend	3:26	Soulless Computer Boy and the Eternal Re...	Trevor Something
14	Turbo	3:00	Cruelty Has a Human Heart - EP	Guilt Chip & MIngo
15	Gimme	3:39	Gimme - Single	BANKS
16	Valkyrie	4:04	Polygon	Battle Tapes
17	As Heaven Is Wide	4:53	Garbage (20th Anniversary Super Deluxe...	Garbage
18	My Favourite Game	3:37	Gran Turismo	The Cardigans
19	Don't Look Back (feat. Angela McCluskey)...	3:20	Rare Remixes	Télépopmusik
20	Never Leave You Alone	2:48	Voodoo Estate	Klasey Jones
21	Sex You	3:33	Sex You - Single	Bando Jonez
22	Wanting You	4:00	One - EP	PLAZA
23	Ocean	3:29	Cruelty Has a Human Heart - EP	Guilt Chip
24	So It Goes	4:55	Amir	Tamino
25	Skin	5:04	LOUD (Deluxe)	Rihanna
26	Body and Soul	2:57	The Essential Billie Holiday	Billie Holiday and Her Orchestra
27	Gone 2 Long (Choir Version)	3:14	Gone 2 Long (Choir Version) - Single	PRETTYMUCH
28	Catch Your Breath (Ødream Remix)	4:18	Awakenings - EP	Verasect
29	Sweet Dreams	3:28	I Am... Sasha Fierce	Beyoncé
30	Liebestraum No. 3 in A-Flat Major, S. 541...	3:55	Beethoven: Fur Elise & Moonlight Sonata...	Walter Rinaldi
31	The Four Seasons, Concerto for Violin, Stri...	2:45	Vivaldi: The Four Seasons - Bach: Violin C...	J.S. Bach Orchestra & Julius Frederick Rina...

twenty-nine

September 10, 2019

And to-night I shall not fear to sleep.

twenty-nine

Mirage has a peak young millennial living space, with thrifted furniture, plants galore, and about a million sources of artificial light in addition to the wide industrial loft windows. His kitchen is full of enough appliances and ingredients to open a third restaurant, but I only need a pot and a spoon for what I'm cooking up: a box of macaroni and cheese.

Mom was a terrible cook and she knew it, but we could never say no to mac and cheese with pepper in it, and a sprinkle of whatever fancy cheese me or Mirage had picked at the store that week.

Mirage is rolling a blunt in homage, because—Mom was also a stoner, and we knew it. Towards the end of her life, her headaches were so bad that she couldn't hide the smell under Febreeze. She'd let us smoke with her from time to time so long as we promised not to make it a bad habit.

This is the casual sendoff she would have wanted.

The water leaps to a boil, and I empty the box into it.

"I wish Helena had told me this was why she wanted to get in touch," Mirage says as he seals the blunt. "I never would've been such an asshole."

"She gets it. I do, too," I say, pointing a wooden spoon at him. "She's excited to meet you."

"In a context that isn't traumatic?" Mirage snickers. "Me too."

Several minutes later, I strain the macaroni and pour cheese powder in, along with a freshly shredded blend of asiago and manchego.

I spoon mac and cheese into two bowls and join my brother

near the window. This isn't our Kansas house with the bay window in the living room, where he and I would sit with Mom after school—us with our homework, her with her favorite synthesizer. It's me and him sitting on the floor in front of the triangular coffee table, facing Brooklyn's eastern skyline with the record player sitting in her place.

Her LP is transparent with an opaque haze of gray, like someone rolled a pin over a monochrome galaxy.

I lower the needle and return to the sofa.

The crackles fade. A low, smooth sound like a dial tone follows.

"That's a sine wave," Mom says.

Four words, and it already feels like my heart's been ripped out through my spine.

"Saw wave. Square wave. Triangle wave. Noise." Mom plays each waveform in turn, trudging up years' worth of lessons that I never retained—that I'm glad I didn't, for the novelty of hearing them posthumously. "Music is just air that moves. It's water for the soul, as life-giving as any element. When I make my sounds, I feel like the god of a universe. I feel all the power I don't have. I forget that there's a whole world spinning under my feet. I never thought I could love anything more than these knobs and sliders and keys but on July 13th, 1996, I met two people."

The waveforms are twisting and layering, slowly shaping into a song.

Mirage brushes his lip with his index finger; I take his hand before he can bite his nail and hold it in both of mine.

"My lush Oasis and my steady Mirage, you know how much I love you both. I also know that there may be times when that isn't enough," Mom says as quiet drums creep into the tune. "No mother wants to die knowing that her death will be the end of her children's childhood. Your father—whatever he does and however he treats you—isn't a reflection of you, and there's nothing he can do for you that you can't do for each other. Know this."

My tears make the streaming sun that much brighter. All I see is light, opening like a mouth.

"I raised you to be two halves of a whole. Oasis, you are my blooming refuge, my fresh water, so full of life that everything you touch lives too," Mom says. "Look out for your little brother. Thirteen minutes wiser makes a big difference."

I clench my jaw. My lungs ache to spill sobs, but my brain

doesn't really want to cry—not with a tune this light and dynamic carrying her words.

"And my baby Mirage, you are not an illusion of water or a taunt to the thirsty. You are living proof that there is warmth and light," she says. "Don't let your sister forget that she needs to be taken care of too."

Mirage takes his hand from mine and covers his mouth. His face is bright, his eyes glassy with tears, his chest rising and falling with repressed sobs.

I put both arms around him and pull him close, resting my chin on his temple.

"If life is a desert, then you two are all I need." The song under Mom's voice is a full-blown jam now, fit to play at a venue or a club. "This is not goodbye. This is goodnight. Death is nothing but a shade of darkness that your eyes might never fully adjust to. *I am not gone*," she says; the emphasis cracks her voice, which has so far been smooth and unbroken. "I'm just so deep in shadow that you can't see me. I'm here, I'm watching, and I love you."

The drums break down into the part where someone on a dance floor might lose their mind.

Mirage is crying so hard that I feel his tears through my jeans.

I didn't have any regrets about almost dying to get this record, and now, I no longer have regrets about not getting it sooner.

To hear my mother say that she's in the shadows—the shadows that kept me alive to hear her voice in the first place—is beyond divinity.

Finally, Mirage wipes his face on the hem of my shirt.

"That was cathartic," he says thickly.

I practically fold him in half reaching for our food.

"Rest in peace, Mommy," I say.

"Rest in peace," Mirage echoes, clinking his bowl against mine in a toast.

"Ope—almost forgot." I put my bowl down and reach for my purse below the coffee table. I uncap the bottle of rust red iron pills and swallow one dry, then proceed to devour my mac and cheese.

*

For a while, neither me nor Talon could stop sulking, splayed in the beanbag chairs beside her bedroom window, overlooking a dense patch of wood and a sliver of river. The space next to her bed is covered in pictures—Polaroids and Kodak moments that feature Talon, seemingly by herself, at various stages of life. In the one nearest to me, she's no more than 10 at the fair on a rainy day, sitting in mid-air at about the height of Laura's shoulders. In another, she's on the floor, drawing someone who looks a little like Cypress.

After watching several Shakespeare adaptations in a row over bowls of homemade Superman ice cream, the misery over her imminent departure abates.

"This is proof of infinite opportunities," I say as we near the end of *Romeo Must Die*, which I haven't seen since I was 12. "There'll be nothing stopping you from adapting *Othello* into a mock reality TV show."

"That's one option. Speaking of *Othello*," she says, sliding down to the floor, "I hope I'm not the only Black person there."

"I'm still available to go with you, T," Cypress says as he enters the room with an overflowing basket of laundry. "I ain't content to sit here while you wander among the Brits with no entourage."

Talon rolls her eyes. "You mean you're tired of Manhattan's produce selection." Then she inhales sharply and looks to me. "Sorry."

"The food chain came before I did, I suppose," I say as noncommittally as I can through yet another surge of shame. "Besides, I wasn't really there."

"Well, *I* was." Cypress dumps the laundry on Talon's bed and begins to sort through the garments, neatly folding sweaters and leggings into her open suitcase. "I haven't partied like that since the '60s, all the drugs that false prophet had 'em doing."

I don't know what to say.

Though the guilt has been a constant, it's difficult to hold it in the same esteem while his laughing brown eyes are on mine.

"Thank you for the good time, Miss Oasis."

"You're welcome, Cy."

*

Not long after Cypress and Talon leave for the airport, Dracula surfaces and gives me a piggyback ride to his dungeon. I resist the urge to look down the back of his sweatshirt for a peek at his wings as he races down the stone steps without touching the ground. Being on his back while he levitates at top speed is like being on the back of a motorcycle, and so I wait until we're over the threshold of his menagerie to remark on this display.

"I can't believe you sacrificed flight for flavor," I say shakily. "What other powers have you been hiding under that hunger?"

"True flight is your flavor. To be quite honest with you, Oaza," he says, pausing to secure his hold on my legs, "you may have ruined necks for me."

I blush and bury my face in his hair, wishing for a moment that I could turn back time and see what the amnesiac Oasis saw when he was looking after her. The octopus is bouncing around in a new pattern, and the brown kangaroo is joined by a black one and a beige one.

Dracula stops at the dark curtain shielding Minty Fresh's lair and sets me down, then draws it open and pulls a lever so that the bars lift. He returns to me and takes my hand. For the first time since we met, he's smiling.

More emotions than I'd like to admit to passed through me on the way down here as I asked myself if I was *really* prepared to see Zeke—if witnessing his torment would please me, or if it would remind me of all he's done and taken. Of all the lives lost to his biblical delusions. But seeing my baby smile pleases me more than Zeke scares me. His green eyes reflect the distant green light of Minty Fresh's flames, and although I'm not afraid, I can't help sidling behind him as a mighty breeze rushes through the theater screen-sized hole.

The sound of flapping wings intensifies. I peek around Dracula's arm, heart thundering; he looks practically giddy, fingers steepled nefariously. Sublime astonishment overcomes me as Minty Fresh comes into view, and I can't help emerging for a closer look. Her scales are a patchwork of jet black and emerald green. Gold spikes protrude from her long face and match the gold membranes of her wings.

She lands with a soft screech, blinking at us with enormous gold eyes, thin pupils the length of my forearm. Spearmint-scented smoke issues from her nostrils. Five of me could probably fit on top of her head, which is warm when I reach out to pat the space between her nostrils.

"Minty Fresh has been guarding the false prophet so that I may torture it within your line of sight," Dracula says excitedly. He points to a spot on the floor. "Minty, you may spit the mongrel here."

The rumble in her throat seems to rattle my bones.

Minty Fresh opens her mouth partway, wafting spearmint over us, revealing rows of sharp white teeth as tall as picket fences. Her wide red tongue rolls out of her mouth like a carpet. Something—several somethings—fall off the forked tip, clattering in the crags of the stone. Some of them roll crookedly across the floor like toys.

A skull stops several inches from my feet, thinly coated with green slime. I spot a ribcage, a femur, and several vertebrae among the regurgitated pile of bones.

"That's Zeke?" I gasp.

Minty Fresh seems to respond in the affirmative with a low growl.

"You digested the false prophet?" Dracula wails.

I look over in time to see him sinking to his knees, eyes pure white and red-rimmed, lower lip quivering like he's about to burst into tears.

"Oh no," I say, hurrying over. "Baby, don't cry."

"But I was to torture and kill him. I gave him a speech," he says frailly. "It had been over a century since I gave a speech."

"You gave a speech while I was concussed on the floor?" I ask skeptically.

He ignores me and buries his face in the crook of his arm, sobbing quietly.

"De ce, Minty Fresh? *Cum ai putut?"*

Her response is a smoking, spearmint belch. She bends her scaly knees and launches herself back down the tunnel, whipping my braids back with wings like hurricanes.

I put my hand on top of Dracula's head, massaging his scalp as he hugs my knees, weeping openly over the glistening pile of bones.

thirty

September 19, 2019

Truly there is no such thing as finality.

thirty

So far, the aftermath of my unremembered visit to Blessed Falls has been about me and my girlfriend—drafting a tentative feeding schedule, putting together a shortlist of restaurants for me to explore, clearing space in my closet for some of Laura's clothes, adding a new bookshelf to the smaller of Dracula's libraries for my growing collection.

My most cherished display of trust is the keypad installed next to my fire escape: entering the five digits of our anniversary vanishes the alley and skyline, and takes me instead to the infinite storage unit of music, where a bicycle with a crate on the handlebars awaits at the doorway.

I wish that all of this could smother everything else—that what the magnitude of us could overshadow the weight of this date.

9/19/19.

The day I was supposed to be an angel.

The rapture I didn't wake up to today is what woke me up every morning for years, inspiring me to live another twisted day as an anorexic vessel.

As badly as I wanted today to mean nothing, it doesn't.

I bled for this date, and I owe it to myself to see the truth behind who that blood was for.

"And you are quite certain you want to do this alone?" Dracula asks yet again. "If Satan has yet to approach me, Oaza, it is possible that the absence of my heart has gone unnoticed, and that you need not introduce yourself."

"I'm certain," I say through the crunch of a carrot initially meant for a snoozing Bunnicula.

He nods and removes the black tome from the top shelf. It thunks on the table, startling Bird Bones from her nap atop an open first-edition Shakespeare folio. I rise from the couch as Dracula unbuckles the book and waves his hand over it. Whispers fill the room as the pages turn of their own accord. I catch glimpses of etchings and illustrations—bats, pentagrams, goats, human bodies, all surrounded by glyphs and symbols.

The movement stops. He plucks a sheath of pages from near the end and unfolds them, then quickly shuffles through.

"October 1937," he reads. "*Dearest Vlad, Pops says to anticipate a more intensive workload in the back half of the twentieth century and the beginning of the twenty-first. Metatron is hinting at another plague, so there is a chance I will be ripping and running again, and therefore will not have much time to write. Although I clearly recall you saying that a technological device that allows anyone to reach you at any time for any reason "truly infernal," I figured I would give you my phone number. I can only hope a human sways you towards modernity. Get with the times, or the times will get you.*" He stops to scowl at the page. "Are you ready to take down the number?"

I'm not, but I take out my phone in a daze anyway.

"Go ahead."

"Six," he says

"Six," I repeat.

"Six."

"Six," I say after a pause.

"Six." He snaps shuts the book, silencing the whispers, then sits beside Bunnicula, who's still curled up in a ball on the couch, and retrieves his *Batman* omnibus from within the cushions. "Give the Devil my regards."

I can't help shaking my head. I look at my own phone—at the three numbers crammed between parentheses, like an area code. My thumb hits the dial button.

It rings once.

It rings twice.

It rings three times.

It rings and rings, but I don't hang up.

I hear the tone louder than I hear my own thoughts.

I feel it in my chest where a heart once beat.

I see it like the frequency waves from my mother's childhood synthesis lessons.

When it stops ringing, I'm not where I was when I first dialed. The cozy library around me is now a long, bright hallway lined with blue lockers, decorated with hand painted back-to-school signs. A nearby sign taped to the wall reads *Flint Southwestern Academy Student Government FAQ: Thursday, September 19, 2019 @ Lunch! There will be pizza!!!* Further down the hall, another sign reads *Need community service hours? Sign up for a water distribution day, Saturdays at Derby Downs. Help keep Flint hydrated!*

A bell rings, prompting me to move my legs.

I haven't set foot in a high school since I graduated, and the only teenager I've been exposed to since is over a century old. Less than a dozen students are in the hallway, rifling in their lockers and meandering to class.

Although I could've used some warning, I withhold the urge to text my girlfriend several question marks and focus on the task at hand: finding Satan. I venture down the hall, battling memories of myself walking down a similar hallway in Kansas, relishing in the fact that I'd soon be in Pennsylvania.

Bitterness threatens to take root, but something at the end of the hall catches my eye, quickening my pulse: a girl with flamingo-colored box braids swings a hot pink backpack off her shoulder.

She's with two friends—one tall and skinny with a red Afro puff, the other, lean and broad-shouldered, wearing a teal letterman jacket. They're holding hands, the redhead orating what looks like a riveting tale while his boyfriend watches amusedly, arm swinging as the redhead gesticulates.

I walk slowly, trying not to stare too hard, bracing myself to be accosted at any moment by someone who can tell I don't belong.

"Aight, Money, we out," the redhead's saying as I come close enough to hear their conversation. "Don't forget my set tonight."

"I would *never*. I know it's at 9 o'clock."

He deadpans as his boyfriend tugs him along. "It's at 8:15."

"*Relax*. You know I'm just kidding." She rolls her eyes and shakes her head. "*Humans*."

"I'm still in earshot," he says, less than a foot away.

"And you're still human," she says, sticking her tongue out.

I'm a few lockers away when she locks eyes with me.

Between her fuchsia nylon tracksuit and gold bamboo earrings, she certainly looks stylish enough to be in Laura's orbit.

"Hello," I say.

"Hi."

"Are you…" I clear my throat, confidence on the brink of collapse. "Are you Satan?"

"Nic."

"Satanic?"

"Monica," Nic says, pursing her lips. She unzips her bag and swaps two notebooks from her locker. "Who gave you my number?"

"Vlad Dracula." Again, I clear my throat. "He's my girlfriend."

Her jaw drops. "*Shut up*," she gasps. "I'm so happy for you, Oasis. You both deserve it."

"You know me?"

"Oh, yeah," Nic says with a nod. "On their way to hell, people get their own personal orientations with slideshows explaining why they're there. I like to walk in with the laser pointer for Christian cult leaders. Putting words in Dad's mouth is par for the course for humans, but my siblings are off-limits." She sucks her teeth, and her eyes seem to flash bright pink. "Today was supposed to be a big day for you, wasn't it?"

"Yeah," I say, heart ricocheting off my ribs. "I was going to host—"

"Gabriel," she finishes, nodding. "That tracks. He likes plaid."

I say nothing.

This is really happening.

I'm talking to an angel.

Somehow, I'm still here, standing on two legs, thinking thoughts that aren't aflame with devastation.

In fact, I'm struggling not to contemplate asking more about the angel my life revolved around for three years.

"I'm glad we met this way," Nic continues, "and not during intake. There's no hell like the one I give to suicides." She traces her neckline, then pulls a golden chain into the open. The pendant glints between her thumb and forefinger. The three prongs of a trident catch the light.

"Noted. How old are you?" I ask, unable to stop myself. "Are you a child?"

"I'm turning 18 next month," she says. "I mean, do you really think a fully grown angel would stage a rebellion in *God's* heaven and *live?*"

"I guess not," I say.

I'd been prepared, albeit barely, for grief to be the dominant emotion while meeting an angel for the first time, but I'm starting to think I should get used to finding bizarreness in the same places that might otherwise burn me, because all I feel now, and as always when it comes to Laura's world, is fascination.

"Anyway, I came to tell you that I have Dracula's heart," I say. "And I'm not giving it back."

"You have *what?*" She scoffs, eyebrows raised.

"I have Dracula's heart," I repeat. "It's mine."

"How can it be *yours*," Nic says, reaching into her locker, "if it's right...here?" She pulls out her empty hand, then scans the locker top to bottom, sifting through folders and textbooks. Upon finding nothing, she drops to her knees, opens her backpack all the way. Her right arm goes in, then her left, then her head and shoulders. Moments later, the entire top half of her body is gone, like her bag is hiding a hole in the floor.

Several minutes go by with me staring at her legs, then looking around the empty hallway, wondering as I do just how often stuff like this—angels reaching into bottomless bags, vampires grocery shopping, and the like—has happened in my vicinity, but beyond my awareness.

Nic resurfaces breathing hard, eyes narrowed. Her formerly laid edges are frizzy, and thin spirals of pink steam waft off her body.

"What the heck did you do?" She demands.

"I found what Lucy Westenra stole," I say calmly.

"You're kidding," she snorts. "Van Helsing stole *her* from me. She was on her way to *me* before he...well, if you've read the book, you know what happens," she mutters as she zips up her bag. Back on her feet, she sighs quietly. "Alright, so I'm not at my most organized, but that heart is my most prized possession, so..."

"So? It's my most prized possession, too."

"*You* don't love Dracula the way *I* do. I fell from heaven again because I ripped his heart from his chest and molded him in my image," Nic says, stepping closer. Her brown irises disappear beneath a lens of pink. "How would *you* feel if your cat went missing, and someone called you to say they found it, but they're keeping it?"

"His heart isn't an animal. And I have no interest in becoming undead, so..." I swallow hard, skin flushed with goosebumps. "It's more of a loan, if you think about it."

Nic smirks. The brown returns to her eyes as she slams her

locker and slings her bag over her shoulder. "Come with me, then," she says, beckoning.

I let out a shaky breath. I hadn't expected such a smooth exchange, and follow her in a slight stupor.

Nic stops at a janitor's closet, then unclasps her necklace and sticks the trident in the lock. She looks left and right, then opens the door.

The scent of concentrated chemicals strips away once it closes, and we're standing at the threshold of what seems to be the top half of a two-family flat, fitted with enough bookshelves for a small store, furnished with a mélange of recliners, loveseats, and sofas. Faygo cans line the windowsills, and clipped bags of snacks sit on top of a mini fridge in what must've been the dining room.

The living room's open bay window frames several blocks of urban prairies, strewn with caved-in houses and rusted cars.

It's the part of the Midwest I'm least familiar with—the urban carcass of the gutted auto industry.

"Where are we?"

"My library. It's different every time I go to heaven and back, same as me." Nic drops her bag on a recliner, gesturing for me to follow her to a room in the back. "You're welcome to swing by and look around next time we hang out, which we *will* be doing if you're holding onto my chimera's heart."

"That's fine by me. I'm short on friends," I say.

She smiles and gestures to the black shelves lining the walls before pointing directly at an empty bell jar perched on top of one.

I scrutinize one of the titles: *Dracula*, bound in dandelion cloth. Next to it is *Dracula*, movie tie-in edition. Next to that is a taller edition, bound in pale red, annotated with a plastic dust jacket. A quick survey of the shelves suggests that this room is dedicated solely to one title.

"*You, too?*" I ask.

"Nah. I'm just the angel who has to clean up whatever those pink flames swallow," Nic says. "Can you believe this is all from this year alone?"

I turn my back on the shelves, sufficiently blown away. She puts a hand on her hip, and with the other twirls her trident pendant around a finger. Then she sighs and grabs a comic from a stack off one of the shelves: a single issue of *The Tomb of Dracula*.

I watch as she moves a green armchair aside to access a

wooden door, then unlocks it with her trident. On the other side is nothing but a wall.

Nic pushes it once, then waits. It swings open slowly, revealing starkly different lighting.

I approach the threshold alongside her.

Her arms are crossed, foot tapping on the wooden floor.

I'm tempted to pose similarly as a familiar book-filled room comes into view.

We're standing behind the same bookshelf from which Dracula retrieved his black book. I see nothing but the top of his head and his phone screen from as he lays on the couch, still playing Candy Crush. Bunnicula is sitting on the armrest, eating a carrot.

I clear my throat pointedly.

Dracula sits up, jostling Bird Bones, who'd been situated on his hip.

"You have returned to me, Oaza," he says. Then his green eyes land on Nic. "Speak of the you."

Nic glowers and storms over to him, rolling up the comic as she goes. I drop my hands and cover my mouth as she proceeds to whack him on the head several times.

"*Stop—burning—books.* You're supposed to be sending bad people my way, not bad writing," she scolds while he sits compliantly on the couch, cringing. "And stop letting humans touch my stuff."

"I did not know Lucy had rambled in your possessions," Dracula says defensively.

"Yeah, well, you're lucky Oasis is so forward. I like her." She reaches for one of the golden bats in his earlobe, one hand on her hip. "Our Father who art in heaven, these are *so* cute."

"I will fashion a pair for you," he says, pouting.

"Bet," Nic says with another, gentler whack upside his head. "You behave. You, too, Oasis," she says, pointing at her eyes, then at me, as her irises flame pink. "No more cults."

"No more cults," I echo.

The bookshelf closes after her, wood scraping on the floor.

Dracula's still sulking when I sit next to him, plucking Bunnicula off the armrest so I can hold her instead. He puts his arm around me, resting his chin atop my head.

"I think that went well," I say.

"The Devil did not procure her trident," he whispers. "It went very well indeed."

"I'm still thinking about it," Nic calls before the shelf hits the wall and seals all the way.

*

The remainder of the day that almost wasn't elapses in the remnants of Castle Dracula—or at least what John Seward and his crowd managed to loot and ship to America. I showed Laura most of what I looted back, save the surprises tucked in the drawer; this earned me a pile of kisses, and this: IKEA has nowhere near the furniture selection that Laura does, and so my venture to make my apartment less of a husk begins here.

Laura rattles off descriptions of all the furniture I pause to look at, including eras, materials, and in some cases, the names of the people who gifted them to her. In the end, I choose a mossy green sofa with blue pillows, both from Vivaldi, and a coffee table with talons for legs, which now hosts a small smart TV.

The ensemble fits nicely to the far right of the fire escape, a fresh place to lounge and, more importantly, to kiss my girlfriend.

Laura's lips are as warm as mine, but her fingertips still leave goosebumps on my body when we touch. "What shall we do to round off the rapture, my love?" She asks, nibbling my ear.

"We can watch a movie," I murmur.

"Smaug?" Laura whispers.

I break away and sit up, taking her hands in mine as she smiles hopefully.

"Baby, I love you, but no. No more Smaug," I say.

She kisses my knuckles with pouting lips. "I am certain you will make a wise choice." She gets up and puts on a hoodie, rolling the sleeves up to her elbows on her way to the kitchen. "How shall I season your popcorn?"

"Surprise me." I grab the remote from between the cushions and scroll through our streaming options. "Is it safe for you to watch *Hunchback of Notre Dame*?"

"No, but the music is worth the flames," she says idly. She takes out a tall pot and a bag of popcorn kernels, humming the film's opening tune while pouring oil.

"Not to me," I mutter. "What about *Devil's Advocate*?"

"What about me?"

Thunder claps outside, zapping the speech from my mouth. I barely withhold a shriek as car alarms blare in a chorus, undercut with the startled cries of pedestrians caught off guard. Lightning flashes like silent gunfire, and the sharp hum of heavy rain filters through the fire escape.

"It's not supposed to rain tonight," I say shakily.

"This is not my doing either," Laura says, frowning over the stove.

A series of door-rattling knocks on the door makes me jump. I spring up, wired with adrenaline.

"I'll get it," I say, shooing Laura back to the stove as the popcorn kernels begin to fire off.

I open the door to a man, standing with his back to me. He has a head of long blond hair, and a white fur pelt draped over his lean shoulders. His feet are clad in brown boots lined with white fur; one of them is planted between the shoulders of someone sprawled facedown on the floor, dressed in a tattered suit. The visible parts of the person's body are bloody and bruised, fingers and limbs bent at odd angles. If it wasn't for the soft, spluttering groans coming from their mouth, I'd think they were a corpse.

The lanky stranger turns around, pelt swishing majestically. He's wearing a pale red tunic under his pelt, trimmed with a maze-like silver pattern. The golden belt around his waist is carved with runes that match those on the bloodstained hammer in his right hand, the head of which is as big as mine.

"Are you Oasis Johnson?" He asks in an accent unlike any I've ever heard.

"Who wants to know?" I ask, looking him up and down.

"I have a gift for your girlfriend," he says curtly, nudging the person on the floor with his foot.

My ears ring.

"Who's this?" I ask.

"The Midgardian who shot my dog," the stranger sneers. "I only skimmed some off the top. There's plenty left for your sweet one to play with," he says, turning away.

"Wait," I say.

He paused and looks back, blond brow furrowed.

"Can I tell her who the gift is from?" I ask.

"Thor."

I hear the stove fall silent, then the patter of Laura's bare feet. Her nostrils flare as she beholds the figure on the floor. Red swarms her irises.

"Seward blood," she hisses, "fouling the air like a carcass."

She looks at Thor, who gazes back with a bored look on his face. "You have brought me this?"

"Are you the girlfriend of Oasis Johnson?"

"Yes."

"Then yes." He turns away again.

"Justina will want to see this, *iubirea mea*. I must depart to the dungeon," Laura says as she grabs Dr. Seward by the ankles, eliciting a strangled groan, and lugs him into the apartment, towards the fire escape. "I should not be more than fifteen minutes. I trust you will have chosen a film by then."

I hardly hear her words or Dr. Seward's whimpers. My heart thunders alongside the storm as I watch Thor's fur pelt ripple with his retreating footsteps.

"Wait," I say again.

Again, he turns around, just shy of my neighbor's door, blinking at me with sky blue eyes.

"What are you up to?" I ask, trailing towards him, fiddling with the recently repaired button on my flannel sleeve.

"Listening," he says. "To you, human."

"Ah," I say, stricken with déjà vu. "Where are you headed?"

"Asgard," he says, twirling his hammer once. In doing so, I notice a tattoo on his left arm—an *animated* tattoo, like aerial footage of a red puppy racing from his bicep to his wrist. Another tattoo of a tree covers the back of his hand and wraps around his wrist. The red puppy disappears into the branches, then races back up his arm with a stick in her mouth and disappears under his pelt. A moment later, the scene replays.

Thor watches me, expressionless. Then he angles himself towards the end of the hallway.

"Wait," I say yet again.

He stops and faces me. Pale red static crackles from his eyes and fingertips as he perches his hammer on his shoulder.

For a moment, I start to reconsider the enterprise of striking up a conversation, but the fact of the matter is being struck down by a Norse god would be a step up from the plans I had for this day three years ago.

"Ásttora said you might take interest in me. I humored her in saying I would at least pretend to care," he says laconically.

My eyes widen.

"In truth, I couldn't have cared less until Heimdallr spoke of you," he continues. "He let you cross the Bifröst."

"Yeah," I say, trying my best to glide past the burn of what I hope was an accidental insult grounded in cultural differences. "Tell him I said thank you."

"Actually, he asked me to thank you," Thor says as puzzlement briefly overshadows the boredom in his blue eyes.

"For what?"

"I asked. He only smiled."

I blink, so stunned that my growling stomach falls silent, and I forget there's popcorn waiting for me.

"Heimdallr's all about the big picture," Thor says. "It made me curious to see him smile at a detail as inconsequential and insignificant as yourself."

My wonderment threatens to buckle under outrage, but since he's still standing here, looking more curious than not, I decide once again to give him the benefit of the doubt.

"I know you're probably not here very often, but it's rude to call people insignificant," I say.

"Then what should I call you?" He asks.

"Oasis."

"Alright, Oasis. My question for you, then, is this." Thor steps closer still, towering above me, holding the hammer behind his neck with both hands. "Can you find it in that fragile human heart of yours to braid Falhófhir's mane as well?"

"Who?"

"She's my horse. She's very shy," he says. "She needs the self-esteem boost."

I almost scream. "I can find it. Not tonight, though," I say. "I just got my first couch."

"I bet you're proud of yourself, aren't you?" He asks curtly.

"Yes, I am," I say, smiling.

He nods, as though satisfied. "As you should be."

"You didn't come all this way just to go right back. Do you wanna hang out with us?" I ask.

"Alright, then," he says. Thor follows me over the threshold, hammer perched on his shoulder.

I put a Ziplock bag over the bloody head before he hangs it and his pelt in the closet. Then he follows my lead and washes his hands in the kitchen sink.

I feel light as a cloud as I transfer the popcorn from pot to bowl. Laura nailed the butter to nutritional yeast ratio like a champion.

"We were just about to watch a movie," I say, gesturing to the sofa.

"Wonderful." Thor sits beside me, gazing around with a deepening frown as I search for the remote. Then he looks to me, his face a portrait of confusion. "Oasis?"

"Yes?"

"What is a movie?"

the end.

acknowledgments

A *Dracula* retelling/rehash/revisit/whatever you wanna call it has been knocking around my brain since 2014. This is the first of several premises to actually take root and blossom, and despite all the [gestures at literally everything], I couldn't be happier with it. I would like to thank:

  - Noah, for being the first person to read this book

  - Angélica, for sharing me with these characters

  - Olivia A. Cole, for not letting me give up on this story.

  - Rysz at tRaum Books, for helping me polish this book into publishability.

  - Stephanie and Sarah "Ink Black" Ahn for the cover of my dreams.

Major shoutout to Earlee, Nazanin, Thom, and Sohmer for years of support, solidarity, and friendship. Thank you to Pheolyn Allen, Brendon Zatirka, Ryan Douglass, Derrick, and Dwyer for being the best cheerleaders I could ask for on my writing journey.

Much love to my friend Tulsi for all the hours spent listening to tunes with me from across the globe, and for teaching me a thing or two about making my own.

Lastly, I would like to thank Courtney Gould, for all the castles we've built in the air: without your readership, no story of mine is complete.

Oh, and of course, I'd like to thank my mother, for the music.